10/21

D0438493

ANY
SIGN
ØF
LIFE

RAE CARSON

ANY SIGN OF LIFE

GREENWILLOW BOOKS
An Imprint of HarperCollins *Publishers*

Any Sign of Life
Copyright © 2021 by Rae Carson

The text of this book is set in 11-point Adobe Garamond Pro.
Book design by Paul Zakris

Library of Congress Cataloging-in-Publication Data

Names: Carson, Rae, author.
Title: Any sign of life / Rae Carson.
Description: First edition. | New York : Greenwillow Books,
an imprint of HarperCollins Publishers, [2021] | Audience: Ages 13 up. |
Audience: Grades 10–12. |
Summary: Paige Miller fears she is the only person left alive in Ohio until she meets a handful of other survivors, and together they struggle with the knowledge that their new reality is the first part of an alien invasion. Identifiers: LCCN 2021008897 (print) | LCCN 2021008898 (ebook) | ISBN 9780062691934 (hardcover) | ISBN 9780062691958 (epub)
Subjects: CYAC: Survival—Fiction. | Extraterrestrial beings—Fiction. | Ohio—Fiction. | LCGFT: Novels. | Apocalyptic fiction.
Classification: LCC PZ7.C2423 An 2021 (print) | LCC PZ7.C2423 (ebook) | DDC [Fic]—dc23
LC record available at https://lccn.loc.gov/2021008897
LC ebook record available at https://lccn.loc.gov/2021008898
21 22 23 24 25 PC/LSCH 10 9 8 7 6 5 4 3 2 1

First Edition

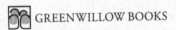 GREENWILLOW BOOKS

For Kristine and Sky

March 13

I LURCH UP FROM THE BED, GASPING FOR AIR. IT TAKES SEVERAL breaths, several heartbeats, before I'm aware how badly my head hurts. Like I have the worst hangover of my life. Which makes no sense. But my mouth is parched, my tongue swollen, my teeth rancid, like something crawled up in here and died.

What the hell? I try to swallow, but my throat snags on itself, making me gag. The gagging becomes coughing—hard, dry waves that feel like they're splitting my ribs open.

Relax, I tell myself. *Breathe through your nose. Relax, relax, relax.*

The coughing stills, and I catch my breath, head tilted back like Coach D taught me. The ceiling fan of my bedroom is motionless. A single fly buzzes around the wooden blades.

I swing my legs over the bed and set my feet on the floor,

blinking to clear eyes that are as arid and hollow as skeleton sockets. I try to stand.

Something bites at the back of my hand, and I lift my other hand as if to smack a bug, but I freeze, palm raised. It's an IV. The entry site is swollen, bloodless, and aching, like a giant hive. The clear IV line stretches up to a 1000 ml bag hanging from a pole. It's daisy-chained to several identical bags. They're all wrinkled like raisins, empty of fluid.

I don't remember getting an IV.

Everything is bright and hazy, silent except for that stupid fly. I peer toward my alarm clock, which is a small plastic basketball with a wedge cut out for the digital insert. My eyes don't want to focus, but through sheer force of will, I make them.

4:17 p.m. I should be on the court with my team.

No, I remember now; I went to bed right after dinner. So I've been asleep almost twenty-four hours.

My throat had been hurting all day. Something about my depth perception had been off, too. At practice, I missed two bounce passes from Shawntelle; both times I put my hands out to catch the ball, but it sailed right past me. *Hey, I hear the JV team has room on the bench*, Shawntelle teased.

Later, at the table with Mom and Paul and Ryan, my whole body started to ache, and I knew with a sinking feeling that I was getting the flu. The one that had put half of Columbus out of commission. Even though I'm completely up-to-date on my flu shots. Mom had made my favorite, baked mac and cheese with garlic bread, but I went to bed without finishing dinner.

Mom must have hooked up the IV. She did that for me once after a grueling practice made my legs cramp with dehydration. But how did she get permission to bring so many bags home from the hospital, and why did she daisy-chain them together? Why did she let them go dry?

"Mom?" I call out in a voice so hoarse I hardly recognize it as my own. No answer. She's probably working an afternoon shift.

I roll my shoulders, trying to get movement and circulation back. Lactic acid burns in my deltoids, and my head refuses to rotate to the right. I must have dropped off to sleep in one position and not budged the whole time. A hot shower will help. If I'm quick, there's still time to make the last hour of practice.

Shower.

Suddenly, I'm craving water more than I've craved anything in my life. Cool, clear water. Gallons of water.

I rip the medical tape off my hand and yank out the needle. The pain makes the edges of the world close in around me—or maybe it's the sight of yellow puss oozing out of the wound. I lurch to my feet and stumble toward my bathroom. I misjudge the doorway and bash my forehead against the jamb, but I don't care. *Oh, god, water.*

I fumble blindly for the faucet, twist the knob. The sound of water flowing makes me stupid. I knock my skull against the spout in my haste to get underneath it, and I gulp like a wild animal. It slides down my throat, a waterfall of wonder, sweeter than honey, more filling than Mom's baked mac and cheese.

My stomach squeezes like a vise, and I don't even have time for a breath before I vomit all that glorious water back into the sink. It whirls down the drain, tinged with greenish bile but not much else.

I'm still so thirsty I could die of it, but I have to be smarter. I grab my rinse cup and place it under the faucet. It takes all my control to watch it fill up, to bring it slowly to my lips, to take only tiny sips.

My stomach heaves again, but this time the water stays down. I pull the cup away from my face and breathe, in for four, out for four. I take another sip. Breathe again. Another sip. Physical gains take patience, Coach D always says. Patience and pain.

I set the empty cup down, wanting more, more, *more* but knowing full well by the way the water sloshes around in my stomach that I need to give my body time to adjust. *Later, Paige. You can have more later.*

I reach into the shower and turn on the hot water. While it heats up, I glance at the mirror. I almost scream.

The face staring back is that of a stranger, with sunken cheeks and corpselike skin and blue eyes that are way too huge and bright. My lips are split and peeling, my chin scaled with flakes of dry skin. Something brownish yellow crusts the edges of my right ear; strands of hair are stuck to it.

And god, my hair is a matted, oily mass, unrecognizable in any way as blond. Half of it is plastered into a towering wall—must have been the side I slept on.

I refuse to look at my reflection as I brush my teeth. My

gums hurt, but the cool mint of the toothpaste is heavenly. I rinse and spit out an enormous gob of toothpaste and blood. There's so much blood that I stick my finger into my mouth to check my teeth. My finger comes out blood-smeared, but my teeth seem to be okay.

My stomach clenches again, a little with revulsion and a lot with wrongness. I know I've been sick, but something . . . something about all of this is *off.*

A hot shower always clears my head. I reach in to test the water and jerk my hand back. Still ice-cold.

"Ryan!" I yell. My little brother is thirteen, exactly the age when boys start taking embarrassingly long showers. "You used all the hot water again!"

No response. He usually thumps the wall—we kind of have this code worked out between us, ever since he was five and I was nine, when we left the Sperm Donor and Ryan started having night terrors. He used to thump the wall when he was scared, and I would thump right back, to let him know that my ear was right next to his, that he was safe. Two thumps from Ryan meant I had to get over to his bedroom right away because he was too scared to deal.

We're past that, and a gorgeous connecting tiled bathroom now separates our bedrooms, but we've never stopped thumping to let one another know, *I hear you. I'm here.* Irritates the crap out of our stepdad.

I rap the wall with a knuckle, but still no answer. Ryan is probably downstairs.

I have two choices: wait for the water to heat up again and

miss practice, or grin and bear it. The state tournament is next week, so of course I'll grin and bear it.

I shuck my clothes—khaki pants, underwear, black tank top, and sports bra. Everything reeks of the sharper end of the musty spectrum. I must have sweated out a fever while I slept.

Taking a deep breath, I plunge into the shower stall.

I squeal as the cold sends shock waves through my whole body. The tile is icy against my bare feet. Shivering, I grab the shampoo and work it through my hair. The water isn't the usual cold; it's more like alpine snowmelt cold. Or maybe my dehydrated body is imagining things.

Still, it feels good. I can almost hear my skin slurping it up. I lather everywhere and rinse, paying special attention to the IV site. It's obviously infected. I'll ask Mom to take a look tonight, see if I need an antibiotic.

But right now I have to hurry, leave the house before Mom gets home from work and tells me I'm too sick to go to practice.

I don't often use conditioner in my hair, but the knots are so bad that I have to. As I finger-comb, strands of hair drop to the tile and whirl away into the drain. The more I comb, the more hair comes out—and more and more.

I'll worry about that later, because I'm already so late. Coach will make me shoot extra three-pointers tonight for missing an hour, but I don't mind. My shooting has been weak from outside the arc this year—down to 36 percent lately, after shooting 40 percent my junior year—and I hate being weak.

Back in my bedroom, I start to squeeze into a clean sports bra. I brush my left breast with the back of my hand and gasp, flinching away from myself. It felt like touching a stranger. The skin against my hand was cold and limp, like a deflated basketball.

Carefully, slowly, I run trembling hands over my deflated breasts, my stomach, around my thighs to my butt. Without the ice-cold water and soap providing a distraction, the difference is obvious. I am thinner. Too thin. A wisp of a girl.

I must have lost ten pounds or more in the last twenty-four hours.

"Mom?" I whisper. Panic edges into my chest, and my legs twitch as if to take flight. *Calm down, Paige. You're a warrior. You can handle anything.*

I plunk naked onto my bed and stare at nothing, the wrongness too heavy in my head to ignore any longer. In my peripheral vision, the red digits of my basketball alarm clock stare back. I turn my head to take them in fully, just looking for something familiar and bright and solid.

And I notice it, the thing I didn't see when I first woke up. Beneath the time stamp, in much smaller letters, is the date: *Mar 13*.

I've been asleep for six days.

Suddenly I'm noticing other things too. The stale urine reek coming from my sheets. My ceiling fan, which is always, always on, perfectly still in the space above me. And barely audible but steady and overwhelming now that I've detected it, the sound of birds. So many birds, squawking, flapping, screeching.

I stumble over to my bedroom window and push aside my

curtains for a better view. It's a beautiful, sunny day, the colors crisp with early spring. The street is empty of people, but birds are everywhere. Crows mostly, some ravens, a few buzzards, hopping around in our front lawn, perched on top of cars, lining the gutters of rooftops. The wrongness blossoms into full-blown horror.

A bird crashes against the window, and I jerk back. It drops away as quickly as it came, leaving a brownish smear on the glass. Did it fall? It can't have survived. I start forward, to look for it on the ground, but wait, I'm standing in front of my window completely naked.

I shudder, creeped out by my own weird responses as much as anything; it's like my mind is swimming through sludge. I need to talk to someone, or at least hug my mom. I grab my robe from the peg outside the bathroom and put it on gingerly, trying to ignore the burn in my shoulders. I throw open my bedroom door and rush into the hallway. "Mom? Paul?"

No, no, it's too early for Mom or my stepdad to be home from work. I open my mouth to call out again anyway when I notice the smell.

Sickly sweet, like fruit gone bad. No, it's gamey, like warm, spoiled milk. With a start, I know exactly what it is. It's the same smell that filled our house when a rat got lodged under the washing machine and died.

A whimper bleeds from my lips. Ryan. I have to find my brother.

I run, just two steps, but my weak knees can't take it and I buckle to the ground. I drag myself along the hardwood floor, my knees getting caught in my robe, my heartbeat a drum in my temples. When I reach my brother's door, I use the door-knob to pull myself to my feet.

I knock. "Ryan? It's Paige."

I stare at his Keep Out sign and the hazardous waste symbol beneath it. "Ry-guy?"

But I can't take it anymore. I have to see him, family privacy pact be damned, and I swing open the door.

Screeching, flapping, black wings, yellow eyes, buzzing insects. A gust of ice-cold air and everywhere that overwhelming, sweet-sick scent. The window is open—no, broken—its jagged edges slick with blood and feathers. Denim curtains sway in the breeze.

My rebelling mind doesn't want to put it all together, but it does, inexorably, and I fall to my knees all over again. I manage to look up, toward Ryan's bed, and I see a small pale hand flung over the edge of the mattress. The pinky finger is a shredded, bloodless stump.

I crab-crawl backward as fast as I can until I hit the wall and then I crash into it again and again, scrambling to get away until by chance I find open air and tumble back into the hallway. I hook the door with my foot and slam it closed.

I'm shaking everywhere and I can't stop. I can't even think. I just grasp my knees to my chest and rock back and forth, back and forth, whimpering like an injured puppy.

Because the crows are eating my brother.

I'm not sure how long I've huddled here. But the haze is clearing, and with clarity comes pain, bone-deep and even more shocking than an ice-cold shower. My brother is dead. *Dead dead dead.* The kid I held in my arms and rocked late into the morning when his monsters kept sleep away. My little Ry-guy, who at eleven years old swore that someday he'd dunk over my head. The boy with the lightning flashes of anger who could go from fierce to gentle in the space of a hug.

Using the wall for support, I gather my feet and stand. Mom needs to know. I need to . . .

There's that wrongness feeling again. I lean against the wall and take a few deep breaths, letting my brain work it out, even as I dread the conclusions.

Oh.

I move down the hallway, putting one foot in front of the other in plodding, wobbly resolve, toward Mom and Paul's room. I half know what I'll find, because Ryan has been dead awhile. Maybe days. Why hasn't anyone taken away his body? Why did my IV bags go dry?

Why are there so many birds outside?

Double doors lead to my parents' suite. We have a beautiful home, thanks to Paul, an engineering professor at Ohio State who shares patents for two types of windmills. A stream of light pours diagonally from the skylight above the hallway, bathing the crown molding and the doors below in pale yellow. Like it's beckoning me home. I've been so busy trying to get my team to the state championship that I haven't taken the time to appreciate what a lovely house I have. What a lovely family.

I don't bother knocking this time. The door opens with a

soft click, and I pad inside on bare feet. Just three steps is all it takes for me to find them. They're atop the comforter, fully clothed, arms wrapped around each other. My mother's blond hair streams across the bottom half of Paul's face, snagged in stubble at least two days old. They seem peaceful, like they're sleeping. Except that the comforter beneath them is stained and damp with . . . something. And Paul's wide-open eyes are filmed over with white like curdled milk.

"Mom," I whisper. "Momma." But then I step back and close the door, finding my first comfort of the day, because at least they died together. I know it's weird as soon as I think it, but I cling to the comfort anyway. Like it's a lifeline. Like I might burst apart if I let go.

Gripping the oak bannister, I make my way down the stairs. Every movement is a little easier now, as my body remembers to pump blood and oxygenate my muscles. When I reach the kitchen, I glance around for Mom's cell phone. I find it next to the toaster and grab it. Though it's plugged in, the battery indicator is red. I dial 9-1-1 and hold the phone to my ear.

Nothing happens. Not a ringing sound, not a dial tone, not even a "please try your call again."

I hang up and try again anyway. Still nothing.

My own phone is in my backpack in the entryway, where I dropped it after practice. Maybe it has some charge left. I stumble past the dining room toward the front door, and I ignore the squeeze in my heart as I kick Ryan's Reeboks aside to grab my pack. I reach into the side pocket and pull out my phone, and breathe a sigh of relief to see the screen flash on.

But the battery icon is red—I may only have a few seconds.

I dial 9-1-1 again.

Nothing. I peer at the screen. No voicemail or text notifications either.

When was the last time I went even a day without getting a text from Shawntelle? I can't remember.

I look closer. Zero bars. A base station must be down. Must have been down awhile for me to not have a single notification from my best friend or my coach or anyone else on my team.

I dock the phone in the charger, but the charging symbol does not come on. I flick the light switch beside the outlet, but the light does not come on. Panic finds its way back inside me as I whip open the refrigerator door.

The smell of rotten vegetables hits my face, and I gag, slamming the door shut.

The electricity has been out for days.

I need to find help. Someone. Anyone. I need a friendly face or a friendly voice more than anything in the world. I'm starting toward the front door again when a wave of dizziness makes me grasp for the counter.

You need more water, Paige. And food.

The thought of eating makes my stomach turn, but I can't let myself be this fragile. I haven't eaten in almost a week. I'll just have a drink and a few bites of something bland, and then I'll find someone to help me with . . . I pause a moment before I'm able to say it, even silently to myself. *The bodies. I need help with the bodies.*

I pour myself a glass of water and drink. It goes down easier this time. I rummage through the pantry and find some saltine crackers. I choke on the first one, but the second is better, and by the third I'm so ravenous that I crush it into my mouth and hardly chew before swallowing. *Careful. Just like with the water.* I force myself to slow down.

The saltines won't be enough. I glance around until my gaze settles on the fruit bowl. It holds a few apples and two splotchy bananas. I grab a banana and peel it, then push it into my mouth. I stare at the bowl as I chew. I made it three years ago in ceramics class. Ryan called it "The Monstrosity" because of its odd bulges and splashes of mismatched paint. I thought I was being artsy. Abstract. Really, I was being ridiculous. But when I brought it home, Mom beamed proudly and immediately retired the old fruit bowl to the attic. The Monstrosity became a family fixture.

I force myself to swallow the rest of the banana, then I wash it down with another half glass of water. That taken care of, I think about my next move.

All those birds—maybe thousands of them—perched right outside are giving me the creeps. I shouldn't leave the house without a weapon. An umbrella, at least, or something that will make a loud noise. And I should change out of my robe.

Getting food into my bloodstream is helping me think. I loose a ragged sigh, grateful for the clarity.

I race up the stairs, and I'm light-headed by the time I reach the top, but I don't care. I throw on a pair of jeans—which never sagged on my hips this way before—a long-sleeved tee, and a zip-up hoodie. The scent of stale urine is overpowering now, and I make a mental note to change my sheets as soon as possible. I rummage around the bathroom cupboard until I find the box of disposable blue-and-white face masks Mom brought home from the hospital after the flu hit. I slip the elastic over my ears, which proves to be a good decision because I don't smell my own pee anymore.

I should put antibacterial cream on my hand, too. Later. I grab my key ring and its resident canister of pepper spray.

Another wave of dizziness hits as I go down the stairs, but I ignore it. I pass the kitchen, promising myself that if the saltines and banana stay down, I'll treat myself to some protein, then I grab my coat from the rack and swing it on.

I pause at the door. The back of my neck prickles, and my feet plant themselves stubbornly. *Are you a doer? Or a don't-er?* Shawntelle would say. I put a trembling hand to the knob and push the door open.

A rush of cold air greets me as I step into sunshine. Shivering, I shut the door behind me and start down the walkway, holding my pepper spray at the ready position. Crows peck at our lawn. They hop away as I pass, eyeing me warily. I wish they seemed more frightened, less bloated and satiated.

The street is silent and empty, save for the flapping of wings and the cawing of birds. It feels like they're watching me. The air buzzes with mosquitoes. No, they're tiny flies. Clouds of them hover around the mix of 1920s and 1940s homes that make up my neighborhood.

Cars sit parked on the street or in their drives, but there's no traffic. Usually by now some of the neighbors are getting home from work, kids are out on their bikes, someone is walking a dog. I glance to my right, expecting to find old Mrs. Carby tending her daffodil beds, her little sheltie, Emmaline, running circles around her ankles. We've had an early spring, and she never misses a day out with Emmaline. But her yard is as silent as everyone else's.

Mrs. Carby! She's one of the few people on the street who still has a landline.

I flip my hood up over my still-damp hair and I start to shove my hands into my coat pockets, but I decide I'd rather keep the pepper spray handy. I cross the grass toward her house, scattering crows in my wake.

Mrs. Carby's home is a neat one story with brick trim, yellow shutters, and a wheelchair ramp—for her husband until he passed two years ago. By the time I reach the top of the ramp, my legs quiver like jelly. Rather than protein and water, what I probably need is another IV.

I press the doorbell, which rings out an awful rendition of "Some Enchanted Evening." Emmaline barks, and the barking comes closer and closer until her nails clatter on the entryway tile, and then she's *scritch-scritch-scritch*ing at the door and whining her little head off.

"Hi, Emmaline," I say through the door, my words muffled by my face mask. "Is your mom home?" *Please be home. Please.* My brain flashes to a vision of dead bodies in beds, but I pull a mental curtain down over it and stare fixedly at Mrs. Carby's door panels.

Scritch scritch scritch.

I ring the doorbell again, and Emmaline goes wild, yipping and howling like a coyote. I put my face to the mail slot and say, "It's okay, sweetheart. It's just me. I promise I'll give you a belly scratch when . . . Oh!"

Death sends sickly, noxious creepers into my nostrils in spite of my mask, and I bend over, gasping and gagging.

Something snaps inside me, and suddenly I'm banging on the door with my fists and then my knees, and kicking and kicking until pain bursts sharp and bright in my big toe. I pause to suck in breath as my toe throbs with my heartbeat. I've probably broken it. I hardly care.

I have to get inside Mrs. Carby's house. I lift the doormat, looking for a key—nothing. I search the nearby planter and above the doorframe. All the while, Emmaline barks raggedly. Her voice is hoarse, like she's been barking a long, long time.

I give up searching and find a big, decorative rock instead. It's half the size of a basketball but ten times as heavy, and I can barely hold it. My heart is huge in my chest, and I think, *I am too thin, too weak, to hold my own heart inside myself.*

You're a warrior, Paige. Do this.

With all my strength, I hurl the rock through the front window. It shatters, and Emmaline comes flying out of the jagged hole. I squat down to hug her as she licks and nips at my face, her tail wagging so fiercely I fear it might fly off. Her long sable coat is horribly matted, and she stinks of poop, but I hug her anyway.

I rise, and Emmaline stands on her hind legs, batting at my thighs with paws that smear blood all over my jeans. Poor thing ran through broken glass to reach me. In any other circumstance, I'd tend to her paws, make sure there isn't any glass left inside, but I have to get to Mrs. Carby's phone.

I remove my coat and bunch it around my fist. With my makeshift glove, I punch out the glass around the edges of the window. Then I unwind my coat and drape it over the ledge to protect myself and climb in, one shaky leg at a time.

The smell is awful. Even worse than at home. "Mrs. Carby?"

I'm not sure why I call out. She's dead, taken by whatever took my brother and my parents. By whatever has taken a lot of people in my neighborhood.

I'm alone.

I know it. No, *accept* it. And something like relief-but-not-quite washes over me. It was part of the fog in my brain, the knowing but not accepting.

Instead of looking for Mrs. Carby, I head straight for the phone, which hangs on the wall beside the refrigerator. On the counter beneath the phone is a cookie jar and Mrs. Carby's brown leather purse. "Handbag," she always called it.

How many times have Ryan and I eaten cookies here, surrounded by stupid porcelain roosters, served with stupid rooster napkins? How many times have we pretended interest while Mrs. Carby waxed on about plans for her flower garden? The new trick Emmaline had learned at puppy school? I'd give anything to do it again.

I take a deep breath and lift the phone from the receiver and put it to my ear.

Nothing.

My knees give way and I crumple to the ground. Emmaline whines in my ear, bleeds all over my hoodie, but I hardly notice because my sadness cup is finally overflowing. Sobs wrack my body and snot drips from my nose. I keen, wild and high, as if the noise can push the pain out of my chest, and though I can't seem to form the words, the sound coming from the back of my throat means *alone, alone, alone, alone, alone.*

Emmaline barks as I sense a shadow near my shoulder. I whip my head around. A big black bird has hopped up onto the counter. He looks at me sideways, raising and lowering his head like a buoy in stormy waters. A funny feeling twinges in my chest. It's like he's sizing me up for meal potential.

Several others fly in through the open window and alight on the floor. Emmaline launches toward them, yipping wildly.

"Emmaline! Come back!" I yell, fearful of what will happen if she runs through broken glass a third time.

She twists midair and dashes back toward me.

"Good girl," I say, patting her head. I clamber to my feet, and I'm about to shoo the crow off of the counter but he flutters off without being prompted and half flies, half hops down the hallway toward the bedroom.

"Oh," I whisper, knowing he follows the scent of carrion.

I stand here in Mrs. Carby's kitchen for a moment, wiping my dripping nose, wondering what to do, but all I can think is, *Home. I want to go home.* The prospect of being in the same house with the bodies of my family fills me with sick dread, but I don't know what else to do, where else to go.

Food. I still need food. And water. I shouldn't have survived so long without. Mom obviously nursed me for a while. She probably saved my life by hooking me up to that IV before she got sick herself. Whatever happened, I shouldn't be alive, and I'm not going to stay that way unless I take care of myself.

So the first thing I need to do is get some strength back. And when I'm no longer dizzy with weakness, as soon as it's safe for me to drive, I'll get in the car and go find help. The hospital, maybe. Or the fire station, which is only a few streets away. In the meantime, I'll stuff rags under the doors of the bedrooms and air out the rest of the house as best I can.

On impulse, I unsnap Mrs. Carby's handbag and root through it for her wallet. It opens easily to a state-issued ID. Not a driver's license; Mrs. Carby stopped driving years ago.

Suyin Carby, it says. Five feet seven inches, wears corrective eyewear, white hair though the photo shows a few remaining strands of black. Born January 13. She's a beautiful old lady with high cheekbones, a single age spot under the corner of her left eye, and a smile that manages to be joyous without showing her teeth. She was born to Chinese immigrants, she told Ryan and me one afternoon over cookies, and she still speaks fluent Mandarin. According to this card, she's in her eighties now. I'm not sure why, but I never realized she was quite so old. I slip the ID into my pocket.

I open the cupboard that I know contains Emmaline's dog food. Only three cans left. I grab my coat from the windowsill and shake it out, wary of leftover glass shards. Crows flap away and hop down the hallway toward the bedroom. I put the coat on and shove the dog food into my pockets. I pat my chest and say, "Up-up, Emmaline," and she launches into my arms.

She's heavy, maybe too heavy for my weakened state, but we only have to make it as far as next door.

"Don't worry, girl, you're not alone anymore," I tell her as I open the door and step back into the light. And it's true. I suddenly love this little dog so much my heart hurts to bursting. "We'll be okay. We have a plan, sort of."

I don't bother closing the door behind me, and I don't look back.

March 14

REMEMBERING MY OWN REBELLIOUS STOMACH, I FEED EMMALINE in strategic intervals. She scarfs everything so fast it's like it disappears by magic. She needs a bath desperately, but I don't have the energy. I eat the second banana, drain another glass of water, then—reluctant to go back upstairs—I curl up on the couch and throw the afghan over my shoulders. I'm barely aware of Emmaline's weight settling in the crook of my belly before I drift off.

It's dark and cold when I wake. I reach for the lamp on the end table and pull the cord, but nothing happens. I stumble past the coffee table to the living room window and peer outside, looking for any sign of light or life, but it's darker than dark. My neighborhood is old, and most of the utilities are still above ground, so we have a power outage or two every year when thunderstorms blow through. But even then, there's always *some* light remaining: candlelight in windows or a glow in the distance, indicating the high-rises of downtown Columbus.

But not tonight. If I didn't know better, I'd think I was out in the country, miles from the nearest human.

I head toward the "emergency drawer" in the kitchen, trying not to consider that maybe I am miles away from the nearest *living* human. Emmaline limps beside me, her nails clicking on the floor. Maybe I can scrounge up enough light to tend to her lacerated paws.

Inside the drawer, I find a flashlight, a crank lantern, matches, and several candles. I turn on the lantern first, glad it's still holding a charge from the last outage—I'm not sure I'd have the stamina to crank it now. By its glow, I find the Neosporin in the downstairs medicine cabinet. Then I light three candles and set them on the kitchen counter near the sink. After indulging in another glass of water, I grab a dish towel, soak it with ice-cold water, and then rub it over Emmaline's coat. She quivers, ecstatic with the attention.

The smell is worse at first, as the water softens the dried poop stuck in her fur, but I keep at it. What I really need to do is take her upstairs and put her in the tub, but I can't go up there. Not yet. Instead, I rub and rub, rinsing the towel several times, until I can't smell poop anymore.

I grab a clean towel and the crank lantern and sit down on the floor, pulling the dog backward into my lap so that her legs splay out in four different directions. I examine each paw. Three of them have cuts, but the cuts look clean. Light glints off a large bit of glass still embedded in her right fore-paw. Before I can feel squeamish, I grasp it between thumb and forefinger and yank it out. She yelps, and blood wells up after it. I wrap her paw in the towel and press down to stem the flow, talking the whole time. "You're such a good, brave girl, Emmaline. And you're going to feel so much better after this, I promise."

Her feathery tail thumps against my thigh.

When I'm satisfied that the cut no longer bleeds, I rub Neosporin all over it and let her go. I stand to rinse the bloody towel, expecting her to lick all the Neosporin off, but she sits at my feet while I work, content to wait until I notice her again.

I dry my hands on a third dish towel—I'm going through towels fast—then slather the back of my hand with more Neosporin. The swelling might be going down already, but I can't be sure. I grab a granola bar from the pantry. While I chew, I rummage through the "miscellaneous drawer" for a pen and something to write on. I discover a small spiral note-book and carry it along with the crank lantern back to the couch. Emmaline hops up beside me. I give a fleeting thought to her paw staining the couch before deciding it doesn't matter.

I have accomplished something, even if it's just wiping down a dirty dog and removing a glass shard. It makes me feel a little braver, a little stronger. Maybe I can start asking the hard questions.

I write, *How many people got sick?*

The flu hit very fast. The last day I attended school, every class had missing students. The principal was debating whether or not to call off school for the next day. A few people had already died in the Cleveland area—mostly the very old, the very young, and those with preexisting conditions—and health professionals were encouraging everyone to wear face masks. When local airports started shutting down to prevent the bug from spreading, I remember being glad that Ohio is a smallish state, area-wise. All the teams would still be able to drive to the tournament, with the airlines closed.

What a selfish thought.

For six days, I was comatose. *Six days.* But my family was fine when I left the dinner table that night, which means they sickened and died in less time. So it kills quickly. Maybe too quickly for the disease to spread.

Could I be in some kind of quarantine area? Every scary movie I've seen rushes through my head. I imagine men in hazmat suits driving camouflage jeeps, Uzis hanging over their shoulders.

I write: *Quarantine?*

I need information. I can't turn on the television or computer without electricity. We used to have a crank radio, until Ryan broke it. The only way to find out what's happening beyond my neighborhood is get in the car and start driving.

The car! It has a radio.

I leap to my feet, dropping pen and paper, and rush over to the kitchen and snatch Mom's car keys from the counter. Emmaline follows at my heels as I dash through the laundry room to the garage.

From habit, I hit the light switch, but it doesn't come on. Briefly, I wonder how I'll back a car out of the garage without electricity to roll up the garage door. I'll figure it out later.

We have two cars—Mom's white hybrid sedan on the right, and Paul's maroon SUV on the left. I squeeze around the front bumper and open the driver's side door to the hybrid. The dome light flashes on, and I breathe relief, so glad for this tiny bit of normalcy. I climb in, slide the seat back to make room for my long legs, then depress the start button halfway—enough to engage the battery but not start the engine.

Music fills the garage, and it's so startling, so wonderful, to have a human voice in my ears that I freeze and listen. It's Guns N' Roses, my mom's favorite CD. I hate this song. Still, I close my eyes and lean back, letting the music wash over me.

I barely stifle a scream when Emmaline leaps over me into the passenger seat. She circles three times before sitting down.

"You scared me, girl."

Her tail thumps twice.

I sigh, realizing I'm putting off the inevitable. My fingers tremble as I lean toward the sound system in the dash.

"Here goes, Emmaline." I push the button to switch to radio.

Static.

I press the seek button; the radio's digital readout blurs as it whips through the frequencies. I hold my breath as it starts over at the bottom, works its way up, passes the frequency where it began.

Still nothing.

My disappointment is so sharp it hurts. I try to think about what this means. The radio seems to be working fine. So none of the stations are broadcasting. The power outage must be regional. What's the range of this radio? Miles. Maybe a hundred. Whenever we take a road trip, we're halfway to Cincinnati before our local stations fade out.

It feels like someone is standing on my chest. No radio stations broadcasting for a hundred-mile radius. Surely some of the stations have generators. But they're still not broadcasting. That means whatever happened is bad. Epically bad.

I flip the dial from FM to AM, not because I'm hopeful but because it's something to do. I hit pay dirt.

A man's voice fills the car, the first live voice I've heard since I woke up. He has a thick Clevelander accent. I start forward in the seat, hanging on every word.

". . . martial law per the Ohio Constitution. The CDC reports that the virus is airborne, with a mortality rate of 100 percent. Therefore, for your own safety, do not leave your homes under any circumstances. Anyone violating this order will be shot on sight. Anyone operating a vehicle will be shot on sight and their vehicle impounded. Roads must remain clear for military personnel."

Shot on sight! Did I risk my life just to walk next door? Is that why the streets are empty? Maybe everyone is hiding, afraid to step outside. Hope flares inside me, only to wink out like a burned-up match.

Because that doesn't explain the birds. Or the flies.

"Do not bury or burn the deceased. I repeat, do not

bury or burn them as this may have a contaminating effect. Recommendations for handling the deceased are posted at emergency-dot-cdc-dot-gov."

Why would anyone bury or burn the dead themselves? That's what morgues are for. And how could burying bodies contaminate anything? That makes no sense. A cemetery, after all, is a very large collection of the dead.

But all of a sudden it does make sense. If there are so many bodies that they're creating some kind of toxic waste. If there are hundreds of thousands. Or more.

"This message is being sent on March tenth at three p.m. This message will repeat. You're listening to AM 1610, the people's choice for Sandusky free radio, with a breaking news update from the capital. The president has declared a national state of emergency and the governor has invoked martial law per the Ohio Constitution. The CDC reports that the virus is airborne, with a mortality rate of 100 percent . . ."

My heart sinks. I'm listening to a recorded message on a loop, not a flesh-and-blood human. I reach out and brush the face of the radio with my fingertip, as if doing so will connect me with the man who spoke these words four days ago. Is he still alive? Is this the last thing he did?

A mortality rate of 100 percent.

And yet, I lived. My smidge of hope is a fragile thing, a tiny wavering flame in a vast landscape of reeking darkness. I will shelter it, treasure it, coax it, because the alternative is despair, and I don't do despair.

"C'mon, Emmaline." I turn the keys to the off position and

grab the doorframe to pull myself from the driver's seat.

Together we return to the living room and my spiral note-book. Morning sunshine streams through the curtains now. I open them so I can observe the street as I work. If anyone is alive out there, I want to know it at once.

I settle back down on the couch, Emmaline beside me. Beneath *How many got sick?* and *Quarantine?* I write, *100% mortality rate* and *National state of emergency.* I underline *National*.

I chew on the pen. On the end table is a framed photo of me and Shawntelle in last year's prom gowns and bedazzled Chuck Taylors. We're back to back, hands on our hips, stand-ing below a fake arbor wrapped in blue and gold balloons. A couple of guys from the boys' basketball team asked me to junior prom, but Shawntelle and I decided to heck with the boys; we were going together. A girls' night out.

How do I find out whether the streets are empty because everyone is hiding, or because everyone is dead? Maybe Shawntelle is holed up at her place, afraid to leave.

I stare at the photo. Shawntelle loves purple. Her prom gown, her corsage, her Chucks, her nails, even her laboriously straightened hair—all violently purple.

My best friend was afraid of nothing. If she were alive, nothing would have stopped her from being at my bedside when I woke up.

I have to go out searching for signs of life, even if I risk encountering someone with orders to shoot me on sight. It's what Shawntelle would do.

In my notebook, I write, *Signs of life: running vehicles, movement, light.*

I tap the end of my chewed-up pen against my lip, then I underline *light*.

A plan forms. I'll wait until dark, wear dark clothes. Carry nothing but a water bottle, a flashlight, and pepper spray. I'll dart from house to house, using the buildings as cover, listening for sound, looking for candlelight or the sweep of a flashlight. If I encounter trouble, I can sprint for the shadows. I'm a very fast, agile runner.

No, I *was* a very fast, agile runner.

In my notebook, in all caps, I write, *GET HEALTHY.*

March 15

I ALLOW MYSELF ONE DAY BEFORE ENACTING MY PLAN. I USE THAT time to drink as much water as I can and readjust my stomach to normal food.

I'm worried about the water. Will it get polluted? How long until the supply from the nearby tower is used up? I could collect rainwater, I guess. One thing you can count on in Columbus is a steady drizzle of snow and rain. But how would I keep it uncontaminated? I would have to keep the birds away, the birds who have been drawn here by death.

What I really need is bottled water. My grocery store has a whole aisle devoted to spring water, distilled water, water in gallon jugs, sparkling water. But until I know whether or not martial law is being enforced, I don't dare go looking.

And I'm almost out of dog food. I have tuna in the pantry,

a little canned chicken. I'm pretty sure Emmaline will eat anything, but I'll need to come up with something else for her soon.

The smell from upstairs is unbearable, so overpowering that I can't function. It's not even the reek that bothers me so much as the reminder. I can't go a single second without being utterly aware that my family is dead. I see photos of my brother pinned with magnets on the fridge, and I revel in his regional championship basketball team picture even as I smell him decomposing. I see Mom and Paul's wedding album on the coffee table, remember the way they kissed after saying "I do"—like giddy, ridiculous teenagers—and then the reek flashes me back to their dying embrace.

My family deserves a decent burial. Some kind of marker, something as immortal as marble or granite that will forever point to these precious souls and the lives they had.

I'm not strong enough to drag the bodies outside. Even if I were, I'm not sure the bodies are . . . whole. And the radio message rings in my head: *Do not bury the deceased.* It's the only voice of authority I've heard since I woke up. It feels good to obey it.

So I'll let nature take its course. I'll even help nature along. This would please Mom, I know. The staunch environmentalist who forced us to reduce, reuse, recycle. She'd like the idea of being part of the circle of life.

I grab a yellow bath towel from the linen closet and wrap it around my nose and mouth. Then I dash into my parents' room—refusing to look at the bed—and I fling open all the windows in the bedroom. I pull on the tabs to yank the screens out of place, and toss them to the yard below. Then I run into the master bathroom and do the same to that window too.

I rush back into the hallway, slam the double doors shut, and bend over against them, heaving.

After getting my breath back, I seal off the doorframe from top to bottom with plastic wrap and duct tape. Then I do the same to Ryan's door.

The crows can have them all, with my blessing.

But by the time I reach the bottom of the stairs, I'm sobbing so hard my back aches. Ryan. Mom. Paul. My family.

Mom never lost faith, no matter how bad things were with the Sperm Donor. And I guess she was right not to. Our lives got so much better.

As the sun sets, I light a candle and sing Mom's favorite hymn into the twilight. My voice is too loud in a vast silence, and no one will hear it but me and Emmaline and the birds. But on the off chance that Mom was right about an afterlife, that she can look down on me now, I want her to know I'll be okay. I sing with my whole breath:

> *When peace like a river attendeth my way*
> *When sorrows like sea billows roll*
> *Whatever my lot thou hast taught me to say*
> *It is well, it is well with my soul*

March 16

IT'S TIME TO GO OUTSIDE.

In spite of our early spring, it's still winter cold at night. But I need to be able to move quickly and easily, so I forgo my heavy coat in favor of thick knee-high socks under black sweats, two long-sleeved T-shirts, and over everything a tunic-length hoodie. The hoodie is deep purple instead of black, but maybe it won't matter in the dark. I tie Paul's black scarf around my neck—ready to pull it up over my nose like a mask if I have to—and slip on my mom's leather driving gloves.

The gloves are too small for my long fingers, so I pull them off and grab the kitchen scissors to slice off the fingertips. I try them again, flexing my hands. Perfect.

I gather my hair into a ponytail at the base of my neck,

noting that it's greasy again and will require another horrifically cold shower soon. I check to make sure I have everything I need—my Mini Maglite, house key, pepper spray.

Emmaline dances circles around me as I get ready, rapturous at the prospect of going for a walk. But I tell her to *stay* in the firmest tone I can muster, and she drops to her belly, rests her chin on her paws, and gazes up at me with such a look of wide-eyed despair that I almost give in.

"I'll be back, Emmy. I promise." And I leave her whimpering in the entryway as I head out into the night.

The moon is full, which lights my way but also makes me uncomfortably visible. I stand in the walkway a moment, listening. The dark shapes of sleeping crows huddle in the grass, line the branches of our winter-bare redbud tree, shift on the rooftops of nearby cars.

I start forward on soft feet, alert for any sight or sound, any change in the air. The night is ice-cold; I should fire up the woodstove when I return. Good thing this happened at the tail end of winter, or I'd have to add firewood to my list of things I'll run out of if I don't find help soon.

The sidewalk is bright, almost shimmering, in the moonlight. I move to the middle of the street where my clothes blend in better with the dark asphalt. I pass Mrs. Carby's house, then the Douglases' yellow Craftsman and its solar walkway lights. My footfalls seem too loud, my breath too fast, as I study each window, looking for a glint of candlelight or a shadow of movement.

I'm three blocks east when I hear it—no, feel it: a *whoomph*, like all the air has gotten sucked away. I freeze, heart pound-ing. I let my gaze dart around, not sure what I'm looking for.

Whoomph.

It's such a ghostly thing, happening just below the level of my senses and yet powerful enough to leave an echoing hollow in my chest, like I've been standing next to thumping concert speakers.

My legs buzz with the need to flee, but curiosity keeps me frozen in place. Because as otherworldly as it seems, it's *some-thing*, the first something I've found since I woke up.

I brace myself to hear—feel—it again, straining with all my senses. Instead comes a soft clatter, like high heels on con-crete. Very close.

I dart between two cars and duck down.

The clatter approaches, unhurried, echoing in the night. I dare to peer around the fender. Dark shapes move toward me. I hold my breath.

The shapes are only two houses away when they manifest in the moonlight into something recognizable. Deer. Three of them. Walking down the middle of the street.

They veer toward the sidewalk opposite my hiding spot and lower their necks to nibble a hedge. Their ears and tails twitch constantly, alert for the slightest hint of danger. I'm as quiet and still as I can possibly be. They're so beautiful and lithe and graceful and *alive*, and I don't ever want them to leave.

All at once they raise their necks and look eastward, ears pricked forward. The world pauses for the space of a breath, then they dart off in the opposite direction, tails lifted high.

Another shape slinks after them, its body low to the ground, skimming it like a ghost.

I lurch up. "No!" I yell after the shape. It's a coyote, maybe. A large coyote.

It stops and turns to face me, ears pressed back, eyes glowing golden in the moonlight.

A *very* large coyote. No, a German shepherd. Or a husky? Whatever it is, it drops its head below its shoulders and studies me.

It circles my position at a slow trot, keeping about twenty feet between us. It has a long-legged, wolfy gait, a straight bushy tail. Never once does it take its eyes off of me.

Surely it hears my heart pounding? Smells the fear clogging my throat?

Slowly, I reach into my pocket for the pepper spray.

There's no sound, no warning, just a huge black shape plunging toward me as it charges.

I sprint away, pumping legs and arms as fast as I can, expecting to feel hot breath at my back, fangs tearing into my calves. I don't dare look back, but claws scrape concrete behind me. Already I'm dizzy, my lungs burning. I can't last. I need to find an enclosed porch or climb a tree.

There! A porch. Not enclosed, but a lattice rises up the side along with a drain pipe. If I time it just right, I can jump from the edge of the porch, up the lattice to the adjoining six-foot fence, and from there to the roof. I'll need both hands.

Mid-stride, I transfer the pepper spray to my mouth and clutch the cylinder with my teeth. Almost there. The footsteps behind clang loudly—the dog has launched itself over the fender of a parked car to cut me off.

I place one foot on the edge of the porch and launch off it, grasping for the lattice. *Please hold, please hold.* I bang hard against the side of the house, but the lattice sticks firm. I climb it like a ladder. My arms shake with the effort.

I'm swinging my right leg onto the fence when teeth close around my left heel. Pain explodes through my leg. I can't hold myself up. The dog is going to pull me down and rip me apart. I'm sobbing from fear and desperation, but my body won't give up. I cling one handed to the lattice, reaching for the pepper spray with the other.

The dog shakes my leg back and forth, and I try to kick it, but it hangs on.

I fumble the pepper spray; it flies into the air. I catch it by its dangling key chain, maneuver it around until I can finger the latch.

I barely remember to take a deep breath and close my eyes before letting loose.

It empties in a *whoosh*. The dog squeals, dropping to the ground. It rolls once in agony, then dashes off, banging into cars as it threads its way haphazardly up the street.

Too soon, I take a breath of relief, and suddenly I'm choking and coughing so hard I can barely breathe. I tumble to the ground, landing hard on my shoulder, sending daggers into my neck.

I roll onto my stomach and try to get my knees underneath me. Tears stream from my eyes and snot pours from my nose as I cough and hack my way to my feet. I take a few experimental steps. My bitten heel hurts like hell, but I don't think anything is broken.

I limp toward home, my eyes and nose on fire, my pepper spray held at the ready, feeling lucky to be alive.

Then, from far away—north, maybe?—comes the eerie not-sound: *whoomph*. Its aftermath shivers in my chest as I break into a staggering run.

I sit on top of the toilet lid in the downstairs bathroom and peel off my court trainers and socks. The skin of my heel is partly shredded and badly bruised around one large, deep puncture. My big toe is bright purple from when I kicked Mrs. Carby's door. Between the dog bite and the kicking, I'm very lucky that nothing seems broken. If I'd been wearing boots, I might have escaped nearly unscathed. I vow to never again leave the house without my Doc Martens.

Emmaline sniffs the discarded shoe and whines, no doubt scenting the other dog.

Was it rabid? It didn't seem frothy or crazed. Just feral. Still, a dog bite can be bad news. Cleaning it is going to hurt.

As I soap up a damp washcloth, I wonder: how long does it take for friendly house pets to go feral? The world has been dead less than six days. I think of Emmaline, darting through broken glass toward a familiar face, someone she knows can feed her.

How many pets didn't make it? How many are trapped inside their homes, starving to death, without even the opportunity to turn feral?

We living creatures get desperate fast. I'm bound to encounter more. Dogs. Maybe people. How am I supposed to handle feral people?

Wincing, I scrub at my heel, paying particular attention to the raw bits. In one spot near the arch of my foot, the skin peels back, revealing the meaty redness of what might be muscle. But if the dog bit all the way down to muscle, wouldn't it bleed more? I start to peer closer but find that I can't bear to. I wish my mom could help me. She would know at a glance what needed to be done.

Muscle or not, Mom would say I need to sterilize it.

I rummage under the sink and find a bottle of rubbing alcohol. I pour some onto the washcloth and press it against my torn flesh. It burns, oh, god, it burns. My breath hisses through clenched teeth, and sweat breaks out on my neck.

I should rub it into the wound. But I don't think I can bear to feel my own flesh separate from my body.

Before I can think about it a moment more, I lift my leg over the sink and upend the bottle, pouring its contents all over my foot.

I scream. Black spots dance in my vision.

I toss the empty bottle into the garbage and bend over my knee, panting, waiting for the pain to fade, but it doesn't. I knock everything off the counter in my hurry to fill the rinse cup with water and pour it over my heel and arch. That helps. It's blessedly cool. I can breathe again.

I plaster a wad of cotton gauze with Neosporin and wrap it against the wound with an Ace bandage.

Gingerly, I rise from the toilet and test my weight against it. Not bad. Then again, I've just discovered that everything is "not bad" compared to pouring alcohol onto an open wound.

Emmaline stretches up to put her forepaws on my thigh. I lean over and let her lap at my cheek as I bury my hands in her thick ruff. "I should take you with me when I go outside, Emmy," I tell her. "I don't think that dog would have attacked both of us together."

I straighten, thinking hard. Actually, it shouldn't have attacked me at all. At six-foot-three, I'm the tallest girl in my school by far. I've always been on the willowy side, but my height alone should have been a deterrent.

Maybe it identified me as weak. Sickly.

"You and me, Emmy, we've got to get healthy. It needs to be our first priority."

March 17

In the morning, I let Emmaline into the backyard for a potty. I listen to the world around me as she does her business, hoping for the sound of a motor, music, talking, anything. But there is only the caw of birds, the flapping of wings, and the buzz of insects. The whole neighborhood smells now. It's like a festering swamp—motionless and muggy and sickly sweet. As soon as Emmaline is done, I hurry us back inside and spray the downstairs with pine-scented air freshener.

I take stock of my food and water options. I have lots of canned food: tuna, refried beans, peaches in light syrup, stewed tomatoes (ugh), crushed pineapple, tons of soup, and creamed corn (double ugh). I also have two boxes of Wheat Flakes cereal, which I'll have to eat without milk, two loaves of bread, peanut butter, honey, two boxes of macaroni and cheese, one and half boxes of granola bars, a can of sour cream and onion Pringles (my mom always kept one in the house for Shawntelle), a jar of lightly salted peanuts, a six-pack of Fruity Juicy boxes (orange flavored—Ryan's favorite), three bottled waters, a bag of long grain brown rice, corn chips, and a sealed pack of flour tortillas.

Easy on the salt before the big game, Coach D always said. I decide to forego eating soup or macaroni and cheese or anything with huge amounts of sodium, even though they'd be easy enough to cook up on the woodstove. Until my body is fully hydrated and recovered, I shouldn't risk it. The canned meat would provide protein, but I maybe I should save that for my dog.

So I make myself a peanut-butter-and-honey sandwich for breakfast, which is wonderful. I decide it's the most wonderful breakfast I've ever had. Emmaline thinks so too. I drop a large dollop of peanut butter on top of her left paw and laugh while she spends the next several minutes happily at war with the sticky stuff.

My water supply is probably intact. Especially if I'm the only one left alive in my neighborhood. What a strange quandary. If I'm alone, my water could last forever. If I'm not, the water tower will empty, and the new water coming from the purification plant could poison me.

I had better start boiling my water. Just in case.

A few years ago, Paul insisted that Ryan and I learn about the woodstove—how to fire it up, how to hit maximum temperature at a slow burn, how to clean it, how to do it all safely.

We complained the whole time. But now I glance toward the stairs and whisper, "Thanks, Paul."

I rummage through the cupboard by the stove and come up with two large pots, which I fill with water from the tap and set on top of the woodstove. I get a fire going inside and shut the doors. Watching the warm glow through the glass flashes me back to Christmas morning, to evergreen garlands and red velvet stockings and our fake tree with its tiny white lights. I swallow hard, remembering how Ryan had presented me with a pair of Nike Air court trainers. He was so excited for me to open my gift. He saved up all year to buy them.

It takes a long time for water to go from ice-cold to hard boil. I turn my back on the stove, grab the pepper spray, and head out the back door, whistling for Emmaline to follow. I have no desire to go outdoors again so soon, but doing something—anything—is better than being sad.

Our backyard is fenced, so we're unlikely to be attacked by the feral dog that took a bite out of my foot. Also, I'm hoping the face full of pepper spray will make him think twice. Still, I study every part of the yard—the winter-brown lawn, the border of daffodils, the small redbud tree in the back corner that could burst with hot pink any day. Except for the crows lining the fence and the stench, it seems like a normal, beautiful spring day.

In the garden shed, I find our extension ladder. It's heavier than I remember and awkward as hell. I bang the wall three times maneuvering it out the wide door. I extend the ladder and lean it against the house, which sends a bunch of crows who'd been sitting in Ryan's windowsill flapping away. I pause for breath, then I start to climb.

Paul would kill me if he saw me using the extension ladder without a partner to hold the bottom steady. *Sorry, Paul.* I pull myself resolutely upward. Emmaline whines at me from below.

I pass Ryan's broken window, refusing to look inside, and clamber onto the roof. It's not a steep pitch, which is lucky; several homes in the neighborhood have rooftops way too steep for safe climbing. I straddle the peak, bracing my back against the chimney, which is already feeling warm from the fire below.

Our house is on a slight rise—as much of a rise as one can find in Columbus—and it's too early for the trees to have greened out. Which means I can see a good half mile in every direction. Only two houses east is High Street, Columbus's main thoroughfare. Everything is still. No smoke from chimneys, no moving cars, no glowing traffic lights, no pedestrians. Never in my life have I seen High Street without traffic.

A few blocks north on High are the remains of a major car pileup. A black Chevy Suburban lies on its side, its roof so dented and scraped that it obviously rolled. A smaller sedan is lodged between its front wheels, its windshield shattered. A pickup is spun off to the side, its nose wrapped around a utility pole. Other cars lie scattered beyond, but I can't see much past the SUV.

I imagine the sounds of horns and tires squealing, the crunch of steel. So much violence happened right outside my door, and I slept through it all. What became of the drivers?

Maybe they're still inside their cars, rotting along with the rest of my neighborhood.

In spite of the bright sunshine, the horizon is hazed and dirty. A layer of gray chokes the earth. It's the bugs, maybe. Or smoke.

What I don't see, what I hoped desperately to see, is any sign of human life.

The icy breeze stiffens my cheeks and my limbs. I'm like a gargoyle crouching on the edge of a roof, gone to stone with cold, looking out over a ghost of a city.

Maybe I'll come back up tomorrow. And the day after that. I can figure out a way to signal from the roof. Maybe mirrors. Or flashlights at night. If someone is out there, I'll get their attention. I'll . . .

No, I'm stronger than this. Denial is not my style. I know what Mom would say. Face facts, Paige. You'll make better decisions. And the fact is that no one else is out there. Not nearby, at least. What I need to do is come up with an exit strategy. Find food and clean water for me and Emmaline. I need to get the hell out of here before all the decomposing bodies make it too dangerous. If they haven't already.

I'll pack up everything I can carry. I'll find a meaningful way to say good-bye to my family. And I'll take to the road, looking for others like me, martial law be damned. Because if I don't, I'm dead anyway.

My heart is heavy as a rock as I scoot down the roof toward the ladder. Emmaline's whimper sifts up to me through the hazy air. I swing my leg onto the first rung, glad to have a living creature waiting for me at the bottom.

The sky blackens with crows—a blanket of them, several feet thick, lifting off all at once. They fly south, skimming the rooftops, and I duck as they screech and flap just overhead. When I sense that the sky is clear, I warily raise my gaze.

The earth rumbles. The ladder shifts, and I grab for the gutter. The metal edges dig into my palms as I steady myself. I take a deep breath, my heart kicking at my ribs. Close call.

A fireball shoots into the sky, high above the buildings, several miles north. A metal disc flips through the air beside it. It looks like a Frisbee.

Emmaline's whining turns to frenzied barks. Another rumble, another desperate clutching at the gutter, as a bigger, brighter fireball launches skyward. Closer. This time I recognize the metal disc as a manhole cover.

It's an explosion in the sewer. No, a series of explosions. Making its way down High Street.

I scurry down the ladder as fast as I can. The earth shakes again, and the ladder slides to the side. My instinct is to cling to the rungs, to ride it to safety, but I recognize this as the wrong play just as the edge slips off the roof into open air. I leap away from the ladder and land hard, stumbling backward, my injured heel screaming agony.

I start to get up, but another explosion knocks me down. Emmaline grabs the hem of my jeans in her mouth and tugs hard. I clamber to my feet and run into the house, the dog at my heels.

I have one minute, tops. What do I absolutely need? Car

keys. Something to drink. Everything else can wait.

I search the living room frantically. Where did I put Mom's keys? Maybe they're in the kitchen. I run to the island. Nothing.

I swing the pantry open and grab a couple of bottles of Gatorade. There are more drinks in there somewhere, but I don't dare take the time. I spy Paul's spare key to the RAV4 hanging by the calendar and yank it from its hook.

At the last second, I grab the bulging Monstrosity from the kitchen island and hitch it under one arm. "Emmy, let's go." Together we dash through the laundry room and into the garage.

Another explosion rocks the ground beneath me, and my elbow slams into the side-view mirror, knocking it askew. Woodsmoke and natural gas prick at my nostrils.

It's too dark to see well, and when I hit the unlock button on Paul's key, I get my first flare of real hope, for the headlights flash and the dome light pops on. So normal.

I open the door and fling the Monstrosity into the passenger seat, and Emmaline follows after.

The garage door is automatic, powered by electricity. Should I barrel through it in the RAV4? No, the door is segmented with steel beams.

The earth shakes continually now as I stumble toward the door, hoping for a latch, some way to lift it manually. I feel along the metal edges in the semidarkness. There! A lever. I crank it and heave. The door rolls upward. Light and air and bugs pour inside.

I run to the driver's side door and swing myself inside. *Please let there be gas in the tank. Please.*

I crank the ignition, but the engine sputters. The car hasn't been started in days. I try again. It roars to life. I jerk it into reverse and squeal out of the garage.

The air outside is hazy with smoke, bright with flame. The fire is too close. Another explosion sends the wheels bumping over the sidewalk, and I tug the steering wheel left to compensate. I speed toward the nearest cross street. I just need to get a few blocks south. Then I can head west on Henderson, across the river and to safety.

Something as bright as the sun flashes in my rearview mirror. My home. Bursting into flame. My diaphragm heaves, like I've been gut punched. Now I've lost everything. Absolutely everything.

I lay on the gas pedal. My vision is blurred with tears and I'm going way too fast for safety, but I don't care. Explosions continue to rock the air, and even though they become more distant as I near the bridge, it doesn't matter because each one pounds the dreaded word into my head: *Alone. Alone. Alone. Alone.*

I don't even realize where I'm going until I take a sharp turn, missing the bridge and heading instead toward Shawntelle's house a couple of miles away. Normally it's only a six-minute drive, but nothing is normal about this drive. I go slowly, looking for signs of other survivors, keeping my eyes sharp for soldiers enforcing martial law, even watching for wolflike dogs hunting the streets. Clusters of wrecked and abandoned cars interrupt the pavement, but nothing moves. I weave my way through the obstacles. A cloud of flies swarms around a dark shape on the sidewalk.

My eyes sting, and at first I think I'm crying again, and maybe I am a little, but the stinging gets worse. Smoke. The scent reaches me a split second later.

This neighborhood got hit with the sewer explosion too. Flames leap above rooftops and trees even before I reach Shanwtelle's street. Heat turns the cab of Paul's RAV4 into a furnace. I roll forward slowly, until my body can't bear it anymore. Several hundred yards away, in the middle of the burning block, Shawntelle's house is an inferno. The windows have blown out. Flames lick the window frames. Black smoke pours from a hole in the roof.

"C'mon, Shawntelle," I whisper, feeling like a coward for not going any closer.

I imagine her running out the door and I shout to her to get in the car and we hug and hug, and then we drive away to safety.

Sparks shoot up in the air as Shawntelle's roof collapses. The front wall of her house gets pushed out into the street, blocking the road completely. No one comes running out of her house or any other.

Everyone in this part of town is dead.

I back up, the air cooling with every car length. I make a three-point turn and drive away, tears blurring my sight of the rearview mirror. Because I'm still watching for Shawntelle to come running down the street. I watch and watch and watch until I turn the corner toward the highway, when I finally tell myself my best friend was definitely dead of the sickness before that explosion hit, because that would be so much better than burning alive.

The onramp to Highway 315 is blocked by orange cones. One has fallen over, which gives me just enough room to maneuver the RAV4 through them. I crane my neck as the ramp rises toward the highway. I'm not sure what I'm hoping to see. A moving vehicle, maybe. A view of the city. Any sign of human life. I would prefer soldiers with gas masks and machine guns to this emptiness clawing at my chest.

But as the RAV4 crests the shoulder, all that greets me is desolation, broken up by scattered bits of strangeness. There's a Mercedes, pulled almost-but-not-quite off to the side of the road. A shape hunches over the steering wheel, but my view is blurred because the windows are slimy.

Farther on, a skeleton lies broken and sprawled in the middle of the highway, its flesh picked clean. The bones are muddy brown, which surprises me. I thought bones would be white. I steer around it, peering over the dash, wishing the skeleton could tell me what happened, what it's doing in the middle of a once-busy highway.

Cars are scattered along the way, some off to the side, some stalled out in the middle of the asphalt. A few have bodies inside. Others don't, or at least not that I can see.

Nothing moves. Even the birds have shunned this place.

To my right, a line of thick smoke runs parallel to the

highway, choking the sky with sickly brown. The air reeks of burning chemicals. Maybe this is why the birds have gone. Everything along the High Street sewer line, my whole neighborhood, Shawntelle's neighborhood, is smoldering rubble.

Now that my heart rate has steadied, now that I'm a little bit safe, questions chase themselves around in my mind. "If no one is left alive," I say to Emmaline, "what caused the gas explosion?"

Her tail thumps.

My grip on the steering wheel tightens, and I lean forward, renewing my search for signs of life. "I mean, maybe someone was smoking. Or had a candle lit. Something ignited that gas. It couldn't just . . ."

I frown. It could *just*. All it would take is an abandoned generator, churning away after its owner died. A blown transformer. A metal gate sparking against concrete as it swung in the wind. It would be easy, if enough gas had accumulated.

Tears threaten again, and my throat is tight and hot. I push it all away and focus on a plan. I need food. Water. A safe place. But the world is suddenly my enemy, full of flies and birds steeped in carrion and all manner of things that could kill me slowly, as well as feral dogs and invisible dangers—like sewer-gas explosions—that could kill me instantly. And I have no phone, no internet, no friends to tell me what lies around the next bend in the highway. I must treat my hometown like a stranger I've never met. No, more like a psychotic stalker. I can't let down my guard for a second.

I should leave the city. Go somewhere rural, where low

population will mean low body count. The air will be cleaner, at least. I glance at the gas gauge. Only a quarter of a tank. That won't get me far. I'll figure something out.

"Food first, Emmy," I say. "Supplies. Then we'll find an old farmhouse to hole up in. Or something like that. And, hey, maybe we'll find someone out there, right? Maybe this awful plague didn't make it outside of Columbus."

I know it for a comforting lie as soon as the words leave my mouth. That radio announcement had called it a "national" emergency. Besides, something so deadly that it makes a wasteland of Ohio's largest city in six days is bad. Unspeakably bad. Apocalyptically bad.

Which strikes me as significant. I roll the thought around in my head as I pass under the exit sign for Upper Arlington. Six days. That's how long it took for my city to die.

"Emmaline?" I whisper. "Six days is not enough time for a disease to kill a whole city." My heart races, and my palms against the steering wheel grow slick. When I was younger, the coronavirus seemed to last forever. And I've played the endemic scenario, Plague Inc., on my tablet like everyone else, but I wish I'd paid more attention in history class when we studied the Spanish flu. Or to my mom when she complained about flu season. Or anything. "It's not enough time for everyone to get exposed *and* incubate a sickness. That would be impossible. Right?"

The more I think about it, the more I'm sure. In order for everyone to die so quickly, we all had to be exposed at exactly the same time.

"Oh, god, Emmaline."

What if it wasn't by chance that some new strain of deadly flu appeared to everyone all at once? What if we were exterminated?

I've always thought the suburb of Upper Arlington was too pristine, like a giant golf course dotted with sprawling ranch homes and perfectly behaved maples. I imagine it's a place where people take tea and play bridge and go to the salon at least once a week, and as I drive through the silent, immaculate streets my impression does not change. It's as if even death does not dare to defy the privileged wealthy who lived here.

Ravens dot the lawns, but they're not as thick as in my neighborhood. The air is less muggy, with fewer flies. Maybe Upper Arlington had better ways to deal with the bodies, in the same way that they have better schools, better snowplows, better paychecks.

Or maybe not everyone here is dead. No, that's naïve. Of course everyone is dead.

I'm wandering aimlessly, wasting what little gas is in the tank, not sure what I'm looking for. I steer into a cul-de-sac and hit the brakes. Above me, a giant sign stretches across the street, hanging from matching light posts. It says, WELCOME TO THE END OF THE WORLD BLOCK PARTY!

Beyond the sign is a haphazard collection of lounge chairs and coolers, garbage pails lined in black trash bags, and outdoor umbrellas. A charcoal grill lies belly-up, its tripod legs pointing toward me. A giant turkey vulture perches on the topmost leg.

I creep forward slowly. The vulture hops down from the grill and ambles away, giving my car the side-eye. The white tip of his beak is a sharp blade of bone. He settles on a lawn, which isn't nearly far enough away to suit me.

I steer the car around the cooler and the grill. All my senses are afire. I'm not sure what I'm expecting. Phantoms, maybe. It's too quiet, too still, made even more so by all this evidence, right in the middle of the road, that *life* was so recent and so vibrant.

To my left, on a fluorescent green lounge chair, is a body.

It's a man, wearing jeans and cowboy boots, a gray hoodie, and a red Ohio State ball cap pulled down over his face. One arm hangs over the edge of the lounge chair, just brushing the pavement. He looks like he's out for an afternoon nap.

His leg moves.

I slam on the brakes, and Emmaline tumbles into the foot well. "Sorry!" I throw at her, even as I fumble to unlatch my seat belt and fling the door wide.

"Hello?" I say, running toward the lounge chair. "Are you awake?"

He doesn't respond.

Emmaline comes to sit beside me as I peer down at him. His chest rises and falls. "Sir? I'm sorry to wake you, but I could really use some help."

No answer. Maybe he's sick.

I reach down to shake his shoulder.

It caves beneath my touch, like pudding, and I recoil, almost tripping over Emmaline. His chest heaves, and something small and white squirms out below the waist of his hoodie. Then several somethings. Then thousands of somethings, tumbling over each other and milling about like plump grains of rice.

I scream, backing away, and then I'm dashing for the car, the dog at my heels. I throw myself inside, and the second Emmaline follows, I slam the door closed. I hug the steering wheel, letting my forehead fall against the center column. The horn rips the air and Emmaline yips in response, but I don't pay any attention. I stay this way a long time, catching my breath, fighting against nausea.

Finally, the sound of the horn becomes intrusive, and I raise my head. *You are not afraid of maggots, Paige. Maggots can't hurt you.*

Emmaline's wet tongue on my hand startles me. She's either giving comfort or asking for it. I scritch her behind the ear. Her tail thumps.

I force myself to look at the body in the lounge chair. He seems a bit deflated now, and the maggots that fell from him cover the sidewalk. From a few strides away the concrete appears to move, like liquid.

Just maggots. Harmless.

I put the car in gear and push forward into the cul-de-sac.

Beyond the scattered remnants of the block party, bright green lawns stretch wide, the grass now ragged and already growing over the edges of concrete driveways. One lawn sports a high flagpole, and the Stars and Stripes whips in the wind.

Below it in the front window is a huge sign with the words I VOTE FOR FREEDOM!

To the right of the window is a lovely porch with a swing. Two bodies sit on the swing's bench. No, they're more like skeletons, with dry clothes hanging over picked-clean bones. They seem to be holding hands.

I park the car and get out for a better look. I'm not sure what pulls me toward them, but I have to know. I have to see.

The skeletons grin at me as I approach. The smaller one is clothed in a pink cotton dress that perfectly matches the explosion of pink peonies bordering the porch. Leg bones descend into gray orthopedic shoes. The larger skeleton still wears a straw hat, though it's a bit askew. Strings of drying flesh hang from one sharp cheekbone, as if the hat provided some protection from the relentless crows. The two are indeed holding hands, their spindly bone-fingers intertwined.

Like Mom and Paul, these two died together, taking what comfort they could.

Did everyone just lie down and die? Was everyone so accepting of their fate? I can't imagine it. If I knew the end was inevitable, I would want to *live*, raging and wild and free, until my very last moment.

But I would also want to be with the people I loved. Maybe that's the trade-off. Maybe dying gently means soaking up every last bit of love.

Emmaline pads forward and thoroughly snuffles the pant leg of the larger skeleton. I click my tongue at her, heading toward the front door, because I'm worried she'll raise a leg and pee on it. Or is that something only male dogs do? I should find a book about dogs.

She follows me happily, but when I clutch the ice-cold doorknob, I hesitate.

I'm hoping the couple outside was older. Retired, maybe. I'm hoping they didn't have any children living at home, and that, since they died outside, their house is unlocked and free of dead bodies.

But it's still someone else's home. It feels deeply wrong to walk right in.

Wind kicks up, bringing the scent of carrion along with a wintry chill. It's going to snow tonight; I'm sure of it. I don't have anything to wear but the clothes on my back. I *have* to go inside.

I release the handle and knock on the door instead, three sharp raps that seem to fill the whole neighborhood with uninvited, echoing sound.

No answer. Of course there is no answer.

I try one more time; it's the right thing to do. I hear footsteps, and my heartbeat notches up a gear. But no, it was just wind whipping a nearby maple branch against the roof.

Somehow, that tiny sliver of dashed hope is the most devastating thing. Tears fill my eyes and I wrench open the door.

I gag on the scent of rotten fruit, but recover quickly because rotting fruit has got nothing on rotting human flesh. I can sniff rotting fruit all day. Inhaling defiantly, I step inside.

This home is a tribute to the 1980s. Mauve carpet stretches from wall to wall. Matching mauve curtains curl and froth at the living room window, which frames a mauve and green floral couch. Above the fireplace mantel is a wooden plaque hanging from a wire, carved to spell out GOD BLESS OUR HOME. To the right is the open kitchen with golden oak cupboards, golden brass fixtures, and fake mauve flowers in pastel blue vases.

It's a decorating disaster, but it looks lived in and loved.

"Hello?" I call out in a wavering voice, just in case.

Waves and waves of rotting fruit make me a little dizzy. Maybe I should leave the door open to help the place air out. A harsh laugh bursts out of me. Leaving the door open would mean letting in the scent of carrion—and its accompanying flies and birds.

I slam the door shut.

"Let's see what we've got, Em," I say, heading toward the kitchen.

I find a long cupboard that seems promising and swing it open. Pay dirt.

It's filled to the brim with specialty cereals ("Heart-healthy Wheat 'ems, for all your fiber needs!"), organic tortilla chips, StayFit Nutrition Bars, and no less than four twelve-packs of Ensure, in vanilla, chocolate, and strawberry.

"Wow, Em, this is nasty. But it'll last a long time."

What I don't find is dog food. Or cat food or any kind of pet food. I rummage through the pantry cupboard and scrounge up two cans of tuna and six tins of Spam, neatly stacked. "Huh. It will have to do."

I find a spoon and a small plate, then peel open a tin

and plop the wobbly, glistening meat brick onto the plate. Emmaline whines at the smell. I set it on the ground, and she sniffs it suspiciously, then plunges her muzzle into it and noisily chomps away.

"Well, I'm glad that worked out."

I help myself to a can of chocolate Ensure, which isn't nearly as bad as I thought it would be. As I sip, my lower abdomen clenches, somewhere deep inside. It doesn't hurt exactly. It's more like a warning. I hold out the can of Ensure and study it with suspicion. Maybe I should have something else. Do I know of anything that prevents diarrhea? Dehydration might be deadly for me right now.

My abdomen clenches again. This time, warmth spreads throughout my pelvis, and the sensation is familiar. I'm about to start my period.

I'm late. It should have started days ago. My sickness must have stalled it, and now that I'm getting regular food and water, it's about to return with a vengeance.

I put my half-empty can of Ensure on the counter and set off in search of a bathroom. A short, dark hallway leads away from the mauve living room. There are three doors, all closed. The first opens to an overflowing linen closet that smells of perfumed dryer sheets. The second is a small bedroom with a double bed covered in the ugliest afghan I've ever seen—black, red, and yellow rosettes lined up in a perfect grid. The third door opens to a bathroom with 1940s era pink and black tile and a metal grab bar that's screwed into the wall by the toilet. I open the under-sink cabinet to look for supplies.

Two rolls of toilet paper sit beside glass cleaner and wet wipes. Behind them is a package of Confidence Women's Underwear ("Now with better fit!") in lavender plastic wrap. Damn. The woman who lived here probably hadn't menstruated in years.

Emmaline noses into the crook of my arm as I sit crouched, staring at the package of adult diapers. "I guess it's better than nothing," I tell her, resigned. I pull one out of the package and unfold it. Not as bad or bulky as I thought. It's stretchy in all the right places, and it just might work.

"Don't look at me like that," I tell Emmaline. "Mom wouldn't want you to stigmatize incontinence wear." Then I start giggling. But it takes on a high-pitched edge, and I gulp it down before the giggling can become something else.

Suddenly I'm tired, so tired. My shoulder and neck throb with the bruising I took leaping from the ladder. My bitten heel throbs; I should check the bandage and see if running for my life shoved something out of place.

I gingerly take off my boots, shuck my jeans and underwear, and pull on the adult diaper. I put my jeans back on and take a few experimental steps. The jeans aren't as loose now, which is a good thing, but I crinkle a little with each step.

It'll do, and my heel can wait until later. My eye sockets feel dry and gummy, and my limbs seem like dead weight as I stumble into the bedroom with the ugly rosette afghan. I yank the bedding down and slide underneath it. Emmaline hops up beside me, and I pull the blankets over us both. I snake an arm around her and bury my nose in her back.

March 18

WETNESS ON MY CHEEK, KEENING IN MY EAR. I SHOOT AWAKE, sitting straight up.

Emmaline laps at my face, whimpering. I force myself to release my death grip on the afghan. My heart rate gradually slows to normal.

Low light filters through the lace curtains, and a chill pricks the air. Birds sing—not just the carrion caw I've been hearing endlessly, but actual singing. It's early morning. I slept for twelve straight hours.

My dog whines again. "Do you need to go potty?" I ask.

She spins around on the foot of the bed, tail wagging.

"You and me both, girl." My muscles are stiff as I drag myself from bed, but I don't feel injured. Lucky break.

Emmaline follows me through the kitchen and dining nook

to the back door. She charges out when I open it and squats to pee. A layer of fresh snow covers everything, but it's already melting with the sunrise. I rub my upper arms for warmth as I sniff the air. Either the smell of decay is abating, or I'm getting used to it.

She kicks up snow with her rear legs when she's done, and I usher her back inside. Emmaline follows me into the bathroom. It's a little weird, having a dog stare at me while I take care of business, but it's better than being alone.

I started my period during the night as expected, so I roll up the old adult diaper and toss it in the trash and put on a new one. As I wash my hands, I think about trash. How long will it take for me to fill up all the cans in the house? A week? Less? What about the garbage cans outside? Without weekly trash collection, I'll have to get creative. Maybe dump everything in a neighbor's yard. How far away should trash be taken to be safe?

I reach for my phone to look it up before realizing that my phone blew up with everything else in my house.

For breakfast I indulge in another can of Ensure—strawberry this time—while Emmaline chomps on canned tuna. While I sip, I set my goals for the day.

First, I need a backpack. Something to hold essentials that I can grab quickly. I'll keep bottled water inside. First aid supplies. A few granola bars. A box of tampons. Maybe I'll add a knife and some batteries too. It wouldn't hurt to find a gun. I've never shot a gun before, and the idea terrifies me, but not so much as the idea of another wild dog chasing me down.

After I have some basic, easy-to-carry supplies, my second goal will be to look for the living. I can't be the only one who survived this thing; I just can't. I'll drive down to University Hospital, where Mom worked. If there are any survivors, that's where they'll be. A big hospital like that has to have backup generators, right? And medical supplies. The swelling from my IV entry site has subsided a lot, but the bite on my foot could sure use an antibiotic.

For once, Emmaline doesn't follow me around as I search the house for some kind of carrying item. I hope that's a good sign that she's settled, that she's less scared now.

Upstairs are two ugly-but-pristine bedrooms, a linen closet that contains approximately one million hand-crocheted doilies, and a spotless, white-tiled bathroom with a cupboard empty but for a can of air freshener. I'm guessing the elderly couple living here didn't make it up the stairs much.

I check the garage next. There's a workbench, two bins full of children's toys—for grandkids?—and a single car. It's hard to see in the gloom, but it's a large four-door sedan that looks like a brick on wheels. Maybe I'll come back for it when Paul's car gets low on gas. They certainly won't be needing it anymore.

But no backpack. I go back inside, and my gaze settles reluctantly on a gigantic purse sitting on the kitchen counter beside a rotary phone. It's covered in quilted material, printed with lime-green and fuchsia flowers. I upend the contents onto the counter—car keys, prescription bottles, cosmetics, a wallet, a small photo album, ballpoint pens, and an honest-to-god checkbook.

I shove the car keys into the pocket of my jeans. I'm about to turn away, but on impulse I grab the wallet and open it to the driver's license.

Hazel Jenkins. Five foot five, one hundred forty pounds. Born July 21. She's a withered apple with a shock of white hair. Something about her wide, wet grin makes me smile; it's rimmed with runny hot pink lipstick, set off by eyes so crinkled they almost seem closed. She's so alive in this photo, uncaring that her teeth are gray or that her hair sticks up at odd angles. Hazel Jenkins was a joyful person, and she loved pink.

I slide the driver's license from the wallet and toss it into the floral purse.

"Let's go, Emmy." I grab the purse and head out the front door, Emmaline trotting behind.

The sky is wrong.

At first I think it's the tinting of Paul's SUV. But I roll down the driver's side window, and the sky is the same: filling with clouds, but with a sickly greenish cast. It's even hazier than yesterday, and my eyes ache from trying to focus through it. It smells of decomposing bodies, burned plastic, and wet fireplaces.

Smoke from yesterday's explosion, I tell myself. That would explain the green tint, right?

Cautiously, I pull into the Tremont Shopping Center. The

store windows are dark. Padlocked chains stretch across the doors of the supermarket. The parking lot is empty of everything except for patches of melting snow and a single Humvee in gray and white camouflage, parked near the pharmacy. I almost hit the brakes and turn around, but snow on the hood and a busted passenger side window indicate that the Humvee has been parked awhile.

It's the first sign of martial law that I've seen. I listen, hardly daring to breathe, remembering the radio warning about being shot on sight. If I hear the sound of another motor, I'll have to find a hiding place for the car. Or possibly turn everything off and duck down in the seat, hoping no one notices me.

I roll across the lot toward the pharmacy. No chains here. Maybe I can break a window. I pull into the accessible parking spot beside the abandoned Humvee and turn off the car. I toss Hazel's floral purse into the backseat beside the Monstrosity, and I quietly slip out.

But I stop short, grabbing Emmaline by the ruff so she can't move forward.

A patch of snow lingers in the lee of the curb. Inside it, clean and clear, is a large shoe print.

It's fresh. It has to be. It only snowed last night. Someone is alive out here. Someone besides me. Maybe the driver of the Humvee? Looking for people to shoot on sight? I put my hand on the fender. It's ice-cold. I was right the first time; no one has driven this thing in days.

I've read the books, seen the movies; I know how this goes. In the apocalypse, humans turn against each other out of desperation and distrust. I have to be careful. See them before they see me, size them up, decide if they're friend or foe.

Emmaline sniffs the print, ears cocked forward. Too bad she's a herding dog and not a tracker. I could have let her sniff them out.

"Let's go, Emmy," I murmur, and I step onto the sidewalk. Every whisper of wind, every birdcall, every swaying tree branch, is cause for alarm. They could be watching me right now.

Soaking garbage is piled up near the door—candy bar wrappers, beer cans, and a raggedy stuffed bear holding a plush heart. Spray-painted on the faded brick wall is a giant oval with a line cutting diagonally through it, in bright, dripping orange. That symbol has been all over Columbus lately, the tag of the notorious street artist who calls himself Null.

I press my face to the glass of the doors. It's dark inside, but my eyes adjust. The store has been ransacked. Shelves are overturned, clutter blocks the aisles, broken glass shimmers on the floor near the cash registers.

Not everything is a mess. Some shelves still hold items, though I can't make them out from here. The entire east wall seems intact. Maybe people were just starting to loot when the Humvee pulled up and scared everyone off.

I turn the door handle. It rattles, but it's locked tight. Worth a try.

The tinted window glass seems impenetrable. Maybe Paul kept a crowbar in the SUV.

I open the back of the car, lift the cargo mat, and hit pay

dirt. Not a crowbar, but a tire iron will do just fine. I gauge its weight, shift my grip, and swing it experimentally. It feels good in my hand. I can break windows *or* faces with this.

Emmaline barks.

I sink down between Paul's car and the Humvee before I realize how silly I'm being. She's probably barking at a bird. Even if it's the owner of that footprint, they've probably already seen me.

Gradually, carefully, I lift my head and peer through the car windows in the same general direction that has my dog's attention.

A flash of something in the sky between the bank and the pharmacy. Unease curls in my belly as I slink around the front fender to get a better look, but whatever it was is already gone. It was so quick. And bright. Like sunshine on silver. No, it was iridescent, like dragonfly wings.

Like a ghost.

Or maybe I'm imagining things. I did recently wake from a six-day coma, exhausted, dehydrated, and starving.

"Am I losing it, Em?" I whisper.

Emmaline's ears are still cocked toward the alley between stores.

My brother Ryan would tell me to run, if he were here. But I hate running from things, and I hate not knowing. "All right, let's a take a look." Tire iron in hand, I creep forward.

Two huge black rats skitter away as I enter the alley. Emmaline tears off after them.

"Emmaline!"

She has already disappeared around the corner. I resist the urge to chase recklessly after, even though I couldn't stand it if something happened to her. I force myself to move forward slowly.

Behind the store, near a huge dumpster, I find the driver of the Humvee. Her body sits spread-eagled, back against the wall, chin to chest. She wears gray and white camo to match the Humvee, a hard, round helmet, and a gas mask. A gun strap drapes over one shoulder, but the gun is missing.

She's misshapen, like she's caved in on herself, and bits of mottled flesh still cling to the bones of her remaining two fingers, which seem a bit gnawed upon. My stomach turns, and I have to put my hand over my mouth as I remember those rats. I'm glad the gas mask covers her face.

Emmaline comes trotting back, tail wagging, and I'm so relieved it's hard to breathe for a moment. Maybe I should get her a leash.

"Heel," I say, and she surprises me by moving immediately to my side and pacing me as I skirt the dumpster.

Lots of trash back here. Whether it was blown in by the wind or left over from looting I can't tell. The area behind the pharmacy is wide. Big enough for semitrucks. A concrete loading ramp leads down to a roll-up cargo door. Beside it is a smaller, employee door.

The door is ajar.

Hope wars with alarm. There are intact supplies inside that pharmacy; I saw them from the window. There might be food for Emmaline. Bottled water. Tampons. And sweet, holy god,

I could use a candy bar or some caffeine.

But there was that boot print. And a missing gun. Reluctantly, I step forward.

Footsteps echo behind me. I whirl.

A young Black man strides toward me. He's tall, even taller than me. A long duster whips at his heels, and he holds the missing gun in his gloved hands. It's an automatic rifle; a gigantic M-something-or-other about four feet long, but this guy wields it like it's a matchstick.

Emmaline moves to stand in front of me. She doesn't growl, but her hackles rise, and she drops her head the same way that wild dog did right before it charged me. My grip on the tire iron tightens. Can I really swing it at another human being if I have to?

He freezes when he sees my dog. We stare at each other. His gaze narrows as he takes in details about my hair, my clothes, my dog. I'm taking in details too; he's frowning slightly, and dirt mars his left cheek. His hand on the rifle slides toward the trigger.

I should run for it. I learned in my self-defense class that it's almost impossible to hit a moving target, even with an automatic weapon. Maybe I can get inside and slam the door shut before he starts shooting.

And then he lowers his gun.

Suddenly, without thinking at all, I'm dropping my tire iron and running toward him and he's running toward me and tears are streaming down my face and his arms engulf me and his gun pokes my back and my hands are clutching his shoulders and he lifts me up and swings me around muttering, "Oh, thank god, thank god, thank god."

I don't know how long we're like that, me burrowing into this stranger's neck, him pressing his cheek to my greasy hair. Finally, we separate. He holds me at arm's length, breathing hard, staring at me like I'm the most precious thing in the world.

"Hi," he says, releasing me at last, grinning the most beautiful grin I've ever seen in my life.

I laugh-choke-cry: "Hi."

Emmaline stands on her hind legs, paws against his thigh, and licks his hand.

His face sobers. "We need to get inside. It's not safe out here."

Just like that, my relief is gone and all the tension of the last few days settles back around me so fast I stumble under the weight of it. As he ushers me through the back door of the pharmacy, I glance over my shoulder, certain that something watches us, but the world is silent and still.

The darkness inside is muggy and stale—a big improvement. He closes the door behind us and snicks the deadbolt into place. I stare at the thin strip of light along the top edge of the door. The sound of his breathing fills the tight space, loud like a stormy wind—or maybe it's been so long since I've heard another human breathe that I'll have to adjust all over again to this not-silence.

Emmaline whimpers, and I realize I'm trapped with him now. A total stranger. Maybe this was a bad idea.

He shuffles around, bumps into something, and light sears the darkness. He holds an army-green plastic lantern. It says "Camp Lamp" in red letters on the side. He sets it on a round table surrounded by folding chairs. It's just bright enough for me to see the small fridge off to the right, the ragged love seat to the left, the sleeping bag rolled out in the corner. We're in the employee break room.

He whips off a leather glove and holds out his hand. "I'm Trey. Trey Dawson."

Familiarity at his name pricks at the back of my brain. I stare at his outstretched hand, thinking of all the pandemic PSAs when I was a kid. *Six feet apart. Practice social distancing.* Then again, we just broke all those rules in the alley, and my blood is probably swimming with antibodies. I take his hand and give it a firm shake. "Paige Miller."

Emmaline is wholly absorbed in the scent of his boots. I add, "That's Emmaline."

"Paige," he says, as if testing it out in his mouth. "Emmaline. Paige and Emmaline."

"Trey," I say, and we're both grinning like idiots again.

"Thought I was the only one left," he says. "Thought . . . just me and bodies and birds and . . ." His voice and his gaze trail off into nowhere. The meager light of the lantern turns him into an imposing silhouette. Maybe I should be terrified of this stranger, but I'm not.

I swallow hard. "Yeah. Me too."

"Hey, are you hungry? I've got beef jerky, canned soup—no way to heat it up, but you know, it's *food*. Pretty much all the

Pringles you can eat. Enough Red Vines to do a Script Ohio."

The earlier familiarity is beginning to crystalize. "You're from Ohio State?"

His smile dies. "Would've been a freshman there next year."

He's younger than I realized, and like me, his plans for the future are as dead as the rest of the world. "Do you have a Snickers bar?" I say gently. "I'm kinda craving that right now. My dog could use some food; Emmy's had nothing but tuna and Spam. Also . . ." I feel weird saying it to a total stranger, but I have to. "I need tampons."

He doesn't bat an eye. "Probably have all of that. C'mon, let's go see." He grabs the lantern and gestures me through swinging double doors and into the bowels of the store.

Trey Dawson, Trey Dawson, I think as I follow him. I know that name from somewhere. He's broad shouldered and inches taller than I am. It's not every day I meet a guy I can't physically intimidate. But Trey could overpower me easily if he wanted to, especially as sick as I've been.

"You've been living here?" I ask, kicking trash out of the way.

"Three days now. My house . . . I just couldn't stay there anymore." He sets the lantern on the counter of the actual pharmacy part of the store. The sphere of light reveals shelves cluttered with pill bottles and white boxes. Everything has been partially looted, but maybe there's an antibiotic back there somewhere.

"I love what you've done with the place," I tell him.

He chuckles. "Well, I didn't want it to *look* like someone

was living here." Trey heads down the nearest aisle. He moves cautiously, keeping an eye on the windows of the storefront.

"Why not?"

He bends down and grabs something, then tosses it to me. I catch it with my right hand. A Snickers bar.

Saliva floods my tongue. I tear open the wrapper and shove the candy bar into my mouth, tearing off fully half with a single bite. "Oh my gog thith ith the beth thig I ever hag," I say.

The way he stares at my face makes me feel funny. I chew fast, swallow, and say, "Why did you want it to seem like no one was living here?"

"I . . . I'm staring, aren't I?"

"You are."

"Sorry." He runs a hand over his head. His hair has about an inch of growth. "I keep thinking you're not real. I haven't seen anyone alive in days, and I . . . I'm just really glad you're here. Hey, let's grab what you need, then we'll talk in the back, where nothing can see us through the windows."

"All right." Where *nothing* can see us, he said. Not *no one*.

A few minutes later, we're back in the break room, me sprawled in the love seat and him in one of the folding chairs. I used the tiny employee restroom to change my adult diaper—which is now wadded up in a plastic bag—for a tampon and maxi pad. Emmaline laps happily at a lump of wet dog food that Trey plopped onto a plate for her. I've finished my Snickers bar and popped some Advil, and now I'm responsibly eating a bland piece of whole wheat bread and washing it all down with bottled water. Cramps tighten my lower belly, but they're not too bad.

"So what part of town are you from, Paige Miller?" he asks.

"Clintonville."

He's silent a long moment. Then: "A big chunk of Clintonville blew sky-high yesterday. You can still see the smoke."

"Came down the sewer line. Gas, I think. I barely got out. My house . . . my . . ."

"I'm sorry."

"Thanks. What about you?"

"Northwest Columbus. Not far from here."

"And your home?"

"Too many dead people. I had a little sister. Teena." He slumps over like a man three times his age. "I watched so many people die, but she was the last. After that, I tried to . . ." He changes his mind about what he was going to say. Straightens. His voice is stronger when he adds, "There wasn't any food in the house. So I came here. Had a key to the back. I've been working here two years. Just promoted to assistant manager. Didn't know where else to go."

Seems to me it's an accomplishment for a high school kid to become assistant manager at an Upper Arlington pharmacy.

"Did you get sick?" I ask.

"Nope. I seem to be immune."

His words give me a stab of hope. If he's immune, maybe others are too.

He lifts his chin in my direction. "You got sick, though, didn't you? When I first saw you, I thought you were a zombie."

"That bad, huh?"

His eyes widen. "No! You look great for a zombie. I mean—"

"I was unconscious for six days. Woke up attached to an IV. My mom is—was—a nurse. I think she nursed me as long as she could, and it saved my life."

"Wow," he breathes. "You're the only person I know of who actually recovered."

"I don't know why Mom didn't just take me to a hospital, though."

"The hospitals stopped accepting people pretty quick," he says. "They didn't have room, and all the doctors and nurses were dying. It happened so fast. People died on the way to the hospital, and the roads were a mess. So the National Guard came, and they made everyone stay inside, but then they all died, too."

"Damn."

"Yeah."

"So we're it? The only ones left?" I mean it to sound flippant, but it comes out high and squeaky.

"I hope not. If there are two of us in this one city, then maybe there are one or two in every city. That adds up to thousands of people. Hundreds of thousands, all spread out. No disease in the history of the world has had a 100 percent infection rate. And no disease in the world has 100 percent mortality when modern medical practices are used."

I study him a little more carefully. "How do you know all that?"

He flashes a grin. "I'm a smart guy."

And nice to look at. Or maybe that's the loneliness of the last few days talking. I never want to be alone again. "So this disease hit everywhere? The whole world?"

"Wow, you don't know anything, do you?"

Something about his tone irritates me. "In a coma for six days, remember?"

"That's what I mean. You woke up and found a whole different planet. But yeah, almost all at once. The Great Lakes area was first, but by the next day, people were dying off in New York City, Moscow, Lagos, Shanghai . . ."

It's like a light winks out inside me. I must have been clinging to the possibility that the disease didn't spread worldwide.

At least I've found someone. Even if it's only one person. I hope Trey is a decent human being. I need him to be. I don't know what I'll do if I find out otherwise.

"Which is impossible, you know," he adds.

"What is?"

"For a disease to hit everywhere at once."

I nod. "They always start with a vector and spread."

"You're smart too."

"I just played a lot of Plague Inc. on my tablet." I grab another piece of bread. Eating was hard when I first woke up, but now I'm craving calories. I could eat until I popped. "So tell me," I say around a mouthful. "Why all the hiding?"

Emmaline has finished licking the plate clean, and she walks over to Trey and sits primly at his feet, gazing hopefully into his face.

"Don't beg, Emmy," I say. She used to do this all the time

when Ryan and I went over to Mrs. Carby's house for cookies. Emmaline recognizes the command and slinks away from him. She hops up onto the couch beside me and curls up against my thigh. "Good girl." Her tail thumps.

"I've been seeing things," Trey says at last. "But I'm not crazy, and I'm not on drugs so don't even say it."

"Um. Okay."

"You're not the first person I've seen alive."

I sit straight up. "What?"

"Four days ago, I saw two kids. Ten or eleven. I think they were brother and sister. There were still a few people left four days ago, but they were all sick. Bad sick. These kids were no different—coughing, holding on to each other like they might fall down. They were going from house to house, looking for food maybe." His voice is thick with sadness. Or maybe fear.

"What happened?" I say it coolly, even though my heart beats rapid fire.

"I called out to them. I was so glad to see someone. They turned. Saw me. We were smiling." He rests his elbows on the table and stares off into space as though suddenly lost. "I started toward them, and something came out of the sky. Something metal. I thought it was some kind of huge drone, but it was shaped weird, like a bug. It had this coating, or aura, or . . . All shimmery and thick, but I could kind of see through it, you know? Like dragonfly wings. Anyway, it swooped down, and a shimmering wave came out of it and suddenly the kids were gone. Just . . . evaporated."

"Oh my god."

"I ran as fast as I could to get under cover. Found an enclosed porch. Stayed there for hours, until it got dark. That's the coldest I've ever been in my life. Finally, I had to move or get hypothermia.

"I snuck over to the place where the kids'd been standing. There were two little shadows on the sidewalk. Like burn scars in the concrete. The concrete was . . . melty."

I'm gaping at him. "That's . . . I'm sorry."

"There's something else out there, Paige. Something that wants us dead. So I've been lying low."

I bury my hand in Emmaline's ruff, gathering courage to confess my own theory. "We were exterminated," I say.

He nods. "Some guy from the World Health Organization said exactly that. His interview was all over the major networks right before everything went dark. He called it an 'engineered virus.' And now whoever released it is cleaning house. Getting the stragglers."

"But who? And why?"

He shrugs. "Probably the Umbrella Corporation."

"Huh?"

"You know, from *Resident Evil*? The people who created the virus that caused . . ."

I stare at him.

"Never mind. Stupid video game joke. I don't know who. No one does. Or, I should say, no one *did*."

We fall silent. I pet Emmaline's head as guilt twinges in my chest. I shouldn't be so happy discussing something so devastating. I guess it's not the topic but the talking itself. I'm sitting in a dank room that reeks of rotting food with a strange guy who has a machine gun, and I'm *delighted*. And I sure as hell don't want him to stop talking.

"There had to have been some theories," I press, just to keep the conversation going.

"Well, sure. You know that pastor from the megachurch in Texas? He was all over Fox News saying it was god's judgment for the homosexuality in the world."

"That's messed up."

"Yep. Some people said it was engineered by the Chinese, others said the North Koreans—I guess they just picked the country they were afraid of most. Pretty much everyone agreed it was biological warfare. Maybe an experiment that got out of hand."

Emmaline stretches out her neck to rest her chin on my thigh. She looks up at me with sad eyes, and I give her nose a light knuckle rub. "What do *you* think happened?" I ask Trey.

He grabs a Red Vine from the open package on the table, gnaws off a bite, chews. "You'll laugh at me," he says finally.

"I won't."

He looks me dead in the eye. "I think it was aliens," he says, almost defiantly. "From outer space."

I blink. "Okay."

Trey rises from the chair and starts pacing. Emmaline lifts her head, ears pricked, but she settles when she realizes he's not going anywhere. He's so large, and the room is so small that he has to turn a lot. Emmy closes her eyes, already readjusting to the presence of another human in her space.

"Think about it," he says. "Human beings don't have the technology to wipe out the entire planet in just a few days, not unless we nuked it all to hell."

"There are diseases that kill quick," I say.

He shakes his head. "I'm not talking about the disease. I'm talking about the delivery. For the whole world to get sick and die so fast, *everyone* had to be exposed at the same time. No one has that kind of tech. But aliens might."

I'd had a similar thought earlier, that not enough time had passed for the disease to spread. It had actually given me hope. In normal circumstances, it would mean that people were still alive in other places.

"You've been thinking about this a lot," I say.

"Ever since I saw that dragonfly thing."

"Aliens, then." I tamp down the giggle that rises in my throat. It's so preposterous. But, I suppose, not more preposterous than everyone on Earth dying all at once. "Exterminators."

"Yeah, exterminators. An alien Orkin Man. We got *sprayed*."

I take another swig of water. "What were you doing today when I found you? Why were you outside?"

He leans against the wall and crosses his arms. "I was heading down to the supermarket to look for a way inside when I heard your car. The food in this pharmacy is gross. I can't live on Cheetos and beer. Also, it won't last forever. Especially now."

Warmth spreads through my chest. Especially now that I'm here, he means.

"We should try again tomorrow," I say. "We'll take it slow.

Keep to the shadows. Emmaline makes a good lookout. She'll bark at anything weird, but I don't think . . . the Orkins . . . will care about her. I've seen dogs around."

His smile is huge, because I've just accepted his offer to stay. "Good plan. There's a display of ugly-ass Snuggies in the store. I'll grab a few. You can have the couch tonight."

"I don't mind the floor—"

"I do better on the floor. Back trouble. Sports injury."

Suddenly, I know who he is. "You're the new quarterback! The incoming freshman everyone's excited about." The *Dispatch* did a whole write-up on him, same week my team won regionals. Our win would have been front page if not for this guy. "You were going to redshirt after wrenching your back."

He shrugs. "Doesn't matter now, does it?"

"Local kid with a 3.7 GPA and a perfect score on the math section of the SAT. You tutored at-risk kids on weekends, led your team to the state high school football championship. Basically, a Buckeye's wet dream."

"I said it doesn't matter," he snaps.

Sore subject, I guess. Don't know that I blame him. I'm not too keen to talk about the total annihilation of all my hopes and dreams either.

"I know who you are too," he says after a moment, and his tone has a combative edge. "Paige Miller. Heading to UConn next year on scholarship. One of the only high school girls in the country right now who can slam dunk. You're only six-foot-three. That means you've got serious ups."

Okay, it's definitely creepy to have a total stranger know all about me. "I can *barely* dunk. And I've never done it in a game."

"Your video upload has over two hundred thousand views."

I swallow the sudden lump in my throat. Shawntelle and Ryan spent an hour with me in the gym that day, trying to get the angle and lighting just right. My voice wavers when I say, "In truth, it took five tries to get a good enough clip. I bruised my hand." Shawntelle used the injury as an excuse to make me practice my left-handed layup.

"Still, that's impressive."

It *was* impressive, and it clinched my UConn scholarship. My stomach twists with the loss of so much—my best friend, my brother, my future. "You're right. Let's not talk about it. It doesn't matter."

We stare at each other a long moment. The Camp Lamp flickers. "Batteries must be getting low," he says.

"I'll take that ugly-ass Snuggie now," I say. "If you're still offering."

"'Course."

"And I could use an antibiotic. Mind if I have a look through the prescription shelves?"

He blinks. "You hurt?"

"Feral dog took a big bite out of my heel."

His face is grave. "Stay off your feet. I'll be right back."

I'm about to protest, but he grabs the lamp and leaves me in the dark. I'm not sure if Trey's obvious concern is sweet or strange. I've been walking around all day; no need to suddenly stay off my feet. Then again, if he were the one who was hurt, I'd move heaven and earth to help him. He's my only human.

Trey Dawson, I muse. Practically a household name in central Ohio. I would have recognized it right away if I hadn't been so wrapped up in my own life these past few months. Shawntelle would have given away her jersey number to meet this guy.

Emmaline jumps off the couch and pads over to the door a second before I hear Trey's footsteps. He turns sideways to get through the doorway with his loot: two large boxes picturing a laughing woman wrapped in a bright blue Snuggie, a white pill bottle, a package of D-sized batteries, and various bandages and gauzes.

He sets everything on the table. "I want to see that bite," he says.

"Sure. Okay." I lean forward to unzip my boot. My hands freeze on the zipper. What if this is just an excuse to get me to take something off? Maybe Trey has a weird foot fetish or something. I mean, what do I *really* know about him?

Chill, Paige. If he tries anything, you can break his face.

With a glance at my tire iron resting on the floor, I remove the boot, then peel away my sock to reveal the Ace bandage and cotton gauze. The bandage comes away easy enough, but I hiss as the gauze unsticks from the wound.

Trey rips open the package of batteries, and everything goes dark as he changes them. The light comes back on, brighter than before, and he lifts it to get a look at my heel.

"Ouch," he says. "He tore into you good."

"I think it's better." The skin flap seems to have sealed shut already, though peeling away the bandage made it ooze a bit. But the puncture beside it aches something fierce, and the pain extends deep into my arch. Like it bruised the bone.

"Was the dog rabid?"

"I don't think so."

"It doesn't look infected," Trey says, "and I'm not sure how, because animal bites are nasty. But yeah, you should take the amoxicillin, just in case." He straightens and goes to the sink to wash his hands.

"I poured rubbing alcohol all over it," I say. "Maybe that helped."

He glances over his shoulder at me. "Damn, girl. That's badass."

"Not really. I almost passed out."

"Still." He reaches a now-clean hand forward. "May I?"

I nod permission, though I'm not sure if I want him to touch me. But I do want to know that I can trust him. So I guess it's a test of sorts.

He gently grips my heel between thumb and middle finger, just behind the wound. He presses gently. Shifts position, presses again. "Does this hurt?"

"A little."

"How about here?" He presses into the arch of my foot, and I lurch out of the love seat as bone-deep pain zings up into my leg.

He lets go. "Sorry!"

I fall back, gasping.

"That puncture is deep," he says. "I'm surprised you're on your feet. And you should definitely take that antibiotic. I'll clean it and re-wrap it for you."

"You . . ." I catch my breath and try again. "You seem to know a lot about this."

He rips open a package of gauze and runs it under the water. He adds a tiny bit of liquid soap, then presses it gently to my heel. "Momma was a PA," he says as he works. "But she was a suture tech while she put herself through school. She helped people sometimes. The ones that didn't have health insurance. I picked up a few things." His gaze grows distant. "I was going to be pre-med."

I study the top of his head. For someone who doesn't want to talk about broken dreams, he's awfully forthcoming.

He takes the rest of my bottled water and pours it over my foot to rinse it. Water puddles on the concrete floor. "I'll clean that up in a sec," he says. "What about you? What were you going to major in?"

"I hadn't decided," I say, bracing myself for pain, but in spite of his huge hands, Trey has a delicate touch as he bandages the wound. His fingers are warm and dry, and they almost tickle. "My stepdad Paul was an engineer, specializing in vertical access wind turbines. He was working toward sustainability and decreasing our dependence on foreign oil and all that. Progressive stuff. I thought he was going to change the world."

"You really loved him." Trey wraps the bandage around the gauze.

I swallow hard. "I wanted to do something important like

that. Something that would change the world for everyone who came after me. After going to the WNBA, of course. I thought I had time to figure it out."

I put my sock back on as Trey grabs paper towels from under the sink and blots the water on the floor. "Maybe you still will," he says.

"Maybe," I say, with a shrug.

He pauses, soaked paper towel in hand, and frowns up at me. "That sounded full of despair."

I frown right back. "I don't do despair."

He grins. "Glad to hear it. Because if there are others out there, stragglers like us, maybe we can figure out a way to help them and see if we can all be . . . people . . . again."

As soon as the words leave his mouth, I know it's what I want too. "I like that plan."

"I'll be honest, I'm not sure who I am without family and football. It's like I have to come up with a whole new reason for living, you know?"

"But trying to find others—that's a reason," I say.

He shrugs. "It's something to do."

I settle back into the love seat, and Trey plunks into the nearest folding chair. We talk for hours as the break room grows chilly and the light seeping around the door fades. In spite of what we said earlier, we end up talking about things that don't matter anymore like music and favorite professional athletes (Me: Sue Bird; Trey: Cam Newton. I roll my eyes when he tells me he's a Pats fan), best home-cooked meals ever (his momma made a righteous lasagna; I tell him about Mom's baked mac and cheese), and worst teachers in school. We argue about which *Star Wars* movie was the best (me: *Empire*, him: *The Last Jedi*), and whether or not the Bengals would have had a shot at the playoffs this year with their new draft picks. Eventually, Trey moves from the chair to his sleeping bag. Our chatter grows soft and sporadic as we drift off to sleep.

Whoomp.

I sit straight up. My insides feel huge and hollow, echoing with the strange not-sound.

"Trey?" I whisper into the dark.

"I heard it."

Something creaks—probably the building settling. Fabric rubs together as Trey shifts in his sleeping bag. Emmaline lets out a sigh as she stretches out against me.

Whoomp.

I startle, even though I was waiting for it. "What *is* that?"

"An explosion, maybe?" he whispers back. "Coming from a long way off."

"I've heard it before. The same night I got bit."

More fabric rustling. A shadow looms nearby. "I'm going to look outside," he says.

"You sure that's a good idea?"

"Hell, no. I won't go anywhere. I'll just peek out the store windows."

I toss the Snuggie aside and feel around on the floor for my Doc Martens. "I'm going with you."

I expect him to protest, but he says, "We should stick together as much as possible."

"Agreed."

Moments later, we're peering through the swinging doors, then slowly pushing them open and creeping down the snack food aisle. Emmaline stays at my heel, her tail wagging ferociously at the prospect of a grand adventure.

Bluish moonlight filters through the storefront, softening the cluttered chaos of the floor. The air is icy, and it's an odd, odd thing to watch our breath frost indoors. It makes the world seem thin. Dreamlike. For a wild instant, I think that none of this is real.

Trey is a huge dark shadow before me, somehow menacing and comforting at the same time. Glass crunches beneath his boot, snapping the dream-sense, and we both freeze. He chuckles softly, which I understand. We're probably being ridiculous. But better safe than sorry, right? We press forward.

A sale bin looms before us, mounded with small items I can't make out. We crouch behind it. The position gives us a perfect view of the parking lot. Paul's SUV is off to the right; it's an unremarkable lump compared to the abandoned Humvee. A few birds clump together on the sidewalk in front of the cars, their heads tucked beneath their wings.

How much has the world changed for them to sleep in the open like that? Are there no predators? No hungry ones, maybe. In the absence of humanity, everything else is well fed.

"Do you see anything?" he whispers.

"No, but I don't have a good view of—"

Whoomp.

The door rattles. A soft glow bubbles up over the horizon,

silhouetting the treetops at the far end of the lot. It fades as quickly as it came.

"Did you see that?" I ask.

"Yeah."

We wait in silence, hoping or dreading that it will happen again, but all is still.

"I think it came from far away," I tell him.

"North of the city," he agrees. "Maybe way north."

"To light up like that, to make that big of a . . . sound? It must be—"

"Enormous."

Emmaline's wet nose prods my palm, and I jump a little. I bury my hand in her ruff, and she responds by leaning against my thigh. My legs are starting to tremble from crouching, or maybe it's just the cold.

"I don't like this," Trey says, gazing out over the moonlit pavement. "This store, I mean. It has supplies, but no cover. We'll be totally exposed as we try to get into the supermarket."

"We'll work fast. Fill our cars with everything we can. Then find a different place to hole up for a bit."

"My family didn't have a car." His voice is suddenly a little bit dangerous.

I'd noticed there are no other cars in the lot, but I assumed his was nearby. On the street, maybe. "How did you get to work and school?"

"Bus, usually. After everyone died, I rode my bicycle. I keep it in the stockroom."

"I can fit everything we need in that SUV," I say. "And

there are plenty of cars lying around that no one needs."

"Let's find a place with lots of trees. And houses close together. A place easy to disappear in."

By silent mutual agreement, we creep back into the aisle, toward the swinging doors.

"What about the dead bodies? Maybe we should go somewhere rural."

He pushes the doors open and lets me go first. "It's a myth that dead bodies pose health risks," he says.

"Really?"

"Really. Unless they're diseased, of course. But I'm immune, and you've already been sick, so we're perfectly safe."

Back in the break room, Trey flips on the Camp Lamp. "But I heard a radio message," I say. "It warned about burying or burning bodies."

He nods. "That was when everyone still hoped we could avoid the apocalypse. Corpses can be disease vectors, and Ohio has a high water table. But it doesn't matter now that everyone is already dead."

I can't help the huge grin forming, which is weird because we're talking about corpses and death and the end of the world, but I guess a lot of things have changed lately. "In that case, I say we find a giant mansion. Something with amazing furniture. We'll live like the one percent."

He grins right back. "It should have a fireplace. A fully stocked pantry."

"I want a wine cellar. I don't even like wine, but I want a wine cellar."

"A workout room!" he says.

"A regulation height basketball hoop!" I say.

"A lawn for crochet!"

"You mean croquet?"

"Whatever. And cornhole!"

"And no dead bodies."

Our grins die. It might be a tall order, to find a grand mansion empty of bodies.

"Tomorrow," he says.

"Tomorrow," I agree.

Neither of us mentions how dangerous it might be to travel anywhere. But I made it from Hazel Jenkins's house to the pharmacy without incident, so it's possible, right?

MARCH 19

IT'S SEVEN THIRTY A.M., ACCORDING TO THE WALL CLOCK IN THE employee break room. Trey and I stare at the door. Light from outside shines around the doorframe. No wonder it got so cold last night; the door doesn't seal well.

"Maybe going out in broad daylight is a bad idea," Trey says. "Maybe we should wait until dark."

"So the Orkin aliens can't see us?"

He shrugs.

"Cats can see in the dark just fine," I point out. "Something from another planet might have a totally different visual range than humans."

"That's depressing. Maybe the Orkins don't see at all. Maybe they use some kind of sonar, like bats."

"Now *that* is depressing." It means finding the mansion of

our dreams with good cover might be a totally worthless goal.

"We know nothing about them," he continues. "We don't even know how to protect ourselves. Or hide."

Actually, we don't even know if there is a *them*. But I keep silent on the matter. I'm going along with Trey's theory because I don't have a better one, and he did see that dragonfly thing. But I'm not sure I'll truly believe it until I see *them* with my own eyes.

"Ready?" I say.

He's holding the rifle in his hands. "Ready."

I grab my tire iron, then unlock the deadbolt and open the door. Light pours in. Emmaline pours out. She dashes across the asphalt to the back fence, where she squats to potty.

Neither of us says a word as we creep around the dumpster, past the dead national guardswoman, and through the alley to the front of the store. All the snow has melted, but thick, greenish clouds have rolled in and wind chills the air. I put up my hoodie to protect my ears.

I unlock the doors to the SUV, and we slide into the seats. Emmaline catches up to us and jumps into Trey's lap.

Trey puts an arm around her as he glances into the rear seat. "Nice purse. And nice . . . dish?"

"That dish is called the Monstrosity, and it's coming with us. Nonnegotiable."

He stares at my profile as I put the car in reverse and back out of the parking space. "Sure. No problem."

We roll across the lot toward the supermarket. I turn us around and back up to the entrance to make for easy loading.

We hop out, and I hand him my tire iron. He hands me the gun. It's heavy. At least ten pounds. Or maybe I'm just weak from being so sick.

"I don't know much about using an AR-15," he warns. "But I guess 'point and shoot' is a good starting place."

I nod, swallowing hard, because I've never held a gun before in my life, and because it's an immense gesture of trust for him to hand it over to someone he just met.

"Stand back and keep watch," he says. "And you might want to hold your dog in case glass flies everywhere." Trey pulls a pair of sunglasses out of his pocket and slips them on to protect his eyes. He zips his duster coat all the way up and pulls the collar over his mouth and nose. His voice is muffled when he says, "Here we go!"

Trey steps up to the thick plexiglass window and swings.

The tire iron plunks against it; the sound is like a deep drumbeat. It bounces off the glass and flies out of his hands, winging end over end. I duck instinctively, even though it doesn't come close.

He stares after it, eyes wide, as it clatters to the pavement. "I could have killed you!"

"You cracked the glass," I point out. It's more like a dent, really, with an impact center and lots of tiny cracks spreading out. "A couple more hits might do it."

As he goes to retrieve the tire iron, our eyes rove the sky, the parking lot, the dense trees beyond, for any kind of movement. I stay crouched down, one arm around Emmaline, the butt of the rifle lodged against my thigh so that the barrel points to the sky. My weak legs shake from the effort, and my breakfast PB&J rolls around in my stomach.

Trey returns to the window. "You may want to get farther back," he says.

"And you may want to hold on tighter." But I do as he suggests, dragging Emmaline with me.

He swings. This time the glass crunches, and the dent turns chalky white. Another swing, and he lifts his shades and peers closer. "I'm through!" he says. "But it's going to take a while to make a big enough hole."

"We should have just shot it," I grumble.

"Too loud," he says, taking another swing. "And we need to save bullets until we can find more."

He's right, but I hate standing here, doing nothing, watching out for the thing that may or may not be watching us. I'm about to give up and go find something I can use to bang on that window right along with him when I see it.

Across the street, above the trees. A whisper of light. Shimmering like a mirage.

"Trey!" I whisper loudly.

He's at my side instantly.

"What is it?"

But it's already gone. Disappeared in the space of a blink.

"I saw something. Or I thought I did. It was like mist. But . . . shiny? A prism made of air."

Trey says nothing.

"God, Trey, I'm sorry. I'm probably seeing things. I was so sick, and—"

His large, warm hand settles on my shoulder and squeezes. "I believe you," he says in a low whisper. "That dragonfly thing was kind of like you just described. Metallic, but also a little translucent? Maybe you caught a glimpse of one."

We stay like this a long time, watching the trees, ears pricked for sound. But there's only the wind, the haze, and the ever-present caw and screech and twitter of birds.

When I can't stand the tension any longer, I say, "I think the air is starting to smell better, at least."

"A temporary improvement," he says.

"What do you mean?"

"It's been at or below freezing for more than a day. All the bodies have been refrigerated. If we hit a warm snap . . ."

"Oh. Right." I really shouldn't have eaten breakfast this morning.

"Come on," he says. "Let's finish that window and get inside."

He knocks out a big enough hole that we're able to kick the rest in with our boots. The glass doesn't shatter. It spiderwebs and gradually crumbles, which is a good thing; this time I won't have to worry about Emmaline lacerating her paws.

My neck prickles as I climb after Trey through the hole, certain that something watches our backs. The air inside dampens my skin and smells worse than it did in Hazel Jenkins's house. I hope it's just the produce section.

Light streams through the enormous storefront windows. While Emmaline trots around sniffing floor displays, Trey and I stand side by side near the shopping carts, taking everything in. The aisles are neat and straight, everything perfect in its place. The only noticeable disorder is a single red apple, toppled from its pile onto the floor. Except for the smell, you'd think the store was merely closed for a holiday.

"So much food," I murmur.

"They locked the place down before the looting started," Trey says.

"Let's grab our carts and get to work." Before the thing I saw comes after us, is what I don't say.

He pulls out a cart, steps one foot on the back, and shoves off with the other. "Momma never let me do this!" he yells as he rattles away.

My answering chuckle dies quickly. I stare after him, wondering at myself. It's so easy to smile back, even to laugh, with another person around. Laughing at anything makes me twinge with guilt, like I don't have a right to laughter. Things are too awful. But maybe it's human nature, to cling to goodness even when it doesn't make sense.

I grab a cart and wheel off in the opposite direction. Trey will focus on food, but my job is to find everything else.

In the pet supplies aisle, I grab the biggest, most expensive bag of dry dog food, along with several cans of wet food, a box of treats, and a few bones. I heft a round squeaky toy and give it a test squeeze. Emmaline wags furiously, but it's loud enough to be worrisome, not to mention irritating. I return it to the shelf.

At the end of the aisle is a display of spring picnic items in cheerful colors: picnic baskets, tumblers, plastic food containers, paper napkins. Before I can stop her, Emmaline raises a leg and pees on it.

I glance around for something to help me mop up. . . . It doesn't matter. It certainly doesn't make the store smell any worse. "C'mon, Em," I say, without even bothering to scold her.

The next aisle contains miscellaneous household items. Most are useless, like light bulbs and printer paper. But I grab a few packs of batteries, emergency candles, and a weird little press-on light that we can hang on a wall somewhere. I find a pack of nails and a small hammer; maybe we'll want to—I don't know, fortify something? Next I grab toilet paper, then several flats of bottled water, a box of tampons. My cart is filling fast.

I'm scooting toward the magazine and book rack when I see the boot. It juts out on the floor from behind the coffee bar. It's shabby-black with worn tread, and the toe is sticking straight up in defiance of all the laws of physics of the universe—except if there's a foot inside it.

"Trey!" I call out. I release the cart and peer around the counter.

A man lies on the floor. He no longer has a face; his head is a wreck of bone bits and congealed blood and rotting flesh. Black-brown blood spatters the floor and the wall behind him. One hand is flung over his chest. It still grips a shiny black handgun.

I sense Trey come up behind me. "Oh, god," he says in a strangled voice. "That's . . . that's . . ."

I stare at the dead hand. It's shrunken and thin, the

remaining flesh the color of wet cardboard. The reek is awful. "Look, Trey. He has a gun."

"I . . . Yes. A gun." He sounds far away, and I look over my shoulder to find that Trey has turned his back on the scene.

Emmaline snuffles the dead man's pant leg.

"It would be a lot easier to find ammunition for that handgun than your rifle," I point out. "We could probably get it at a Walmart. Or a sporting goods store."

I watch the back of his head nod. "Sure," he says.

Trey isn't going to be any help. I'll have to pry the gun from cold, dead fingers all by myself.

I creep forward, wary though I'm not sure why. It's not like he's going to jump up and attack me. His other arm is flung off to the side. Beside his wrist is an open wallet and a piece of paper, neatly folded. It's damp with . . . body juices? . . . which makes the ink of the handwriting show through backward. My stomach turns over, but I think of Trey freaking out behind me and I ignore the nausea. One of us has to be strong.

I'm not sure what makes me do it, but I bend down and gingerly pick up the wet piece of paper. Carefully so it doesn't rip, I unfold it.

The ink is blurred, but I can still read the writing. "Wow," I breathe.

"What?" Trey demands. "What is it?"

"Listen to this:

"*Marta, I'm trapped in here. They said there would be riots, so I sent everyone home early and closed the place up myself. I tried to call, but the phones are out. Then the tornado sirens went off, and a big military jeep pulled up and now I can't leave. You must be worried sick. Sick. Ha. I'm sick now, too. I'll be dead in 2–3 days. I won't wait to die, Marta. I'm just going to do it. Get it over with. I know you won't get this note. I'm writing it to make myself feel better. But in case you do, I love you.*

"That's it. That's all there is."

Trey says nothing as I reach down and grab the wallet. It's open to a picture of a smiling, middle-aged Latina. Lines crinkle her eyes, and she has a large beauty mark above her right lip. He was looking at her picture when he died.

"This store is intact because of him," Trey finally says. "We have all the food and supplies we need because this man closed down before the looting started."

Next to the woman's picture is the dead man's driver's license. I slide it out. Barry Stockton, born in 1977, brown hair, brown eyes, five-foot-eleven, 220 pounds. I shove it into my pocket.

I take a deep breath, which is a mistake because Barry Stockton smells like rotting meat soaked in fermented fruit juice. I make a hard, cold fist of my stomach, of my soul, as I reach down for the gun. His fingers are cool and dry—not like skin at all—as I pry them from the grip. I'm careful to point the barrel away in case it's still loaded.

His forefinger is stubborn, curled around the trigger. If I push the wrong way or let the finger slip, the gun could go off again. Maybe letting the gun fire isn't the worst thing that could happen, so long as it's pointing away. I'm about to warn Trey when I notice a mote of red on the side of the gun behind the barrel. Beneath it is a tiny lever. On a hunch, I flip the lever up so it covers the red mote.

It's the gun's safety; I'm almost certain. Even so, doesn't hurt to be careful. The man's yellowish fingernail digs into my flesh as I push it off the trigger. Something in his hand pops, but I keep pushing, gently, slowly, until the finger is through the trigger guard and the gun comes free.

"Got it!" I say, turning to share my triumph with Trey, but he has disappeared.

I look down at the gun in my hand. My heart races, just to feel its weight. So much power in something so tiny. "9mm" is engraved on the barrel. I have no idea what that means. Something about the ammunition, I guess. At the top of the barrel is a narrow silver piece about an inch long that says, "Loaded when up." It's up.

Behind the trigger are buttons, one on each side. I push them, and the magazine slides out and clatters to the ground before I can catch it. The gun is instantly lighter, and I feel approximately seven gazillion times better knowing I'm holding an empty gun.

If I'm going to use this thing, I'll need to practice. Figure out how to use it safely. Figure out how to not be afraid of it.

Footsteps come up behind me. It's Trey, carrying a large ivory blanket. "Found it in the home goods section," he says. He pauses a moment, a muscle in his jaw twitching. He closes his eyes and steps forward, blindly flipping the blanket over the body. His shoulders relax the moment the body is covered.

Together, we stare at the lump on the floor. The edges of the blanket already soak up moisture.

"Thanks for the gun, Mr. Stockton," I say.

"And the food," Trey adds.

I shove the gun in one pocket, the magazine in the other. "I need to wash my hands," I say.

Trey nods. "Restrooms are by the meat counter. I'll watch your back. Then we'll finish up."

I turn to grab my cart.

"Paige?"

"Yeah?"

"You're pretty brave."

I smile thinly. "Thanks."

I drive us from the parking lot while Trey keeps watch out the windows. Emmaline sits in his lap, just as intent on the outside world as he is. The SUV is full to bursting with every dry good we could possibly need. The hole we put in the front window of the store is now sealed with plastic and duct tape. Hopefully, it will keep flies and birds and maybe even aliens away from our supply source.

"So, where are we going?" I ask.

He cranes his neck for a better view of the sky. "What about Victorian Village? Or the Short North? The houses are close together. Lots of trees."

I turn right onto Fishinger Road. "I do like the idea of being near the hospital. Lots of medical supplies."

"They might have power," he agrees. "Hospitals have generators. Maybe we could take hot showers."

"Sold." I'm a walking grease bucket. Also, if anyone is left alive, they'll probably be at the hospital. "Let's go there first, then look for a house."

"We could just live in the hospital," he says. "If there's power, I mean."

Two large sedans block the road. I steer left and bump up onto the sidewalk to get around them. "That's not a bad idea. No, wait. What about all the bodies?"

"Right. Let's *not* live in the hospital. There are probably thousands . . ."

As his voice trails off, I glance at his profile. That muscle in his jaw is twitching again.

I say, "It's okay to be grossed out by all this, you know. It's epically disgusting."

"That's not it." His voice is suddenly low and dangerous.

"Oh?"

He's silent a long time, and I just let him be. We turn south on Kenny Road. I'm only a few minutes away from seeing the place where my mom worked.

"Does the sky look weird to you?" he asks finally. "It seems a little green."

"Smoke and decomp, I guess."

He ruffles Emmaline's fur, and she leans against his chest in rapture. "That makes sense. Billions of humans dying all at once probably released a ton of methane into the air."

I barely stop myself from hitting the brakes. "Is that

toxic? Are we breathing bad air?"

"I doubt it. The extra methane is a lot at first, but it can't possibly make up for everything else. Think about it: we've had a 100 percent reduction in vehicle emissions. So it will be gross for a few more days—maybe a week if the weather stays cold—but then it should clear up."

"Okay. I guess we have scarier things to deal with."

"You mean like figuring out who wanted humanity dead and why? And how we can avoid something we don't even know enough about to avoid?"

"Yeah, that."

His arm around Emmaline tightens. "Well, I'm keeping an eye on that sky all the same."

We fall back into silence as I steer through the deserted streets. A cardinal wings by, a bright red flash in a quiet, hazy world. The carrion birds are nowhere to be seen.

I turn onto Medical Center Drive, curve around the four-story parking garage toward the main entrance, and suddenly I can go no farther.

"Damn," Trey says.

Cars and ambulances choke the area. There must be a hundred, maybe more, bumper to bumper along the sidewalk, filling the street, even squeezed together on the green divider that used to serve as a picnic area. There's no order to the mess; people parked wherever they could, and fenders point in all directions.

I pull on the brake and turn off the engine. "There's no way through. We have to climb over."

"Let's go then." Emmaline darts out as soon as he opens his door.

I open my own door and climb out. My knees buckle. Suddenly I'm flat on the pavement, my shins bruised and my right elbow stinging with a scrape.

"Paige!" Running footsteps, then Trey is looming over me as Emmaline laps at my face.

"I'm fine." I take his proffered hand and shakily gain my feet.

"What happened?"

"I lost my . . ." I bend over, hands on my knees, and take a few deep breaths. I'm dizzy and light-headed. My bones ache with heaviness, like I could sleep for days. God, I hate being weak. "I'm sorry, Trey. I just woke up a few days ago, and I think I almost died of dehydration, and—"

"And you just spent all morning on your feet, hauling groceries. Here. Sit."

Emmaline sits prettily.

I smother a laugh. "Good girl."

Trey guides me back toward the car and sits me down. He disappears, and I hear him rummaging in the backseat; then he returns with a nutrition bar and a bottled water. "We can scout the hospital tomorrow," he says. "Let's find a place to camp for the night."

I tear off the wrapper and take a big bite. "I'll be fine," I say around a mouthful of something that's not-quite-chocolate. "I always get a second wind." I brandish the partly eaten nutrition bar at him. "You realize these are pure crap, right? That whole nutrition bar fad. Total scam."

"First-world problem."

"Huh?"

"When I was little, before my mom graduated from PA school, anything that wasn't ramen noodles or boxed macaroni and cheese was a rare delicacy."

"Oh." I swallow guiltily.

"You'll get healthy," he assures me. "You already look better than when I first saw you."

"Thanks."

"Sure you don't want to find a place to stay for the night?"

The possibility of a hot shower makes me say, "We're here, and we might as well investigate."

Emmaline trots around, sniffing bumpers, daffodil shoots, and park benches. I expect her to raise her leg like she did in the grocery store, but I guess peeing is reserved only for *really* interesting discoveries. I finish my nutrition bar and wash it down with some water. I stand, carefully this time. "Let's go."

Trey opens his mouth to say something, and I expect to hear my mom's words: *Use better judgment . . . No one can be a hero all the time. . . . You're not invincible, Paige.* But he changes his mind. Instead, he stretches an arm out in a "lead the way" gesture.

I climb onto the hood of the nearest car—a white Ford sedan—and walk over it toward the next car, which is an older Hyundai. They're so close together that I can step from one to the other with little effort. Trey follows, then Emmaline, and our boots and claws make hollow drumbeats as we go from hood to hood toward the front of the nearest hospital in the huge complex.

My gun is in one pocket, my flashlight in the other. Trey carries his rifle and the tire iron. The grocery store glass was tough enough; I can't imagine what it will take to break into a hospital. We might have to use precious bullets after all.

But, no, someone has already done the work for us. The wall of glass is shattered, the steel framing buckled. The nose of a huge black truck with a king cab is mashed into a bent silver crossbeam that may have been part of a doorway once. Glass shards litter the ruined cab and the cars around it; they glint like ice in the sun.

"Well, there's an idea," Trey says. "Next time we need to get inside a place, we'll just drive a huge truck through it."

"We'd end up like that guy," I say, pointing toward the dry but mangled corpse face-planted into a deflated airbag.

"We could get a car rolling and jump out," he says.

I slide off the last fender and grab Emmaline before she can walk through the glass. She doesn't protest when I pick her up, just pricks her ears forward and thumps her tail against my waist. The entrance is shadowed by high-rises on either side, so it's a lot darker here than in the grocery store. Muggy, too, thick with rancid meat and old urine.

A null symbol in glittery blue spray paint shimmers at us from right outside the doorway.

"What kind of vandal tags a hospital?" Trey says as we step inside.

Glass crunches beneath my boots, then sticks to my soles.

I peer at the floor and discover that much of it is covered in still-gummy bird poop.

"No sign of power," Trey says.

I lift my foot up to the edge of the reception counter and scrape my sole against it to get the sticky glass off. "Maybe in ICU?"

"Hospitals are required by law to have emergency power, but I don't know for which sections or for how long. Generators might have run out of fuel days ago." Trey pulls a flashlight from the pocket of his long coat and flicks it on.

I set Emmaline down and do the same with my own flashlight. I sweep it around and discover that Trey and I guessed right: there are so many dead bodies.

They sit slumped in the waiting chairs, curled up in the hallway, and even collapsed against giant potted ficus trees. Several gurneys are lined up behind the reception desk, each containing a corpse watched over by an IV tree and a dangling, empty IV bag.

"You still want to do this?" Trey's whisper echoes through the corridor.

I stare at the gurneys.

"Paige?"

"That was me," I say. "That's how I woke up. With my bag empty like that. And my sheets . . ." I stop myself from saying, *soaked with pee.*

"I'm sorry."

I didn't fully realize until this moment how very close to death I had been. "Yeah, I still want to do this."

He nods. "Let's see if ICU or NICU has power."

"Nick-you?" I should have paid more attention when Mom talked about her workplace.

"Neonatal Intensive Care Unit."

"Oh. That's not depressing or anything. Actually, the *last* thing in the whole world I want to see right now is a whole ward full of . . ."

"Okay, let's skip the NICU. We should try to find the generators. There might be leftover fuel drums we can hook up."

As we head deeper into the wide, dark hallway, I say, "You know a lot about this."

"My mom worked in a hospital."

"Mine too. The heart hospital connected to this one, in fact."

"I spent more time at Riverside than I should have." His echoing voice makes the hallway sound cavernous. I look around nervously, but I resist the urge to shush him. "Momma made me and my sister volunteer after school," he continues. "While she was paying off school loans. Cheaper than childcare. Each shift got us a free meal in the cafeteria."

A dead woman lies sprawled in the hallway, and we carefully step over her legs. The floor beneath my boots is slippery. A lump beside her resolves into a dead crow as my flashlight sweeps across it.

I'm relieved when our path begins to brighten, thanks to a skylight down the hallway. I ask, "How did you find time for—"

Emmaline growls, a split second before something clatters, echoing down the hallway toward us.

Trey reaches out with the tire iron to block my path.

"Could be animals," I whisper. "Dogs or birds."

He doesn't budge. We stand still as statues, listening.

Footsteps approach. A slow, heavy one-two, one-two.

Trey yanks me into a dark side hallway and ducks down. I crouch beside him, my arm around Emmaline. I'm not sure why we're hiding, but when he flicks off his flashlight, I do the same.

I didn't get a good look at our surroundings as we dashed into the cover of darkness, except to notice a gurney across from us with a vague child-sized lump under a hospital blanket. And as we crouch here, the unmistakable scents of old urine and decomposition prick at my nose. Emmaline huffs, then starts to sniff in earnest. She's not interested in the corpse, though. Instead, her whole body is rigid, keyed in the direction of the footsteps. I tighten my arm around her neck.

Our dark hallway begins to glow.

It's subtle. Soft. Blue-white. Not like a flashlight beam at all. As the footsteps get closer, the glow brightens.

Emmaline jerks forward under my arm. I ruffle her fur to calm her, but she whines.

Panic edges into my throat as I resist the urge to shush her. I sense movement beside me. Trey has lifted the rifle and is now pointing the barrel forward.

A shape edges into view. It looks human, except for the fact that its body is blurred by a radiating glow. Except for the fact that it's unimaginably tall.

I hardly dare to breathe as it rises off the floor, no longer stepping but *floating* down the hallway, the top of its head almost brushing the ceiling. Something flows from its head all the way to the ground, but it's not hair—not exactly. It's nearly transparent, and it shifts with the creature's movement. It might be a hood, made of silk like water.

Emmaline whines again.

The creature freezes. Turns its head.

It has no eyes.

A long forehead extends all the way down to a small flattened nose. Instead of eyes, there are vague hollows smoothed over with whatever passes for skin, as if this creature had eyes once upon a time but gave up on them and closed them forever. Beneath the small nose is a wide mouth with lips as black as tar.

My heart knocks against my ribs as that black mouth opens. And opens, and opens.

Until it's a huge black maw, glistening with something slimy. I think of a snake unhinging its jaw.

Trey flicks off the safety of his gun.

The creature *breathes* at us. One long breath, followed by several short pants.

Emmaline growls deep in her throat.

My legs twitch with the need to flee. Even if the creature can't see us, surely it can hear us. Or smell us. Surely it senses the pounding drum of my heart.

It howls. Like a wolf, but deeper, and as the sound echoes around us, thrums in my head, all the hairs on my arm stand up straight. "Oooowww?" it says.

It's talking to us. I'm sure of it.

"Owww? Howww you?"

Trey gasps.

"Hooww do you I? Howw do you aliving?"

We should make a run for it, I know we should, but I am utterly frozen.

"How do you aliving?" Its voice resonates like a plucked guitar string, each word a note that twangs in my skull.

It stretches out a hand toward us. It has six fingers and no thumbs, though its palm is almost cylindrical, with all the fingers opposing each other. At the end of each finger is a long black fingernail.

A clicking sound. Something ripples down the glowing flesh of its arm and hand.

Pain sears my shoulder and something darts past my ear a split second before I register that the black nails have detached from the hand and bulleted toward us.

Trey launches to his feet, pulling me with him. He yanks me across the hallway, and it's all I can do to hold on to Emmaline as my right shoulder starts to go numb, but not so numb that I can't feel hot blood dripping down my arm and pooling in the crook of my elbow.

He pulls me down beside the gurney and its resident corpse.

What the hell is he thinking? We need to run for our lives. We need—

"Wheeeere?" the creature moans. "Wheeere you?" Its black maw of a mouth widens, and once again it breathes at us.

Emmaline growls, and her body quivers with the desire to defend, but I hold tight. The smell from the corpse is unbearable. Something drops from the gurney and splats onto the floor.

The creature's mouth snaps closed. It turns away. Resumes its slow, gliding journey. It disappears down the connecting hallway. The glow gradually fades.

Relief threatens to overwhelm me, but I won't let it. By silent, mutual agreement, Trey and I remain frozen in our hiding place. We wait and wait and wait.

When I'm certain the creature has had enough time to get far, far away, I release my grip on Emmy and whisper, "There's another way out of the hospital." I stand, yanking Trey up with my good hand.

"There could be more," he whispers back as we retreat deeper into the corridor.

I glance down at Emmaline, who is little more than a lump in the dark, but it's not so dark that I can't see her relaxed ears and gently waving tail. "Em says the coast is clear. She'll let us know if something's coming."

"Can you get us there without flashlights?"

"I think so. Once we cross over into the heart hospital, there'll be plenty of light. Lots of windows."

He gestures with a lift of the rifle. "Lead the way."

"Did it get you? With its nails, I mean?"

"Took one in the thigh. Can hardly feel a thing now. You?"

"Shoulder."

"Let's get out of here quick. Before . . ."

I'm not sure what he was going to say. Before the poison in the creature's nails kills us? "Can you walk?"

"Well enough."

The corridor is narrow, the ceiling low, the cold air clammy with wetness. Trey's gait is lopsided as we travel in silence, skirting corpses—mostly human, but also a few birds, and one large furred creature with a white, pointed snout and a frozen, toothy grin. Opossum, maybe.

"What happened to the animals?" I whisper.

"Who knows?" Trey says. "Animals die by the billions every year. It's just that humans are usually too disconnected from nature to bother noticing."

And that's all the talking I can handle because the smell of death is so thick it seems to tingle on my tongue. I clamp my mouth closed. Trey pulls his scarf up to cover his nose.

As we turn a corner and head down a sloped hallway, the air brightens. A few paces more and it's bright enough to see easily. The corridor breaks into a wide reception area several stories high and lit by a massive wall of windows.

I glance around to make sure the coast is clear. No aliens as far as I can tell, but corpses are everywhere. Instead of on gurneys, they're laid out on the floor in neat rows, covered in blankets. More are stretched out on the leather seats in the waiting area. There must be hundreds. Maybe a thousand.

"Storage," Trey murmurs.

The exit lies ahead. Outside are more cars, parked bumper

to bumper haphazardly. I can't see the SUV from here, but it shouldn't be far away. "Let's get the hell out of here."

"Watch your step; the floor's slippery."

The bodies are so close together that they're hard to avoid. We're almost to the door when my foot squishes down on something lumpy, almost tripping me. It's a bloated hand, snaked out from beneath a striped hospital blanket. Something wet oozes from cracks in the skin.

I jerk away, practically leaping for the door. I step on something else, but this time I refuse to look down, just reach for the door handle and push with all my might.

The door is locked.

"Oh, god." I rattle the door, then bang, then kick. My insides feel like they're crawling out of me. "Oh, god, oh, god."

Trey settles a hand on mine. "Paige, you're panicking." He gently peels my hand off the door, reaches for a deadbolt, and flicks it. He pushes open the door and fresher air pours in as I stumble outside, choking and gasping.

"We'll have to climb over the cars again," Trey says. "Can you make it?"

It's all too much: the glowing creature, the bodies everywhere, my exhaustion. My legs tremble, and my breaths are shallow and weak. *You're not invincible, Paige.* "Honestly, I'm not sure. You? Your leg—"

"That thing might still be around, so we'll take it slow and quiet. Grab on to me if you need to, okay?"

"Sure, okay," I say, relieved that he's taking charge.

We clamber over cars, alert for danger. My neck prickles

with the expectation that I'll be impaled by more fingernail projectiles at any moment.

The air has warmed, and I'm slick with sweat by the time we find the SUV. I think about what Trey said earlier, about warmer weather making the bodies decompose faster.

"You want me to drive?" he says.

"Can you?"

"I only need my right leg."

Don't drive drowsy, Paul used to say. *It's as bad as driving drunk.* "Yes, please."

As we climb in, I glance down at my sleeve, which is stained dark red with blood. I melt into the passenger seat as Emmaline settles in my lap and Trey starts the car. "Trey?"

"Yeah?"

"You're pretty brave too."

His hands on the steering wheel tighten. "Thanks."

We pull up to a detached garage behind a giant, three-story brick Victorian with a gray slate roof. "Wait here," Trey says. "I'll be right back."

He grabs the tire iron as he steps from the car, then he disappears beyond the garage. Glass shatters, and Emmaline tries to leap from my lap out the open door, but I hold her back.

A few minutes later, Trey returns. He's limping from the injury to his thigh, but a huge grin splits his face. "It's empty," he says. "No bodies."

I bang my shin against the door panel in my rush. Dizziness threatens to put me on the ground again, and I'm forced to slow down as we circle the garage and navigate the winding path of the tiny backyard. We step inside the house, and I vaguely register granite and stainless steel and shiny wood floors as Trey leads me into a small bedroom with a queen-sized bed. "Lie down," he orders. "I'll bring you some food and water and take a look at that shoulder."

I'm asleep before he returns.

March 20

I WAKE TO WARMTH AND THE SCENT OF WOODSMOKE. LONG, ochre-colored velvet curtains cover the windows, but sunshine pours through a transom above the bedroom door. The ceiling is a fleur-de-lis pattern of pressed tin, painted off-white. I'm nestled in a thick down comforter, surrounded by jewel-toned decorative pillows. On the nightstand beside me is a bottled water and a plate full of blue corn tortilla chips.

The bed creaks as I rise, and a split second later comes the clatter of claws on the floor, then a *scritch-scritch-scritch* at the bedroom door. "Coming, Emmy," I call out, and she responds with a little yip.

I reach over to grab the bottled water and realize my shoulder is thickly bandaged. I roll my arm experimentally. No more numbness, but it aches a little. I take a swig of water and shove a few corn chips into my mouth, then I pad over to the door and crack it open. Emmaline plunges inside and runs circles around my ankles. "Up-up, Emmy," I say, and she jumps into my arms. I snug her tight while she laps at my face.

I set her down and head into the hallway, following the scent of burning wood until I reach a large living room with plush couches and a massive flat-screen television. Another scent pricks at my nose: coffee.

Trey squats before a cheery fire, poking at embers. Beside him is a pot of steaming water and a long glass cylinder full of dark liquid.

Relief washes over his features when he sees me. "I found a coffee press," he says. "Want some?"

"Dear god, yes."

"You slept all night. I was getting worried." As he pours me a mugful, I can't help but notice his arms. He wears jeans and a gray tank top now, and he looks every inch the scholarship quarterback, with rounded deltoids and corded forearms. Without his duster coat, he's not bulky at all, but rather lean and elegant. Even simple movements like filling up a coffee mug are done with an efficiency of motion that puts me in mind of a hunting cat.

He hands me the mug, saying, "I fed Emmaline and took her outside to do her business."

"Thank you." I take a sip—it's divine—and stare into the dark steaming liquid. "You also bandaged my shoulder." My face flushes a little. He must have pulled back the sleeve of my hoodie to do that. Weird that I slept through it.

"Paige, we need to talk about what happened at the hospital."

My cheeks warm even more. "I really lost it out there, didn't I? I'm so sorry—"

"Stop it."

I snap my gaze to his. "What?"

"You keep saying you're sorry. Stop apologizing."

"But I can hardly stay on my feet. I'm slowing you d—"

"You're an athlete. A leader on the battlefield, like me. I get it. But you almost died, and no one recovers from that overnight. So relax already. Focus on getting healthy."

I take another sip and weigh his words.

"My freshman year of high school," he says, "I decided I wanted to move up to varsity. Once I got the idea in my head, I became obsessed. I trained really hard. Came home after practice and went for an extra run. I did a hundred pushups every morning. On weekends, I went to the park with Teena and made her come after me for the sack while I practiced my footwork."

"But you burned out?" I guess.

"Badly. Got stress fractures in my right shin and pulled my shoulder. I was benched for the rest of the year."

"So you're saying take it easy before I make things worse."

"Yep."

My mom would have agreed with him. She was always worried that I was doing too much, never cutting myself a break. Working out her own guilt, Paul told me once in confidence. For turning me into a mini-adult before I'd really had a chance to be a kid. "Okay, Coach, you win." I take another sip. "Thanks for helping me."

He shrugs. "You're my best friend in the whole world."

I choke on my coffee. Then I'm laughing. Then tears are pouring down my cheeks. I look up to find him grinning ear to ear. God, he has a great smile. "That's pathetic," I manage.

"Well, you *and* Emmaline," he amends, which gets me laughing all over again, even though it's the opposite of funny.

His face turns solemn. "So, about . . . that thing."

I set my coffee on the side table and lean my head back. A chill runs down my spine as I flash back to that eyeless face, that glowing aura, those airborne fingernails. "Definitely not human," I say to the ceiling.

"Check this out." He pulls a wadded napkin from his pocket. No, it's a bit of gauze. He unwraps it and spreads it out on the coffee table. In its center are two black slivers.

I bend to get a closer look. They're slightly larger than human fingernails but a whole lot sharper. The black surface is striated with dark, iridescent blue.

"Did you pull one of these out of my shoulder?" I ask.

He nods. "And the other out of my thigh. Both bled a good bit; they were in deep. The numbing wore off fast, though. A mild neurotoxin, maybe? If one of these lodged in your spine or near your heart, I think you'd be in big trouble."

"Or if it nicked an artery. Of if you were hit by a bunch at one time."

"Right. Higher concentration of poison."

Gingerly, I pick one up and study it. "Maybe this is one

reason I slept so soundly through . . . everything." It's cool and smooth, pinched between thumb and forefinger, except for a crusty spot of dried brown blood. Is the blood mine or Trey's?

"I'm sorry I didn't ask permission before . . . ," he says. "But you were knocked out cold, and I thought it might be because of that thing in your shoulder, so I was afraid to leave it in, and—"

"You did the right thing. Why did you pull us down behind that gurney?" I ask him. "Why not make a run for it?"

"Lucky guess. It seemed like it was sniffing us. Through its *mouth.*"

I shudder, remembering the way its mouth gaped open and shimmered oily black. The fireplace pops, startling me.

"It breathed at us," Trey adds. "Taste and smell are interrelated, you know."

"You think that body disguised our scent. It was dripping with decomp."

"Maybe." His gaze seems focused on the mantel, though I'm fairly certain he sees nothing but the image in his head. "I couldn't shoot, Paige. I had the rifle in my hand. I had it pointed at that . . . thing. And I couldn't pull the trigger."

I chuckle.

His face gets a wounded look. "What's so funny?"

"I had a gun too, remember? And it didn't even occur to me to pull it out of my pocket. I mean, I would have had to shove the magazine back in and find the safety and . . . Can you tell I know nothing about guns?"

Trey allows himself a weak grin. "We're not exactly Commander Shepard, are we?"

"Who?"

"Another video game thing." He runs a finger along the fireplace mantel. It's a giant slab of polished oak, carved with vines and flowers. Displayed on it are a handful of shiny trophies. Behind the trophies, hanging from the wide brick chimney, is a huge framed Ohio State flag.

"Whose house is this?" I ask.

"Coach Buckell's," he says. "Head coach of the Ohio State basketball team. I came here last summer with a bunch of other football recruits for a mixer." He snickers. "The athletic department had to pay a ten-thousand-dollar fine to the NCAA for holding that mixer. Violated some rule. Anyway, the plague hit a few days after Coach Buckell and the team had their big tournament send-off, so I knew the place would be empty."

"Good call," I say, though without enthusiasm. Nothing like staying in the abandoned house of a famous basketball coach to remind me of the total annihilation of my future.

"Also, you said you wanted a regulation-height basketball hoop. There's one out by the garage."

I sit straight up. "Is it safe to be outside, do you think?"

"Probably not."

I sink back into the couch.

"But he's got a workout room with a treadmill and some free weights so you can do some conditioning. Come into the kitchen with me," Trey says. "I'll make us some gourmet peanut-butter-and-honey sandwiches, then I'll give you the tour."

I wouldn't mind a break from peanut butter, but my stomach growls as I follow him into a sunny dining area. Both the cherrywood table and the granite counters are piled high with our grocery loot. "Thanks for unloading the car," I say.

He finds bread, peanut butter, and honey and makes a space on the counter to work. I slide onto a barstool to watch. He slaps on peanut butter like it's going out of style, and I get the feeling his mind is far away.

"It talked to us," he says finally.

I nod. "'*How do you aliving*,' it said. As in, 'Why are you alive?' Or 'How did you survive?'"

He shrugs.

"It's like it *almost* knew how to talk. Like it was figuring it out."

"Maybe it was surprised to see us."

"To see us 'aliving,' anyway. There are plenty of dead people."

He pauses, butter knife poised in the air. "It floated. And it was huge. Did you notice that? Its head almost brushed the ceiling, and that ceiling was at least ten feet high."

My stomach flutters. "I noticed."

He grabs a plastic container in the shape of a bear and squeezes honey out of it. "So this is what I think. I think it couldn't see us. But it heard us. And it tried to sniff us out but couldn't because of the decomp." He hands me a sandwich.

"We should put the theory to the test." I take a bite and close my eyes to savor. I'm definitely still into peanut butter. How much has the world changed that I can enjoy my sandwich while discussing decomposing bodies?

"How would we do that?" he asks.

"Not sure," I mumble around a mouthful.

"We should avoid the aliens whenever possible."

I swallow and look him straight in the eye. "What we don't know about them could get us killed."

"Purposely seeking out giant creatures who shoot poisonous fingernails could get us killed too."

"What do *you* think we should do?"

His lips press into a firm line. He stares off into space, eyes slightly narrowed—a look I'm already starting to identify as his thinking face. "We should stay here a couple of days," he says. "I want to see you get some strength back before we make any big moves."

"And then?"

"And then we get the hell out of Dodge. Hole up someplace rural where there are fewer bodies to deal with. Maybe we can find a house with a big propane tank that will give us some hot water."

"But if your theory is right, bodies give us protection," I point out. "Like camouflage. The smellier the better."

"If this warm weather holds, we only have a week or so of camouflage left anyway."

I stare at my sandwich. "You think there will be fewer Orkins in rural areas."

He shrugs. "Maybe."

"Just because humans work that way doesn't mean aliens do. Maybe they *prefer* rural areas. Maybe the small towns of Ohio are crawling with them."

He gives me an angry frown. "Don't you think it's worth a try?"

"My point is that we don't *know*."

He starts slapping his own sandwich together, attacking the peanut butter with vengeful purpose.

"Are we about to have our first fight, Trey?"

This coaxes a grin out of him, but he sobers quickly. "We do know there's at least one Orkin at the hospital. We know they have at least one big shiny flying thing that kills people right here in Columbus. And we know that they have the technology to wipe us out with an engineered disease."

Softly, I add, "And we know I'm not healthy enough to run or fight or whatever we have to do."

"Not *yet*," he amends.

"Not yet," I agree. "So I'm on board with the first part of your plan. We should stay here two or three days. I'm feeling better already. My heel hardly bothers me at all anymore."

"Good. You should walk around the house a bit. Go up and down the stairs a few times, see how your heart and lungs handle stress."

I nod. This is a language I understand, the language of my life for the past several years, and I cling to it as to a lifeline. "I've been hydrating pretty well, but I need to replace lost muscle mass."

"And fat stores. That's why I put so much peanut butter on your sandwich."

"Thanks."

"We can work out together," he says cheerfully. "We'll start with easy isometric exercises, then move on to weights when you're ready."

"I'd like to work with Emmaline too," I say. With my forefinger, I wipe a dollop of peanut butter from the side of my sandwich. I lean down so she can lick it up, which she does with gusto. "She's pretty well trained already, but I'm worried about her running off. What if we have to hide again? Can't have her whining and growling."

"We have a plan then," he says. "For the next few days at least. Then we'll figure out what to do next."

The decision won't be any easier for putting it off, but I'm in no mood to argue, so I just nod.

March 22

Something shakes me awake. I lurch up from my bed, heart hammering, before I realize it's Trey.

"You need to see something," he whispers.

I slip out from under the covers. Emmaline uncurls from the foot of my bed and indulges in a full body shake before hopping down and following us into the hallway and up the stairs.

Trey has been using the upstairs corner bedroom. He says he likes to look out the window when he can't sleep, and the room gives him a good view of the street. I've heard his footsteps on my ceiling in the middle of the night. Often enough to wonder if he sleeps at all.

The floorboards creak as Trey brushes past his rumpled queen-sized bed and pushes aside the curtains. The moon has been waning, but enough moonlight remains to make sense of the neighborhood. Three-story Victorians rise from tiny front yards that are lush with weeds and bulb sprouts and overgrown grass. Mature oaks shade broad lemonade porches, and fading solar lamps line brick walkways.

"In the house across from us and two doors down," Trey whispers. "Watch for it in the bay window."

It's the biggest mansion on the block, with a giant, castle-like turret on one corner. The bay window juts out beside it. A neglected plant wilts from the window box at its base.

I'm not sure what I'm watching for, but Trey is tense in the space beside me, both hands on the sill.

Something flickers in the window.

"There!" he says. "Did you see that?"

"A flashlight?" Hope wars with dread. It could be another human being. Or it could be something else.

It flickers again, stronger this time. Yellow-orange. Diffuse.

"Candlelight," Trey says with conviction.

We stand shoulder to shoulder, watching. The light steadies, like the candle has been set down. A silhouette ghosts past the window.

My heart is racing now. "Should we go knock on the door?"

Trey leans forward so that his nose almost touches the glass. "I don't know! Maybe it's an Orkin."

"But they don't need light, right? I mean, they can't even *see*."

"Just because the one we saw doesn't have human eyes doesn't mean . . ." He makes a frustrated sound. "Actually, I don't know what anything means."

"It wasn't that glow-y light like in the hospital. It was . . . flickery. Let's go knock."

He turns from the window to stare at me. Moonlight makes deep shadows of his eyes. "You're not a very cautious person, are you?"

I blink up at him, wondering what he'd think of me leaving my house alone in the middle of the night, or climbing up onto my roof, or driving straight into a burning neighborhood. "No one ever got anywhere in life without taking a few risks." It's something Paul used to say to me, but I know it's bull crap the moment it leaves my mouth. Things have changed. The old rules don't apply. "No, you're right," I add hastily. "It's just that I hate not knowing something."

His mouth quirks. "Well, you're right too. About what you said the other day. What we don't know could get us killed."

Which means we need to find out what's inside that house.

"Let's keep watch," I say. "We'll do it in shifts. Eventually, whoever—whatever—is inside has to come out, right?"

He's peering at the house again, his breath fogging the window. "Maybe there are binoculars around somewhere."

I can't help the chuckle that escapes. At his questioning look, I say, "If it turns out to be a person, we're going to look like total creepers."

He grins. "I'm willing to risk it if you are."

Neither of us feels like sleeping, so we watch together. Some time later, the light goes out. The moon sets. We shove the bed around so we can sit on it side by side, staring into the darkness.

March 24

WE'VE BEEN WATCHING FOR A DAY AND A HALF. IT'S MY SHIFT. I'm in the upstairs bedroom, and Trey is asleep on the couch downstairs as late-morning light pours through the windows. But I'm barely paying attention to the mansion across the street because I'm working with Emmaline. At first, she loved her treats so much that she whined when she scented them. At the slightest noise from her, I put a hand on her muzzle. When she quiets down, I release her nose and offer the treat. She's getting better at it, and most of the time she'll quiver with excitement as the treat nears instead of whining. When she does whine, my hand on her muzzle shushes her instantly.

I'm guessing wildly about how to train my dog, and I hope I'm not damaging her in some way. But the alien in the hospital keyed to the sound of her soft whining so fast it was uncanny, so I need a way to keep Emmaline quiet if we have to hide again.

A door slams.

Emmaline barks.

I grab the binoculars from the nightstand and dart over to the window, Emmy at my heels.

A flash of movement outside the mansion. Hidden by trees. My heart pulses in my throat.

I follow the movement down the sidewalk. The trees break wide, and I gasp.

It's a girl. Partly shaved head, black hair swept over to one side, black combat boots beneath a black knee-length overcoat. A camouflage backpack is slung over one shoulder.

I drop the binoculars and race down the stairs. "Trey! Trey, wake up."

He rolls over on the couch, blinking sleep from his eyes.

"It's a girl!" I pant out. "That's who was in the mansion across the street. She just came outside."

He launches from the couch like a bullet, yanks on his court trainers, retrieves the rifle from the coffee table. I throw on a jacket and grab Emmaline's brand-new leash, which makes her whip around in tiny circles.

As I clip the leash on to her collar, Trey pauses. "You sure it was a human? Maybe you saw . . . something else."

"Only if 'something else' looks like an emo teenager."

"You think we should talk to her?"

"Hell, yeah."

"Take your handgun."

"In my right pocket. Magazine clip in my left."

Trey heads for the door. "We need to find a better carrying solution for your gun than your pocket."

"Agreed."

He opens the door, and cold air rushes in. The sky is cloudy, the air murky with haze—tiny flies and dust and that greenish tint. Emmaline whimpers with excitement, and that changes my mind about bringing her along. I say, "Sit. Stay."

She gives me a single piteous whine, but she plunks her bottom down on the entry tile. "Good girl," I murmur, and I close the door.

"There." Trey points. The girl is two blocks away now and walking at a fast clip.

"Let's go." I head after her at a slow jog, not bothering to see if Trey follows. I open my mouth to call out after the girl, but decide against it. What if more of those nail-shooting things are lurking around?

Trey catches up to me. "You okay to run like this?" he whispers, keeping pace.

"Yep." But my gasping breath gives me away. "Not for long though."

We're gaining on the girl. Our footsteps seem too loud, even though we're running mostly on our toes, the crunch of fallen leaves echoing through the trees and the silent, ghostly mansions to either side of the street. But she walks on, caught up in her own thoughts, I guess. Her backpack jounces against her back. It looks deflated and empty. Maybe she's making a supply run.

She whisks around a corner. Trey and I exchange a glance, then we sprint to catch up.

My diaphragm heaves with oxygen debt, but I don't dare slow down. She's only the second person I've seen alive since I woke, and I won't lose her.

We round the corner. The girl is just ahead, close enough that I won't have to shout. She's tiny, barely more than five feet tall, and her side-swept hair reveals a thin, delicate neck.

"Excuse me," I say. "Hello?"

She whirls.

Her huge brown eyes are rimmed with thick black eyeliner, her lips plumped with blood-red lipstick. She's pale and small, with a heart-shaped face that ends in a perfect, pointed chin. She looks elfin. Vampiric, even. And she stares at us mouth agape, eyes wide with surprise.

No, not surprise. Rage.

"You've got to be fucking kidding me," she spits out.

"I'm sorry?" Trey says.

"Get the hell away from me," she says.

I gape at her. "Why? I mean, you're *alive*. I . . . we're really glad to see you."

Her body is wound tight, a coil of fury about to explode. "Just back off."

Trey puts his hands up. "No worries," he says. "We're not going to hurt you. We just—"

"Leave me alone."

"We could help you," I insist. "We have food. Supplies—"

Her tiny hands become fists. "Oh, my god, did you not hear

me the first fifty thousand times? I said back. The fuck. Off."

She turns tail and sprints away, leaving Trey and me to stare open-mouthed.

I say, "Should we go after her?"

Trey shakes his head.

"But—"

"Momma taught me that a lady's no means no. I expect that holds true even in the apocalypse."

I frown. "It's not like we're asking her out."

"She was very clear about what she wants," he says.

We're standing beneath the awning of a stranger's porch, surrounded by trees, and the breeze rustles the bare branches around us. Tiny buds are poking out all over, promising an explosion of green in the coming weeks. The trees don't care that humanity has died. They're going to keep budding and blooming and drying up, a stubborn cycle of life and death and rebirth.

"I suppose you're right," I say finally. "At least she knows we're here. If she gets into trouble, maybe she'll change her mind and . . ."

Birds explode into the sky, a dark cloud of wings and screeched warnings. They disappear, and just as suddenly, a hush falls.

A large shadow passes over the street. A mechanical whine fills the air.

"Get down!" Trey says, yanking on my arm.

I drop to the ground beside him. Together, we huddle in the lee of the awning.

"What is it?" I whisper.

"Not sure, but it might be—"

It appears through a break in the rooftops, following its shadow. It's silvery and shiny in the sun. Sleek and winged, the size of a one-man fighter but shaped a little like a giant dragonfly. There's no propulsion system I can see. No windows. No door. Just a sleek narrow body and gossamer wings with lines so fluid and aerodynamic they seem almost like water, gently flowing through the sky, the slight whining sound the only indication that it's actually a machine.

It's heading in the exact same direction as the girl.

"That's the thing I was telling you about," Trey says, his voice trembling. "The thing that killed those kids."

"We have to go after her," I say, as Trey simultaneously says, "We should stay in cover until it's gone."

We stare at each other for a long moment, our faces close. Trey's lips press into a hard line, and then he nods once, curtly.

He takes off running at a low crouch, and I'm happy to follow his lead. We keep to the shadows, sprinting from porch to porch, tree to tree, following the flying thing. We have to get to the girl, warn her away or save her or . . . I don't even know what we'll do. I just know that I couldn't stand it if she died.

We round a corner, and there she is, her empty backpack jouncing against her shoulder. But her pace has slowed, and she glances about in apparent caution. She knows she's being followed. Above her, the flying thing slows, drops altitude.

There's no way to reach her in time.

"Look out!" I scream.

The girl whirls.

I point frantically at the silver thing as Trey waves her toward a nearby porch. "Take cover!" he yells.

The girl's mouth opens as she gapes at the sky. Her pack slides off her shoulder and drops to the ground.

The mechanical whine grows louder. Heat begins to shimmer off the hull.

I'm sprinting toward her, yelling, "Go, go, go! Run!" but she remains frozen, transfixed by the thing that's about to kill her.

Part of me understands that if I reach her as the thing fires, we'll both be obliterated, but I can't stop my feet from pounding against the pavement, my arms from waving her aside.

A hole opens up in the flying thing's hull, a maw of black emptiness. Its edges turn white with heat as something rumbles in the cavity of my chest.

I'm not going to reach her in time.

A huge shape blurs past me. It's Trey at a full sprint. He grabs the girl's shoulders and dives toward a nearby lawn, taking her with him.

Light flashes, blinding and hot. I instinctively put up a hand to shield my eyes, as heat singes the skin of my cheeks. All the hair on my head lifts for a brief moment, as if full of static.

I stumble toward the space I last saw Trey and the girl, knowing I need to get under cover, but spots dance in my hazy vision, like I've been staring at the sun.

"Over here, Paige!" Trey calls. "Run!"

My ankle turns on a dislodged brick, and I almost go down, but I keep my feet and hobble as fast as I can in the direction of Trey's voice.

There. Huddled in the doorway of someone's walkout basement, protected by concrete and brick.

I half run, half trip down the few steps and crouch beside them. The three of us are thigh to thigh, shoulder to shoulder as we hug up against the brick wall that defines the stairwell. If we can't see the flying thing, it can't see us, right?

Then again, as Trey and I learned in the hospital, these alien creatures might not rely on sight at all. Maybe the flying thing is sniffing us out, or listening for movement.

I don't know how long we stay here. Minutes? An hour? None of us dares move, or even speak. Not when the steady mechanical whine starts up again and gradually fades into the distance. Not even when a crow flaps down and perches on the brick wall above our heads, less than an arm's reach away. It studies us, occasionally shaking its tail feathers, walk-hopping along the wall as if waiting impatiently for us to die.

Finally the girl, who is smooshed between the two of us, gives a great shudder. And it's like a dam breaks because she begins to cry softly, her shoulder heaving against mine.

"I'm sorry," I say. "We were going to leave you alone, but we saw that thing following you."

"If you want us to let you be, we will," Trey adds. "We promise."

The girl heaves a few more times, but no sound comes out. Her hands clench into fists. She's trying to stop crying.

"I'm Paige," I tell her, keeping my voice even and casual, as if nothing is amiss. "Paige Miller. This here is Trey Dawson."

Trey says, "Hi."

The girl takes a deep, ragged breath and says, almost defiantly, "I'm Tanq. With a *q*."

Trey and I exchange a look over her head. He gives a slight shrug, as if to say, *If she wants to be called Tanq, we'll call her Tanq.*

"Nice to meet you, Tanq," I say. "We have a dog, too. Her name is Emmaline, but she's back at the house."

The girl says nothing.

"Where were you going, Tanq?" Trey asks. "Is there something you need? We can help you get—"

"Just shut up," Tanq says. "Shut up and let me think."

We shut up.

She works on catching her breath and stilling herself, while Trey and I listen hard to our surroundings. The birds, at least, think the alien flying thing is gone; they're chorusing again, just the normal twitters and chirrups of springtime.

Finally, Tanq says, "I need to get my backpack. I dropped it on the street. Do you think it's safe to look for it?"

Trey nods at me above her head.

"Probably," I say. "The birds are acting normal again. But we'll be cautious." I stand, craning my neck to view the street. It seems empty.

Trey and Tanq gain their feet. The top of her head barely reaches my shoulders. She looks up at me and frowns. "My god," she says.

"Huh?"

"You're freakishly tall. Both of you."

A harsh laugh bursts from my chest before I can stop it.

"What?" she demands. "What's so funny?"

"Nothing's funny," I say. It was a laugh of anger, not mirth. "It's just that we're in the middle of the apocalypse, and I'm still *the tall girl*."

I had a huge growth spurt the summer between fourth and fifth grade. The first day of school that year, I made the mistake of wearing a dark green hoodie. The kids in my class mocked me mercilessly, calling me "The Jolly Green Giant." I started hunching over to hide my height. Until years later when my stepdad sat me down and told me . . . Actually, I don't want to think about Paul right now. "Let's find your backpack," I say gruffly.

I climb out of the stairwell, Trey and Tanq right behind me.

"Eyes to the sky," Trey says in warning.

"You a gamer?" Tanq whispers to Trey as we creep toward the spot where Tanq dropped her pack. The girl clutches her left shoulder as we go.

"I was. Your shoulder okay?" Trey says.

"I'm fine," she snaps.

Her pack lies in the gutter. It's made of camouflage denim with leather detailing. One strap is detached. It trails into the street and ends—or rather, is melted away—where it touches a huge burn scar in the pavement.

Tanq dashes forward before I can warn her. She grabs her pack by the half-melted strap, then yelps, dropping it and jumping back.

She stares at the pavement, cradling her hand. The ground scar is about the diameter of a trash can lid, black as char, and sunken an inch into the pavement. Its edges glimmer with heat. "What was that thing?" she says, and her voice has an edge of panic. "The street . . . it's . . . melted."

"Laser blast," Trey says, stepping forward. He gingerly lifts her backpack, using the strap that didn't get caught in the blast. "Did you see how bright it got? It turned parts of the street into glass. Or obsidian. Like a volcano would."

"I saw," I tell him. "It was like looking at the sun."

Trey hands the backpack to Tanq. "Don't let the hot part of the strap touch you," he warns.

She takes it from him absently, still staring at the mini crater.

I say, "We need to get off the street before the Orkins come back."

"Huh?" says Tanq. "Orkins?"

"Do you want us to leave you alone now?" Trey says. "Or do you want to come with us?"

"We have plenty of food and water," I say. "And Trey can take a look at that burn on your hand."

"And your shoulder," Trey adds. "I may have broken your clavicle when I knocked you to the ground. Sorry about that."

"You hurt me for my own good, is that right?" she says bitterly.

"Huh?" Trey says.

"Nothing. Never mind." She stares off into the distance, taking a few deep breaths. Finally, she says, "I'll come with you. For now."

We're back inside the coach's mansion, sitting on the couches—Trey and I on one, with Tanq across from us—while the fire crackles cheerily. Maybe the fire is a terrible idea. Surely the Orkins can see or smell the smoke coming from the chimney? But it was damn cold out there, and as I lift my mug of hot coffee to my lips and sip, it seems worth the risk.

Trey already checked Tanq's shoulder. She has a little road rash on her skin, but nothing seems broken. Now her feet are tucked up against her rear, and her shoes are off, displaying mismatched socks—one thin and dressy black, the other a thick, red knit. She cuddles her steaming mug close, like it's a stuffed animal, and she stares over the rim at nothing at all.

Emmaline has sniffed our new guest thoroughly, and she now lies curled up on the couch beside the girl, gazing at her adoringly.

I take a sip of coffee, swallow, and say, "I'm pretty sure the flying thing was a vehicle. It made a sound that was . . . I dunno, mechanical?"

"Agreed. I got a better look this time, and it definitely seemed metallic. But different. It was flowing. Liquid. Like quicksilver." Trey leans forward, elbows on his knees, his fingers steepled before him. "What kind of energy must that thing be able to produce? To melt concrete? To obliterate anything organic in the space of a second?"

"Well, they're spacefaring, right?" I say. "That already puts them way beyond our technological capacity."

"Right."

"I just wish . . ." Well, a lot of things.

"You wish?" Trey prompts.

"That my stepdad were here to ask. He was always going on about *Star Wars* and laser blasters and how a saber made of light, by its very nature, would be invisible, and blah, blah, blah, all this stuff about physics that I never really understood. He would have been . . ." I almost choke on the word. "Fascinated. Thrilled to able to observe something so magnificent and strange. Even if it was the end of the world."

Tanq snorts. "Sounds like a douche to me," she says. "And what are you going on about? Orkins? Spacefaring?"

My temper flares, but I tamp it down and instead quickly explain our alien theory, along with the likelihood that we were purposely exterminated.

Trey starts to tell her about the hospital, but Tanq seems to curl in on herself when he describes all the dead bodies, and he stops before he gets to the part about the creepy, floating alien. "And, uh, yeah, we got back here as quick as we could," he finishes with an apologetic look my way.

Tanq is silent for a long time. And then longer still. Emmaline nudges Tanq's elbow, hoping for a scritch. Something pops in the fire.

"So, um, are you hungry?" I say. "Trey makes a mean PB and honey, and we have a lot of stuff to eat before it goes bad. I was thinking of chopping up a fruit salad for us. Just apples and pears and bananas, but still."

Tanq is tiny and tense, eyes darting every which way. I think of bombs about to go off, the way they *tick, tick, tick,* right until the very last moment.

"Why are you being so nice to me?" she says, but it's more like a hiss, like she's a cornered cat. A feline bomb.

The fire pops again, and I sidle closer to it. It's cold in this house, colder still outside, and the fire is the only thing keeping this place livable. That, and the humans inside it.

Tanq is staring up at me, eyes wide with a need she's failing to hide. I'm not sure what that means, but I do know that how I answer her is important. My next words could change everything.

I decide to go with stark honesty. "Because Trey and I are nice people. You're a bitch, sure. You're angry at everything for some reason. But you're . . ." I give Trey a sliver of a grin. "Our best friend. Whether you like it or not. Whether we like it or not."

She doesn't respond, just sits there staring wide-eyed, so Trey adds, "You're not stuck with us. If you want to go your separate way, that's fine. But Paige and I have been talking, see, about finding survivors and maybe building a community back up somehow. So we really hope you consider sticking around."

Tanq lets her hand drift down to Emmaline's thick ruff. Emmy shifts, guiding Tanq's hand to the exact spot behind her ear that she likes rubbed the most. Finally, Tanq speaks. "That thing almost killed me."

"Yes," I say.

"It's still out there."

"Yep."

"Are you going to stay here? In this house?"

Trey says, "We don't know. Once Paige gets her strength back, we'll figure out what to do next."

Her gaze snaps to me. "Get your strength back? Why? What happened? Is that why you look like an anorexic cheerleader?"

This time, as my temper flares white hot in my chest, I don't bother tamping it down. "Look, girl, I don't know what your problem is, and I don't know why you think you have to be insulting and combative, but I know—knew—a lot of cheerleaders and not a single one was anorexic, and maybe you—"

"Paige got sick," Trey interrupts gently. "She wasn't immune to the plague like I was. Like you must have been. She was in a coma for a week before she started to recover."

Something flits across Tanq's face that might be shame. "Oh." Then she adds, "Sorry." But she punches the word out like it's a weapon.

"Whatever," I say, rising from the couch. "I'm going to make myself a sandwich." Emmaline jumps down from the couch to follow me.

We're halfway to kitchen when Tanq calls out, "Wait! Paige."

I turn around.

"I want to stay," she says, peering over the back of the couch toward me. "I'll go wherever you two are going. It's just that I have some business to take care of first."

"What kind of business?" I ask.

"That's none of your . . . business."

Another deep breath. "I'm not trying to be nosy," I tell her. "But maybe we can help."

That fleeting look of shame again. "Oh. Right. I guess it's not safe out there, is it?"

"It's really not," Trey says. "We don't even know if it's safe *here*. We're learning as we go. But in the meantime, Paige and I have agreed never to leave this house alone."

She sighs heavily. "Alone. I thought I was all alone in the world. The last girl left alive. It was amazing. The best thing that ever happened to me."

Trey and I share a puzzled glance over her head.

"And then you two show up, and it's like, I can't even have one nice thing. Not even in the apocalypse. But maybe being alone isn't so great, huh?"

"Yeah," I say. "Not so great."

She rises from the couch and stands strong, hands on her hips. Her voice is fierce when she says, "There's a house in New Albany. I have to get there. With my paints."

New Albany is about twenty minutes away by car, and I'm not sure it's safe to trek over there, but Trey gives me a slight nod, so I say, "Sure. Whatever you need. We'll go tomorrow."

It's full dark. Tanq and I sit side by side on the bed upstairs, Emmaline at our feet. Trey is sleeping in another bedroom across the hall, though I won't be surprised if he joins us at some point. It seems that guy never really sleeps.

Coach Buckell's house has four bedrooms, plus a huge finished basement. Plenty of space for more people, if we can just find them.

"So this is where you first saw me," she says, staring out the window toward the mansion with the tower.

"Trey and I started keeping a watch," I explain. "We were hoping to run across more survivors. We saw the light in your window. Hey, do you have any personal belongings over there? We can go and grab all your stuff and—"

"Everything important is in my backpack."

"Okay. Is that your house? Or were you just camping there?"

"I grew up on the east side," she says. "Well, Whitehall. I bailed as soon as my mom got too sick to come chasing after me. Wanted to see how rich people live, so I holed up in the nicest empty house I could find. What about you? Is this your house?"

"I lived in Clintonville."

"Nice neighborhood."

"Yep."

"But not as nice as this one."

"Nope."

Whoomp.

Tanq shoots up from the bed. "What was that?"

Out the window, the dark horizon glows soft blue for the space of three seconds.

"It's happened a few times now," I say. "Or maybe every night; I sleep through it sometimes. We don't know what it is. Comes from somewhere up north. Wait a moment. It'll happen again."

She settles back onto the bed, hands clasped, shoulders tight in the space beside me, making herself as small as possible. Her wide eyes have a feral glint.

Whoomp.

Tanq recoiled as though struck.

"Weird, huh?" I say, trying to sound only casually concerned.

She nods. "North, you say?"

"Like, directly north. As north as you can get."

"Sandusky, then."

"You think?"

"That's where that radio signal's coming from," she says. "It's the only thing still broadcasting."

So Tanq has heard it too, the looped warning from the CDC declaring martial law.

"You think they're related?" I ask.

She shrugs. "I'm going to get some sleep now. You promised, yeah? Tomorrow we go to New Albany?"

"We promised."

March 25

After a breakfast of coffee and chicken noodle soup, all heated over the fireplace, the three of us climb into Paul's car and head east on the 670 freeway. The SUV has less than a quarter tank of gas. I'm not sure what we'll do when we run out. The easiest thing would be to dump this car and find a new one; cars are everywhere we look, some abandoned, some grimy with decomposition. Enough cars to last us a lifetime.

But maybe I don't have to give up Paul's car. Maybe we can figure out how to gas it up and keep it running.

Tanq sits in the passenger seat while I drive, sorting through her backpack, which is full of tubes of acrylic paint in all different colors. Turns out, when we first saw her leave the mansion, she was on her way to the art supply store for more.

Her seat is pushed all the way forward to make room for

Trey, who sits behind her, his knees practically to his ears. He cranes his neck to watch the sky. Emmaline is in his lap, her nose occasionally darting toward his face for a stealth lick.

"See anything, Trey?" I ask.

"Just bugs and birds," he says.

"You've been quiet this morning," I say, just to take my mind off the fact that we might be taking our lives in our hands driving across town. One of those quicksilver ships could blast us at any moment. It would happen so fast. Maybe I won't have time to dread it, or even feel much pain.

"Been thinking," he says.

"Yeah?" I prompt.

He's silent a long moment. I steer around a semitruck that's angled across three lanes of freeway.

I add, "You don't have to share if you don't want to. Just trying to keep my mind off—"

"What if we're it?" he blurts. "The last people left alive in the whole world?"

"You said no virus has ever had a 100 percent mortality rate," I remind him.

"Yeah, no earthly virus."

"We're not the only ones left," Tanq says with such casual conviction that I nearly brake the car.

"What do you mean?" Trey says.

"That guy in Sandusky," she says. "The one with the radio broadcast."

"It's a prerecorded loop," I tell her. "Not an actual person."

"Until three a.m.," she says, "when he goes live."

"What?" This time I do brake the car, bringing us to a screeching stop in the middle of the freeway. I twist in the seat to face her. "Who?" I ask, while Trey simultaneously says, "What does he say?"

Tanq blinks up at me. "He says he's low on fuel for his generator, and he won't be able to broadcast much longer, but if anyone is out there, he wants them to come to his broadcast location in Sandusky."

"Is that it?" Trey says. "Anything else?"

"We should go!" I say. "As soon as . . ."

Again Tanq shrinks inside herself, as though she's trying to make her body too small a target. Suddenly, it's my brother Ryan in the car beside me, before his growth spurt, with his sandy blond hair and his cowering shoulders, listening to the rumbling warning of the garage door that signaled the Sperm Donor getting home from work.

In a quiet voice, Tanq-not-Ryan says, "Maybe you should listen to the broadcast yourself."

"Does he give an address?" Trey pushes, because he can't see the deepening panic in her eyes. "Does he say anything about other survivors? Does he—"

"We'll listen tonight," I interrupt. "All of us together."

In the rearview mirror, I note how Trey presses his lips tight. I give him a subtle nod.

No one talks as I get the car rolling again. We glide toward the handful of skyscrapers that mark downtown Columbus. The giant rectangle of the Nationwide building looms over us, like a cement brick standing on end. It's the ugliest building downtown by far, but everyone loves it anyway because the windows always light up at night for the holidays, forming a heart on Valentine's Day, a triangle-shaped tree on Christmas.

"The Nationwide building will never light up again," says Trey, like he's in my head.

Then he gasps. The freeway has curved around just enough that we can glimpse the front of the building. Below the massive "Nationwide" marquee is a small crashed plane, a Cessna maybe, like the ones always coming in and out of the OSU airport. Its nose is deep in shattered windows, its cockpit, rudder, and tail protruding precariously into the sky. It looks as though a stiff breeze could send it toppling to the street hundreds of feet below.

"Some people died so fast," Tanq whispers. "So fast that planes fell out of the sky."

"I thought you were glad about that," I say, in a tone more accusing than I intend.

She whips her head toward me, gives me a weird look. "I wanted everyone to fuck off, not fuck off and die. I'm not a *monster.*"

"Okay," I say, even though it doesn't make sense. I don't understand how anyone would choose aloneness. It's like having a constant, aching hole in your heart.

Filling that hole is the only reason Trey and I would agree to help Tanq with her "business." It's not safe to go anywhere, do anything, except lay low until we figure stuff out.

But with my family, my best friend, all my hopes for the future gone like smoke in a breeze—Tanq is *here*, an actual person, and I can help her, even if it might not be the smart thing. This is how we stay human.

"North on 270, right?" I say to Tanq.

"Yeah. I'll give you more directions as we get closer."

Tanq guides us through a neighborhood of million-dollar brick mansions overlooking winter-brown lawns as vast as football fields. We turn into a narrow drive and wind through rows of poplars that are just beginning to bud with green, then around a pond shimmering with a thin layer of ice toward the biggest house I've ever seen in real life. It boasts a columned entry, long casement windows, three full stories, and several brick chimneys. To the left is a bay of garage doors—enough for six cars.

We curve around the circular drive and park at the front door. Tanq is the first to step out, hefting her backpack. Her gaze has grown fierce, and she glares at the massive double door like she's sighting down the barrel of a gun.

"You expect anyone to be home?" I ask as Emmaline trots over to the grass to pee.

"No."

"How do you know?" Trey says. His neck is craned, his eyes constantly scanning the sky.

"The owner of the house is in Europe. Well, he's probably dead, but he was in Europe when the virus hit."

I'm curious how she knows, but something tells me not to push. "How are we going to get in?" I ask instead, and with forced cheer I add, "I stand ready to bust through a window."

Tanq ignores me, reaching toward a small panel beside the door and whisking it aside to reveal a touch pad. The screen lights up, which means it has a backup power source.

She keys in a seven-digit code. The deadbolt clicks, and Tanq pushes the front door open to reveal a marble foyer framed by twin staircases that wind toward a balconied second story. Paintings line the walls of the foyer, each labeled with a gilded plaque—like in a museum. In the very center is an honest-to-god tree in a giant pot, reaching toward a skylight high above.

Trey whistles. "This is the fanciest house I've ever stepped inside."

"Same here," I say, gawking at the skylight. Emmaline's claws make an echoing *tap-tap* as she scurries everywhere, sniffing everything in reach of her muzzle.

"Show yourselves around," Tanq said. "Feel free to snoop. Extra points for vandalism."

"Wait, for real?" Trey says.

She heads unerringly through an arched doorway toward a gleaming white kitchen. "I'll be in the garage," she calls over her shoulder.

"She knows the person who lived here," Trey observes quietly, staring after her.

"She *hates* the person who lived here."

"You know something weird?" Trey says.

"What?"

"I don't think we saw a single dead body while driving through this neighborhood."

He's right. Not even a car accident. "Rich people lead weird lives. They probably got out as soon as the trouble started. They died in fancy places like Europe or the country club or whatever."

"Or maybe there was literally no place fancier than home, and they all died inside, without making a single fuss."

Something in his face makes me ask, "Others made a fuss, though?"

"God, yes. Thousands of people got trampled in a stampede in Hyderabad. A shooter walked into the Mall of America and gunned down a bunch of kids. A Paris AirWays pilot flew his jet full of passengers into the Eiffel Tower. Some billionaire tech guy threw a party on the rooftop deck of a Manhattan hotel; a bunch of people got drunk and jumped . . ." He runs a hand over his hair, and his jaw goes tight.

It finally occurs to me that I had it easy, getting sick. I didn't have to watch the trauma unfold.

"That sounds awful."

"I can't unsee any of it."

"We've got to get to Sandusky." I punch out the words. "We don't have time for Tanq's drama."

"Let's listen to that broadcast first," he says. "Do you think Tanq would come with us?"

"Maybe. If we let her do . . ." I make a vague hand gesture as I echo his words, "Whatever this 'business' is."

"Is that why you shut me up when we were in the car?" He raises an eyebrow at me, as if in challenge.

"Sorry about that. Tanq had this look on her face, like my

little brother used to get when he was scared, and then he would go into these panic-rages. . . ."

"Ah. Figured you had a good reason." He fingers one of the bright green leaves of the tree. It's waxy and thick, though it's showing a bit of wilt, maybe from lack of water. "I think it's an orange tree," he says.

"It's going to die without someone to take care of it."

"And it's too big to take outside." We both stare at it a moment, then he says, "If Tanq doesn't want to come with us, then what?"

"Then we go together. The two of us."

His smile is one of relief.

"But you're right; we should listen to that broadcast tonight," I add. "Just to make sure."

He nods. "In the meantime, let's see if there's anything to eat."

"Maybe I can find something for Emmaline." I should get into the habit of always having dog food on hand for her.

She comes toward me at the sound of her name. Emmy and I follow Trey into a vast kitchen that overlooks a sprawling family room. Everything is decorated in light gray and white, with splashes of turquoise. This house is spotless, the floors and counters gleaming, the cushions on the sofas plumped to perfection. A wall of windows overlooks a covered cedar deck and a built-in barbeque with a sink.

"Check this out," Trey says, peering at the oversized refrigerator. It's covered with photos, haphazardly tacked on by magnets. He indicates one in the middle, canted at a slight diagonal. The photos feel odd, a splash of disorder in an other-wise pristine showroom. "Doesn't that look like Tanq?"

He's pointing to a middle-aged man in a red polo shirt. His arm is wrapped around a woman's shoulders; she's red haired and aggressively curvy and seemingly not that much older than me. Standing waist high are three young children, all boys. Everyone smiles at the camera as though their lives depend on it.

I can see why the photo stopped Trey in his tracks. The man in the polo shirt stares at us with Tanq's wide, anime eyes, and his white, white smile spreads out over Tanq's delicate elfin chin.

"Whoa," I say. "Maybe that's her dad?"

"It would explain why she had the code to get inside."

"But she said she grew up in *Whitehall*."

He opens the fridge, and our noses are walloped by a wave of rot. The entry lock may have had a backup battery, but the rest of the house sure doesn't. Emmaline thinks the scent is delightful. She wags furiously, thrusting her face into the open fridge.

I turn away from the stench, but Trey bumps my shoulder with something. A glass bottle of Coca-Cola, wrapped in a Christmas sleigh graphic.

"Whoever lived here collected holiday-themed Coke," he said. "There's a ton of them in here."

"Is it still good, do you think?"

"One way to find out."

Using his giant hands, he pops off two bottle caps. Brown

stuff threatens to froth over the sides. He hands one to me, and we clink bottles, grinning at each other.

Feeling brave, I take a long swig. "It . . . tastes like cola. Warm cola." Emmaline whines, certain my bottle holds a delicious treat.

Trey follows my lead, then wipes his mouth and says, "I'm a little bit scared of whatever they put in this stuff to preserve it for years and y—"

Glass shatters. A girl screams.

Our cola bottles crash into the sink as Trey and I drop them and sprint toward the sound, Emmaline at our heels— through the family room, down a short hallway, past a laundry room, and through a doorway into the six-car garage.

Tanq stands over the hood of a jet-black Porsche, a tire iron raised toward the ceiling. Paint is everywhere, splattered over the fender, the windows, the garage's epoxy floor, in all conceivable colors—as though Jackson Pollock suddenly discovered that Porsches make the best canvas.

With another scream, Tanq whips the tire iron down and shatters a headlight. She lifts it again, this time aiming for the windshield.

"Emmaline, sit," I command, imagining wet paint all over my dog's paws.

Tanq freezes at the sound of my voice, the tire iron held high. Tears stream down her cheeks, made into foggy gray rivulets by her eyeliner.

"What are you staring at?" she demands.

I look around the garage to avoid her glare. More cars—a

Ferrari, a Lexus, and a couple sleek showpieces I don't have a name for. The Ferrari is also splattered with paint, mostly greens and blues to contrast with the car's candy-apple red. The color choices are vicious. They make the car look cheap.

"I'm looking at art," I tell her in all seriousness.

Her lips part with surprise. Then: "I was going to do the Lexus next, but if you have an idea, help yourself to my paints."

"Okay," I say, stepping toward her backpack, which has been flung onto a workbench. "Extra points for vandalism, right?"

Tanq actually smiles, maybe the first I've seen from her. That man in the photo is definitely her dad.

The Lexus is pearlescent white, and it looks like it's never been driven. Such perfection demands giant black splotches. As I sift through the pack looking for a tube of black paint, Trey says, "I have an idea," and runs back into the house.

Tanq and I exchange a shrug, and then we get to work. She continues screaming and smashing, while I put dollops of black paint on the Lexus's bright fender. Using my forefinger, I smear each one around, creating Rorschach-like inkblots that look like they *should* mean something but actually don't.

"Fuck you, you fucking loser!" Tanq screams as she attacks the Porsche's hub cabs. "Fuck you and your fancy cars and your trophy wife and your slimy hell spawn."

She steps back, wipes a bit of sweat from her forehead with her sleeve, and takes a moment to admire her handiwork. Her breathing comes heavy, but the tears have stopped.

"Hey, that's not bad," she says to me, indicating the Lexus

with her chin. "That one looks like blood splatter." She points to one particular blob.

"I was thinking an eagle in flight."

"Definitely Barack Obama's profile," Trey says suddenly from the doorway. A silk comforter is balled up in his arms. "I found this in the master bedroom. I rubbed dirt from the orange-tree pot all over it."

Tanq peers at the balled-up comforter, thinking, thinking, thinking. . . . "Let's attach it to the rear bumper of the Lexus," she says. "It will look like the train of a nasty wedding gown."

I'm not sure it will look like that at all, but the blob definitely did not look like Obama, so who even cares? Trey and I rush to comply.

Tying a comforter to a bumper proves difficult work, but we manage it. When we're finished, Tanq hands me the tire iron. "The honors?" she says. Her eyes are measured, like this is some kind of test.

I take the tire iron from her and eye the Lexus's left headlight. I suppose some kind of screaming is in order, but I'm not sure what she wants me to say. So I take a guess.

I holler, "Just one!" *Crash.* "Of these cars!" *Crash.* "Could have paid!" *Crash.* "For Tanq's college!" *Crash.*

I've obliterated both headlights and the right side-view mirror and put a huge spiderwebbing dent in the windshield. I stand back, breathing hard, my shoulders throbbing with the impact. Vandalism, it turns out, is really hard work.

I look up and discover that Trey is trying not to laugh. Emmaline is so trusting of all of us now that she has taken it all in stride and is busy licking one of her paws. But Tanq stares at me with wide-eyed wonder. "It's perfect," she whispers. "The Lexus is perfect."

"You want to do that Caddy next?" Trey asks, pointing to a giant black brick of a car, one I didn't have a name for.

She blinks for a moment, seemingly a little stunned. "You know, I think . . . it's fine. I think I'm done now. No, wait. Just one more thing."

Tanq reaches for her pack and retrieves a can of pink glitter spray paint. She shakes the can as she heads toward the Cadillac's fender. A grin splits her face as she carefully paints a large oval with a diagonal line through it. The null sign, in sparkling pink.

"You a Null fan?" Trey asks.

"I admire his work," Tanq says, gazing at the Caddy with pure smugness. "I wish I owned a phone. I'd take so many pictures of this shit."

After cleaning off as much paint from our hands and clothes as possible, the three of us are gathered with Emmaline around the kitchen island.

"So what now?" I say. "Do we go back to Coach Buckell's house?"

"Not gonna lie," Trey says. "It makes me nervous to drive anywhere. Every time we do it, we're taking a huge risk."

"All our food is back at Coach's house," I remind him.

"There's plenty here," Tanq says. "I see you've already found the Coke. Oh my god, Francie would die if she knew you drank some." Then she choke-laughs. "I mean, I guess she died anyway, yeah?"

"Is Francie your stepmom?" I ask, with a glance toward the redhead grinning at us from the refrigerator.

"I guess? Sort of? It's hard to be a stepmom when you deny any relation."

At Trey's and my confused looks, Tanq adds, "That's my bio dad." She points to the guy in the polo shirt. "It was a drunken one-night thing with my mom. They never expected to see each other again. A few years later mom ran into him at the post office, told him he had a kid. It was nice at first. We hung out. I came over here a lot. He took me up to Buckeye Lake a few times. Taught me how to fish, how to jet ski. Then he got married."

Trey reaches into the fridge, retrieves collector Cokes for all of us. While we sip, Tanq continues, like vandalizing those cars has caused a dam to break, and suddenly she can't stop talking. "Francie didn't want anything to do with me or my mom. I think it was because my mom, uh, didn't have the best reputation? I dunno, there's a bunch of details my mom never told me. Anyway, we never asked for child support or anything, but after Francie moved in, that woman convinced my dad I wasn't really his. I mean, we'd never done a paternity test or anything. So he . . . cut me off. Just like that. I tried to see him a couple of times, called him. He ignored me. When my mom went back to meth and started hitting me, he refused to help. Said I wasn't his problem, that he had a real family now."

Her face is stoic and perfect as she talks, like that of a porcelain doll, but there's something a little looser about her too. She's not curled in on herself; her arms drop naturally from her shoulders.

"You look just like him," Trey points out. "I mean, *just* like him."

"I know, right?" she says. "There was never any doubt. Francie just wanted me out of her life, and my dad didn't have the balls to stand up to her. To be fair, I may have gone too far. I came over after school one day and . . ." She changes her mind about what she was going to say. "Anyway, Francie took out a restraining order on me."

"Dang, girl," I say, flashing back to the way she screamed while attacking her dad's car with a tire iron. "Couldn't your mom sue for a paternity test?" I asked.

Tanq snort-laughs. "Spoken like a rich bitch. With what money? My mom wasn't even sober enough to walk into a law office most of the time. We lived in a cramped apartment with another family; I shared a room with three other kids. What the hell were we supposed to do?"

That *had* been a pretty insensitive thing to say. *Check your privilege, girl,* Shawntelle used to tell me. "I'm sorry. And I'm sorry you had to go through that," I say.

She shrugs. "The boys had it worse than me, the kids I shared a bedroom with, I mean. They were Black. Cops were always giving them shit. They couldn't walk into a grocery store without people looking at them funny. By the time the virus hit, their dad was in prison. Ten-year sentence for selling a little MJ. The boys were awful, and we fought all the time, but then, yanno, they died." Tanq says it flippantly, but she's staring out the window to avoid our gazes, and her left hand is clenching into a tight fist.

She gasps, and Terrified Tanq is suddenly back—the wide eyes, the rounded shoulders. "What's that?" she says.

Trey leaps toward the window. I spot it the moment he does: a silver glint, followed by a high-pitched mechanical whine.

"Get back!" Trey whispers. "Behind the island. Crouch down."

We all bump knees to comply. "Emmaline, come," I say, and it's such a relief when she trots over. "Sit."

"Not a sound," Trey whispers. He's heavy in the space on my left; though he's crouched low, the top of his head almost reaches the height of the kitchen island. Tanq is coiled into a ball on Emmaline's right, eyes squeezed shut. After a moment, she reaches out blindly and wraps her arm around my dog.

We wait a long time. I expect to hear the window shattering, to feel the heat of the aircraft's weapon. Even if it happens fast, there will be at least a split second of agony, a moment when I have utter assuredness of my own death.

But nothing happens. Trey and I look at each other, the same question in our eyes. His face is very close. A tiny bit of stubble darkens his chin. "I'm going to check," he says in a whisper so soft I strain to hear.

I nod, and my heart is in my throat as Trey slowly pushes his head up to peek over the top of the island.

"I don't see anything," he whispers. "Wait here." Maintaining his crouched position, Trey creeps around the island toward the wall of windows, then hunkers down in front of a sofa. I peer around the edge of the island to keep an eye on him. I'm half tempted to look away, though. I couldn't stand to watch something bad happen to Trey.

The sun must be high now, and natural light pours into the house in spite of the clouds. I used to spend hours on our sunporch, doing homework or texting with Shawntelle. In summer I would take a towel out to the backyard and lie down on the grass, soaking up as much light as possible. Mom always called me a sun worshipper. Paul used to say I was solar powered.

But now all this light makes me feel vulnerable, exposed. It crawls across my skin like a sickness, its spreading warmth a warning instead of a comfort.

"I think it's gone," Trey says at last. He crawls along the length of the sofa, which brings him to the edge of the window. He reaches up for the curtain pull and yanks. Miles of velvet curtain come out from the wall like magic, smooth and easy, hanging from some kind of rail system. Trey keeps pulling until they cover the entire wall, leaving us in gloom. Blackout curtains, useful for watching that giant TV.

I stand up from my hiding place. "You think that'll keep us safe?" I ask.

Trey shrugs. "I don't have a better idea."

I don't either. We've only seen those silver flying things outside, so it stands to reason we're safer under cover.

"I don't want to drive back to the other house," Tanq says in a tremulous voice. "Not with that thing flying around."

I think of all the food we left behind. Trey and I risked our lives to break into that grocery store for nothing.

Well, not nothing. We had the foresight to stash some bottled water and snacks in the car. And the Monstrosity, I remind myself. Along with Hazel Jenkins's ridiculous purse. We haven't lost everything. Not yet.

"I agree with Tanq," I say with obvious regret.

"There are eight bedrooms," she says. "Plenty of room."

"Do you know where your dad's car keys are?" Trey asks her.

"No. Why?"

"We need a radio to listen to that Sandusky stream tonight."

"Paul's SUV has a rad—" I begin.

"It's parked outside," Trey says. "I'd rather put off going outside as long as possible."

"What Trey said!" says Tanq.

I take a deep breath, knowing that by tomorrow, they're probably going to want to drive out of here in a fancy sports car, leaving the SUV behind. Guess I'll fight that battle when it comes. "Okay, let's look for those keys."

March 26

It's almost three in the morning. After a late-night snack of peanut-butter sandwiches—Tanq smashed up Oreo cookies on hers—we've crammed ourselves inside the Ferrari, which is a two-seater. Trey is precariously perched halfway into the driver's seat, his left leg and shoulder hanging out the door. I'm smooshed into the middle, one knee bent up to my nose to avoid the gear shift. Emmaline is on Tanq's lap in the passenger seat. Tanq holds a bottle of bourbon, and she's a little tipsy. She found it in her dad's office and helped herself.

I used to drink. Not often, but too much at parties. Shawntelle and I made a pact to quit drinking after we lost a home game to a crappy team. We were only mildly hungover from the party the night before. But we also weren't at our best.

I'll do anything to be the best. Shawntelle got that about me.

Tanq takes another swig, elbowing my ribs in the process. We'd be a lot more comfortable in the Cadillac, but none of us have ever been inside a Ferrari before.

My fears about ditching Paul's SUV for something sportier proved unfounded. The Cadillac gets terrible gas mileage, according to Trey. The other car I didn't have a name for turns out to be a Bentley, but it's blocked by some boxes and a motorcycle with a flat tire. The rest have messed up windshields thanks to Tanq's tire iron and paint, so they're going nowhere.

Trey has the Ferrari's key fob in one hand. With the other, he presses the "start" button halfway down to engage the radio. I expected something fancy: a touch screen, maybe. But the Ferrari sound system is hardly different from the one in Paul's car. I reach forward and turn the dial to AM 1610.

Static at first. Then: ". . . your own safety, do not leave your homes under any circumstances. Anyone violating this order will be shot on sight. . . ."

"That's just the repeater message," I say. It cuts in and out, barely discernable. The radio signal isn't as strong here in New Albany as it was in Columbus.

"Give it a minute," Tanq says.

We wait. The message repeats three times, the broadcast becoming stronger and clearer. Emmaline gets restless, lapping at Tanq's face, then shaking her head like she was stung; probably got a little taste of bourbon. My shoulder is crammed too tight against Trey's, but I don't hate it.

The message cuts off abruptly. More static. Finally comes a man's voice, lower than that of the recording. Cracked and old. Not a radio announcer at all.

"This is Manny Gomez on AM 1610, Sandusky's only pirate radio station. I am live. I repeat, this is a live human voice. You are not alone."

"Holy shit," Trey whispers.

"Told you," said Tanq.

"Our signal boosters have the potential to reach most of Ohio, parts of Indiana, Michigan, and Ontario. Within that targeted geographic area, we anticipate there were fourteen survivors of the virus. Of those, we hope that six to eight survived the ensuing chaos. If you are one of those survivors, please meet us here in Sandusky. Drive or walk or ride carefully. Stick to cover when possible. Do not travel after dark, as this will put you at a disadvantage."

"Holy shit," Trey repeats. "Six to eight survivors. In that whole area."

"And we're three of them," I point out.

Tanq shushes us as Manny Gomez continues. "Our generator is low on fuel. To save power and for added safety, starting tomorrow, we will no longer broadcast the loop message. But tune in every night at three a.m. for updates. We'll be on air as long as we can."

"He keeps saying 'we' and 'us,'" Trey says.

"We can't give you an exact address," Gomez goes on. "The wrong entities could be listening. But if you head toward the president's park, you'll find something to guide you. Or I guess you could just follow the rail."

The channel goes messy with static.

"Wait, is that all?" Trey asks.

"Park . . . ," I muse. "Did he mean Cedar Point, the amusement park?" Ryan and I spent a whole day there once, getting sick on apple fritters and trying in vain to win stuffed animals. No roller coasters, though. Ryan was terrified of them.

"He said 'the president's park,'" Trey says. "Not sure what that means. I've never been to Sandusky."

"Me neither," says Tanq. "I didn't know it had a railroad."

"All small Ohio towns have railroads," I say. "Railroads and meth."

"That's bigoted, don't you think?" Tanq says. "Hashtag not all small towns—"

The broadcast clarifies again, cutting her off: "—no mistake, it will be a perilous journey. But if you can make it here, you'll find temporary safety and answers to a lot of your questions."

Through the ensuing static comes the susurrus of someone whispering near the mic.

"Okay, okay, I'll tell them," Gomez says in a muffled voice. "Wyatt here wants me to remind you that firearms are too noisy and should be considered a last resort against the Farmers. Keep quiet, stay under cover, move slow and steady, and don't panic. Wyatt made it here safely, and so can you."

"The Farmers?" Trey echoes.

"Wyatt?" I say.

"The Farmers will figure out we're broadcasting from this location soon enough, but we'll wait here as long as we can. Manny Gomez signing off. God bless, stay healthy, see you in Sandusky."

The radio goes silent—no looped message, no static, just dead air.

Tanq raises the bottle to her mouth and swigs. Then she says again, "Told you so."

"Why didn't you head to Sandusky?" I ask as Trey peels himself out of the driver's seat, stands, stretches. I follow after, arching my back to avoid the gear shift.

"Oh, hell, no," Tanq says from the other side of the car. "I didn't want to see *people*. You wouldn't either," she adds, gesturing with the bottle, "if you'd never had a moment of privacy in your life and everyone you ever met either hit you or wanted something from you or rejected—" Her words are cut off by a tiny burp. "Think I've had enough," she says, and with all her might, she throws the bottle at the hood of the Lexus. The bottle bounces off, leaving a small dent, then shatters on the ground. The air suddenly reeks of booze. Quality booze, I'm sure, but a faint headache stings at the base of my skull as the alcohol smell mixes with the scent of still-fresh paint.

"Let's go inside," I say.

Tanq's stepmom loved candles. On the coffee table is what looks like a hunk of driftwood, with four holes carved into it for tea lights. We light them all, bathing the family room in soft orange. The air begins to smell of vanilla.

Tanq and I sit on the sofa. Trey plunks down across from us in an easy chair. Emmaline is conked out at our feet, curled so tight she looks like a cinnamon bun. It's almost three thirty in the morning. The fatigue from earlier is back in full force, weighing down my limbs like my bones are made of lead, and my eyes feel swollen and gummy.

But none of us feel ready for bed.

"So, let's review what we've learned," Trey says in a take-charge tone that reminds me so much of Coach Dalrymple that a knot of tightness stings my chest.

"Manny Gomez," I say. "Wyatt. Two survivors besides us."

"I bet Wyatt is a douche," Tanq says. "I mean, that name. *Wyatt.*"

"Isn't that bigoted?" I say. "Hashtag not all Wyatts . . ."

"I want to go to Sandusky," Trey says. "Tomorrow."

"Me too, Trey," I tell him. "As long as I eventually get some sleep." *Driving sleepy is as bad as driving drunk.*

"Of course. Your health is our top priority."

"Gomez said to look for the president's park."

"And that we might find something to guide our way," he says.

"Something about following the rail?"

"I'm sure we'll figure it all out, if we can just get there."

Tanq has been looking back and forth between us as we talk, and she blurts, "God, you two sound like mini adults, all business and logic and . . . well, not *mini.* You're both enormous."

I still can't tell if Tanq's being deliberately provocative or if she's just socially clumsy. I decide to give her the benefit of honesty.

"I haven't been a kid since I was ten years old," I tell her.

"What do you mean?"

"After the Sperm Donor ditched us, my mom worked two jobs, and I basically raised my kid brother and took care of all the household stuff. Chores, homework, getting him to and from school every day, cooking, errands, making all these decisions that . . . actually, it's not a very interesting story. And it all turned out fine. Until the virus."

I feel Trey's gaze on my face. He has a slight smile, and for some reason, I'd give anything to know what he's thinking.

"Sounds like me and Teena," he says softly. "Taking care of ourselves."

"It's adorable," Tanq tells him, "how much you and Paige have in common."

She says it mockingly, but I don't feel like answering that volley. Refusing to look at Trey, I say, "Are you coming with us, Tanq? To Sandusky?"

She shrugs. "I could live here by myself a really long time. Even with those things out there." Tanq looks up at the ceiling, which is painted a darker gray than the walls to make it appear depthless. "I always imagined living here," she adds in a distant voice.

"That guy on the radio said to keep quiet and under cover," Trey says. "So if you live here, you'll have to stay inside except for supply runs and not make any noise."

Tanq raises her chin. "I can do that."

"You can do that just as easily with us," he points out.

"Are you serious?" she says. "Driving to Sandusky is *not* staying under cover. It's open farmland from here to Lake Erie."

"I was going to suggest we take back roads," he says. "Hit some of the small towns along the way. Back country roads don't have as much vegetation clearance. It will add an hour to our trip, but it might be safer."

"I'm not sure Paul's car has enough gas for the scenic route," I say.

Tanq says, "I can siphon gas out of the Lexus for you."

"You know how to do that?" I say.

"Growing up poor gives you an interesting skill set," she says.

"Does that mean you're coming with us?" Trey asks.

"No. I don't know what I'm going to do."

"You said if we helped you do your 'business,' you'd come with us."

"Jesus, Trey, why do you want me to come with you so bad?" She gives him a vicious smile. "Admit it, you think I'm hot."

Trey launches from the easy chair, and Tanq and I both wince, but he just stretches. "I'm going to find a bedroom and get some sleep." His voice is tight and angry. "And I'm going to Sandusky tomorrow. Both of you are invited to join me."

He leaves without a backward glance. A moment later, his heavy footsteps plod up one of the staircases.

"So, tell me," Tanq says when he's out of earshot. "What's going on between you two?"

"Nothing."

She raises a delicate eyebrow. "Don't bullshit me."

"We met just a few days before we found you."

"But he's hot, right?"

I study her carefully. Tanq regards me with open curiosity, not challenge. A slight smile quirks the corner of her mouth.

"Scorching," I concede. "But truly, the apocalypse has been all I can handle. I woke up from a coma and realized the world had died. I haven't really been thinking about . . . romance stuff. Besides, Shawntelle—that was my best friend—would have warned me off of him; she was suspicious of jock types. Well, she had other reasons too. Like, she used to say that white women fetishize . . ." On second thought, I don't care to let Tanq in on all the late-night talks with Shawntelle about race and racism, privilege and activism, allies and friendship. They were hard talks, and precious. Just between Shawntelle and me. So I say, "Why? You into him?"

She rolls her eyes. "Of course not. Not my type."

"You prefer women?"

"I prefer no one. Tried sex a couple times. It was boring and messy."

"Then you definitely shouldn't do that again."

Tanq narrows her eyes at me. "Usually, when I tell people I'm ace, they say I just haven't met the right person."

This is another kind of test. *There's no such thing as "normal" sexuality*, Mom used to say. "My mom would tell you there's no rule that says you have to want sex."

I half expect her to respond with something disparaging about my mom. Instead, she says, "I read this science fiction book last year about a group of people who return to Earth after a disaster in order to repopulate it. I keep thinking about it. Like, what if everyone thinks it's my *duty* to . . ."

So that's it. "Tanq, if you come with us to Sandusky, and we meet people who want to have sex with you and won't take no for an answer, I'll punch them in the face. Trey would too, I bet. 'No means no,' he says."

"Really? He says that?"

"He said it when I insisted on chasing after you even when you told us to get lost."

"Huh." She hunkers down into the sofa, arms around a pillow.

"I'm going to follow Trey's example and get some sleep," I say, getting to my feet. "I really hope you join us tomorrow, but neither of us will force you."

She doesn't meet my gaze as she whispers, "I'll think about it."

The double doors to the master bedroom are thrown wide, the room lit from the soft blue digits of a battery powered alarm clock. The king-sized bed is without a comforter, but the heavy blankets should suffice. My eyes are hot and dry with exhaustion, and I'm winded from going up the stairs—a reminder that I'm still not well. My shoulder seems okay, but my heel is aching again; my body needs sleep as badly as it needs oxygen if I'm going to heal up for good.

I fall onto the bed and sink into the plush mattress. I'm drifting away when a small bulk on the nightstand catches my eye. Curious, I reach for it.

A wallet. I flip it open, revealing a library card and a driver's license. Tanq's dad grins up at me.

Kenneth Anderson, it says. It's too dark to read his height and weight and other details. He must have taken his passport to Europe. Apparently, he didn't plan to do any driving. I guess a guy like him can afford to have people drive for him.

I slip out the driver's license. "Thanks for the peanut-butter sandwiches, Mr. Anderson," I whisper. "And the house. And the gas. You might have been a terrible person, but I'll still take the help."

I shove the license into my pocket and lower my head to the pillow. I'm vaguely aware of Emmaline's weight as she jumps onto the bed and curls up at my back.

I wake shivering. The alarm clock reads one p.m. Even with the plantation shutters closed, I can tell it's going to be a gray day with thick, low clouds.

The scent of unwashed skin pricks at my nose, and I realize it's me. After splashing water on my face in the marble-and-quartz master bathroom and finger brushing my teeth with some toothpaste, I raid the giant walk-in closet for a fresh set of clothes, especially fresh underwear.

A week or so ago, I would have never considered wearing another person's underwear, even if it had just come out of the wash. But then I also would never have considered going more than a day without a shower or eating peanut butter sand-wiches for almost every meal.

Francie had a *lot* of underwear, and most of it is lacy and vibrant and not meant to be worn for very long. I finally find bikini briefs in shiny, stretchy black. After putting them on, I stare at myself in the full-length mirror.

My knees seem too knobby in my emaciated legs, but my cheeks are a little fuller, my hair not quite so limp. I've already gained weight since waking up, though I'm sure it's mostly water weight. I don't look like *me* yet, but I'm getting there.

A lace thong in satiny blue catches my eye. For a brief moment I imagine grabbing it and smuggling it out in a pocket. I feel a little foolish as I turn my back on it and search for more clothes.

I hit pay dirt near the back of the closet. It's dim in here, with just the open door for light, but it's obvious Francie was an exercise fashion junkie. I find multiple yoga pants, sports bras, sweatshirts, even some jogging scarves. Tanq's stepmom was shorter than me, but also fuller of figure. I pick out a set in scarlet and gray—Ohio State colors in honor of Trey—and nothing fits perfectly, but it's all good enough, and this particular set has pockets deep enough for my gun. I've been storing the gun in the floral handbag, mostly. But it's good to know I can keep it handy if I need to.

I find a stash of pads and tampons beneath one of the sinks. My period is winding down, but I'm glad to refresh my supply; I left all my essentials back at Coach Buckell's house.

I shove Kenneth Anderson's driver's license into the pocket

of my new sweatshirt, then I throw away all my old clothes—my dark hoodie, my underwear, bra, and jeans. It's not like I can toss them in the washing machine. But I can't help staring at the jeans for a moment, all wadded up in the trash can. Another piece of my life before the coma is gone.

A drawer full of hair accessories provides a hair band, which I use to throw up a quick ponytail. The clatter of claws greets me as I leave the bedroom. Emmaline is ecstatic to see me awake, running circles around my ankles, making it difficult to navigate the stairs.

In the kitchen, Tanq sits on a barstool at the island, noisily munching, her arm deep in a bag of corn chips labeled "nacho cheese-jalapeño." Trey stands at the counter, cutting a sandwich in half.

They both brighten when they see me. "I'm coming with you," Tanq blurts around a mouthful of chips.

"That's great, Tanq."

"I fed Emmaline," Trey says.

"Thank you."

"And we put gas in the car," Tanq says. "Are those Francie's clothes?"

"Mine were gross. And I didn't think she'd mind."

"I threw some food from the pantry into the back of the SUV," Trey says. "And more bottled water. Enough for three or four days." His grin turns sloppy. "Hey, those are Ohio State colors."

"Go Buckeyes," I acknowledge half-heartedly. "It should only take a few hours to get to Sandusky. Even using the scenic route."

"Yeah, sure," Trey says, but I hear doubt in his voice. "All those supplies are probably overkill."

"Better too much than too little," I say. "I'm ready to go whenever you both are."

"Eat something first!" Trey orders. "I made you a tuna sandwich. Is that okay? Do you like tuna?"

"Did you put anything else in it?" The area north of Columbus is a reality-warping black hole where an innocent girl can ask for mayonnaise and get Miracle Whip instead. I learned a long time ago it's best to have your tuna plain.

"No, nothing else."

"Then yes, I love tuna."

They watch me eat, especially Trey, as though he's worried I might sneak it to Emmaline—who stares up at me with the purest, rawest hope that I'll do just that. I chew fast, trying to decide if Trey's commitment to my health and well-being is touching or irritating.

Touching, I decide. He's an older sibling, just like me. He probably can't help himself.

We sling our meager things over our shoulders—my floral purse, Tanq's backpack, Trey's rifle—and head for the RAV4. It's parked sideways in the driveway now, as close to the door as possible. So Tanq could siphon gas into it, I realize.

It's bitterly cold, and a line of crows stares at us from the peak of the garage roof. I was right; the day is gray and cloudy—how long has it been since I've seen the sun? Like me, Trey and Tanq constantly crane their necks, keeping an eye out for flying craft as we strap into the car. Trey sits in the passenger seat this time. Emmaline hops into the back with Tanq.

"We'll never see them coming," I say, "with the clouds this low."

"Maybe they won't see us either?" Tanq says.

"If they even *see*," Trey says. "The one at the medical center didn't seem to have eyes."

"Wait," Tanq says. "Waitwaitwait. You saw one?"

Worried she'll change her mind about coming along, I quickly put the car in gear and aim it toward the road. Trey recounts our experience at the medical center—the impossibly tall, eyeless creature that seemed to float down the hallway, its odd attempt at speaking, the projectile fingernails that launched from its hand and embedded themselves in our skin.

"Oh my god," Tanq says, over and over.

I have no desire to relive it all, so I mostly ignore their conversation, focusing on the road, searching the wide gray sky ahead and the fields around us for a telltale silver glint. A couple of warmer days have transformed the world, and green is poking out everywhere: grass spreading along the roadside, trees budding with new leaves, crocuses blooming lavender in winter-brown lawns. Even daffodils and tulips are sending their first shoots out of the mud. Within a few weeks, this roadside will be a riot of color.

Ohio is cold, cold, cold, Mom used to say. *And when you can hardly stand it, it's cold some more. Then suddenly, one day you blink and it's spring.*

North of New Albany is a whole lot of nothing, just dead

winter wheat fields as far as the eye can see, which would have gotten rotated out with corn or soy in the summer. Too bad the virus didn't hit later in the year. Cornfields would have provided plenty of cover.

We agreed to avoid major thoroughfares like Interstate 71 or U.S. Route 23. Instead, we'll weave our way to State Route 61 and head toward Mount Gilead for the first part of our journey. There might be safer ways, small-town roads and access lanes that could get us there just as well. But in spite of years spent traveling the state for basketball, I'm just not familiar enough with the back roads of Ohio to keep us from getting lost. A small state route seemed like the right compromise.

Still, I'm ready to steer us off the road and into cover at a moment's notice. My hands are already sweaty on the wheel, my neck tense from staring, staring, staring at the sky. It's going to be a long trip.

We pass a newly paved road with a huge sign advertising a home development. STARTING IN THE LOW 300KS! it says. In the distance, a bunch of limp balloons hang from a marquee sign, marking model homes. Most of the balloons are completely deflated, flapping back and forth in the wind, but a single red one remains stubbornly full. I have no idea how.

A few miles later, I'm forced to hit the brakes. A coyote saunters out from a stand of trees and into the road. It's the biggest coyote I've ever seen, still plush with its winter coat. A moment later, two tiny, fuzzy gray pups come stumbling after.

Emmaline growls.

The mother gives us this yellow-eyed look, like she's saying

What the hell are you doing on my road? Then she casually leads her young into a gully and disappears.

"Holy shit, was that a wolf?" Tanq says.

"Coyote," says Trey. "A big one."

"Not my first weird wildlife sighting since I woke up," I say, getting the car rolling again. "Animals own the world, now that humanity has died."

"The Orkins—or Farmers?" Trey says. "They didn't go after animals. Just people."

"Seems like," says Tanq.

"I bet a lot of animals died by default," I say. "House pets like Emmaline, stuck inside their homes with no one to take care of them. So many dogs and cats. Even birds and hamsters and—"

"Okay, Paige, we get the point," Tanq says. "Dammit, now I'm depressed."

"What's that smell?" Trey says, just as I catch a whiff of stench. It's both rotten and sweet, like manure in syrup.

In the rearview mirror, I watch Tanq pull her jacket over her nose. "My god," she says, her voice muffled. "That's awful."

"Don't forget to help me watch the sky," I warn them both.

We roll along a few more miles, the stench getting worse and worse. My eyes are starting to water; the back of my throat stings like we're traveling through noxious gas.

"We may need to find . . . ," Trey chokes out. "Another route—"

"There!" Tanq points out the window toward something on the left.

A steel fence hems in sprawling acres of black, churned-up mud. In the distance, low, metal-roofed buildings stretch long and narrow. Then I see it. A dead Holstein cow, on its back just inside the fence, belly bloated to an impossible girth, swarming with flies. Her four legs stick straight out, stiff as posts.

Trey says, "That smell couldn't come from just one cow."

"It doesn't," Tanq says in a squeaking voice.

A massive blanket of flies lifts into the air, darkening the sky, and suddenly the churned-up mud clarifies into corpses. Hundreds—no, thousands—of decaying cows. Dead from starvation or thirst or cold or even trampling? There's no way to tell. All I know is that are *so many*.

Trey stares out the window, a look of sick fascination on his face, but I can't stand to see any more. I stare straight ahead, but tears blur my vision. "Eyes to the sky," I say, because I need a little help right now.

"It's probably like this all over the country," Tanq says, ignoring me. "All over the world."

"Dairy farms like this one, chicken farms, meat-packing plants," Trey says.

"Every single one a sea of rotting corpses," I say.

"Maybe not," Trey says, and I'm relieved because he finally tears his gaze away from the dairy farm and starts watching the sky again.

"What do you mean?"

"If you were a farmer with a chicken coop, and you knew for a fact that you and your family were all going to die and no one would come to take care of your farm, what would you do?"

"I'd let out all the chickens," Tanq said. "I mean, the coyotes would probably get them, but at least they'd have a chance."

"Exactly," Trey says. "I bet more than a handful of ranchers let their cows and horses loose. I bet some pet owners even left windows open for their pets."

The thought fills me with light and hope, because I know for a fact some people used their last moments to do something caring. Something good. Like my mom, who daisy-chained multiple IV bags together before she died, just to give me a fighting chance.

"If we're all alive in a couple of years," Trey continues, "don't be surprised if the earth is covered in flocks of wild chickens and sheep."

I think of the huge dog that took a bite out of my foot. "Apex predators will make a comeback if that happens," I point out. "Wolves, the big cats."

"I've personally always thought the world would be better off without humans," Tanq says. "Maybe it's time to give another species a turn at the top."

"Like the Farmers?" Trey asks.

Tanq frowns. "No, not them."

The smell begins to fade, and a few miles later I'm able to blink the tears from my eyes for good. We pass a sign that indicates we've entered Harlem Township, which turns out to be a meager collection of small homes, a grocery market, and a pizza joint. Out of habit, I slow down, even though no one's around to enforce a speed limit. Several cars are parked in front of the pizza place, as though the good folk of Harlem chose to gather there to die.

Then it's more fallow fields as far as the eye can see, with no cover anywhere. We are totally exposed.

"I'm going east," I say, turning abruptly.

Trey says, "But we agreed—"

"We'll eventually hit the Hoover Reservoir. Lots of trees and houses there. I can follow it north and get back on track."

"Are you sure—"

"I won't be so cavalier with directions once we hit Mount Gilead, I promise," I tell him. "But I *know* central Ohio. I've driven all over the place for club basketball during the summer, high school basketball during the spring."

"Okay, Paige. I trust you."

"Trees are good," Tanq says.

Even so, Trey and Tanq seem as tense as I feel, and the air in the car grows tight and claustrophobic. I'm tempted to roll down a window, but we could hit another dairy farm at any moment.

About ten minutes later, the sprawling homes outside of Westerville come into view. I was right; there are way more trees here. So many trees that when we turn north onto the road that hugs the edge of the reservoir, we often can't see our way clear to the water. My shoulders start to relax a little. Tanq drifts off to sleep, and I let her, knowing she went to bed just as late as I did, but got up so much earlier.

The trees thin as we pass the reservoir and roll through the village of Galena. Not far now to Sunbury, a town just big enough that I'd rather avoid it.

Trey gasps. At exactly the same moment I see it: a glint out of the corner of my right eye. Maybe it's nothing. Maybe we're about to die.

"Get off the road," Trey whispers.

"I'm trying!" The cemetery on our left would provide no cover. I crank right onto a small road that leads toward scant trees and hit the gas. Or maybe I shouldn't go fast. Manny Gomez said to travel slow and quiet. Maybe driving fast will just attract that thing's attention.

"There!" Trey says, pointing toward a copse of trees. One is a tall fir, still green. I bump off the pavement and roll through dirt and mud to reach it.

Tanq startles awake. "What? What's going on?"

"We're taking cover," Trey says.

"Shit."

I angle the car as best I can to take advantage of the tree's shelter. Evergreen trees don't have much of a canopy. Wood screeches against metal as I bury the RAV4's fender in the branches. A few bare trees around us provide a little cover too, so it isn't exactly like an ostrich burying its head in the sand, but it feels like it.

I turn off the car and unhook my seat belt.

"You sure you saw something?" Tanq says, peering out the window.

"No," Trey says.

"We should slip out of the car," I suggest. "Get under that tree."

"Or maybe that would be worse," says Tanq.

Emmaline's nose is pressed against the window, and her tail is a whip of excitement at the prospect of stepping outside.

"I'm getting out," I say, fingers to the door handle.

"Paige!" Trey says. "Tanq's right. It might be worse out there."

"I have to see," I tell him. "I have to know if it's nearby. We won't be able to tell from inside the car. Here." I toss him the keys. "If something happens to me, you and Tanq should make a run for Sandusky."

"Jesus," he says as I open the door.

I don't open it much, just wide enough to slip out. Before I can close it back up, Emmaline dashes out after me.

"Emmaline, heel," I whisper, and she obeys instantly, attaching herself to my lower leg. I send a quick prayer up to Mrs. Carby, thanking her for spending so much time in obedience classes.

I creep around the fender of the RAV4 and push through pine needles toward the trunk. Sharp pine scent tickles my nose, and spiderwebs are sticky against my face, but I resist the urge to brush at them, to make any unnecessary movements. The tree branches are thick, leaving little maneuverability and no more than a spotty view of our surroundings, but I *can* see.

Emmaline flips over and starts scent rolling on the ground, and instead of worrying about what she's found, I'm glad she's occupied. While my dog rubs pine sap and needles and who knows what else into her thick fur, I peer through the branches, looking for that terrifying silver glint.

There. Above and slightly behind a tall water tower. Still

too distant to make out an exact shape and size, but its path is more hovering than linear, occasionally darting quickly to the side. Not like any Earth aircraft I've seen.

Slowly, carefully, I push aside a branch so I can see into the RAV4. Trey and Tanq watch wide-eyed from within its dimness. I put a finger to my lips, indicating silence, then I point toward the aircraft.

They crane their necks to follow my gaze. I can't tell if they spot the craft or not, and I guess it doesn't matter. I just needed to warn them.

Keeping an eye on the metallic dragonfly, I hunker down against the trunk. Emmaline approaches, a stick in her mouth to tempt me to play. "Sit," I whisper, and she complies. "Good girl." I wrap an arm around her. She doesn't drop her stick, but she leans into me, which is great because the cold is seeping through Francie's clothes and into my skin.

Absently, I scritch the spot on her cheek that she loves, right where her ruff explodes. Ahead of us, the craft darts around, like it's searching. I tell myself it's a good thing it hasn't come straight for us. Maybe it lost sight of us. Maybe it never spotted us at all.

Or maybe it knows exactly where we are, and it's just waiting for us to show ourselves.

How long will we have to wait? Hours? Days? I should have bundled up better, maybe searched Francie's closet for a good coat.

Trey fidgets in the car, looking back and forth between me and the direction of the aircraft, as if deciding whether or not to join me. In the backseat, Tanq is a huddled shadow of terror, as still as I've ever seen her.

Suddenly, I blink and the dragonfly is gone, like it ceased to exist. I scan the sky as best I can through the tree branches. No silver flash, not even the exhaust of contrails. Birds start chirruping all around me; I hadn't even realized they'd gone silent.

Still, I wait. It feels like a trap. Like that thing is just waiting for me to let down my guard.

The door creaks as Trey eases out the passenger door. Crouching low, he weaves through branches to join me. Emmaline thumps her tail in welcome.

"I think it's gone," he whispers when we are shoulder to shoulder.

"We have to be absolutely sure," I say.

"Then let's wait a bit."

He smells good, like aftershave, which makes me notice that his stubble is gone. He must have found a razor at the house.

Now that my gaze isn't laser focused on the dragonfly, I take better stock of our surroundings. We're in a community park. Rickety picnic tables spread out behind the car. A green area leads to a playground and—

I gasp.

"What?" Trey whispers. "What is it?"

"A basketball court." Regulation-height net, freshly painted lines. "It's nothing. Sorry to alarm you. It's just . . ."

I can't finish aloud. It's just that seeing that pristine court wallops me all over again with how much I've lost. Basketball was everything. I can close my eyes and feel the ball in my hands, hear the squeak of my trainers on the gym floor. It wasn't just the sport I loved. It was my *life*; inextricably entwined with my family, my friends, my home, my future. I can't think about basketball without remembering the afternoon Shawntelle and I got our scholarship notices on the same day. Playing one-on-one with Ry-guy. Paul cheering from the bleachers at every single game, waving his ridiculous pompoms. Mom helping me glitter up a pair of Converse to wear to junior prom.

I feel Trey staring at my profile. I'm afraid to look at him. If I see understanding there, I won't be able to keep these hot tears from leaking out of my eyes.

He shifts in place beside me. Then his huge hand wraps mine and squeezes. "I know," he says.

His hand is warm. And strong. We sit like this a long time. With Emmy snugged against me on my left, Trey's fingers around mine, I'm almost okay.

Eventually, the cold becomes too much to bear. "I'm getting back inside the car," I say, gently untangling my fingers from Trey's—and suddenly my empty hand is the coldest part of me.

I creep toward the RAV4; Trey snaps a few twigs as he follows. Before getting in, I order: "Emmaline, go potty." She obliges by squatting, and not a whole lot comes out, but I appreciate the effort. "Good girl."

After we slip into our seats and close the doors behind us, Tanq says in a weak voice, "Is it gone?"

"I don't know about 'gone,' but it's definitely out of sight."

"Maybe we should wait here a little longer," she says.

"Maybe," I say.

"We just don't know," Trey says. "It could be waiting around the next curve in the road. It could have some kind of radar technology showing it exactly where we are. . . . I hate not knowing."

I say, "That guy in Sandusky said some of our questions would be answered."

"What if it's a trap?" Tanq blurts. "What if he's luring us there? Maybe he's made some kind of deal with those alien things."

Trey and I exchange a look that says, *Tanq has a point.*

"We just don't know," Trey repeats.

This feeling in my belly is like pregame jitters. Sometimes, it made me throw up. Other times, it made my limbs so antsy to move that I expended too much energy in pregame warm ups. Lots of athletes learn to harness those jitters. But not me. No matter what, pregame anxiety always made me less than my best.

So I take a deep breath, and I imagine Coach Dalrymple's voice in my head: *Let the fear and panic flood your being, accept it, examine it . . . let it go.*

I *am* afraid. And that's just how it's going to be. I say, "Our odds of survival are low, but they go up if we get some answers." There. Truth, unvarnished. Accepted, examined.

"You're saying it's worth risking our lives, if it means we have a chance of getting those answers," Trey says.

"Yeah."

Tanq says nothing.

"So we stick to the plan," I say.

"Sandusky," Trey says.

"Any objections? Comments?" I say, looking at Tanq in the rearview mirror. It's another thing Coach D used to say, after reviewing the game plan with us.

"No," she whispers.

"All right then," I say. "Here we go." I stare at the gear shift, and it's a moment before I can force my hand to put the car in reverse. Another moment before I depress the gas pedal. Pine branches screech along the fender as I back us out from under the tree and toward the playground area.

"Eyes to the sky," Tanq mutters.

I steer us toward the main road, slowly, noting escape routes as I go—a driveway that leads to a carport, a covered picnic area, a straggly copse of trees. Trey reaches forward and turns up the car heater. "If we're going to die," he says, "we're going to die warm."

Emmaline barks, nose pressed against the window, and I accidentally jerk the steering wheel trying to see what she's seeing. The tires screech, and I barely manage to correct our course before we bump off the pavement and into a ditch.

"Jesus, Paige," Tanq says.

"Sorry."

"It was just a squirrel," she says. "How about Trey and I watch the sky and you just focus on driving."

"Yeah, okay, I said I'm sorry."

We're silent a long time.

Our road takes us through Sunbury, which feels like a ghost town. Several storefronts are boarded up. Outside an insurance office, bodies are piled up on the sidewalk. I steer away, into what would normally be oncoming traffic, so we're not forced to look too closely.

A speed sign says 25 MPH. I could speed through this town at eighty right now, and no cops would stop me. Maybe I should go one hundred miles per hour all the way to Sandusky, get there as quickly as possible.

I'm forced to hit the brakes. A fallen marquee stretches across almost the whole street. ASK FOR THE FARMER'S BREAKFAST SPECIAL! it says. $9.99 FOR A LIMITED TIME.

Our right front wheel bumps up onto the sidewalk as I aim around the marquee. There'll be no speeding for us after all, not with so much debris in the roads.

As we clear Sunbury and head into the flat, wide-open land we Central Ohioans call the "wilderness," I can't get that sign out of my head. Farmers. Why does Manny Gomez call the aliens "Farmers"?

A few miles later, we begin to see signs for Interstate 71.

"We're not getting on the freeway, right?" Tanq says.

"No way," I assure her. "We're going under it."

"All this wide-open space is making me nervous," Trey says.

"Me too. See anything?"

"Just clouds," he says.

"And grass," Tanq adds.

"*So* much grass," Trey agrees.

"Cows!" Tanq says. "Not dead!"

I'm glancing in the direction she's pointing, but Trey gasps. "Something just flashed. On our right."

"Shit," I say. There's no cover anywhere. Not for miles. "We're almost to the interstate. We can lie low in the underpass."

"Maybe step on it a bit?" Trey says.

"Or would that attract attention?" I say.

We push doggedly forward, rolling at about forty miles an hour—fast enough to make progress, slow enough that I can make quick maneuvers if I have to.

"You're right," Tanq whispers. "This not-knowing is going to get us killed."

We pass a church with peeling white paint and a steeple that's seen better days. Like us, it's out in the middle of nowhere, completely exposed and alone. I'm tempted to head toward it, try to find a way inside. But a closer look shows several broken windows and a driveway covered in broken glass. The last thing I want to do is risk our tires.

My palms on the steering wheel are getting damp again, so I wipe them on Francie's sweatshirt and try to keep a lighter, more relaxed grip on the wheel.

"Damn these clouds," Trey says, scanning the sky. "It could be on top of us."

"We're almost to the travel center," I say, just as we round a bend and a giant FLYING J sign comes into view.

"There!" Tanq says, pointing above the sign. "One of those things."

"It's coming right for us," Trey says.

"Hang on," I warn, and I hit the gas.

Do I imagine the metallic whine as it approaches? Does the temperature in the car really rise several degrees?

In every horror movie I've ever seen, someone is dumb enough to run in a straight line. Not me. I drive in a zigzag pattern, as fast as I safely can.

A shadow darkens the windshield. Then it's gone. Then back again. It's struggling to adapt to my erratic driving.

"Shit, shit, shit," Tanq mutters.

"The gas station!" Trey says.

I see it. The fueling area is covered. Not exactly out of sight, but better than nothing.

Light explodes on our right, strobing into my brain, as I zag left. I'm blinking to clear my vision as the gas station looms closer.

That thing fires again, lighting up my rearview mirror. Something pops, like a bullet, and suddenly the RAV4 is fishtailing wildly, and Emmaline starts to whine but a concussive *flap-flap-flap* drowns her out.

"Grazing hit," Trey yells. "Blew a tire!"

We can't go far on a blown tire.

"When we get to the gas station, we bail," I holler over the noise. "All of us, in all different directions."

"We're safer in the car," Tanq shouts back.

"That covering is too high," I say. "The dragonfly can swoop right under it."

"Ah, hell," she says.

If we take off in different directions, maybe one or two of us will survive. It can't fire on all four of us at once, right? Unless it has some kind of split beam technology . . .

No time to second-guess. The steering wheel vibrates like it's going to fly off. The rear tire squeals like metal gears grinding. No more tire left, just rim sparking against asphalt.

I zip under the overhang. "Get ready!" I say, unclipping my seat belt. I pull us in behind a blue van, hit the emergency brake, and swing open the driver's side door. "Go!" I yell. "Go, go, go!" Like I'm at an honest-to-god basketball game, and I fling myself from the car and sprint with everything I have for the storefront and the Subway sign above it.

An explosion rocks the earth, and I stumble. I refuse to look back, only forward. The door is padlocked. No way inside, but there's an ice machine beside the doorway, and I dive for it, squeeze in behind it, scraping a layer of skin off my hip.

I force my body to stillness, though I want nothing more than to heave great big breaths of precious air. Even stilled, my breathing is too loud in my own ears. Surely every Farmer for a hundred miles can hear it.

If the dragonfly saw me hide here, I'm a goner. If it didn't see me, I have a small chance. I hope Trey and Tanq found cover. And Emmaline.

Oh, god, my dog. I hope she got out of that car. I hope she ran as fast as her little legs could carry her. Maybe the Farmers don't see dogs as threats. Hopefully, she's safer than all of us.

I crouch here a long time, my back against the scratchy brick wall of the travel center, my head twisted sideways to allow room, my cheek pressed into the ice machine. It stinks of motor oil and old urine.

Please be okay, I think, over and over like a prayer or a mantra. I can't be alone again. I just can't. I imagine Trey's warm smile, the way he dropped his gun to hug me the first moment we met. I see Tanq's delicate elfin face and the way she gazed wonderingly when I said I'd punch a guy in the face for her. I hear Emmaline's clattering claws on tile or pavement whenever she came running toward me . . .

No, those really *are* claws coming toward me, then a little yip, and suddenly a black nose is nudging at my thigh and somehow I've managed to crouch enough to bury my arms in her ruff as tears soak her sable fur. "Emmy, oh my god, Emmy."

She laps at my face, her tail wagging so fast I fear it might fly off. I rub my hands all over her body, assuring myself she's all right, and she looses a tiny whimper when my fingers find a bald patch on her flank. I twist to get a better view—no small task behind this ice machine—and see that a neat circle of fur has been burned off, her underlying skin bright red. Just a first-degree burn. It will heal fine, if I can keep her from licking it too much.

I bury my face in her ruff again. She smells funny, almost chemical. Burned hair, I realize. "Oh, Emmaline, that was *close.*"

But it gives me hope. Maybe Tanq or Trey survived too.

After several minutes of cuddling my dog, I dare to peek out around the edge of the ice machine.

The parking lot of the Flying J is bare except for the few cars that were already there when we arrived. But the RAV4 is missing, along with the blue van it was parked behind. My gaze sweeps the lot, searching. Maybe the car was thrown somehow? Maybe it rolled away? Even though I'm pretty sure I remember hitting the emergency brake . . .

No, wait, it's right where we left it, except it's not a car at all. My view from here is poor, and the light dim with cloud cover, so I can barely make it out: an inkblot of shimmering black, cratered into the pavement, still sending up tendrils of smoke. Paul's RAV4 was completely obliterated.

All the air around me has been sucked away, leaving me nothing left to breathe. In spite of the cold, my neck flashes hot, and my hands in Emmaline's ruff tremble uncontrollably.

I've lost everything now. The last bits I cared about—Paul's car, the Monstrosity, Hazel Jenkins's floral purse. Probably even my new friends.

Paul.

I close my eyes and try to imagine his face, afraid if I don't, he'll slip away from me. His slightly crooked teeth, his short graying beard, the way he squinted when he left his glasses on top of his head. A memory comes unbidden: *Are you wearing Chucks to the prom because you're afraid of looking so tall?* he asked. *Of course not,* I said, waving it off, but my face was filling with heat, because as usual, he knew me too well. *Fine,* he said. *Wear whatever makes you feel good. But it wouldn't hurt my feelings if you wore six-inch heels and strutted in like you owned the place.*

How was I not aware, every second of every day, that I had the best stepdad in the whole world?

Suddenly, a different face fills my memory. Younger, with much darker skin and an impossibly beautiful grin. Brown eyes that exude warmth and understanding. Listening eyes, just like Paul's.

I lurch out from behind the ice machine. I have to find Trey. I *have* to.

I'm not so lost in grief and memory that I forget to scan the sky. The aircraft is nowhere to be seen as I cautiously approach the smoking crater that used to be Paul's car. Emmaline's nails click on the asphalt beside me. What if they're not supposed to click? Should I have been trimming my dog's nails this whole time?

"Emmy," I whisper as we step into the shadow of the covered parking area. "I'm so sorry if I'm being a bad mom to you. But I'll figure it out, I promise."

I'm not sure what I'm hoping to find here. A clue as to where Trey and Tanq ran off to? Footprints, like in all the movies? Looking down at this crater, the asphalt glittering like melted glass, there's no way to know if either one was still inside when that thing hit.

I should have done more. I should have found better cover or driven faster or listened to Tanq when she said we should stay at her dad's—

"Paige?"

I whirl. Trey's head is peeking out from around an island of gas pumps. He stands, sweeps toward me in his duster coat, the rifle still hanging over his shoulder.

"Trey!" I run at him, laugh-crying, and he hardly has time to straighten before I throw my arms around his neck.

"Thank god you're okay," he whispers, and his lips press against my hair as the butt of his rifle pokes my ribs. "I thought we . . . I thought . . ."

I pull back to arm's length and look him up and down. "Everything all right? Were you hurt at all?"

His gaze fixes on my face. "No. You?"

"I'm fine. Emmy has a burn patch on her side, but I think she's okay. You smell bad."

"Hid behind a trash bin. It was gross."

"Any sign of Tanq?"

"No. Heard her scream, though. If she bailed out her door and ran in a generally straight direction . . ."

I follow the line of his pointing arm. "Then she's out there somewhere," I say. Beyond the parking lot is the road, and beyond that is tall grass leading to a patch of alder trees, thin trunked with grayish bark and branches just starting to bud. "We should look for her," I say.

"Yeah," he says.

But our feet don't budge. "Okay, I admit, I'm terrified to go anywhere," I say.

"But are we more terrified of losing Tanq?"

I'm honestly not sure. The first time we met her, the answer was yes. But a body can only take so much fear. It's terror after terror, weight after weight piling up onto a barbell, and after a while I just can't budge it anymore.

What I'm left with is: "I'd want her to do it for me," which probably makes me selfish and not heroic at all.

But Trey says, "Same."

And as one, we step forward, out from under the covering into the open air.

"Tanq!" I whisper, edging forward, keeping one eye on the sky.

It's a massive journey, the longest walk I've ever taken, my skin warm and prickling as we creep over the cold pavement of the Flying J, across the road, into the slight ditch on the other side.

"Tanq!" Trey whispers. "You okay?"

"Maybe we should split up," I say.

"Or maybe we should stick together. Honestly, Paige, if finding Tanq means losing you, I'm not sure I . . . I mean, she's important too, but . . ."

My stomach does a funny little flip. "We'll stick together."

We search the grass, already tall so early in the year. Something loud skitters away, crunching through dried leaves. A squirrel, or maybe even a groundhog.

"There's no guarantee she went this way," Trey says.

"Let's try the trees," I suggest, and head in that direction. "Tanq?"

The trunks are close together, making it hard to walk, and it's a good thing I have decent socks and Francie's thick yoga pants, or I'd have itchy grass scratches on my legs for days. After we find Tanq, I'll have to check Emmaline for ticks.

"Is that her?" Trey says, pointing.

A lump of black fabric is bunched against a tree trunk. "Tanq?" I say, thrusting myself through the trees. "Is that you?"

The lump manifests into a huddled mass of human—a torn sleeve, a scratched pale cheek. Her arms are wrapped around her knees. Maybe she's dead. Maybe she dragged herself all the way here only to . . .

No, she's alive. Relief washes through me like a cleansing flood because she's rocking, back and forth. Murmuring something. Totally unaware of our approach. "Tanq?" I whisper again, but she doesn't respond.

Trey squats, puts an arm on her shoulder.

She lurches away, baring her teeth.

"It's us," Trey says, hands up. "Are you okay?"

I see the exact moment she snaps back to herself. It's like her vision clears and she takes a great gulp of air, as though she hasn't bothered breathing at all the last few minutes. "Uh . . . hi," she manages.

"Anything hurt?" I ask.

She blinks. "I don't know."

"Can you walk?"

"I think so."

As Tanq shakily gets to her feet, Emmaline trots over to greet her and solicit pets. Tanq gazes down at the dog, a strange look on her face. "You're all right, Emmaline," she says, and I get the feeling she means in general, like she's conferring approval.

"We need to find a car," Trey says. "And food. Everything we had was . . . is gone."

"Not everything," Tanq says, turning around and bending over. She lifts something out of the grass and hands it to me. Hazel Jenkins's floral purse. "Sorry I couldn't grab that ugly serving dish. This was all I could reach."

"Oh, my god," I say, taking the purse. "Tanq. I can't believe you saved this. Thank you."

"I knew it was important. Even though it's ugly as hell."

She wasted a precious second grabbing this. She risked her life for it. Thanks to Tanq, we have bottled water, a few bandages, some granola bars, a handgun. And all the photo IDs I've been collecting. I stare at her, wondering how I thought, even for a second, that this girl might not be worth saving.

On impulse, I reach out and hug her. She's stiff as a tree trunk for a brief moment, but then she relaxes against me, and her own arms wrap around my back.

I'm the first to pull away. "I'm sorry. I should have asked permission—"

"Whatever," she says, shrugging. "So, what next?"

"We find another car," Trey says.

"So we can get blown up again?" she says.

"We could walk," I say. "All the way to Sandusky."

"How long would that take?" Tanq asks. "It might be easier to keep under cover. Like that ditch running alongside the road. Lots of tall grass, easy access to trees."

"How far is it from here?" Trey says. "About eighty or ninety miles?"

"Seems about right," I say. A flash of red startles me, but it's just a cardinal, flitting among the alder branches.

"So, averaging three miles per hour, walking eight hours per day . . . ," Trey mutters. "About four days. *If* we can keep up that pace. And frankly, Paige, I'm not sure you're ready for that kind of physical exertion, especially with your foot just healed. . . ."

"Wow, you're a math nerd," Tanq says.

"Thank you," he says solemnly.

"So let's estimate five or six days," I say.

"Honestly? More like seven," Trey says.

"Okay, seven. Manny Gomez said they were running out of fuel, that they'd keep broadcasting as long as possible, but—"

"But they might not even be there in seven days," Trey says.

Tanq deflates. "So we find a car."

I study her, her wilted shoulders, her whipped puppy face. Moments ago, she was practically comatose, so frozen by fear that she didn't hear us approach. I shouldn't make the mistake of assuming she's okay, just because she sometimes puts up a front of defiance.

I say, "Let's head back to the travel center, see if we can find a car that still has some gas."

At Tanq's panicked stare, Trey adds, "We'll go carefully."

"Would you rather stay here, Tanq?" I say. "Trey and I will find a car, swing by to pick you up."

"Just relax here and catch your breath a little more," Trey adds.

"Yeah, okay, I'll stay . . . No. I'm coming with you. Grabbing another car is the right play and I . . . I'm in."

I hide my smile. "Okay, let's go."

The return journey isn't quite so long, though we creep quietly, constantly scanning the sky.

The first car we reach is a gray sedan. It's empty, and all the doors are locked.

"I'd be willing to risk the noise of breaking in," Tanq whispers, "but I don't see car keys anywhere."

"Next one," Trey says.

Near the ice machine where I hid minutes before is a Chevy truck with a king cab. I reach for the driver's side door, and it opens easily.

A wave of sweet rot hits my nose as a moist body slips out of the seat and splats onto the pavement. I catch a glimpse of plaid work shirt and faded blue jeans before I turn away, retching.

"The keys are in the ignition," Tanq says.

Trey isn't looking either. He's gazing off toward the Subway sign, his jaw and neck muscles hard at work. I remember the way he avoided looking at Barry Stockton's body in the grocery store. He's the biggest and strongest of us all, but apparently he has the weakest stomach.

I take a deep breath, and ignoring the decomposing corpse at my feet, I peer into the truck's cab.

The seat is wet and dark, soaked in decomposition.

"I can't . . . I won't . . . ," I stutter.

"Well, I'm not sitting on that either," Tanq says. "Trey, would you be willing to drive while sitting on top of—"

Trey heaves in answer.

Tanq looks up at me and says matter-of-factly, "This is not the car we're looking for."

"Let's try another."

We try them all. Each car is either locked, or it holds a dead body. One white Acura contains two bodies, though the windows are so damp and fogged we can't see much more than that. We also try getting inside the travel center, but it's locked down tight.

"The empty cars," Trey muses. "Maybe their owners are inside the travel center? Maybe we can find keys."

"Remember how hard it was to break into that grocery store?" I remind him. "Do we want to make that much noise right now?"

"What else can we do?"

"We walk. For now. Just until we find a farmhouse. It's easier to break into a farmhouse than a humongous store like this. Eventually, we'll find a house with keys to a car."

"We can travel in that ditch," Tanq says. "Crouch down in the grass if we see anything."

Trey stares at the ditch.

"Trey?" I prompt. "Thoughts?"

He frowns. "On rough ground, we won't even hit three miles per hour. But I don't have a better idea. Let's go."

We've been walking for hours, and it's getting colder. Or at least I think it's been hours. I have no phone to check the time, no clear sky to gauge the position of the sun. The bones in my legs weigh a thousand pounds. My bitten heel aches, though as long as it doesn't start to sting—indicating the wound has opened up again—I'll choose to ignore it.

We have not seen a single farmhouse.

A church rose up in the distance, about two miles back, and we headed in its direction just long enough to note that its parking lot was empty. So after we took a quick break to share water from the bottle in my purse and eat granola bars, we passed by and pushed on.

The drainage ditch alongside State Route 61 is spongy with dampness and thick with reeds, but Tanq was right; it will provide a little cover if we need it.

"Hey, there aren't any snakes out here, are there?" Tanq says, startling me, because we've all been silent so long.

"Nothing venomous," I lie. I saw a northern copperhead once, outside a gymnasium in southern Ohio.

"Okay, that's good."

Trey leads us, and he glances back over his shoulder and says, "You doing okay, Paige?"

"What about me?" Tanq says, and I can see in her face that she's mostly teasing. "You never ask about me."

"You weren't in a coma a week ago."

"Fair point," she says.

Trey stops in his tracks, but he doesn't duck for cover, so after a confused mutual glance, Tanq and I hurry to catch up.

"What?" I say. "What is it?"

He points.

A billboard rises high, topping out over trees and distance. It's at least a mile away, but I can still read it because the lettering is so huge, stark black against weathered white. It says, HELL IS REAL.

Tanq laughs.

"Well," says Trey. "No argument from me."

"Let's keep going," I say in a voice that's shaking a little because that sign reminds me of the Sperm Donor, who made Ryan and me go to Sunday school every single week, like that made up for the fact that he was a mean drunk who sometimes got mean on his kids. I asked him about it once, why he took us to church when he ignored Jesus the rest of the week. I was only about seven years old, but I remember it clear as day. He said, "I don't want to go to hell."

We trudge along, and my shoulder starts to burn with the weight of Hazel Jenkins's purse. Emmaline is the only one who's been enjoying the walk; I've let her dart here and there, sniff whatever she wants, just so she can get her wiggles out. But even she's beginning to look haggard, and every now and then she keeps pace with me for a few steps, whining softly, and I finally realize she's hungry.

Emmaline isn't the only one. My stomach is rumbling now, and hunger is a painful pinch beneath my breastbone. Moisture from the drainage ditch begins seeping into my shoes, making me shiver. The clouds grow thicker and grayer, and I can't tell whether it's due to a coming storm or the day growing late. Tanq's arms wrap around herself, and she forgets to watch the sky. Like me, she's concentrating on putting one foot in front of the other.

All my emo musings about mortality were too romantic. I

imagined myself in a hospital bed, surrounded by a loving husband and children, painkillers within easy access. Everyone would tell me what a wonderful life I'd led, how much they'd miss me.

Turns out, it's much more likely I'll die cold and hungry in a lonely ditch.

It takes us several hours to pass under the HELL IS REAL billboard and put it out of sight.

"Is that a farmhouse?" Trey says, pointing. I stretch onto my tiptoes to see what he's seeing: a white two-story house with a wraparound porch, surrounded by wheat fields growing wild. Beside the house is a huge red barn with the state of Ohio painted in bright white on its side.

We cut through the wheat fields toward it, and it's rough going, but at least it's not wet. More critters skitter away as we travel. In the distance, something yips. Something else answers.

"Dogs?" Tanq says.

"Coyotes," I say, remembering the giant one we saw in the middle of the road.

"Oh, god," she says, picking up the pace.

We break into a clear area, with a gravel drive and an overgrown lawn, then step up onto the porch.

Trey knocks, which I'm finally accepting as a ridiculous gesture because if anyone is inside, they are certainly not alive, but maybe these little gestures are important anyway.

"Hello?" Trey calls out. "Anyone home?"

Tanq presses her nose to a window, shading her face with her hands. "No one in the living room."

"We'll need something to break the glass," Trey says. "Maybe the handle of the gun . . ."

I reach for the doorknob. It twists like it's just been oiled, and the door swings open. "Finally," I say. "A bit of luck."

A wave of decomp wallops me in the face, but it's not as bad as Mrs. Carby's house or even that Chevy truck at the travel center. Whoever's in here has been dead a little longer.

"Ugh," Tanq says, but she bulldozes past me and goes right in.

It's a pretty house, with hardwood floors made of old railroad ties and a giant fireplace mantel with built-in shelves to either side, enclosed in leaded glass. The furniture is used but comfortable—lots of wood in simple, clean designs, possibly made by the local Amish. Through the family room is a small kitchen with pots and pans hanging from a ceiling rack over an antique stove in avocado green. Somehow, the owners made it look trendy next to soft yellow walls and cupboards covered with calico curtains instead of doors.

A doorway leads to a small area that does double duty as both pantry and laundry room.

"Yahtzee!" Tanq says, grabbing a bag of corn chips.

There's plenty of food on the shelves. I find some canned chicken, then rummage through drawers and cupboards for a can opener and a plate, and within minutes, Emmaline is happily chomping away.

It's a relief just to feed my dog. Like that one simple act

reminds me that I can do things, take care of things.

"We should avoid the upstairs," Tanq says, grabbing a jar of peanut butter.

"Agreed," says Trey. He reaches for a keychain hanging from a peg by the refrigerator, shakes it at us. "Let's hope there's a car matching one of these keys in that barn."

"Manny Gomez said to travel during the day," I say.

Trey's face falls. "Yeah, you're right. We should sleep here tonight, hit the road early in the morning."

The mere thought of resting almost makes my knees buckle.

"Paige, you can have the sofa," he says. "I sleep fine on the floor."

Tanq rolls her eyes. "Don't worry about *me*, Trey," she says pointedly. "I can sleep on the floor too."

Trey just grins at her.

I take just enough time to find something to eat. The pantry contains so much dried pasta—spaghetti, boxed macaroni and cheese, elbow macaroni, bow-tie pasta . . . pasta would be amazing, but we have no way to boil water. Maybe in the fireplace? But it feels like so much trouble, and I'm so tired. I settle for some mixed nuts and a can of cold clam chowder. Dinner of champions.

As I collapse onto the sofa, I'm vaguely aware that I promised myself I'd check Emmaline for ticks, but I can hardly keep my eyes open. I hate being weak.

March 27? 28? I'm losing track

I WAKE TO HEAT ON MY FACE AND THE ACRID TANG OF BURNING pine. My neck hurts from being cricked into one position all night, but it feels so good to be warm.

I sit up on the sofa. It's light outside, but the curtains are drawn, so I have no idea what time it is, and there's no sound but the crackling fire; I'm all alone in the house. Tanq and Trey must have taken Emmaline outside with them.

My eyelids are still heavy, and it would be the easiest thing to roll over and go back to sleep, but hunger tugs at my belly along with something else, a different kind of emptiness I'm coming to recognize. It's because the house is so, so quiet, and the smell of decomp is still sharp enough to tug at my nose.

Alone, alone, alone.

I won't be weak, and I don't do despair. So I heave myself off the couch and head to the kitchen to find something for breakfast. A peanut-butter-and-jelly sandwich sits on the counter, leaking grape jelly through the paper towel it's wrapped in. Beside it is a sheet of white printer paper, and someone has written in blue ballpoint pen: *Eat up. We're in the barn. T.*

"T" could refer to either Tanq or Trey, but somehow I know it's Trey. His handwriting is neat and spare, beautiful in the way of the simple but perfect furniture in this house.

After shoving down the PB&J, I do my business in the downstairs half-bath, and splash some water on my face. Near the bathroom is a door to the rear yard, and beside it is a small table with a pile of mail. A man's wallet lies open beside the mail. I grab it, flip to the driver's license. Kent Williams. Born 1958. Five-foot-ten, one hundred ninety pounds. Brown eyes, gray hair, corrective lenses. "Thanks for putting us up last night, Kent," I whisper.

I slip the license into Hazel Jenkins's purse and exit the house via the front door.

Crows line the porch railing, and they barely react to my presence. Cold wind is like a block of ice to my face. Maybe I *should* go upstairs and face the inevitable corpses—on the chance one of the closets contains a decent coat.

But the barn door is open, and my feet take me forward, toward the comfort of friends.

I'm nearly there when Tanq manifests in the doorway and waves me inside. "We have good news and bad news," she says.

Emmaline greets me when I enter, trots circles around me while my eyes adjust to the gloom. A squat car stretches before me, like a flat rectangle on wheels. Trey is loading something into the car's . . . truck bed?

"We have a car," Tanq says. "It has a full tank and decent tires. That's the good news. The bad news is that it's a 1987 Chevy El Camino."

"Hey!" Trey says. "This car is a classic."

"A '69 El Camino is a classic," Tanq retorts. "This? Is a travesty."

They've obviously been having this conversation all morning. "It's . . . brown," I say. "Mud brown."

"I was thinking baby diaper brown," Tanq says.

"It's *cinnamon*," Trey says, "and someone was lovingly restoring it when the virus hit."

All I care about is: "Will it get us to Sandusky?"

"I think so," Trey says. "We'll be lucky to get ten miles to the gallon, but it should last. Someone will have to sit in the back."

"Which will be cold and horrible," Tanq says. "But me and Trey, we figure whoever's in the back will be our spotter. Should have a good view of the sky from there."

I nod. "We'll take turns, do it in shifts."

"Did you eat?" Trey asks me.

"Yep. Thanks for the sandwich."

"I pulled five ticks off of Emmaline this morning," Tanq says.

I gape at her. "How did you know to do that?"

"I used to pull them off the boys I lived with. They always played in the creek behind . . ." Her gaze darts away. "Anyway, keep an eye on her. We should all be careful, if we have to walk like that again."

"Good thinking," I tell her. Something glimmers outside the barn, and I'm ducking reflexively when I realize it's just a goldfinch, flitting through the trees. Mom and I used to make a game of it every spring, seeing who would spot the first goldfinch of the year.

"You okay, Paige?" Trey prompts.

"You both let me sleep in again," I accuse.

"You needed it," Trey says, closing up the hatch as gently and quietly as he can.

"What I need is to contribute," I say. "You don't need to baby me."

"You looked terrible," Tanq says. "Pale like a zombie. I would have painted you while you were sleeping if I still had my paints, because you looked so dead. It was great."

I blink at her. "You lost your paints. Your whole backpack. When the RAV4 exploded." I was so absorbed in my own terror that I didn't even notice. "You grabbed that ugly purse instead."

Tanq shrugs. "Everyone makes mistakes. Anyway, we're ready to go. Me and Trey put some supplies in the back."

They both seem somber. Like they know something I don't. They've been hanging out all morning without me, and I sense that I'm being left out of something. Or maybe my fear of being alone again is making me petty. *Get a grip, Paige.*

"I'll take first shift as spotter," Trey says. "Found some sunglasses to protect my eyes. I'll rap the window if I see anything."

"Tanq, we'll find more paints for you," I tell her. "Somehow."

"Whatever," she says, but she still won't meet my gaze.

Trey comes around the rear of the El Camino to join us. "No, really, Tanq. You're an artist, and it's important that you keep creating."

Tanq glares at him. Glares at me. Glares at Emmaline. "Do you expect me to fall all over myself with gratitude?" she says.

I'm about to say something sharp, but Trey takes a different tack. "I accept payment in Red Vines," he says gravely. "And you must address me as His Holy Majesty Trey Dawson, King of Ohio."

Tanq stares at him. I expect her to blow up. Instead, her lips start to twitch and she says, "Very well, Your Majesty . . . and all that other stuff."

But our mood is subdued as we climb into the El Camino. Trey wraps himself in a quilt he found inside the house, then he and his long legs stretch out in the truck bed, while Tanq, Emmy, and I cram into the cab.

I turn the ignition, and the engine makes a sound like boulders rolling down a cliff. The Farmers will be able to hear us from miles away.

If they even *hear*. We have to get to Sandusky. We have to get our questions answered.

I ease out of the red barn. The El Camino has the turning radius of an aircraft carrier, and I'm forced to back into a corn field to make a three-point turn, but soon enough we're back on SR-61 heading north to Sandusky. If all goes well, we'll be there in two hours.

o o o

We drive through Mount Gilead without incident, then Galion, and we're nearly to Norwalk when it starts to snow. It melts when it hits the ground, darkening the asphalt with slick wetness.

"Would someone please tell Ohio it's almost April?" Tanq says. "God, I hate this state."

"Really? I love Ohio."

"Ew. Why?"

"I don't know, I guess because it's home. My whole life was here. I traveled the entire state several times a year with my teams. It's beautiful. Green and lush. I love summer thunderstorms and winter woodstove tea. There are cute little towns everywhere. And everyone is . . . was . . . nice."

"They were nice to you because you were a rich, white cheerleader," Tanq says. "Try being a poor kid from the wrong side of town. Or worse, Black, like Trey. Ohio wasn't as nice to us, you know."

"Hey, I was never a cheerleader, I was a basketball . . ." At her disgusted look, I say, "Okay, fair point."

The snow falls in blinding spirals, getting thicker. The edges of my side window are starting to collect the stuff. Trey's quilt won't protect him from this kind of cold; he must be freezing back there.

Our road turns white with the dropping temperature. Everything that got wet will now freeze, making our route treacherous.

"Lake effect," Tanq says.

"Yup," I say.

Everyone in the Midwest understands the lake effect, when a cold front blows in from Canada, sweeps over the relatively warm Great Lakes, picking up power and moisture, then dumps it on us with a vengeance.

A few miles later, I can no longer make out lines on the road. I find the knob that controls the windshield wipers, which helps brush the snow away. If the storm gets much worse, we'll have to stop.

We reach a gas station, and I pull in under the overhang.

"What are you doing?" Tanq asks.

"Checking on Trey." I roll down the window and stick my head out. The cold air stings my cheeks; the temperature must have dropped at least ten degrees. "You okay, Trey?"

"Yeah," he hollers. "Just cold." His voice comes out muffled, like his mouth is full of marbles.

"Do you want to drive for a while? Warm up in the cab?"

"No, you should be the one to stay warm. We can't risk you relapsing—"

"Trey!"

"Oh. Right. No more babying you."

The whole car lists sideways as Trey gets to his feet and leaps out of the truck bed. He shakes off the quilt, and even though he's aiming away, the wind pushes all the collected snow into our faces.

I open the door and step out of the cab. Emmaline follows after, thinking this is a pit stop, so I tell her to go potty and watch while she squats in the fresh layer of snow.

"Here," Trey says, wrapping the quilt around my shoulders. Then he takes off his sunglasses and hands them to me. "It's impossible to see anything right now, but these will at least keep the snow out of your eyes."

"Thanks." We stare at each other for a long moment, neither of us moving. A bit of wetness rims his eyes, melted snow that the sunglasses couldn't block. Finally, I remember to tell him, "The road is really slick, and this car doesn't handle well, so take it slow and careful."

"Will do. Rap the window if you need anything, just once. Twice if you see one of those alien things."

A few minutes later, we're back on the road, and my nose is already so cold it's starting to run. I discover it helps cut the wind to lie flat in the truck bed, a section of quilt bunched under my head.

I stare at the sky looking for any sign of trouble. The endless gray-white and blinding snow makes it impossible to see. I suddenly understand the true origin of "white noise." The bright white is relentless, drowning everything out, making the world vividly silent.

We pull into Sandusky as the snow turns into a light drizzle of rain and everything begins to melt, leaving puddles and mud. Then again, maybe Sandusky's location, hugged up against Lake Erie, makes it a generally marshy place. The air is damp and smells faintly of algae and fish. The El Camino's cab caught plenty of snow during our drive, and it seeps cold and wet into my back. Even though the air has warmed, my toes have gone numb, and my cheeks are blocks of ice.

Trey drives past several car dealerships and approximately fifty thousand fast food restaurants before heading into the parking lot of a strip mall. He parks beneath a sprawling dogwood tree that's so heavy with white blooms it looks like it's holding midwinter snow.

He gets out of the car, and I try to clamber from the truck bed, but my legs are so cold and stiff they refuse to move.

"Why'd we stop?" I ask as Trey lowers the back and helps me down.

"Time for a team meeting," he says. "Also . . ." He points.

Beyond the dogwood is a Hobby Trader store.

"For Tanq," he explains.

"I said you didn't have to stop for me!" she protests, angling toward us.

Emmaline lifts her leg and pees on the tree trunk.

"Team meeting, remember?" he says. "And if we *happen* to find a way inside and get you some paints, that's just bonus. Paige, are you all right? Your face is bright red."

"It was a rough ride," I admit. "My ass hurts, but I'm fine. So, now what?"

"I don't want to wander around aimlessly," Trey says. "The broadcast clearly said 'Sandusky' and we have reason to believe the Orkins—Farmers?—know some basic English. So we have to assume they have a presence here."

"We didn't see a single aircraft," I point out. "I mean, not after they blew up the RAV4." I say it casually, but this small boulder in my chest might never go away.

"When you were sleeping last night, Tanq and I heard that sound again."

I know exactly what he's talking about. *Whoomp*.

"It was really loud," Tanq says. "And the whole sky lit up. We couldn't believe you slept through it."

Trey says, "No big deal, right? I mean, it happens every night. But while driving it occurred to me that we must be getting closer to it. So I don't want to take any chances."

I can't stop my gaze from sweeping everything around us—the parking lots, the mix of brick and cement buildings, the trees, the sky—as if the mysterious cause of that sound might suddenly manifest and make itself known to me. Everything looks normal. Well, except for a slightly greenish cast to the sky and the five giant turkey vultures across the street, sitting in the drive-thru of the White Castle. The new normal.

"So let's review," Trey continues. "What did Manny Gomez say?"

"Something about the president's park," I say.

"I saw a sign to Washington Park," says Tanq. "Maybe that's what he meant."

Trey brightens. "That could be it!"

"He also said we could 'just follow the rail,'" I say. "But I haven't seen any trains nearby, or even train tracks."

"Maybe the park has a kiddie train?" says Tanq. "You know, the kind where you pay a couple of bucks and throw your toddler into a bin with a bunch of other drooling little brats and—"

"So let's head to the park and have a look around," says Trey.

"He said it was a pirate radio station, right?" Tanq says.

"Yeah, why?" says Trey.

"Shouldn't there be a tower or something? An antenna?"

Trey nods. "Tanq, that's really smart."

Tanq fails to hide her satisfaction.

"It would probably be in a weird place," he adds. "On top of a building, or sticking out of someone's backyard."

"So we head toward the park, while keeping an eye out for a transmitter thingy," Tanq says.

"After we get you more paints," I say.

The Hobby Trader's door is unlocked. It was partly looted, and most snack items remaining from the cashier displays are strewn about the floor. Several aisles were devoted to Easter-themed crafts, and even unlit, the store is nauseatingly pink and yellow. Emmaline finds a bag of Peeps and rips the plastic to shreds before I can intervene. I'm relieved when she lets me remove everything from her mouth.

The acrylic paint aisle is nearly untouched. Tanq finds a new denim backpack and fills it to bursting with tubes of paint, rolled-up canvas, spray paints, brushes, and two bottles of glitter.

At the last second, as we're heading out the door, Tanq rushes toward a cash register and yanks a package of Red Vines from the display. She hands it to Trey. "For His Majesty," she says, with a little bow.

We're in and out within ten minutes. Tanq insists on riding

in the back this time, saying it's "my turn." Trey drives, and I sit in the passenger seat with Emmaline between us.

"I think Tanq is warming up to us," I say as he aims the El Camino toward Washington Park.

"Of course she is," he says. "We're awesome."

"Definitely some of the coolest people in the world."

"She's really worried about someone trying to make her have babies," he says, frowning.

"She told me. Brought it up in the most awkward way possible."

"There's more to that. I guess she'll tell us when she's ready."

We're all haunted, I suppose, by the people we've left behind. The things that have happened to us. I say, "It's weird how, even though our lives before are gone—and I mean deader than dead—they're still clinging to us. Sucking away at us. Like ticks."

"Oh?" he says, looking away from the road ahead to glance at me. "What part of your past life is still clinging to you, Paige?"

Emmaline takes a break from watching out the back window and lays her head on my lap. I absently scritch the soft spot behind her ears and say, "That came out wrong. I don't mean in a bad way necessarily. I don't *want* to forget my life before or let it go."

"What's still clinging to you in a *good* way?"

It's a moment before I can make the words come out: "I feel responsible for everything. It's like I'm ten years old again, and the world is terrifying, and if I don't make all the right decisions, the people I care about will suffer."

"So . . . you're saying you care about me?" I whip my head around to stare at his profile. His grin is huge.

"What about you, Trey?" I say in challenge. "What part of your past life is unshakable?"

His lips press together. We turn left, following a sign, and find an idyllic downtown area with brick shops and trees blooming along beautifully maintained sidewalks. Just when I've given up on getting an answer, he says, "I can't stop thinking about my mom. And my sister Teena. I was going to declare for the NFL at my earliest opportunity. Then I was going to buy Momma a house and a car. So she'd never have to work again. I designed that house over and over in my head. Indoor laundry, kitchen cabinets with pull-out shelves, a working fireplace, a craft room for Momma's sewing. It kept me going, thinking about Momma's house."

"What keeps you going now?" I ask. "Anything?"

"Not at first," he says, frowning. Then he shrugs it off. "But now there might be a little something. . . ." His voice trails away, but before I can press, he points ahead. "I think that's the park."

It's a vast expanse of green lawn over artificial hills, with walking paths throughout. The word "Sandusky" is formed on a hillside using some kind of pink flowering plant, though it's already overgrown and knocked around so that the *n* looks a little like a *p* and the *k* is more like an *l*.

"Let's circle around the park," I suggest. "Look for a tower."

We do, and each time we hit an intersection, the break in

buildings and trees leaves an unobstructed view to Sandusky Bay, stretching flat and gray. Sometimes we even catch glimpses of the swirling Wicked Twister and the towering Millennium Force—two of the tallest roller coasters of Cedar Point. Which makes me think of Ryan, who was terrified of roller coasters, though he made me swear to tell no one. Maybe I'll honor that secret to my grave.

Tanq bangs on the window, and Trey nearly loses control of the wheel in his attempt to find cover. But she keeps tapping, and I realize she hasn't spotted an aircraft; she's trying to tell us something.

I twist in the seat as she mouths, *Pull over!*

"Tanq says to pull over," I tell Trey, and he does, parking near a giant clock built out of the ground with hedge bushes and flowers.

Trey flings the door open and rounds on Tanq. "You nearly gave me a heart attack!"

"Follow me," Tanq says, ignoring him. "I saw a sign." Eyes to the sky, she splashes through puddles in the street, heading away from the park.

She leads us to an old brick house that looks like it was built at least a hundred years ago. It's surrounded by modern buildings, which makes it stand out. A sign in the front lawn establishes it as the LUCAS BEECHER HOUSE.

"Not that sign," Tanq says, and she points, shifting our gazes to the right. "That one."

It's a historical marker that says UNDERGROUND RAILROAD in big bronze letters across the top. Below is more text, but the writing is obscured by a big tag—a circle with a diagonal line through it—this one spray-painted in bright red.

"Did Null get as far as Sandusky?" Trey says. "I thought he operated mostly in Columbus and Cincy."

"If so, that's racist as hell," I say. "Nullifying the Underground Railroad?"

"That's not what this is," Tanq says. "It's what we're looking for. 'Follow the rail,' remember?"

"How do you know?" Trey asks.

"I *know*. Trust me."

Trey says, "Sandusky was a major stop on the Railroad to Canada. There might still be hidey-holes all over this city."

I study the Beecher House, looking for some kind of ham radio tower. "Harriet Beecher Stowe talks about Sandusky in *Uncle Tom's Cabin*. We had to read it in senior English class. You think she was related to Lucas Beecher?"

"A cousin." Trey stares off into the distance. "Wouldn't that be something?" he says, his voice tinged with wonder. "More than a hundred and fifty years later, and the Underground Railroad is still saving lives."

"Guys, keep up," Tanq says. "The guy on the radio said to go to the president's park and look for a sign. Then he said we could just 'follow the rail.' So help me look for another sign. Something that would mark a trail."

Trey nods, considering. "Another Underground Railroad marker?"

"Or," I say, scanning our surroundings. "There! Another Null sign." It's smaller than the first, but still bright red. This time it's splashed up against the concrete wall of a county building.

"Let's go!" Tanq says, heading off, her new pack bouncing against her back. Emmaline scampers after, her tail furious with joy at going for a walk with her people, as if we're in no danger at all.

We reach the second Null sign. Tanq puts a finger against it and gives it a swipe. "It hasn't been here long," she says, staring at her finger. "It's not wet or anything, but it also hasn't been here for months like some of the tags in downtown Columbus. This kind of paint cracks in the weather after a while."

"Let's look for another one," Trey says.

"Don't forget to keep an eye out for good cover," I warn, noting the awning of the sandwich place across the street.

The breeze picks up, and I shiver. It's been a cold, late spring, but I also wonder if I've been so cold because I was sick. Like my body doesn't have the energy or even the flesh to keep me warm.

We find a symbol on the door of a brewery, another on a picnic table outside a bistro, yet another behind a sign advertising ferry rides. Then we're stuck. No more symbols anywhere, no matter how hard we look.

"We must have missed one," Tanq says. We're standing beneath a redbud tree, staring out at an empty street. Sandusky is a ghost town now, quiet except for the whistling wind and the screaming of water birds. We've encountered fewer bodies than we did in Columbus. Maybe this far north it was just too cold to be outside when everyone started dying.

"Look," says Trey, pointing to a nearby parking lot. Few cars remain in the lot, unrecognizable under a green-and-gray patina of bird droppings. Not from crows, for once, but rather a flock of seagulls, scrabbling about, occasionally fighting over a tidbit.

"Those gulls seem out of place, yeah?" I say.

"Not the gulls. The manhole."

"Oh."

It hadn't occurred to me to look at the ground. The manhole is a bronze shield pressed into the pavement's surface, and it's half obscured by gull droppings. Painted on top is the Null symbol.

"We have to go down into the *sewer*?" Tanq says.

"Maybe there's another symbol nearby," I say. "Maybe that's not the end of the trail. We just have to keep looking."

But Trey is already walking forward. "This Null sign is different," he says. "See the triangles beneath it?"

"Like something you'd see on a quilt," I say.

Emmaline plows into the flock of seagulls, and birds scream their rage as they scatter. "But there's no power anywhere," Trey mutters, as though talking to himself.

"Huh?" says Tanq.

"Anything below ground would be flooded by now," he explains. "We're two blocks from Lake Erie! Without sump pumps constantly pushing out the water . . ."

"That can't be where we're supposed to go," I insist. "There has to be another symbol nearby."

I'm so wrapped up in searching for another Null symbol

that I don't notice the aircraft until its shadow passes over our heads.

"Run!" Tanq screams.

It arrows toward us, pointed nose silvery and slick, close enough that it blocks out the low sun.

My feet are frozen. We stand in a wide-open parking lot, no escape in sight. I don't know what to do.

"This way!" Trey yells, beckoning, and I plunge after him. I don't know where he's leading us and I don't care; I'm just glad someone is taking charge.

Tanq's footsteps pound behind me; Emmaline keeps pace at my heels. I expect to feel a blast of excruciating heat at my back, a split second of blinding pain that heralds oblivion.

Trey's long legs eat up distance, and we struggle to keep up. He takes a sudden hard left; we follow. Something zings in the air, and all the hair on my skin stands straight up. A wave of heat blasts the skin of my face. I waste precious energy looking over my right shoulder. A glassy crater takes up the space our feet were moments ago.

"Here!" Trey yells. "In here."

He motions us into a tight alley between buildings, barely wide enough for my shoulders. My upper arm scrapes brick as Trey motions us through. He doesn't follow until we're inside. "Keep going," he orders, and I'm glad to obey.

It's musty and dark in here. I kick an empty beer can in my hurry; it pinballs against the walls before settling at the base of a struggling vine. The alley is too narrow for the dragonfly to follow, but it could still shoot at us. Or whatever its weapon does. I don't remember seeing a bullet or laser or any kind of projectile. Just light and heat. Maybe it's a different technology altogether.

I hit a dead end. Nothing ahead but a brick wall streaming with black moisture—either dirt or mold.

"There's nowhere to go," I say.

Trey crouches, yanking Tanq and me down by our sleeves. "Remember the hospital?" he says. "No sound, no movement. Maybe it will lose track of us."

I nod, then look up at the strip of cloudy sky between buildings. A shadow passes overhead, but the angle is all wrong and I can't tell what it is.

It passes again from a different direction, and this time I catch the telltale silver glint. It's higher up this time, and it suddenly darts away—eastward, I think—like a dog that's just seen a squirrel.

Beside me, Tanq begins to rock on her heels. Her eyes are glassy, and her fingers clutching her backpack tremble violently.

I grab one of her hands, and she jolts as if to skitter away.

"Tanq!" I whisper. "Stay with me, okay? Breathe. Like this." I demonstrate, inhaling through my nose for four counts, exhaling through my mouth for four. Just like Coach Dalrymple taught me.

She follows my lead. Inhaling, exhaling, her gaze never leaving my face. After a minute, her hand in mine wraps around my fingers, but she keeps breathing.

Emmaline looses a single bark and dashes away, toward the alley entrance. "No! Emmy, come back!" I rip away from

Tanq's hand and try to chase after my dog, but Trey is in my way, and the alley is too narrow to maneuver.

"You can't, Paige," Trey says, yanking me back down. "I'm so sorry, but you can't go after her."

I nod, gulping down a sob. Visions fill my head of Emmaline getting zapped out of existence, of a brand-new crater forming in the parking lot—

"Hey!" comes a male voice. "This way. Hurry!"

A shadowed face peeks at us from the alley entrance. I can't see more than pale skin and sandy blond hair.

"Holy shit, it's a *person*," Tanq says.

Suddenly Emmaline is there too, bouncing around beside her new friend, this mysterious human I can't get a good look at.

"The drone won't be distracted for long," he calls toward us. "You've got to hurry. C'mon."

Trey is the first to dislodge himself and squeeze back toward the entrance. I help Tanq to her feet, and we follow. Part of me twitches to run. Another part urges caution. A lifetime of "stranger danger" warnings is hard to shake, even in the apocalypse.

We exit the alley and blink against the relative brightness. A boy stands before us, seventeen or eighteen years old, with close-cropped blond hair, hazel eyes, broad shoulders, and smooth skin stretched over a jaw like a cinderblock. A pit bull in human form.

"I'm Wyatt," he says. "I'll explain more later, but for now you gotta follow me. We have to be quiet and fast, yeah?"

Trey gives him a sizing-up look, but he says, "Lead on."

Wyatt darts back into the parking lot. There's nothing else to do but chase after him.

He reaches the manhole cover with the Null sign on it, flips it up—turns out, it's on a hinge. "Down the ladder," he says. "Sorry, but I don't think the dog—"

"She's coming," Trey says. "Nonnegotiable. I'll carry her."

"Down the ladder?" Wyatt says incredulously.

"We don't leave teammates behind," Trey says. Then he squats, pats his chest, and says, "Up, up," like he's seen me do a hundred times, and even though they haven't practiced this together, Emmaline launches for him and buries herself in his arms like it's the most natural thing in the world.

Wyatt shrugs. "Okay, then. Follow me. Whoever's last has to pull the hatch shut."

I stare at the boy's back, thinking how Trey always makes everyone else go first, makes sure they're safe, before he looks to himself.

Wyatt descends feetfirst. Trey indicates for Tanq to follow. "Paige, you have to be the one to close the hatch," Trey says, his tone apologetic. "I only have one hand free."

I nod and watch him descend into the hole, using his legs to hug the ladder as he lowers himself with one hand. "Good girl, Emmaline," I hear him mutter. "Just stay still and this will all be over soon."

I don't know how deep the ladder goes, and I won't overestimate my strength. I'll have to be slow and careful.

Once Trey's head is out of sight, I hold on to the edge and

lower one leg until it finds a rung. Then the other. I'm halfway submerged into the ground when a glint of silver catches my eye.

I practically leap for the handle welded to the bottom of the hatch and yank it down, knocking the top of my skull. I teeter on the ladder for a terrifying second before realizing that I didn't hit my head very hard, and that the rung beneath my feet is perfectly sturdy. I duck down, pulling the latch fully closed; the clang of it snapping shut is so much louder than I anticipated.

Darkness closes in. There is only cold metal under my fingers, the purse swinging from my shoulder, the squeak of soles against metal and the heavy breaths of my friends as we slowly descend by feel and by faith.

The ladder goes on forever. Surely we're well below the surface of the lake by now. Below me, Emmaline starts to whine, and I worry that she'll panic and wiggle free of Trey's grasp and fall—

A drumbeat sounds, and light explodes around us, strobing into my brain. It's a moment before I realize that I'm only two rungs from the bottom, that Tanq, Trey, Wyatt, and Emmaline are waiting for me in a cement corridor that's bright with fluorescent lights. Wyatt stands by a wall, his hand on the giant switch he used to light the place up.

I hop the rest of the way and land lightly on my feet.

"This way," Wyatt says, his voice echoing. "Hurry. We're low on power, and I need to turn off the lights as soon as possible."

We follow him down the cement corridor. Dampness mars the edges where the walls meet the floor, and the fluorescent lights buzz above us. It's a little warmer down here than outside, which I did not expect.

"How did you know where to find us?" Trey asks. "Did you see us coming?"

"Yeah, we were watching on the vids. Hoped you'd figure out the manhole yourself, but then the drone came."

"You distracted it somehow," I say. "I watched it dart away."

"We set off some fireworks over by Cedar Point. Had them rigged remotely. That trick will only work once or twice more, though, before they get smart."

"I can't believe that worked even once," Tanq says.

"They seem really keyed to motion and light," Wyatt says. "We're not sure why. But it doesn't matter if it's a drone or one of their walkers—if you find yourself a decent shadow to hunker down in and keep real still, you're almost invisible to them."

That's why we escaped the one in the hospital by diving behind the gurney. Or how we avoided notice by crouching down in a basement entrance right after we found Tanq.

"The broadcast said not to travel at night," I point out. "Because it would put us at a disadvantage."

"They see better at night. Like maybe light is a distraction for them? I dunno, but during the day the shadow thing really works. Here we are." The corridor ends at a metal door. He reaches for the knob and opens it, and ushers us all inside.

We enter a huge hexagonal room with a lofted ceiling. High

shelves full of supplies stretch along one of the six walls, bunk beds poke out from two others, and a threadbare couch and a coffee table huddle up against another. In the very center of the room is an array of flat-screen monitors, all showing various live feeds around Sandusky.

A couple of doors lead to parts unknown, but before I can wonder about them, a man steps out from behind the flat screens. He's older, maybe late fifties, and short enough that his head would barely reach my chin. His black hair is halfway gone to gray, and a dyed black mustache shows white roots against his skin. Small black eyes are made brighter by a pair of round glasses that have slipped partway down a wide nose.

His smile is huge, revealing slightly crooked but bright-white teeth, and his small black eyes fill with moisture. "I'm so relieved you made it," he says. "I'm Manny Gomez. Welcome to the Sandusky Cell."

"Cell?" I say.

But Gomez ignores me, heads straight for Trey. He reaches out a hand to shake. Trey grasps it with obvious hesitation. "Trey Dawson. It's an honor and privilege to finally meet you."

"*What?* How do you know my—"

"Ethel Betts," Gomez says, moving on to Tanq. She stares at his offered hand without taking it. "I've heard so much about you. I'm glad you and Trey found each other."

Tanq continues to gape at his outstretched hand.

Gomez drops his hand. "Ethel, I know you've been through a lot—"

"Her name," I snap at him, "is Tanq."

"With a *q*," Trey says, just as emphatically.

Gomez blinks, stepping back.

He peers into Tanq's face. "No, you're definitely Ethel Be—"

Tanq crosses her arms, raises an eyebrow. "You heard my friends," she says.

He seems to catch himself. "I see. In that case, welcome, Tanq with a *q*. I can't tell you how happy I am to see you."

"How do you know our names?" I say. "Explain, please." Manny Gomez seems friendly enough. But this frisson of being known without knowing is making my belly squirm.

He walks over to me, lifts his chin, narrows his eyes. "My, you're tall. You and Mr. Dawson both."

I exchange a wry look with Trey. "Yeah, we get that a lot."

"Are you Becky Reese? You don't look like her photos except for that white-blond hair. But maybe—"

"I am not Becky Reese."

Manny Gomez opens his mouth. Closes it. Finally, he asks, in an almost-timid voice, "What is your name, please?"

"Paige Miller."

He gasps.

Wyatt steps forward. "The basketball player?" he says. "The one who can slam dunk?"

I'm suddenly even more uncomfortable, and I'm not entirely sure why.

"My god," Manny Gomez breathes. "You were *not* on my list. Young lady, I was not expecting you *at all*."

I don't know what I'm supposed to say to that.

"What's that mean?" Trey says. He angles his body protectively in front of me.

"Manny," Wyatt says, tapping his wrist where a watch should be.

"Yeah, thanks," Manny says. "We need to shut down the generator soon. So do you want answers to your questions? Or do you want hot showers and hot food now and answers in the morning?"

Trey answers, "Hot showers," at the same time that Tanq blurts out, "Hot food." Manny looks to see what my answer is. I nod toward my friends and say, "What they said."

But as he leads us through one of the doors, I'm still wondering what he means by *not expecting you at all*. Like maybe I don't belong here.

Late March?

I AM *CLEAN*.

The shower stall was narrow and low and made of cheap plastic, like in an RV. I had to duck down and contort myself to lather and rinse. But the hot water was the greatest thing that's happened to me in days. My shoulders and neck feel looser, my eyes clearer, my feet less sore.

We followed showers with a dinner of scrambled eggs, bacon, and sautéed bell peppers. Then we conked out on surprisingly comfortable cots.

Now, it's seven a.m., and all five of us and Emmaline are congregated at a metal fold-out dining table, eating hot cinnamon oatmeal with a side of buttered toast. The only indication it's morning comes from the vid screens, which show a tentative gray daylight creeping across the city.

I take a bite of oatmeal and catch Trey staring at me. His glance darts away when he notices me noticing. My face warms.

Manny Gomez—*Call me Manny!* he told us—pushes back his chair and dabs his mustache with a napkin. "You have been very patient," he said. "Thanks for agreeing to put this off last night—we're doing everything we can to save fuel. I know you have a thousand questions. So don't hold back. Everything I know is yours; you have but to ask."

I have *so* many questions, and they all compete in my head with such ferocity that I can't focus on a single one.

"Start with how you knew our names," Tanq says, indicating her and Trey. "But not Paige's."

"Yeah, start with that," I say. Emmaline puts her paws on my thighs, and I am the worst pushover, because I slip her a bite of toast.

"Very well," says Manny. "To understand that, we have to go back. About seven years."

Trey's eyes widen. "Seven years?" he says.

"Buckle up," Wyatt says. "This story is quite a ride."

"Manny?" I prompt.

"About seven years ago, we began to receive some strange transmissions."

"We? Who is 'we'?" I demand.

"Sorry, I am bad at telling stories," Manny says. "Back then I was a staff member for Congresswoman Joffries, who was chair of the House Committee on Science, Space, and Technology. It was a token chair position, a place where the house speaker often tossed someone they needed to keep happy, but didn't want to offer too much power to. I'm proud of the work we did, even though it rarely got covered in the press. We worked with NASA, SETI, the National Science Foundation, labs and institutes all over the country. We coordinated with the other congressional committees to—"

Tanq makes an exaggerated yawning motion.

"Okay, I'll get to the point. One of our SETI consultants approached the chairwoman with the most outlandish claim: Earth was receiving transmissions from an alien source."

"Wait, stop," says Tanq. "SETI?"

"Search for Extraterrestrial Intelligence," Trey says. At her expression, he adds, "I know it sounds wack, but they're cool. They use the search for extraterrestrial life as a framework to discover more about the origins of life in general."

"Nerd," she says, smiling.

"Trey has it right," Manny says. "Their contributions to science, particularly in regard to exoplanets and astrobiology have been . . . well, I'll be honest, I don't understand all that. I just know that one day we aides went in for our daily morning briefing with Congresswoman Joffries, and instead of the usual meeting around the conference table, she ushered us downstairs into a SCIF . . . uh, that is a Sensitive Compartmented Information Facility . . . to tell us that our friends at SETI had made contact with a hostile alien civilization, and that the world would be ending in approximately seven years."

We gape at him collectively. "You *knew*?" Trey says.

"Yes," Manny says.

"Then why didn't you tell anyone?" I ask, my voice coming out a little shrill. "We could have prepared, we could have stopped this from—"

Manny is shaking his head. "There was no stopping it," he says.

"He's getting to that part," Wyatt says. "Be patient."

"The Farmers were already here on Earth," Manny says. "And they had already infected us with the virus. They were just waiting for it to spread to every living human on the planet before hitting the kill switch."

"A ghost virus," Trey says. "Like a prion. Engineered to spread undetected until it was time to murder everyone at once."

I have no idea what a prion is, but Manny nods, saying, "It's definitely an engineered bug, tiny machines swimming through our blood, undetectable by us. I think the closest human technology equivalent would be nanobots, but again, I'm not really a science guy. Anyway, the aliens who contacted us were a splinter group, philosophically divided from the majority on how galactic life should be treated. They argued for granting us sentient status—which would have made our world off-limits for harvesting—but when their government refused, they went rogue and decided to warn us on the down low."

"Why couldn't it be stopped?" Tanq said. "You had seven years to come up with a way to stop it!"

"Because the only material known to neutralize the virus is something not found on Earth or even in our solar system.

You see, the *cure itself* is extraterrestrial."

"Holy shit," says Tanq.

"So, why didn't this splinter group bring the cure?" I ask.

"They did," Manny says. "As much as they possibly could without being detected. It's rare, even where they come from, and processing it into a human-compatible vaccine was almost beyond our capability."

"That's why we're alive," Trey says, his voice almost accusing. "Somehow, we got the cure."

"Yes," Manny says.

"That's what your 'list' is about," Tanq says. "It's people who got the vaccine."

"Exactly," Manny confirms.

"How?" says Trey. "How was it administered?"

"Flu shots," Manny says. "You and Tanq might not remember, but you attended the same flu shot clinic on the same day—you, Trey, did it as part of an Ohio State football team initiative—remember all those cameras?—and Tanq, you received it as part of a community welfare program for low-income families."

"I remember," Tanq whispers.

"When our selected candidates came in, they got a special shot. A little extra."

"I got a flu shot too," I say. "But I definitely did not get your vaccine."

"You must have," Manny says. "Or you would be dead. I suspect you accidentally got a vaccine meant for someone else. Which worked out fine; I think you are a stellar candidate."

"Wait," says Trey. "Candidate? You're saying you *chose* who lived and died?"

Uncomfortable silence settles heavy over the table.

"There was no other way," Wyatt says softly. "Each vaccine cost . . . tell them, Manny."

"Wyatt is correct. We had limited time and resources. Each vaccine cost hundreds of millions of US dollars. Well, first we had to create a secret facility to manufacture them, which alone cost 3.2 billion. Then we made as many as we could, every single year, until our informants in the splinter group told us it was time to deploy."

My chest is tight, and heat stings my eyes. It feels like I'm losing the people I love all over again. All those family dinners, car rides to Ryan's and my games, late night comedy shows with Paul, painting and decorating my bedroom with Mom, Netflix binges with Shawntelle . . . They were the walking dead all along, and we never even knew it. I lean forward against the table. "How many?" I ask. "How many vaccines did you deploy?"

Manny's lips press together, and it's a moment before he gathers himself enough to say, "Three thousand, four hundred, seventy-two. In all the world."

"And of those," Wyatt adds, "probably less than half survived the chaos."

"Planes fell out of the sky," Manny says, and his face grows haunted. "Cars piled up on freeways all over the world. Some people went full *Purge* and just started indiscriminately killing, then came a rash of suicides. . . ."

"And now drones and walkers are cleaning up the leftovers," Wyatt says.

"I watched a drone take out two kids," Trey says. "They were just walking down the sidewalk . . ."

"Were they infected?" Manny asks. "I don't remember two kids on our list."

Trey shrugs. "It was about two weeks ago, when there were still a few people left alive. I'm pretty sure they were sick, and after it happened, I got the hell out of there."

"You did the right thing," Manny says.

"How did you choose?" I ask. "How did you pick who got to live?" *How did you not pick my brother?* I want to scream. *Or my mom or stepdad? Or Shawntelle?*

"Oh, Paige, I know this is hard," Manny says. "All I can say is that we had so little time to figure everything out. So we prioritized those who were young—mostly late teens and early twenties—healthy, and smart, people we hoped would give humanity its best chance of survival."

"So, no disabled people?" Tanq says. "That's . . . gross."

"Oh, we definitely chose some disabled people," Manny says. "Though, to be honest, all candidates were exceptional in some way we hoped would be useful to survival. Several members of our committee argued that for humanity to survive, we had to make moral, human choices, that we couldn't let our selection process dissolve into a kind of eugenics. We also chose from all different ethnic groups, different societal strata. We prioritized indigenous peoples. We gave special consideration to those who had already lost many of their loved ones, hoping they'd have fewer people to mourn—this might have been silly on our part; I don't even know. And after all that, there was an element of randomization. We had far more candidates than we had vaccines. By a factor of thousands."

"You were short by about seven billion," Tanq mumbles.

"Hey, they did the best they could," Wyatt says. "And they picked *you*."

My face feels warm. They didn't pick me. The fact that I'm alive is an accident.

"Paige, you okay?" says Trey.

Tanq peers closer. "She looks like she's about to puke," she says.

"I shouldn't be here," I whisper.

"Of course you should," Trey says.

"I wasn't chosen. I wasn't a candidate."

"*Someone* gave you the vaccine," says Manny. "It might have been accidental, but I suspect someone recognized you and made a judgment call on the spot."

"No," I say. "At least I don't have to worry about that. I did not get a vaccine meant for someone else. Honestly, I couldn't live with that."

Manny says, "I understand how hard—"

"Dude, she got sick," Tanq says.

Manny's eye grow as wide as basketballs.

"She was in a coma for more than a week," Trey says. "She's getting healthy fast, but when I met her she looked like something out of a zombie movie." At my raised eyebrow, he says, "Sorry, Paige, but you know it's true."

Manny is still gaping, but his gaze roams my face, my body. My skin prickles under his scrutiny.

"I just thought she was really skinny," Wyatt says.

I hate this feeling, that my body is a thing for everyone else to study and evaluate, like it's not really my own. If I could crawl out of my skin and disappear somewhere I would. My foot starts to bob with nervous energy.

"If this is true," Manny says slowly, "then you might be the only person in the whole world who has recovered from the virus naturally. You might have blood plasma that could . . . eh, I guess it doesn't matter if everyone's already dead. But years down the road, if we get a chance to study this virus in depth, you might provide some answers."

He probably means it as an encouragement or something, but I flash to a potential future: me lying on a cold metal table, tubes sticking out of me, while people in lab coats and face visors poke and prod and nod knowingly to each other.

Which is ridiculous, because where is anyone going to get a clean lab coat these days?

"We thought the virus had a 100 percent mortality rate," Manny says. "The fact that you survived . . . Even if the mortality rate was only 99.99 percent, there could be . . . If you don't mind, Paige, I'd love to hear more about your experience. Some of the details of your illness might be helpful in—"

"Why didn't you tell anyone the end was coming?" Trey interrupts, with a glance toward me.

I give him a quick smile of gratitude.

"You could have warned us all," he says, "and given us a

chance to put our affairs in order . . . If I could have said good-bye to Teena—"

"We almost did," Manny says. "We debated for days. Even after we were full speed into our plan, we continued to debate. But I think we made the right decision."

"How do you figure?" Tanq says.

"Well, first of all, we didn't want to cause panic."

"Like the panic that ensued when everyone started dying?" I practically yell. "You mean *that* panic?"

"No," Manny says calmly. "I mean a different kind entirely. The kind where people who have access to a nuclear arsenal and nerve gas and weapons of mass destruction panic and think they can contain an alien virus by bombing it into submission."

The thought of nuclear bombs makes me fall silent, but I'm still seething.

"Our president at the time had already bungled a pandemic," Manny adds. "And we were concerned that he would do everything in his power to save his family and billionaire friends—and no one else."

"Wow, you didn't even tell the president," Tanq says.

"We did not. It was a time of growing autocracy all across the world. We felt strongly that several world leaders had the potential to respond with excessive force. So the congress-woman built a secret coalition of politicians, scientists, and business leaders—those she *knew* she could trust—and no one else."

"How did you pull the resources together to manufacture

the vaccines?" Trey asks, his voice softer than before. "If each one cost hundreds of millions . . ."

"We took money wherever we could find it. We diverted funds from the science budget, the defense budget. We got dark money from the Ways and Means Committee. We made deals with private investors, inside the US and out. We made compromises. For example, the owner of some acreage we needed outside Toluca, Mexico, got a vaccine in exchange for funding the construction of an underground facility. The facility itself cost less than the vaccine, but we were able to accomplish it in secret with very little red tape, which saved us years of time." Manny's eyes grow distant. "Maybe he's alive down there right now. I hope he kept his word to broadcast and attract survivors."

Emmaline has given up on begging more breakfast tidbits, though I suspect Tanq and Trey both helped fill her belly, and now she noses around the hexagonal room, sniffing every bit of furniture or electronics.

"A facility like this one?" I ask. "How many are there? Are they all broadcasting?"

He points at me, saying, "A very smart question, and I'm so glad you asked."

Emmaline whimpers.

"Before we get into that," I say, "is there a place I can take my dog potty?"

Manny appears vaguely disappointed to have his lecture interrupted, but he says, "There's an egress tunnel behind the kitchen. It'll dump you out near the yacht club. Lots of trees for cover there, but you still have to be very, very careful."

"I'll show her," Wyatt says, standing from the table.

Trey jumps up, so quickly he knocks the table with his knee. "I'll go, too," he says, then adds, "I don't mind seeing the lay of the land."

"I'm going to keep eating," Tanq says around a mouthful of toast.

"Emmy, come," I say, and she trots over, eyes bright with anticipation.

Wyatt leads us into the kitchen, an industrial-looking affair with stainless steel counters and more fluorescent lighting. He's several paces ahead, when I whisper to Trey, "You don't trust him, do you?"

He shakes his head no. "I especially don't like the way he's looking at Tanq," he says.

I hadn't noticed. I'll have to pay more attention.

At the far end of the kitchen, Wyatt opens another door, revealing a dark, round tunnel made of faded bricks. The tunnel is unlit, so Wyatt flicks on a flashlight.

"Is this a sewer?" Trey asks.

"Used to be," Wyatt says. "The city closed off this tunnel when they upgraded their sewer system a while back. Manny and his friends did some work on it, I think, to make it useable again."

"Are all the 'facilities' underground?" I ask. "Like the one in Mexico?"

"Almost."

"How many are there?" Trey asks.

"I'll let Manny answer all those questions for you," Wyatt says. "Watch your step; this part is slippery."

Emmaline runs ahead, and I let her, hoping she'll get her wiggles out and be able to settle down when we get back.

"So where are you from, Wyatt?" Trey asks.

"Ann Arbor."

A long silence. The air in this tunnel is suddenly humid and thick.

"So, a Michigan fan?" Trey asks, and his voice is cold, cold, cold.

"I was headed there for school in the fall," Wyatt says. "I know you were going to Ohio State. Everyone expected you to be starting QB your sophomore year. I guess that makes us sworn enemies."

"Guess so."

"You're both joking, right?" I say. "We have more important things—"

"Of course," says Wyatt. "But the greatest rivalry in all of sports history should live on, even in the apocalypse."

"Maybe it shouldn't," Trey says.

"Huh? Why not?"

"Paige asked me a question on the ride here, about what keeps us going," Trey says. "And it's got me thinking. So many of our hopes and dreams—our reasons for living—are determined by sociocultural constructs. Here's one dumb example: every year on Michigan Friday my mom would bake a huge cake that said *Beat Michigan*. She spent days planning that cake, hours making it. Teena and I looked forward to it every year." Trey takes a deep breath. "So what happens when all of that goes away? No football scholarship, no big game, no Christmas, no future. Is life worth living *intrinsically*? Is the world even worth saving after you've lost everything you were living for?"

"Of course it is!" Wyatt says. "Just because you can't eat cake—"

"Okay, but *why*? So we can have a sports rivalry?"

"Sure. Why not?"

"Is that really what you're fighting for? Tanq would probably prefer that humanity die off entirely; it hasn't exactly been good to her, and I'm not sure I blame her. Paige, what do you think?"

Emmaline bounds back to us and circles around, trying to coax us to move forward at a faster clip. Herding dogs are going to herd, I suppose.

"Some things are instinct," I say. "Like my need to survive. I can't even explain why. My survival instinct is so strong that even though everyone I love died and everything I was working so hard toward disappeared like smoke, I want to live. I have to try. I don't have a choice. And I'm glad I didn't give up right away, because I have Emmaline now, and you and Tanq, and it kind of feels like we've been together for years, and if something happened to any of you, I would . . . I just want to live. I want *all* of us to live."

Our steps echo for a moment as the boys consider what I said. It's too dark to see well, but I feel Trey's gaze on my face.

"Sorry if you were looking for something deep and philosophical," I add.

"I agree with Paige," Wyatt says. "I want to live too. And maybe later, we can start rebuilding some of the social-collateral constructs Trey was talking about—"

"Sociocultural," Trey corrects.

"That's what I said. Let's rebuild those. Maybe we don't ever have a rivalry again. Or Christmas. Maybe we'll start something new."

"I like that idea," Trey says tentatively. "Trying to recreate everything we've lost would just *hurt*, you know? So let's rebuild, but with something new. Maybe even something better."

"Yeah, something better," Wyatt says.

"Michigan still sucks," Trey says.

The tunnel dumps us into a green area surrounded by trees, which provide plenty of cover. Emmaline goes potty without me giving her the command; poor girl held it all night and all morning. We let her run around sniffing stuff for a few minutes, using the time to breathe the fresh air. Trey and Wyatt watch the sky. It's warmer today, though drizzly, with not a trace of sunshine. To our right is a marina filled with yachts already in their spring berths. Directly ahead is a view of Lake Erie beyond the peninsula, stretching all the way to the horizon, just like an ocean. But it's not an ocean to anyone paying attention. It smells different, for one, and the color—a steady slate blue in winter that turns to pea-soup green during the summer algae bloom—is like no ocean I've ever seen.

Reluctantly, I recall Emmaline, and we head back through the tunnel to the "facility." At the dining table, Manny and Tanq are chatting happily about modern art, while Tanq pours a gallon of sugar over her second bowl of oatmeal.

"Any trouble?" Manny asks.

"None," says Wyatt. "I was worried the dog would run off or bark, but he's a really good boy."

"Emmaline is the *best* girl," I say.

"You were about to tell us about the other facilities," Trey says as we settle back into our seats.

"Yes! Facilities!" Manny says. "There are a few on each continent. Three in North America, for example. Four in Asia. We scattered them strategically and made sure a handful of potential survivors were within a reasonable geographic distance of each. They're mostly underground, like this one. They're equipped with broadcasting equipment, power, supplies. They're basically safehouses for survivors. There are other mini-facilities throughout the world also, though most of them aren't quite the secure bunker this one is. We left caches of supplies everywhere, marked so survivors could find them but the Farmers could not. Before the chaos hit, every single facility had reported that they were in good working order.

"But then, one by one, we lost contact with them all. The last one we heard from was the Ak-Chin Cell outside of Phoenix. Then all the power grids in North America went down for good."

Tanq scrapes oatmeal from her bowl. Trey rubs at his chin.

"What good are bunkers," I say, "if they're all just going to run out of power, like this one?"

"Some have solar power," Manny says. "Even this one has a small solar array that powers a few lights and ventilation. We could survive here a long time; we just won't be able to broadcast much longer or keep our food refrigerated or heat water. . . . Anyway, like I said before, limited resources and time. We threw together what we could with what we had, as fast as we could. If we'd had another year or two to work with, this facility would have been fitted with full solar or wind."

Emmaline has finally decided that Manny is interesting enough to check out. She creeps toward him, stretches her neck forward to give his thigh a sniff. To his credit, Manny does not react, just calmly lets her do her thing. "I'll be honest," he says. "This was not a foolproof plan. Solar tech needs maintenance. All the facilities need maintenance. Without manufacturing infrastructure to support them, I expect they'll begin to fail within a few years."

"You should have picked my stepdad," I say, my voice tight. "To get the vaccine, I mean. He knew all about wind power."

Manny gives me a sad smile. "We should have done a lot of things, Paige."

"Tell us how to find these caches of supplies," Tanq says, and she's leaning forward, eyes bright. I'm not sure what it is about supplies that has her so excited.

"They're marked," Manny says. "We used a symbol

common enough throughout the world that they wouldn't attract Farmer suspicion."

"The Null sign!" Tanq blurts.

"Yep. Only the red ones mark caches. All the others are just there for camouflage. The Farmers are colorblind."

"Interesting," Trey says. "And they don't see into shadows very well. . . . Their vision must have evolved completely differently than ours did. The one we saw didn't have eyes—more like depressions in its face, like it had eyes once upon a time, but they were a vestigial organ that gradually disappeared. . . ."

"Wow," says Wyatt. "You don't talk like a Black guy at all."

Trey's face freezes. He takes a deep breath through his nose.

"Holy shit," Tanq says.

"Huh?" says Wyatt.

"Congratulations on being racist even in the apocalypse," Tanq says.

"What? I was just observing . . . There's nothing wrong with—"

"Wyatt," I say. "Now is not a good time for you to talk." It's something Shawntelle used to tell me whenever I said something ignorant.

"One of the reasons Trey was chosen," Manny says carefully, not seeming to address any one of us in particular, "was his natural curiosity and his aptitude for STEM fields." He pins Trey with a gaze. "So, you saw one? A walker?"

Trey squares his shoulders, as though throwing off what just happened. I wonder how many times throughout his life he's had to brush away moments like this. "Yeah, at the

Ohio State Medical Center. Strangest thing I've ever seen. But also strangely humanlike. Maybe humans and Farmers had a common ancestor?"

Manny nods. "Some of our friends at SETI speculated about that exactly," he says. "I mean, the panspermia hypothesis has been around a long time, and—"

"Back to the Null sign," Tanq says. "We look for the red ones?"

"Exactly. We spent the last couple of years blanketing the whole world in null signs. Well, and theta signs, but that was mostly in Russia. The Farmers will see those symbols everywhere. But only survivors will be able to tell which ones mark caches or lead to facilities."

Tanq starts giggling, and I think I know why.

"That graffiti artist in Columbus," I say. "Called himself Null. He tagged the whole city with that symbol."

"Columbus cops hated him," Trey says. "Several guys on my team had to do community service one summer. Spent the whole time painting over null signs. Seemed pretty useless. They'd just reappear."

"Null was not just one person," Manny says. "There were many, many Nulls, all over the world. It became a cultural touchstone in Ohio. In Madrid too, though there they call him El Nihilista."

"Wyatt, did you ever see a null symbol in Ann Arbor?" Trey asks. A peace offering.

Wyatt is sitting back in his chair, arms crossed. "I'm not allowed to talk. I'm just listening."

Before I can tell him he's an ass, Tanq doubles over with laughter.

"Tanq?" I say.

"I can't believe it," she gasps out. "All that time. The null symbol was literally marking the end of the world. I wish I'd known. I would have. . . . " Laughter overtakes her so that she's unable to speak.

"I'm very confused," I say. I'm not the only one. Wyatt's gaze is fixed fast on her face.

But Manny is grinning at her. "Meet one of our Nulls. Ethel here—sorry, *Tanq*—was hired to do some tagging."

I gasp. "You're Null?"

Tanq nods, wiping tears off her cheeks. "It was great. I got paid to vandalize. It's the only way I could afford my . . . I had no idea who was hiring me or why, but when you need cash as bad as I did, you don't ask questions. I never did any red ones though. Someone else must have been hired to do those."

Trey claps her on the back. "I've been hanging out with a celebrity this whole time."

Tanq rolls her eyes, saying, "And yet you're the one who demanded tribute in Red Vines."

"My next Red Vines are yours," he says, putting his hand over his heart as though swearing an oath.

"So, all three of you are famous," Wyatt says, glaring. "Household names, newspaper coverage. You realize none of that matters now, right?"

I'm not sure what he's trying to say, or why he's so angry. It's a shame that an ass like Wyatt was considered a "candidate" and given the vaccine.

Or maybe that's too harsh. I need to be better than this. Better than Wyatt, at least.

"You're right, Wyatt," I say. "None of that matters. Manny, we have more questions."

"Hit me," says Manny.

"Why? Why did the Farmers come? What do they want?"

Tanq adds, "And why do you call them the Farmers? Trey and Paige called them the Orkins, because we all got exterminated. 'Farmers' sounds less . . . badass."

"Orkins," Manny muses. "I like that. Our friends at the Ak-Chin Cell call them the Colonists." Manny rubs his upper arms as though he's just gotten a chill. "You can call them whatever you want. I just know they came here to harvest the earth's resources. According to the Allies, they've done this to dozens of worlds. For some reason, they desperately need planets with carbon-based life, which are rare. The Farmers are so much more advanced than us in most technological areas, so it was no problem for them to engineer a way to destroy the earth's dominant species and take our carbon-rich planet for themselves."

"What do they need carbon for?" Trey asks. "Do they eat it?"

"I don't know," Manny says. "But everything that's happened so far is just the beginning."

"You mean it's going to get worse?" I say.

"Oh, yes. The drones, the walkers—they are merely a vanguard, tasked with preparing the planet. The full invading force is yet to come."

"Oh, my god," Tanq says. "When are they coming? How many?"

"Millions," Manny says. "Maybe more. We expect them to arrive in about three years, give or take."

Silence around the table. My chest is tight, and I can't seem to get enough air. Emmaline nuzzles my hand, aware that something is wrong.

"That's how you've been able to survive so far," Manny says. "There just aren't very many of them yet. Right now, you can travel miles without encountering one. But when the full invading force arrives, they will swarm across the planet and there will be no safe place to hide."

"Then why bother with all this?" Tanq says, making a vague but expansive gesture. "What's even the point? If we're all just going to die in a few years anyway?"

Manny is nodding. "That," he says, "is the right question, Tanq. We did all this because the next three years provide a window of opportunity. A chance. It's a small chance, don't get me wrong, but for the next three years, we might actually be able to fight back."

"Still sounds like you should have given the vaccine to a bunch of soldiers," Wyatt mumbles.

Manny opens his palms. "If we'd had more time . . ."

"*How* are we supposed to fight back?" Trey says. "That's not enough time to find all the other cells, form a fighting force. We certainly can't cross an ocean, and if we could, it's not like anyone here speaks Russian or Chinese."

"You're thinking like a quarterback," Manny says. With a

look in my direction, he says, "You need to think like a point guard."

"Huh?" says Trey.

"How is being a point guard different from being a quarterback?" Manny asks me.

My cheeks warm at being put on the spot. But I know exactly what he's getting at. "I only have a five-person team to work with," I say, looking around the table. Me, Trey, Tanq, Wyatt, and Manny make five. "On the court, I'm always looking for penetration. Holes in the defense."

"I do that too—" Trey starts, but I put up a hand.

"I know you do, but I don't have a bunch of offensive lineman to bludgeon a hole for me. And I can't push an opposing player out of my way to make my own hole, or they get a free chance to score. Football is like a semitruck compared to basketball."

"Football is a precision sport," Trey says. "Probably even more complicated than basketball."

"But it's a *contact* sport," I say. "I'm know I'm oversimplifying, but in basketball, too much contact gets you penalized. When I'm looking for penetration, I'm looking to dodge, feint, pass . . . tricky stuff."

Manny is nodding along like his head is a buoy on a stormy day. "Small teams, no contact, tricky maneuvers. That's how we'll do it."

Trey is leaning forward on the table, his hands steepled, his eyes narrowed. "Do what, exactly? Tanq warned us this might be a trap, you know. And right now it feels like you lured us here to use us for something."

"No!" Manny says, looking horrified. "No, no, no! You don't *have* to do anything. I will present you with choices, and you get to decide."

Trey seems skeptical.

"What choices?" I say.

"Well, first," Manny says, ticking off his forefinger, "you may choose to do nothing. Stay here for a while and wait to see if any others respond to our broadcast. Lie low, use the supply caches and safe houses when and if you need them. Survive as long as you can. Who knows? Maybe you'll find a place where you can hide for years, or even decades. Maybe you'll make peace with the invaders. Maybe just by surviving long enough to learn more about them, you'll equip yourselves to make better decisions later. This is a valid option and a logical choice."

"Second choice," Wyatt says, "is to start establishing contact with other cells."

"Yes," Manny says. "That's the one Wyatt likes. Safety in numbers, right? It would be dangerous, though. With all the power plants in emergency shutdown, there's no way to communicate long distance. The only way to reestablish contact is to travel there in person. I expect it was difficult just getting here from Columbus, yes?"

We nod confirmation. I flash back to the crater in the Flying J parking lot, smoking and glassy where the RAV4 once sat.

He says, "Imagine how hard it will be to traverse a whole continent? With walkers and drones possibly waiting around every corner?"

"But not impossible," Wyatt says. "Like you said, there aren't that many Farmers yet. We can travel miles without encountering one."

"Wyatt," Trey says. "Why does Plan B get your vote?"

Wyatt hesitates, like Trey is laying some kind of trap for him. But he says, "I figure if we're going to find any of the other cells, we have to do it now, before the full invasion. We won't be able to travel at all with swarms of Farmers crawling all over the earth. So we should find as many as we can, while we can."

"That makes sense," Trey says.

Encouraged, Wyatt continues, "And I'd like to compare notes with the others. Like, maybe they've been able to observe stuff we haven't? And even though I have the skills to handle a northern winter without modern conveniences, not everyone does. I think my particular talents—the reason I was a 'candidate'—are best used helping other people. Oh, and yeah, what Manny said about safety in numbers."

"So you're one of those survivalist people?" Tanq says.

"I'm not sure what you mean by that, but, yeah, I know some stuff," Wyatt says, his gaze steady on her face.

"That's great, Wyatt," I say. "That'll come in really handy."

Tanq glares at me, as if saying, *Why are you giving that dog a cookie?*

I ignore her, telling myself I'll explain later how, even though Wyatt is an ass, there are *only five of us.* "What's the third choice?" I ask Manny.

"We fight."

"Like a point guard," I say. "What does that mean exactly?"

"Fight against what?" Trey asks. "You know a way to take down those drones?"

"I'm not fighting anything," Tanq says, crossing her arms. "I like Plan A, lie low and eat all the Red Vines of the world right up until the very end. Go out painting shit."

"I like Red Vines," Wyatt blurts.

"Like I said, all valid choices," Manny says. "You may vote on it later, if you like. Or you may go your separate ways, if that works best for you. But to answer your question, Trey, yes, I do know a way to take down those drones."

"What?" I say.

"Well, the ones in our area, anyway."

Trey says, "Let me just echo Paige with another *what?*"

Manny's lips press together into a mirthless smile. "Come with me. I will show you."

We're huddled together before the flat-screen array. One screen shows the yacht club; I'm willing to bet Manny and Tanq watched over us as we took Emmaline out to do her business. Another focuses on the parking lot with the manhole we used yesterday. Still another shows the grassy, rolling hills of Washington Park.

Manny reaches for a wireless mouse. A "toggle camera" prompt pops up on the Washington Park screen, and Manny clicks it. The view of grassy lawn cuts out and is instantly replaced by the vast slate-blue water of Lake Erie. The camera must be mounted on the edge of a dock, because there's no land anywhere in sight. Just endless water stretching slightly curved across the horizon.

"You want us to fight . . . water?" Tanq asks.

"Give it a minute," Manny says. "It's almost time."

"That's not the view from Sandusky," Trey points out. "You'd be able to see islands, or maybe Cedar Point."

"You are correct. You're looking at a live camera feed from farther east, closer to the Pennsylvania border. It was a lot of hard work, setting up this camera feed and powering it long distance."

I say, "Why would you—"

"Just wait for it," Wyatt says.

We wait.

With no landmarks anywhere, I don't trust my internal distance gauge. But it sure seems like I'm viewing miles and miles of water. Occasionally, on clear days, you can see Canada from one of the islands off the coast of Sandusky, but certainly not from this camera. I reassess the idea that Lake Erie does not seem like an ocean.

"There," Wyatt says pointing. "See?"

He indicates a tiny bubble at the farthest edge of our view. The bubble grows, turning white. No, it's more like an arrowhead, pouring water as it thrusts upward from the lake, reaching ever higher.

"What in holy Hades is that?" Tanq says.

We stare as the thing grows and grows, stretching up in telescoping layers until it's impossibly tall, taller than the tallest skyscraper. Water continues to fall down the sides for several seconds. Then the pinnacled top unfurls like a daisy, metal petals stretching wide, revealing a glowing stamen.

I hold my breath as the stamen grows bright, bright, brighter. Suddenly, a beam of light shoots upward, an eye-searing laser of white that burns away the thick storm clouds, forming a hole in the sky.

"My god," Trey says. "Is that a spaceship?"

"No," Manny says. "It was transported here."

The stream of light continues unabated. I can't tell how high it reaches; the clouds block our view.

"It does that all day long," Wyatt says.

Water suddenly blasts the camera, then slips away, leaving the lens dripping. It took a minute for the waves caused by that thing to reach the shore.

"It's a terraforming machine," Manny says. "Well, not *terra*forming so much as Farmer-planet-forming. They're remaking our planet to be more like theirs. Surely you've noticed the relentless clouds? The greenish color of the sky?"

I snap my head to look at him. "I thought it was from all the dead bodies."

"Smart girl," he says. "It *was*, partly. So many decomposing bodies caused a quick injection of methane into our atmosphere, which gave the Farmers a jumpstart on terraforming. We think they breathe methane instead of oxygen."

Tanq's eyes are wide with horror. Trey's are widened too, though I suspect with fascination. "How does that thing in the lake help them terraform?" he says.

"Not sure," says Manny. "But several appeared in the final

days of the chaos, every single one landing in a body of fresh water. We rushed to put cameras in place; that one is literally duct-taped to the end of a dock. Other towers landed in Lake Tahoe, in Lakes Tanganyika and Victoria in Africa, Lake Baikal in Russia. . . . I suspect they're mining them for hydrogen."

Trey's gaze is fixed on the giant machine tower. I get the feeling he would reach through the screen and touch it if he were able. "So this . . . thing . . . pulls hydrogen from the water, mixes it with carbon somehow, and shoots it into the upper atmosphere."

"I think that's about the size of it," Manny says. "I don't know why they don't use ocean water."

"Maybe sodium chloride interferes with their process?" Trey says.

"Could be. In any case, this is one of the biggest ones, or so we observed before everything went completely dark; a day or so after everyone died, all the power plants went into auto shutdown, and we couldn't talk to each other anymore. But I figure that three other Great Lakes drain into Erie, so it could go a long, long time before the lakes are depleted. Or maybe it will drain Lake Erie and then move down to Lake Ontario or up to the much deeper Lake Huron. We just don't know very much yet."

An invading force. Depleted lakes. An atmosphere full of methane. Manny was right: everything's going to get a whole lot worse.

I take a deep breath, profoundly conscious of air's passage

through my nostrils, the way my chest rises as it fills my lungs. It feels *good*. Air suddenly seems like a precious extravagance. "How long?" I ask. "Until we can't breathe our own air anymore?"

"Not sure. Three years until it's comfortable for the Farmers. You've seen a walker, so you know they're already out and about. The keeper assigned to the Nanjing Cell in China theorized that the alien cloaks trap and retain methane from the atmosphere, their version of an oxygen mask, I guess. Which gives them a way to function outside. Methane is not toxic to humans, so we hope our atmosphere will remain breathable to us for a very long time."

Wyatt says, "It might cause some health problems over time, though. If anyone lives that long."

"Maybe," Manny agrees. "If it displaces too much oxygen, or burns up, creating carbon monoxide. And we expect it will cause planet-wide ecological catastrophe. Methane is a greenhouse gas, after all, and the more the Farmers shoot into the air, the hotter this place is going to get. Between that and the depletion of our freshwater lakes, well, let's just say the earth as we knew it will cease to exist."

Tanq collapses into a chair beside the keyboard and drops her face into her hands. "I didn't want everyone to die," she mutters. "But when they did, I wasn't too sad. Humans are shit. But the earth? I don't want *anything* to happen to *her*."

"Does this mean you want to fight?" Trey asks. "Plan C?"

"I don't know," she murmurs. "I just don't know."

I point to the giant tower filling the vid screen. "Manny, when you say 'fight,' you mean that?"

"Yep."

"With a five-person team," I clarify.

"Definitely."

"I don't want to go anywhere near that thing," I say.

Wyatt raises his hand. "Another vote for not going near it," he says.

But Trey is leaning forward, eyes bright. "What did you have in mind?"

"I'm so glad you asked, Trey." Manny points to the screen showing the yacht club marina. "We have a boat. See that beauty? Her name is *Tardis*, after the greatest show on television. She can take us where we need to go."

He's indicating a white boat with bright blue trim. The camera isn't close enough to make out much detail.

"She's fueled up, sleeps four, even has a tiny kitchen—"

"Manny, your boat is nice," I say. "But we could get there in a rowboat if we had to. How do we *take that thing down*?"

He grins. "Easy peasy. We blow it up."

"It's from *another planet*," Tanq says.

"It's vulnerable," Manny says. "The Farmers do not expect resistance. Their structure has no defenses. It's made of some kind of organic polymer, just like our plastics. It's probably sturdier than anything we could make. Likely impervious to weather. But it's not indestructible."

I stare at the tower on the vid screen. It sure looks indestructible to me.

"Those dragonflies seem like pretty good defense to me," I say.

"Dragonflies?" Manny asks.

"Sorry, I mean the drones. That's what we called them on the way here."

"Hmm, they do look like dragonflies. I like that."

"You said you knew a way to take them down?" Trey reminds him.

Manny nods. "Take down the tower, and the . . . dragonflies go down with it."

"Really?" Trey says. "You know that for sure?"

"That's what the Allies said."

"These Allies," I say. "Do you have a way to contact them? Will they help us?"

Manny frowns. "I have no idea how to communicate with them, or even if they're still here on Earth. Any contact with them was way above my pay grade. I never even saw one."

So, really, Manny knows nothing. Everything he's telling us is something he heard secondhand. We came here to get answers, and instead we're getting speculation.

Well, maybe that's not fair. Manny is doing the best he can. Everyone did the best they could when this thing hit. I don't know what I would have done differently, except make sure my family and Shawntelle would be saved.

Which might be why it's a good thing I wasn't in charge. I would have fought with my last breath to save the people I loved. If everyone had done that, the five of us would not be standing here in this bunker right now.

"So," I say. "How do we blow it up?"

Manny's face turns sheepish. "Actually, I was hoping you all could help me figure out that part."

"What?" Tanq says. "You want us to consider risking our lives and you don't even have a plan?"

"I have a boat," Manny reminds us. "We just need an explosive."

"And a delivery method," Trey says. "Is there a military base nearby? Maybe we can find a cache of weapons."

Wyatt brightens. "Like grenade launchers, C4 charges, or maybe rockets."

"Nothing nearby," Manny says.

"Even if we could figure out a way to blow it up, why bother?" I ask. "There are a bunch of towers, right? What good does it do to take this one down?"

"It's the biggest," Manny says. "Take this one down, and the Farmers will be forced to delay their invasion. Also, it's proof of concept. If we succeed, we know it's possible for the others to be destroyed too. At one point, the Allies suggested that if we became enough of a nuisance, the Farmers might stop their invasion altogether. It would be too costly. We could literally save the world by destroying this one tower. We could definitely save the world by destroying two or three."

We are silent a long moment.

Then Wyatt says, "Plan B isn't looking too bad, yeah?"

"I'm still leaning toward Plan A," Tanq says. "Eat Red Vines and paint until I die."

A movement on the vid screen catches my eye. In front

of the tower and slightly left is a boat, distant and small, its hull flashing white between lake swells. It lists to the side, unmoored and unguided. A ghost ship drifting on the water.

Maybe there's a dead body or two inside.

I peer closer. Now that I'm attuned to the idea, I notice a few other blots against the water, rolling with the waves, lumpy and vague at this distance. Lake detritus, tossed there by wind and wave. Or maybe they're boats—or the remnants of boats, come loose from their docks, pounded by surf and other bits of garbage.

The Great Lakes are probably filled with ghost ships right now.

"Does anyone know how to make a bomb?" Tanq says. "What about you, Wyatt? You know all that survivalist stuff."

"How is bomb making 'survivalist stuff'?" he asks. "And no, I don't know how to make a bomb."

"Too bad the internet is down," Trey says. "You could always find info like that on the internet."

I look around at all of them, unable to keep the surprise from my face. Are they actually considering this? Am *I* actually considering this?

"Paige?" Trey says. "Any secret bomb-making expertise?"

"God, no," I say. "But . . ." I look back at the ghost ship drifting across the vid screen. Almost against my will, an idea is forming.

"But what?" says Manny.

"We could drive a ship right into that tower," I say.

"Not the *Tardis*!" Manny says, too quickly. "She's not big enough to do any real damage."

"No, I mean a real ship," I clarify. "Your puddle-putter is safe."

He gives me a mock glare.

"You really want to crash that tower?" Trey says.

"Yeah. Maybe. Well, not just crash. Crash *and* explode. Like . . ." I gasp. "A coal barge! Those things are huge. We could light the coal, plant some kind of explosive in the prow, push it right up to the wall . . ."

"Wow," says Tanq. "You want to take out an alien invader in the most Ohio way possible."

"The tugboats that push those coal flats don't go very fast," Wyatt says.

"No, but they're really powerful," says Manny. "Even a small impact, magnified by some kind of explosion, could sink that tower. Paige, you might be a genius."

"Or an idiot," I say. "I can't believe I'm considering this."

"Consider," Manny says, looking around at all of us. "That's all I ask of you. There is no wrong decision, and whatever you decide, I'm behind you."

I'm not sure he's right about that. Plan A is less likely to get us killed right away. But Plan C is more likely to save humanity. Plan B feels like a compromise between the two, but when it comes to my life or the lives of my fellow humans, I'm not sure compromise is something I'm interested in.

"Take a day or two to think about it," Manny says. "Talk it out. I swore an oath to collect as many survivors as possible, and that's what I plan to do until that generator fuel runs out."

"When will that be?" Trey asks.

"About two and a half days. So eat up all the perishable

goods and enjoy your hot showers while you can."

Tanq shoots up from her chair and heads for the kitchen. Since meeting her, I'm pretty sure I've watched her consume more calories than Trey and I combined. Wyatt stares after her for a moment, then decides to follow.

As one, Trey and I go after them, neither of us wanting to leave her alone with Wyatt, but at the last second, Manny's hand reaches up and grabs Trey's shoulder.

"Give Wyatt a chance," Manny says under his breath. "He's a good kid. Lots of potential. He'll learn."

Trey shrugs off his hand. "I've heard that my whole life. Why do people like him get so many chances?"

"They shouldn't," Manny says. "It's not right. Believe me, I understand. But we can't afford to lose even one person."

Trey says, "So you're telling me his privilege extends even into the apocalypse."

Manny opens his mouth. Closes it.

I say, "Manny, if you really feel that we can't afford to lose even one person, why are you encouraging us to attack that tower? We could all die."

"Or we could all live," he says. "Now go. Play cornhole or something. I have work to do."

I've never played cornhole indoors before. We're in the kitchen, in the middle of our third game. Trey and I won the first, tossing bean bags onto a board that says "Life is good, but it's even better at the Lake." Tanq and Wyatt won the second game. This is the tiebreaker.

Between turns, Tanq is gobbling strawberry yogurt like it's going out of style. Emmaline runs back and forth between us and the board, making herself part of the game using a set of rules I'm not privy to. Whenever a bag flies through the air, she gives a little yelp, like it's the most exciting thing that's ever happened to her.

Wyatt is fixated on the board, his pit bull jaw frozen like a block of ice as though afraid to say too much. Maybe he feels like the odd man out, which is fine with me. I can't help but wonder, though, what potential Manny sees in him.

So I throw the poor puppy a bone.

"Wyatt, did you leave a lot of family behind to come here?" I ask as I toss the bag. It lands just south of the hole, but remains on the board. One point.

"Sure. I mean they were all dead, but yeah." He says it casually, but his cheek muscles work overtime to conceal something.

"Sisters? Brothers? Parents? You don't have to talk about them if you don't want to, but if we're going to be hanging out, we might as well get to know each other."

It sounds clumsy as soon as it leaves my mouth, but Wyatt surprises me by responding in earnest. "Three sisters, no brothers. I was the second oldest. My mom was a homemaker. My dad was a high school social studies teacher and football coach."

"You miss them?" Tanq says, tossing her own bean bag, but she throws too hard and it slides off the board.

"Of course I miss them. My older sister Willa most of all.

And my dad. It's weird; I never realized I had favorites until I lost all of them. I loved my mom, but . . . I'd cut off an arm to see my dad again, get his advice, ask him which of Manny's three options he'd go with."

"I miss my sister so much it's like a knife in my stomach," Trey says. His toss lands right in the hole. Nothing but net. Or plywood, I guess.

"I don't miss anyone. Not a single goddamned person," Tanq says. "Though I wouldn't be sad to see the boys again. I don't miss them exactly, but I never wanted anything bad to happen to them."

"The boys?" Wyatt says.

"My mom and I shared an apartment with another family. They had three boys, all younger than me. We bickered all the time. I hated it. But not them. I didn't hate them."

"Did you ever play football? Your dad being a coach and all?" Trey asks Wyatt. Looking for common ground, no doubt.

"Naw," Wyatt says, and his gaze gets shifty. "Dad tried to get me into it, but I guess I had different interests."

"Like what?" I ask.

"Orienteering. Hunting." Wyatt's bag hits mine, shoving it into the hole. His teeters on the edge, but doesn't go in.

"Sandusky rules!" I say. We agreed during the first game that if an opponent's bag pushes yours in, you get the score.

"I could never kill a living creature," Tanq says.

"Not even to survive?" Wyatt says.

She shrugs. "Maybe?"

"What about the aliens?" Wyatt asks.

Tanq blinks. "Huh. I'm not sure. I wouldn't like it, but . . ." Her voice trails off.

"Orienteering," I say. "Isn't that where you find your way around the wilderness with a compass or something?"

"Yeah," Wyatt says. "I'm really good at it. One time, just to prove I could do it, I had my dad drop me off in the middle of the woods with a knife, a topo map, and a compass. I built a shelter, found food and water, and stayed there for five days. Then I found my way out."

"Wow, your dad let you do that?" I say.

"He believed in me. I had emergency flares in case something went wrong. But nothing did."

"All of us were really good at something before the virus hit," Trey says. "But I think you and Tanq might be the only ones who'll get to keep doing your thing. I admit, I'm a little envious."

I know the feeling.

"What are you good at, Tanq?" Wyatt asks.

Tanq freezes, like it's some kind of attack.

"She's good at art," I say.

"And vandalism," Trey says.

"And eating," Tanq says. "You forgot eating."

"Art and vandalism and eating," I amend.

A few turns later, Tanq and Wyatt are leading. I miss the next toss on purpose. Trey gives me a knowing look, but he doesn't say anything.

"So what do you all think of Manny's options?" Trey says.

I remember Tanq, rocking back and forth in mindless

terror after the drone took out Paul's RAV4. I say, "We're still not over last time we were attacked. I don't know that we're ready to do anything."

"Maybe that's something you never get over," Trey says.

"I still want to find the other cells," Wyatt says. "See if we can help each other."

"I don't care about other people," Tanq says. "And even if I did, traveling is dangerous. Why risk it? I say we find a mansion and hunker down. Live like royals for the rest of our short, terrified lives."

"Traveling would be safer without those dragonflies," Trey points out. "We take out the tower, and we could travel halfway across the country before finding another dragonfly."

"Makes sense," Wyatt concedes. "Plus we buy ourselves some time with that whole methane thing."

Our score is tied. I consider missing another shot on purpose, which isn't like me at all. I've always been the most competitive person I know. But something about this moment is different. I *want* to put Wyatt at ease. Make him part of the team.

It's not your job to put men at ease, Paul used to say. *Not about your height, not about your ambitions, not about anything.*

I aim for the hole and give the bag a soft underhand toss. It flies right in, barely scraping the edge.

"Nice," Trey says. "I think that means we win."

"You two are pretty used to winning, yeah?" says Wyatt, a slight edge to his voice.

"You'll get us next time," Trey says.

I barely refrain from rolling my eyes.

"Maybe next time we'll change up the teams," Wyatt says. "Not fair to have two pro-level athletes on the same team."

"Hey, Tanq was pretty good," I point out.

"I was awesome, actually," Tanq says. "I used to play cornhole all the time with the boys. There was already a set in the backyard when we rented the apartment. It didn't cost anything. Got me out of the house." She turns to Wyatt. "Even if you change teams, you'll still be the weak link."

He recoils like he's been struck, and his giant pit bull jaw clenches so hard I expect teeth to come shooting out of his mouth. I can't imagine why Tanq's words have wounded him so deeply. It's just cornhole.

Trey claps him on the back, grinning like it's no big deal, because, truly, it's no big deal. "Trash talk is half the fun, right?" he says.

Wyatt noticeably gets ahold of himself. "Yeah, sure," he says with a weak smile. "All in good fun."

"Wyatt, I'm happy to play cornhole with you anytime," Tanq says with a roguish grin that would make me hide my valuables if I had any.

The effect on Wyatt is immediate. His return grin is sloppy and unsuspecting. "Okay."

"Wyatt, did you bring a gun?" I ask, to distract his attention from Tanq. "You're a gun type."

"Nope. My dad kept our guns in a locked metal cabinet. I have no idea where the key is. I was going to break into a Walmart or something to find one, but then I heard Manny's message and thought it would be best to get here as fast as I could." Wyatt stares at the rifle strapped to Trey's shoulder. Trey has hardly let it out of his sight.

Trey stares right back.

Then he clears his throat. "So, hey, I think I'm leaning toward Plan C," Trey says.

I hate to say this, but I'm going to anyway: "Me too, Trey. Leaning toward Plan C. I mean, I don't want to go near that tower. But I also don't want to die young, and all of humanity and planet Earth along with me. And I think my not wanting everything to die is greater than my not wanting to go near the tower."

"I can understand that," Wyatt says with obvious reluctance. "And look, I'm not going to lie, I'm sad all the time now. Sometimes it's so bad I forget to breathe. I have to *do* something. Otherwise . . ."

Tanq says nothing, busying herself with another yogurt. She's hyperfocused on it, swirling it with her spoon, studying it like it contains the mysteries of the universe. After a moment, she absently piles a dollop of yogurt onto her spoon and offers it to Emmaline, who laps it up eagerly.

"I'm sad, too," Trey says gently.

"Yeah," I say.

"But Plan C is only viable if we have a ship," Trey reminds us.

"That's easy," says Wyatt. "I saw a bunch on the way here from Ann Arbor. They're all just floating out there, drifting. It was creepy."

"Any coal barges?" I ask.

"Sure. There was one just off Port Clinton. Coal barges are huge. Hard to miss."

"And where's that?" Trey asks.

"About twenty miles northwest of here," Wyatt says. "The barge looked weird, though. Kind of sideways? Might be stuck on something."

Trey starts pacing, and even though the kitchen area is huge, his long legs eat up distance so that he only gets four strides before he has to turn. "Probably drifted there from Toledo," he mutters, half to himself. "If it has fuel, we might be able to power it out of there. Then we find some kind of explosive, or at least lighter fluid . . ." His head snaps up. "Wyatt, how many barges was the towboat pushing?"

"Four? I think?"

"Four flats of coal," Trey muses. "That's enough to do serious damage."

Tanq says, "It's also enough to pollute the crap out of Lake Erie."

"Like you Ohioans care," says Wyatt. "Hey, remember how that river in Cleveland used to catch on fire?"

"Remember that town in Michigan where everyone got poisoned by drinking the water?" Trey snaps back.

The air in the kitchen is suddenly thick as the boys glare at each other.

"Trash talk is half the fun, right?" Wyatt says tentatively.

It's like a balloon pops, and all the air rushes back into the room as suddenly the boys are both grinning ear to ear.

"Anyway," says Wyatt, "I'm not sure we could make Lake Erie any grosser with a little coal dump."

"Fair point," says Trey. "And a polluted lake is better than a wrecked planet."

I ask, "Wyatt, do you think you could find your way to that barge again?"

"I can find my way *anywhere*. But . . ."

"But you still prefer Plan B," I say.

He shrugs. "That tower is only one Death Star."

"And there's always another Death Star," Trey says.

"Taking it down means the Rebellion lives to fight another day," I point out, glad that I finally understand one of Trey's pop culture references.

Wyatt says, "*If* we did this, we could reach the barge in less than thirty minutes by taking the bridge across Sandusky Bay. That's risky, because if a dragonfly came after us, there'd be nowhere to go except into the water. By boat, it would take at least a couple of hours."

"We'll need to find lighter fluid," Trey says. "Shouldn't be too hard. This is a summer grilling town."

"Maybe Manny knows where we can get some," I say.

"Or the best way to get to Port Clinton while avoiding dragonflies," Trey says.

"Let's go talk to him."

Trey and Wyatt move to follow me out of the kitchen, but Tanq plunks down at the industrial steel table. "I'm going to hang here with Emmaline," she says, avoiding our gazes.

Emmaline slaps her bottom down at Tanq's feet—over and

over, eyes wide with the hope that demonstrating her "sit" will earn herself more strawberry yogurt. I hope yogurt isn't bad for dogs.

"Sure, Tanq," I tell her. "We'll let you know what Manny says."

Manny sits beside a computer terminal, poring over a giant binder filled with pages and pages of pictures, handwriting, charts—all in plastic sleeves. He closes it when he hears us and swivels around in his chair, but he leaves the binder out in the open. On the cover it says, in bold, colorful, handwritten caps, THE BOOK OF MANNY.

"We might have a plan," Wyatt tells him.

"Part of a plan," I add.

"Tell me!" says Manny.

So we do. His eyes narrow, and he fidgets with one end of his mustache. "Interesting. Half-formed, yes, but I think this plan has potential."

"You do?" I say.

"There's an outdoor cooking supply store close by," he says. "Barb's Barbeque. Most folks these days are using gas grills, but you can still find all the lighter fluid you want. Enough to light up a whole barge."

Then his face freezes, and I know what he's thinking. Most folks these days aren't grilling anything at all.

"Any ideas on getting to Port Clinton safely?" Trey asks.

"I made the trip once already," Wyatt says, "so I know it's possible."

"Ah, but we've been sighted here now," Manny reminds us. "I've seen drones fly by on the cameras half a dozen times this morning."

Something shivers down my spine. What if they're actively looking for us now?

At the expressions on our faces, Manny hurriedly adds, "I do think such a trip is feasible, though! In fact, this might be time to test a theory I've been playing with."

"What theory?" says Trey.

"Well, the tower retracts every night around two a.m., right?" he says.

"It does?" I ask.

"Yep. I suspect it powers down to cool off or refuel or maybe process more lake water for energy. My friend at the Kisumu Cell in Kenya thought the towers might be solar powered, and that their energy stores deplete after a few hours of darkness. Whatever the case may be, the towers all over the world disappear beneath the surface of whatever lake they're parked in during the night—surely you've heard? It makes a deep, alarming sound. Like your chest is suddenly a kettle drum."

"Whoomp!" says Trey.

So *that's* what that was. "We heard it all the way down in Columbus!" I say.

"Here, it's really intense," Wyatt says. "Like you're standing next to giant speakers at a dubstep concert."

"I must have slept through it last night," I say wonderingly.

"You did," Manny says. "You slept through my broadcast, too. That's why I broadcast at three a.m. I'm hoping fewer

Farmers might be listening. Well, that and the fact that radio waves travel a longer distance at night when there's less—"

"Why do you think submerging the tower prevents the Farmers from listening?" Trey asks.

"Because up until that point, the dragonflies in the area are really busy. Even when it's dark you can see them flashing across the vid screens, like they're doing final sweeps. That's one reason I warn people in my broadcast not to travel at night. The dragonflies are very, very active at night. Until the tower goes down, that is. Then they disappear. Every single one. I just confirmed it by going back over my notes. Since taking up my station here as keeper of the Sandusky Cell, I haven't seen a single drone after two a.m."

We stare at each other in collective silence.

Then I say, "Manny, are you sure?"

He shakes his head. "Of course not. Just because *I* haven't seen any doesn't mean they're not out there. My camera views are limited. It's not like I can keep an eye on the entire Midwest. As I said, it's a theory that needs testing. But I am fairly certain that—at the very least—their activity is greatly lessened while the tower is down."

Trey is rubbing at his chin. He needs to shave again. His stubble is a bit patchy, like he couldn't grow a full beard if he tried. I decide I like the stubble, though, and I have a sudden urge to reach for his chin with my fingertips. . . .

"So we have a window," Trey says, smiling a little, maybe because he's caught me looking at him. "An opportunity. We might be able to get to Port Clinton without being seen."

"The way back would be a long trip on that barge," Wyatt says. "I don't think they move very fast."

I say, "Maybe if we left right after the tower went down, we'd have five or six hours before the tower came back up and the dragonflies went back on patrol."

Trey is nodding along. "This could work."

Manny says, "We bring the barge back here, park it outside Sandusky Bay, hole up for the day. The next night, we can get it into place right before the tower rises again in the morning."

"We?" I say.

"Of course I'm going with you," he says. "You need a boat to reach a boat. My *Tardis* can do that."

"So we head there in the yacht?" Wyatt says. "It will take hours."

"We split up," I say, and when Wyatt gives me a weird look, I add, "We can't be sure Manny's theory about the dragonflies will hold. So we go separately, in the *Tardis* and in the El Camino. That way we don't create a single target."

"Good idea," Manny says. "Give me a head start. We'll meet in Port Clinton. If we get the barge working in time to drive it back here, great. If not, we lie low until the next night."

"Paige and Trey said something about an explosive earlier," says Wyatt. "If we head over to Barb's Barbeque for lighter fluid, I bet we can find propane tanks too. The one my dad used for his grill weighed about twenty pounds. We load half a dozen onto the end of the coal barge, make a fuse with lighter fluid . . ."

"Wyatt, that's genius," says Trey, and Wyatt beams. "Coal

burns really hot, definitely hot enough to explode some pro-pane tanks. I bet we could blow that tower back to the stars."

"We have to get close enough first," I remind him. "And we have to do it during the day, when the tower is up and the dragonflies are zipping around."

"I notice that Tanq is not here," Manny says. "Is she . . . uninterested in this plan?"

"She'll come around," says Wyatt.

I give him a warning glare. "We won't force her to do any-thing," I say.

"There might be a job for her right here," Manny says.

"Oh?" says Trey.

"Remember how we created a distraction with fireworks to get you all inside the bunker? Tanq can do that for us. She'll be able to see on the vid screen when our barge approaches the tower. She can trigger the fireworks, and hopefully the drones will fly away for a few minutes to investigate."

"Giving us a chance to ram the tower," Wyatt says.

"Hopefully," I echo. "If they haven't gotten smart to that trick."

Manny claps his hands together. "So we have a plan! A beginning of one anyway. Tonight, we can grab supplies from Barb's Barbecue. And tomorrow night, we head to Port Clinton."

Surely it's April by now

IT'S THREE THIRTY A.M. MANNY HAS FINISHED HIS BROADCAST, and he and Wyatt have left the bunker to retrieve lighter fluid and propane tanks. Their goal is to load as much onto the *Tardis* as will safely fit in preparation for our trip tomorrow night.

They both insisted that they could handle it, that Trey, Tanq, and I all seemed exhausted when we arrived yesterday, and we should take the time to catch up on sleep. They're probably right. But I'm going to worry about them the whole time they're away.

I'm lying on the bottom of one of the bunked cots, the back of my hand resting against my forehead. Surely sleep will come soon. There are enough bunks that we each get our own, which is good, because Tanq is a noisy sleeper, tossing all over the place and snoring softly. If she were right above me, I'd have no chance of drifting away.

Emmaline senses my restlessness and stirs. She's been curled up into a tight ball of fur at the end of the cot near my feet, but now she's readjusting, as if she can't get comfortable. Maybe she has to go potty. Tanq fed her a lot of yogurt today.

Giving up on sleep, I swing my legs over the bed and settle my feet quietly on the floor. I tiptoe toward the kitchen, my path lit only by the soft glow of two vid screens on auxiliary power. Emmaline's claws clatter against the floor as she paces at my ankles.

I'm reaching for the door that leads into the old sewer and outside when footsteps patter behind me, and I whirl.

My stomach does a little flip because it's Trey, his tall, lanky form unmistakable even in the near dark.

"I couldn't sleep either," he whispers.

"I'm taking Emmaline potty. Wouldn't mind the company."

He opens the door and gestures as if to say, *Lead the way.*

I didn't think to bring a flashlight, so I trail my hand along the wall to keep my sense of direction. But I'm not frightened. The sound of Trey's heavier footsteps is welcome company.

We travel the tunnel in silence, and when I open the door leading to the grassy area near the marina, icy wind rushes in, and Emmaline rushes out immediately to squat.

The clouds have broken a little, and moon shimmer turns the grass faintly blue. Crickets squeal, and spring-peeper frogs chorus like bells in the trees and bushes all around us. The air reeks of wetlands and fish, but I don't find it unpleasant. It smells natural. Good, even.

"All this," I say, gesturing vaguely, "is worth saving, don't you think?"

Emmaline finishes her business and scrapes at the grass with her hind legs, so it's a moment before I sense that Trey has been staring at me.

I turn, and sure enough, his gaze is fixed on me, his eyes bright with reflected moonlight.

"Paige," he says.

I'm not sure what he wants or what to say, so I wait.

He reaches for my face, grazes his thumb across my chin. He says, "I want to kiss you so badly right now."

The fresh air makes me bold. I smile at him, maybe a little drunk with this sudden feeling of power.

"Honestly, I've wanted to kiss you for a while now," he confesses.

"Why haven't you?"

Everything comes out in a rush. "Well, you were sick, and we haven't known each other very long, and I didn't know what kind of person you were at first, and I was too lonely to have good judgment. I mean, after I lost Teena, things got so bad for me that I almost . . . and then I was so glad and relieved to find you that everything was all jumbled . . . then suddenly we were running for our lives, and then we met Tanq. . . ."

"And now it's the end of the world, and you think we might not have much kissing time left?"

"Something like that. No, it's closer to 'now it's the end of the world, and I might lose the chance to *tell* her that I want to kiss her.' That's all. For now, I just want you to *know*."

I consider a long moment. Trey shifts on his feet. Maybe I could make it happen. Right now.

My body cants toward him almost of its own accord, but I stop myself, and blurt: "Shawntelle made me swear off of Black guys."

"*What?* Why?"

Emmaline is sniffing around now. She pounces on something, though I have no idea what.

"She said that white women fetishize Black guys. That it's a form of racism. And she was my best friend, so . . . I listened."

"I see. And now?"

"I think," I say slowly, carefully, "that all oaths taken pre-apocalypse are null and void."

Breath leaves his body in a relieved rush.

"And even if it wasn't the apocalypse," I add, "I would have asked Shawntelle to make an exception."

His grin is huge. "She sounds like an amazing person."

"I'm so lucky to have known her."

Emmaline has given up sniffing stuff and begun stretching and yawning like she's finally, genuinely tired.

"Time to head back," I say, and I turn to go, but Trey grabs my hand, turning me back around. His hand is warm, and so, so much bigger than mine.

I think maybe he's changed his mind about kissing, but he

says, "I don't want to move too fast. It's tempting. You know, the apocalypse and all."

"We have a lot going on," I concede.

"But just so you know," he says. His face is very close. I love that I have to look *up* at him. "Even if we weren't in the apocalypse, I would have wanted to get to know you better."

"Yeah. Me too."

"Shawntelle was right, you know. But I wouldn't hate it if you developed a healthy attraction."

I swallow hard. "I'll keep that in mind."

After talking with Trey, I expect to be buzzing awake all night, but suddenly, heavy footsteps are plodding through the bunker and the generator is rumbling and lights are flashing on and I'm blinking sleep from my eyes.

Wyatt and Manny have returned, both grinning in triumph, and even though I've known them for approximately three seconds, I'm so very glad to see them. I sit up and cover my yawn with a fist.

"Success!" Wyatt says. He's hefting an enormous red backpack, stuffed full. Sales tags swing from one of the straps.

"The *Tardis* is loaded up and ready to go," Manny says.

Across the room, Tanq rolls over on her cot, showing her back to everyone, and pulls her blanket over her head.

"How many propane tanks did you get?" Trey asks, rolling stiffness from his shoulder.

"Eleven!" says Manny. "Also, Wyatt brought back something for everyone."

Wyatt beams, reaching for his backpack, unzipping it. "There's a sporting goods store next to the barbecue place. So I grabbed this."

He pulls out a brand-new, bright-orange basketball and tosses it to me. I gasp, snatching it from the air instinctively. The rough texture at my fingertips is so familiar, the rubber smell, the smooth black ribs. I roll it around in my hands, feeling that it's a 29.5 inch ball, not 28.5 like I'm used to. But still.

I can hardly get the words out: "Thank you, Wyatt."

He yanks a football out of his backpack next and tosses it to Trey.

"Thanks, man," says Trey.

Wyatt says, "I was thinking about what you said, how you and Paige won't get to do the thing you're good at anymore, and I think that's bullshit. We'll find a way for you to keep doing it. I know we can't bring back the NCAA or whatever, but maybe we'll invent something new, I don't know. Anyway, you shouldn't have to erase what you love."

Trey is as lost for words as I am, and he can only nod acknowledgment.

"I got something for Tanq too, but . . . she's sleeping." Wyatt reaches into his backpack and pulls out a giant plastic tub of Red Vines. He tiptoes across the room toward Tanq and sets the tub gently on her cot at her feet, like a supplicant with an offering.

She does not stir, but I'd bet my new basketball that she's faking.

"Let's let Tanq sleep," Manny says. "I need to log today's

outing in my book. Why don't you head into the kitchen, and I'll join you in a minute?"

In the kitchen, Trey puts coffee on. Manny didn't make breakfast for us this time, so it's up to us to scrounge our own. I'm suddenly overcome by indecision—eggs again? A smoothie? Plain old cereal? Having choices again is strangely paralyzing.

Manny enters a moment later and plunks down at the table.

"Hey, what did you mean by 'log today's outing'?" I ask as I grab a bowl from a metal shelf, a box of cereal from a cupboard. It's the least complicated breakfast possible.

"I document everything," he says. "I mean, *everything*. We know so little about the aliens. Even though they contacted us, gave us the base for our vaccine, communicating was so difficult. They're too different. Incomprehensible, in fact."

"Trey said we might have a common ancestor," I point out.

"Well, sure, but we also have a common ancestor with chimpanzees. That doesn't mean we speak the same language."

"Oh, right."

"Anyway, every cell keeper across the world was tasked with recording observations. We hope that eventually the weight of data will provide some insight or patterns—anything to help us understand them better. Today, for example, I logged the date and time of our outing, the weather, the fact that we spotted no Farmers." His face falls a little. "I know it doesn't seem like much. . . ."

"I think it's good idea," Trey says, sipping his coffee.

"How'd you get this job?" I ask. "There must have been a

lot of competition for it. Everyone would have wanted a vaccine to survive what was coming." I pour milk into my bowl and carry it to the table.

"Some competition," he concedes. "Not as much as you'd think. This job is a really big commitment. I got it because I have training in statistical analysis, and because I had no family to leave behind. No divided loyalties. I could be 100 percent devoted to this bunker and the people who would eventually live here."

Trey's eyes narrow. "Exactly how long have you been here? Underground, I mean?"

"I moved to Sandusky five years ago to oversee completion. Moved into this bunker full-time about a year ago."

Wyatt is scanning the contents of the refrigerator. "Did everyone in Sandusky know about this place?" he asks, pulling out a yogurt.

"It was an open secret among nearby businesses," Manny says. "We told them it was a disaster preparedness bunker, where the state would run scenarios and experiment with living in isolation—kind of like the Biosphere projects—which was close enough to the truth to be unsuspicious."

"You said you didn't have family," I say around my cereal. My mom would give me her signature glare right now for talking with my mouth full. "Did something happen to them?"

"They were all killed in a hurricane many years ago," he says, his voice distant with memory. "Just . . . disappeared. The house I grew up in on Puerto Rico was literally wiped off the face of the earth."

"Oh, wow," Trey says. "Sorry to hear."

"It was a rough time. I threw myself into my studies—poli sci with an emphasis in statistics and probability. There's a compartmentalization that happens sometimes, when a person goes through something awful. Grad school saved my life."

"So you know what it's like," Wyatt says softly, staring down at his yogurt. "To lose everyone all at once."

"Yeah," Manny says.

Tanq barrels into the kitchen and heads straight for the refrigerator. Her black hair is disheveled, refusing to stay swept over to one side, and her eyes are bleary. Without saying a word to anyone, she pours herself a giant glass of milk and mixes in a truckload of Strawberry Nesquik, turning the milk bright pink.

"Trey," Wyatt says, with an eye on Tanq. "That semiautomatic rifle of yours. Do you know how to use it?"

"Nope."

"Wanna learn?"

"Not really. But maybe I should."

"I'd like to teach you. All of you," Wyatt says. "But I don't know how to do it without making a ton of noise."

"Wyatt, you're saying *you* know how to use a semiautomatic rifle?" I ask.

He nods. "My family never owned one, but, yeah, I've shot them before."

"We've been careful with the guns," I tell him. "We figured out how the safeties work. We keep the magazines separate from the guns themselves, make sure there's never a round chambered. But that's as far as we've gotten."

"That's good, Paige."

"You know what?" Trey says, suddenly rising from the table. "I'll be right back."

He's gone only a moment. When he returns, he's carrying the AR-15. He offers it to Wyatt. "I think you should be the one to hold on to this," Trey says.

Tanq whips around to stare at Trey. Manny's eyebrows go up.

"Trey," Wyatt says, staring at the gun. "Are you sure?"

"Yeah, Trey, are you *sure*?" I echo. He's not just giving Wyatt a gun. He's handing over power.

"I'm sure," Trey says. "It's safest in the hands of someone who knows how to use it."

Wyatt takes the gun reverently, fully understanding how much trust Trey is placing in him. "I'd feel more comfortable if we all carried guns," Wyatt says. "And I promise to teach everyone as soon as it's safe to do so."

"So, Tanq," Trey says, brushing off the gun thing like it's no big deal. "Are you going to come with us tonight?"

"Hell, no," she says.

"Why not?" asks Wyatt.

She spits out: "Because I'd rather feel alone by myself than alone with people."

But it's even more than that. Her wide eyes are terrified.

"There's something you can help us with right here," Manny says.

"What?" she says.

"When I took this job, I swore an oath that I'd do everything

I could to gather and protect as many survivors as possible," he says. "So while I'm gone, I'd sure appreciate it if you kept an eye on those monitors. If anyone else heard our broadcast and comes knocking, someone needs to guide them inside and welcome them to our bunker. I don't want to miss a single person."

She purses her lips, considering. Then: "I can do that."

Tanq strides from the kitchen, taking her glass of strawberry milk with her. On her way out the door, she throws over her shoulder, "Thanks for the Red Vines, Wyatt."

April-ish

When I was fourteen, Paul took Ryan and me camping up here at Sandusky Bay. I'll never forget watching from our campsite as a family of bald eagles frolicked at the shore, dancing in the lapping water, blowing up spray with their wings. They were huge and beautiful, graceful in the air, so cheerfully awkward on the beach. Two of them didn't yet have the white head and tail feathers of their parents, but there was no mistaking the shape of their yellow-orange beaks or the immensity of their wingspans.

Bald eagles used to be endangered. Their population got so low it seemed likely the species would be wiped out.

I'm in the El Camino with Trey, heading toward the bridge that will take us across the bay, and I find myself wishing it was daytime so I could *see* the water. I remember it being beautiful—sparkling blue, filled with sandpipers and cattle egrets and of course endless gulls. I loved watching sailboats go by, loved the ferries full of vacationers waving to the shore. There are no people now, of course, and any boats we saw would be ghostly and lifeless. But I bet there are more birds than ever. I might even see those juvenile eagles again, all grown up.

"I hope Wyatt and Manny are doing okay," Trey says, and he has an iron grip on the steering wheel. We're moving slowly because we agreed to keep our headlights off, just in case any walkers were around. Before we left, Manny disconnected the brake lights so they wouldn't flash red every time we slowed.

I say, "Wyatt insisted they didn't see any dragonflies when they went to Barb's Barbecue last night, so Manny's theory is looking pretty good."

"I'm still worried," Trey says. "It's really dark. They're running that boat without lights, too, and keeping close to shore. I imagine it's easy to run aground if you can't see. . . ."

"Yeah."

"It'll start getting light soon," he says.

I was so antsy with anticipation and terror that I hardly slept a wink last night. It was a relief to send off Manny and Wyatt right after the three a.m. broadcast, even more of a relief to climb into the car with Trey around five thirty.

He's right; it will start getting light in about thirty minutes. But not before we have to cross the bay.

The car goes over a small bump, and the pavement is suddenly singing to us, like the tires are a bow across violin strings.

"I think we're on the bridge now," Trey says, slowing the car to a crawl. "And I can't see *anything*."

He's right. We don't have even a yard of visibility. It's pure blackness ahead, like we're about to fall off the edge of the world.

"I know we agreed not to use running lights," I tell him, "but I think we have to."

Something clicks in the dashboard, and the street ahead of us suddenly lights up. Just in time, because a white pickup looms in our view. Trey swerves right; our bumper clips the fender, wrenching my neck, and Trey has to swerve again to compensate.

I hold on to the dash for dear life as we fishtail for a few seconds, but Trey gets the El Camino under control and brings it to a full stop.

We sit together for a moment, just breathing.

"Well, that was exciting," he says.

"Good thing you were going so slow," I say.

He takes a deep breath. "Okay, let's try that again. Gonna keep these fog lights on, if that's okay with you."

"Definitely."

We press forward through the inky darkness. We maneuver around another car that's parked in the middle of the lane. Then we approach a black sedan whose nose aims sharply away from us. It's not until we're halfway beyond that I see it has busted through the guardrail, that the car's nose hangs off the bridge precariously. I imagine the dark cold water far below.

"Paige, if a walker jumps in front of this car, I'm going to run right over it. No swerving, no nothing. Just lay on the gas."

"Good," I say with vehemence.

I have a sudden urge to grab his hand and squeeze, but he needs both hands for the steering wheel, so I don't.

"Talk to me," he says.

"About what?"

"Anything. Frankly, this is terrifying, and I don't want to think too hard about what might happen tonight, so talk to me. I like your voice."

"Okay." I like his voice too. Deep and resonant, always gentle. I should tell him back. Last night, I should have specifically told him that I want to kiss him too. I'm not sure why that kind of thing is so hard for me.

What I say is "Have I told you about my bio-dad? Ryan and I called him the Sperm Donor."

"You've mentioned him. When was the last time you saw him?"

"Four years ago he showed up to my eighth-grade graduation uninvited." I still remember the shock on my mother's face, the way Ryan tried to shield himself with my body, how Paul was the one who stepped forward and shook my dad's hand, his grip firm, his smile grim, as if saying: *Make no mistake, I will not let you harm them.*

I tell Trey all about it. I talk about the years of verbal abuse, the way he "spanked" Ryan for the slightest thing, how even after my mom packed us into the car along with all the clothes and food that could possibly fit, he continued to harass us with phone calls and e-mails. I talk about the restraining order that finally started us down the path of getting him out of our lives for good. And how even though I liked my new stepdad, part of me was terrified of him until the day Paul showed up to my first game as a varsity starter, his face painted in school colors, waving those stupid pompoms. It was a big deal. I was starting point guard as a freshman; everyone in school just knew me as "the tall girl," and several of my teammates and their parents resented me deeply at first. But Paul made friends with every single person in the stands that year, and by the end of the season, his friendliness and grace and enthusiasm had somehow extended to me, like an umbrella of protection.

Trey brakes as something furry scampers out of our way. A raccoon maybe. "Is that how you met Shawntelle?" he asks.

"We met in seventh grade, played middle school ball together. One day our coach cut practice short again. I was complaining that no one was taking our team seriously enough. . . . I was really loud and obnoxious about it. Coach suspended me from the next game for back talking. Shawntelle snuck over to me after and said she had a couple of balls at home, and if I wanted, I could come to her house and we could do drills together. So that's what we did. After a year or so, we practically lived at each other's houses. My mom kept her favorite Pringles flavor in the cupboard. Shawntelle's mom kept microwave popcorn for me. . . ." I pause a long time. He wants me to talk. Needs me to, but the lump in my throat is so huge—

"You miss her," Trey says softly.

"Yeah," I choke out.

"The person I miss most is Teena," he says, understanding that he needs to be the one to fill the space for a minute or two. "She was so soft-hearted, wouldn't even let me kill a spider we found in the house, always made me take it outside and set it free. She loved royal blue. Almost everything she owned—her phone, her sunglasses, her sneakers—she decorated with bright blue glitter. And she was smart, way smarter than me. Curious about everything. Always making up stories. I thought she would be a famous author someday, probably win the Pulitzer or something. And even though I always imagined myself going to the NFL, I knew that eventually I would just be known as 'Teena Dawson's big brother.'"

I can't help chuckling.

"What's so funny?"

"I can't imagine anyone being smarter than you. You might be the smartest person I've ever met."

"Really?"

"It's . . . hot."

"Then I accept your assessment! But seriously, I was Forrest Gump to her Einstein. She was doing calculus online by the eighth grade. Reading every book she could get her hands on. Excelled at everything she tried. Well, except dancing. She loved to dance, and Momma got lessons for her, but she was pretty terrible. We all decided it was good for her to have to actually try at something."

"I wish I could have met her."

"Me too."

It's Trey's turn to have a lump in his throat, so I say, "I miss my coach too, Coach Dalrymple. My middle school coach was . . . not great. But Coach D believed in me enough to make me a starter my freshman year. Made me earn it though. Do extra practices, more physical training. She said I was tall and talented, but my body was still young, that I would have to build strength to go up against the big girls. So that's what we did. And when it was clear that Shawntelle and I were college scholarship bound, she pulled together extra funding to get us a shooting coach. She sent videos of us to recruiters, did everything she could to give us every opportunity."

Trey steers around a bicycle lying flat in the road. Beside it is a lump of something that I definitely do not want a closer look at. "Sounds like you took basketball as seriously as I took football."

"Did you have a coach who helped you?"

"There's not a single five-star recruit in the NCAA who did not have someone to help them," Trey says. "It's a dirty little secret of sports. You hear these amazing success stories about inner-city kids given a second chance through athletics, but there's always a determined, supportive coach or recruiter who identified them early and gave them a leg up. Makes you wonder about all the wild talent that goes missing every year, all those kids who don't get lucky, like we did."

"This year, no one got lucky."

"Truth. But yeah, my high school coach was pretty great. Ricky Pallini. He . . . Pre-med would have been a pretty tough major to maintain while playing football. Coach Pallini brought in some tutors for the whole team—but I know a lot of it was for me. To help me study for AP exams. I was going to enter Ohio State with more than twenty credits, which would've let me take on a lighter course load the first year, all thanks to Coach Pallini. And my job at the pharmacy. Those tests are expensive. Paige?"

"Yeah?"

"I *really* wanted to play in the NFL someday. And I *really* wanted to be a doctor."

The El Camino bumps off the bridge onto regular asphalt, and the humming of tires against pavement ceases.

"I wish I could have seen you do both those things," I say.

"I wanted them so bad that I gave up things. Like, I hardly had any friends at all. Sometimes I'd get together with the guys on the weekend to play *Madden*, but definitely no one like Shawntelle. I was just working and practicing and studying, twenty-four seven, and it left no time for anything else. Now I'm wondering if I made the wrong decision. I didn't make any memories with people. All that time was wasted."

In the passenger side mirror, I see light edging the cloudy horizon behind us. "Hey, we can turn off the fog lamps now," I say.

He flicks them off. It's still dangerously dark, but we can make out the general shapes of things, and the dawning light is just enough for the street reflectors to mark our lane.

"Should be okay if we go slow," he says.

"You have memories of Teena and your mom," I remind him. "I don't mean to be flippant. Those aren't wasted moments. You're sharing them with me, and now I get to remember them, too."

"Yeah, I guess."

"Besides, you have friends now, and we are going to make our own memories."

"Honestly, the fact that it took an apocalypse for me to make friends makes me feel like a shitty human being."

I shake my head. "You were a *busy* human being, and now that everything is different, you're shifting priorities. That's all."

He smiles a little at that. "So what kind of memories are we going to make, Paige? Running from creepy alien creatures? Scrounging for food?"

"Damn right," I say. And then, because I'm feeling brave: "Also, I'm eventually going to kiss you. You'll remember that for sure." There. I've said something.

His smile widens. "I'm taking that for a promise," he says.

"Please do."

"But not until we take down that tower," he says.

"That's . . . arbitrary. I mean, I know you said you didn't want to rush, but—"

His smile disappears. His gaze is straight ahead, on the road where it should be, but I sense that he's as deeply aware of me as I am of him right now. The El Camino's cab is not large. I could slide across the bench seat and be shoulder to shoulder with him, if I wanted to.

"Taking down that tower will be like playing in the big game," he says. "It's about focus. Compartmentalization. And once I start kissing you, I don't think I'll stop for a while. I'll want plenty of time. No distractions."

I'm silent a good long minute as my heart does dribble drills with my stomach.

"Paige?" he says, sounding suddenly vulnerable.

"I find your terms acceptable," I manage.

We settle into an easy, comfortable silence. The horizon behind us becomes a line of greenish yellow, and all along the roadside, bushes and short coastal trees begin to manifest against a gradually brightening sky. Emboldened, Trey picks up speed a little.

Out of habit, I press my face to the window and scan the sky for dragonflies.

"Anything?" Trey says.

"Nope, not a single—"

I gasp.

"What? What is it?" Trey is already aiming off the road and into the trees.

"No, it's okay. Just stop the car for a second."

He does, and I can't help myself; I open the car door and get out so I can get a better look. Over the tops of the trees, drifting like it's untethered to the earth, is a long neck and a giant head topped with horn-like protrusions and wide-spaced, twitching ears.

"A giraffe!" Trey says, delighted.

We watch, hardly daring to breathe, as it bends its neck to reach the foliage below, opens its mouth, and chomps down. A rustling heralds a companion giraffe, not quite so tall, coming up from behind and joining it for breakfast.

"There's a zoo or some safari thing nearby," I explain, keeping my voice at a whisper. "I bet someone let the animals out."

"We should definitely not tell Tanq that lions and tigers might be roaming North America now," Trey says.

"Definitely not."

"It's awfully cold for giraffes," Trey says. "I hope they make it."

"Yeah. Me too."

We watch a few moments more, and then reluctantly return to the El Camino. As we drive away from the giraffes, Trey says, "Even if the world survives, it's going to be so different from now on. No NFL, but there might be giraffes! In Ohio!"

"I hope we see it, Trey. I don't want to miss what happens next."

We pull into a campground edging a rocky section of Lake Erie coastline. Sure enough, just as Wyatt described, a coal barge floats a few hundred yards offshore. It's canted at a diagonal, the flatboats stretching into deeper water. Mounds of black coal shimmer with wetness; it must have rained a little last night. The wind has kicked up some waves, but the pusher towboat hardly moves at all, indicating that it has run aground.

"Let's hope that thing has enough fuel to dislodge itself," Trey says as he sets the parking brake. We get out of the El Camino and circle around some rickety picnic tables. The breeze is brisk and wet and smells faintly of gasoline. Another cloudy day has turned the lake slate gray.

Out of habit, I look down to check on Emmaline before I remember she's not here. She's back at the bunker with Tanq, probably getting fed Red Vines and yogurt. The little sheltie has been practically attached to my leg ever since I busted through Mrs. Carby's window to rescue her. It's odd to be without her grinning face and ground-sweeper tail, like part of me is missing.

The breeze today is fierce. Trey shields his eyes against the wind with his hand and peers toward the barge.

"Any sign of the *Tardis*?" I ask.

"Not yet." His nose twitches. "Smell that? Something leaked fuel into the lake."

"Not the barge, I hope."

A large object bobs in the water down by the rocks. I start forward to get a better look, but turn away almost immediately. The thing was bloated and pale, and it wore a faded Penn State hoodie.

"Makes you wonder," Trey says softly, "what it was like in other towns. Other cities. Places like New York or Los Angeles, where the population density was so much higher than here."

"It must have been a nightmare," I say.

"Probably still is. Let's never go there unless we have to."

A rumble draws our gazes back to the water, and my heart leaps with relief. The *Tardis* is rounding the bend, cutting the surface of the lake with ease, its engine rumbling like rocks in a blender.

Wyatt stands in the prow, the skin of his face soaked with

spray, and he waves when he sees us. Trey and I wave back.

"Ever driven a boat?" Trey asks.

"Nope. You?"

"Nope. Good thing Wyatt and Manny seem to know their way around one."

"I bet neither of them has driven a coal barge before."

He says, "I guess they'll figure it out."

Trey's right, but the thought fills me with misgiving. The barge is so huge, and the towboat that pushes it so small by comparison. I can't imagine how that contraption actually works.

The *Tardis* rumbles toward a nearby dock, which is laden with paddleboats still tied up, probably for rent to campers during the spring and summer. Manny's face is barely visible through the glass of the cockpit. He guides the yacht so that it slows and stops perpendicular to the end of the dock.

"We can't get any closer," Wyatt hollers. "Might be too shallow."

Trey sucks in a breath. "You ready?"

"Hell, no."

"Me neither. Let's go." And we take off at a jog onto the dock. The wooden slats sway beneath my feet.

Close up, the *Tardis* is elegant and streamlined, perfectly white with bright blue trim that has a slight sheen. The boat is smaller than I expected; more the size of a charter fishing boat than a yacht. Manny waves to us from the raised bridge area; it's high enough that I assume the galley he mentioned fits beneath it. The stern has royal blue cushioned seating for six people, though there's not much room to maneuver because all the space is taken up with ivory-colored, twenty-pound propane tanks.

Wyatt wears a bright orange vest. He stands on the edge of the boat, reaching down for me. I grab his hand, and he yanks me up. I teeter as the boat rocks. It rocks again when Trey leaps aboard.

"Ever been on a boat before?" Wyatt asks, noting my imbalance.

"Does a paddleboat count?" I ask.

He frowns. "This way." He leads us to one of the bench seats. It lifts up on a hinge, revealing more bright orange gear. "Lifejackets," he says. "Required, so don't argue."

"Wasn't planning on it," Trey says, pulling a lifejacket over his head and adjusting the straps. It barely reaches halfway down his chest.

"Sorry, that's the biggest one we have," Wyatt says. "You can swim, though, right?"

"Yep."

"Paige?" Wyatt asks as I strap into a lifejacket of my own. It's a snug fit. A few weeks ago, before my coma, it would have been way too small.

"I'm a champion dog paddler." At his skeptical look, I add, "Kidding! I can swim just fine."

"Okay, good. Let's go see Manny."

The boat jerks as Manny hits the throttle, and I nearly lose my balance.

"You'll get used to it," Wyatt says, leading us up a short set of metal stairs to the bridge.

"Welcome aboard the *Tardis*!" Manny says, but he barely glances at us; all his attention is focused on edging away from the dock. He sits on a padded stool with a short back. His control panel seems strange and complicated—multiple gauges, a steering wheel, a hand throttle, and a screen showing black and gray lines. Manny's eyes keep shifting to it as he steers us away from the dock. It hits me that he's checking the lake depth as we go to keep from running aground.

"Any trouble getting here?" Trey asks. "Any sign of dragonflies?"

"It was perfect, easy sailing," Manny says. "But the wind is picking up quite a bit. Look at that chop!" He indicates the water, which is starting to froth with waves. "Erie can blow hard, so we'll have to be careful."

Once we're a safe distance away from the shallows, he increases speed and aims us toward the barge.

"We circled around it a few times before you got here," Wyatt hollers over the sound of the engines. "She's moving a bit with the water, so we think she's not stuck too hard."

"Do either of you know how to drive that thing?" I ask. As we approach, the pusher tugboat looms huge, with three full decks. But it's not so large as the four-section barge it's pushing. They lie flat in the water, mounded with black coal, each one about two hundred feet long. The bulk of their cargo is hidden beneath the waterline, though. I have no idea how deep those barges go.

"It's going to be a tough job," Manny says. "Those towboats

usually have a full crew of six or more sailors. But we don't have to break and build tow, or maintain the pusher over the course of a long haul, so I'm planning to just steer her true and hope for the best. Come here, Paige."

He gestures me forward, and I comply.

"Take the wheel," he orders, stepping aside.

The steering wheel is wrapped in white leather and warm beneath my palms. The vibration from the engines shivers my skin.

"It's just like driving a car," Manny says. "Except instead of a gas pedal, your throttle is there, to your right. Go ahead; speed up a little."

I seem to have left my bravery back at the bunker, because the thought of learning to drive a boat fills me with as much trepidation as crossing the Ohio countryside while avoiding drones. But as I've learned plenty of times playing basketball, you don't need bravery if you're determined enough. I grab the throttle with a vengeance and give it a tug.

The engine revs. The *Tardis* shoots forward. Water sprays up against the bridge windows, blurring my vision. The lake swells are definitely getting higher.

"That's good," Manny says. "You're a natural."

"She's already got her sea legs," Wyatt observes.

They're lying liars. My thighs already burn from compensating for the sway, and I worry I might re-experience my breakfast.

A large wave rolls toward us, at least the height of the yacht. My stomach leaps dangerously.

"What should I do?" I ask, but my hands are already trying to steer away.

"No, don't avoid it," Manny says. "That's how boats capsize, getting hit in the side. Steer right for it. That's it. Now give it a little gas as we crest the wave. . . ."

All my instincts scream at me to do the opposite of Manny's instructions, but sure enough, the *Tardis* climbs the base of the wave and cuts through the top like it's nothing. My stomach drops into my toes as the boat plunges down the other side.

"See? No big deal," Manny says.

"I'm really bad at this," I observe.

"You'll get better," he says.

Manny lets me drive a few more minutes, then motions for Trey to take a turn.

"Steering the barge won't be this easy," Trey says. "It's just too long."

"It's a very different experience," Manny says. "That thing is like an aircraft carrier. But I'll still feel better going through with this plan if you both have a basic understanding of how to drive a boat."

"Fair enough," Trey says.

We circle the barge twice, Trey and I taking turns at steering, slowing, even reversing. Finally, Manny signals for Trey to pull up alongside the pusher tow. "There," he says, pointing. "That low spot on the port side. We can hop up onto the deck there."

The towboat is shaped like a layer cake, with three stacked rectangular decks, each progressively smaller than the one below. Wyatt throws out some pontoons to keep the sides of the boats from scraping as Trey delicately pulls alongside the much larger craft. Wyatt grabs the rail on the other boat and ties us up with a nylon rope, using a flurry of fancy-looking knots. He's the first to leap up. As he lands, a curtain of black sweeps across the sky, and I duck instinctively. It's a flock of crows rising en masse from the deck and streaming away.

"Guess that means there are bodies up there," Trey says. "Be prepared."

"We have to do this, no matter what's up there," I remind him.

"Yeah."

Seeing death everywhere hasn't exactly been a picnic for any of us, but Trey has seemed the most squeamish. Strange trait to have if you want to be a doctor. Then again, maybe he was planning on going into private practice. It's not like pediatricians see dead bodies every day. I have a sudden, fierce urge to protect him. Maybe there's a job he can do that won't require him to look at bodies. Or maybe we can find a tarp to cover them with. Or maybe we'll get lucky and there won't be any bodies at all.

We don't get lucky.

A slimy skeleton sprawls across the lowest deck, tattered clothes hanging from bones that are covered in wet gray bird droppings. Bits of flesh still cling to the socket areas. The boots are round and bloated with rotted flesh where the birds couldn't reach, the boot laces straining, so that the skeleton looks like it's wearing clown shoes. A half-smoked cigar lies on the deck beside the grinning skull.

"Just don't look," Manny says at our backs. "Head up that ladder to the next deck."

We obey eagerly, jogging down the port side of the boat past portholes that likely mark crew cabins, maybe a galley. More bodies are probably inside, but I'd rather not know.

We climb the ladder to the second deck, which appears clear at first glance, then climb another ladder to the third deck, which houses the bridge. Like the *Tardis*, it's enclosed with glass and has a complicated-looking piloting station. Unlike the *Tardis*, the windows are a bit slimy.

The door to the bridge is closed. Wyatt is the one who reaches to unlatch it.

A wave of decomp hits like a punch to the face, and we all recoil.

"We'll let that air out a bit," Manny says, blinking against tears brought on by the smell.

Wyatt says, "I'll find a blanket or tarp or something," and he disappears down the ladder.

This boat—no, it's a small ship—doesn't rock with the swells as much as the *Tardis*, but I'm still aware of the rising waves, the wind becoming more punishing with each passing moment. At least it makes short work of the fetid air in the bridge.

I'm the first to peek inside.

A body lies curled up in the back corner, a few strides away from the piloting station. She's petite, even more so now that her body has gone past the bloating stage and started caving in on itself. Long brown hair flows from beneath a wool cap, and stained, stiff blue jeans end in bright red deck shoes. She was wearing a short-sleeved shirt when she died. The skin of her tiny arms is wrinkled like a raisin and bright red, like she's been in the sun all this time.

Above the steering wheel is a glass hummingbird, hanging from a suction cup on the window, like fuzzy dice hanging from the rearview mirror of a car. Along with the hummingbird is a laminated badge on a lanyard. The woman on the floor smiles up at me from the badge. Her brown hair frames a wind-chapped face and peeling lips, but her smile is bright, her cheekbones high. She has old skin but young eyes—no more than thirty years old. The badge identifies her as Captain Mercedes Wade, employee of the Toledo Barge Company.

I grab the badge and shove it under my lifejacket, into the pocket of my hoodie.

"Thanks for the boat, Captain Wade," I whisper.

"Everything okay in there?" Trey calls.

"Fine. Not as gross as some of the stuff we've seen."

"Here comes Wyatt," Manny says. "Where did you find that, Wyatt?"

"Don't ask," Wyatt says, and his blocky form suddenly fills the doorway. He's holding a sailcloth, folded into a neat but heavy square. Together, Wyatt and I unfold the sailcloth and drape it over the body of Captain Mercedes Wade.

"Okay, it's clear," I call out, and Manny and Trey tumble into the bridge cabin. "So," I say to Manny, mostly to distract

Trey, who looks a little queasy, "do you think you can drive this thing?"

Manny moves toward the driver's seat, examines the controls. "Key's in the ignition; that's good. Let's see if she starts up, shall we?"

We hold our collective breath as Manny gives the ship a bit of gas and turns the key. The engine gives a little cough, but nothing happens. He tries again. Still nothing.

Manny slumps over, looking defeated.

"Try again," Trey orders. "Don't give up."

Manny shakes his head. "I'm not giving up, but I have to wait a moment. Otherwise we'll just flood the engine. If this boat even has fuel."

We wait. The sky has darkened with storm clouds, and the lake is responding with ferocity. Something knocks the side of the ship, making an echoing sound in my chest. The *Tardis*, I realize. I hope those pontoons are staving off any damage.

Manny reaches forward, primes a pump, hits the ignition. The engine flares to life, gauge needles flick over, screens light up. "She lives!" Manny exclaims. He points. "And look at that. Three quarters of a tank. My friends, we got *so* lucky today."

"I'll count us lucky if we can dislodge her," Wyatt says.

Manny does something to a button in the middle of the throttle and says, "Here goes nothing."

The floor rumbles beneath my feet. The boat edges backward an inch. An inch more.

"This might work," says Trey.

The engine grinds. Manny gives it more gas. Something whines, like the poor thing is straining with all its might. "C'mon, girl," Manny mutters.

A single knock sounds, deep like a kettledrum, and suddenly the towboat springs free. The floor rocks; the coal flats before us undulate on top of the water.

"I think we're clear," Manny says. He slows the boat, yanks the wheel to the side, and steers away. Everything is so much slower to respond than the *Tardis*—slower to accelerate, slower to turn—but gradually, he has us pointed forward into the deeper water of Lake Erie.

"I can't believe that worked," Trey says, his eyes wide. "We actually have a coal barge."

"Let's unload the *Tardis*," Manny says. "I'll be glad to get all that explosive stuff off my boat. Then we'll drop you off at the dock so you can drive the El Camino back to the bunker."

Lightning rends the sky, tearing through some of the most menacing storm clouds I've ever seen, as we transfer cargo from the *Tardis*. The waves and wind have reached us, making this a more dangerous outing than any of us expected. Manny asks us if we want to hide out for the day, see if the storm clears up by tomorrow morning. But none of us wants to quit.

Which is why I'm soaking wet as I haul a propane tank over my shoulder, stepping carefully toward the bow along the edge of a barge filled with massive mountains of black coal. I expected raw coal to be lumpy, but it's much finer than that, almost powdery.

Leaping from the towboat to the cargo barges is dangerous work, it turns out. They're connected by the thinnest of
paraphernalia—a few wires and levers and hooks—so that
the cargo barges occasionally separate from the boat, leaving
a gap. Then, when the waves hit just right, that gap disappears,
the parts slamming back against each other. Manny says many
a towboat crewmember has lost their life falling into that gap.

So Trey and I have been taking it slow and careful, leaping
farther than it looks like we ought to, just in case of separa-
tion. At the bow, Wyatt is knee-deep in coal, shoveling out
pockets of space for the propane tanks. He's covered in black
stuff, and a bandana is pulled up across his mouth and nose
to protect his lungs. Waves hit him from behind as he shovels,
and his sweatshirt and jeans are drenched with lake water. The
moisture might be a good thing, though, keeping the coal dust
down.

I'm halfway to Wyatt with another propane tank when he
bends over, gasping for air.

"Wyatt, you okay?" I call.

He nods, though he's leaning heavily on the shovel. After a
moment, he picks it up and gets back to work. But he's moving
slower now, taking deep breaths between each shovelful.

I pick up my pace. We only have two hours to get the barge
loaded and drive it back to Sandusky before the dragonflies are
out in force again. I should volunteer to take a turn shoveling,
give him a rest.

My body is holding up surprisingly well. I've been lugging
these tanks, leaping to the barge, keeping my balance with each

angry wave. My legs burn with effort, but it's a good burn, the kind you get during a satisfying workout. I revel in it a little, enjoying the spray on my face, the feel of my lungs pushed to their max. My dog-bitten foot doesn't even hurt anymore.

I barely register my name being called beyond wind and waves. I turn. Trey is on the lower deck, waving both arms at me.

"What?" I holler back.

He points, gesturing wildly—toward Wyatt, maybe?

"Trey, I can't hear y—"

He leaps to the barge and sprints toward me, shouting, arms still waving. He points at Wyatt—no, *beyond* Wyatt. To the water.

"There's something out there!" he yells, finally near enough that I can make out his words. "In the water. Moving fast." He beckons with his hand, urging me to come back, as he yells past me: "Wyatt! Get out of there!"

I flash back to every shark movie I've ever seen. But there's *nothing* like that in Lake Erie. A big channel cat, maybe. Or a really huge walleye. Even so, I turn back around and yell for Wyatt, since I'm so much closer to him than Trey. "Wyatt! Come on back. There's something in the water."

His cheeks are smudged with coal, his bandana gone from yellow to sickly brown. He gives me a thumbs-up and says, "Just a little more—"

Something launches out of the waves, rocketing into the air behind him. Water streams away from a glistening, quicksilver body as it stretches its arms wide like wings and lands as lightly as a butterfly on the bow of the barge, not two yards away from Wyatt.

"Wyatt!" I scream, dropping the propane tank and sprinting forward. I don't know what I'll do, I just know I have to get there.

Wyatt turns. Freezes.

The alien creature lifts its hand, points its strange fingers with their black-tipped nails toward Wyatt's chest.

I'm almost there. I'm going to hit that thing like I'm a linebacker. Knock it back into the water. Count on my life vest to—

A wave bludgeons the barge, and I teeter, then bounce against the edge of the coal trough, flipping over the rail, landing hard on a mountain of coal. I scramble to get to my feet, but they just dig in until I'm sunk up to my calves. I can't move. I can't even breathe; the wind was knocked out of me and now my diaphragm is an unyielding boulder in my belly.

I'm gasping for air, trying to dislodge my legs from hundreds of pounds of coal, when Wyatt's head—just barely visible from my half-buried position—jerks awkwardly to the side, right before he crumples out of view.

My breath unlocks, and I breathe in the entire sky before screaming, "Wyatt!"

I try to yank up my right foot, but it's stuck, lodged against something. Maybe it's just coal, heavy with water and the settling of time, but I pull and pull until I feel a sickening pop in my ankle and pain zings up my calf.

It's not dislocated, not yet, but another hard tug might do

it. I plunge my fingers into the coal and dig with my hands.

"Paige!" comes Trey's voice. He saw me fall in. He's coming for me.

"In here . . ." I start to yell, but the alien creature's head crests my view, its translucent cloak still streaming water, its eyeless face focused straight ahead. On Trey.

"No!" I scream. "Down here! I'm down here!" Which I realize is a terrible plan, because I'm stucker than stuck, and I have no way to evade that thing. I'm still shoveling coal with my bare hands as it cocks its head. Like it heard me.

Its black-tar maw of a mouth opens, and it says, "Wherrrre you?"

If one of us is to die, it should be me, not Trey. I wasn't even a candidate. "Here!" I yell. "Right here!" I can save Trey and Manny by buying them time. They can jump into the *Tardis* and jet away from here.

The creature seems to peer over the edge of the trough, right at me. Then it rises—no, floats—up and over the rail, into the trough itself. Its depthless maw hangs open, as though it's scenting the air with its mouth.

It's so close now I can smell it—lake water, and hot metal, and something like talcum powder—and I cease shoveling. There's no point. This is the moment I die.

Tanq will take care of Emmaline. Maybe Mom was right. Maybe heaven is real, and I'll see my family again.

I close my eyes and await the inevitable. Then I change my mind and open them. I'm a warrior. I don't give up just because the scoreboard doesn't look good.

So I glare daggers at this creature, this thing that has stolen my life, everything I loved, my planet. My fingers clutch handfuls of wet coal, readying to throw it in the creature's face.

It cocks its head again, ghosting closer, closer—its cloak brushes my cheek, and it feels like a cloud of raw cotton. Then it moves beyond me, leaving me behind in my prison of coal.

What the hell?

One of my fingernails is broken and bleeding but I don't care. I resume shoveling and shoveling until I've freed my left leg, which makes it easier to access my right ankle, the one that popped.

I free my ankle. Wiping coal onto my sweatpants, I launch to my feet, then wince at the pain. Quick as I can, I climb back over the rail and use it for support as I limp along the side of the barge after the creature.

I don't know why that thing passed me over, but it's going after Trey and Manny now, and I have to do something.

At the other end of the barge, relief floods Trey's face when he sees me, but his expression snaps back to deadly serious as the enemy approaches, gliding in perfect silence, immune to waves and the sway of the barge.

"Run, Trey!" I yell.

He shakes his head, even as he stares down the alien creature. Trey won't leave me behind.

Manny exits the bridge and scurries down the ladder. "Come on, Trey!" he hollers, pointing to the yacht parked alongside the tugboat. "We can escape in the *Tardis*. Pick up Paige and Wyatt on the way out of here."

If Wyatt is even still alive. There's no sign of him. He's probably bobbing around Lake Erie right now. A blot of orange in angry gray water.

I'm almost there. The creature has raised its arm, pointed its toxic nails toward Trey's chest. Last time, they caused only a mild reaction. We might not get lucky again.

"Hey!" I yell. "Stop!"

It doesn't seem to hear me, so I throw a handful of coal with all my might at its back.

The coal doesn't fly well, but a big-enough chunk hits it in the shoulder, causing it to turn.

"That's right," I yell. "Come and get me. Run, Trey!"

The creature ignores me, turns right back around, raises its arm to Trey again. I don't understand. I'm yelling, throwing coal at it. Why is it so focused on Trey?

A projectile flies from the creature's hand, almost faster than I can see, and Trey lurches back, hit in the shoulder. Another embeds itself in the breast of his life jacket. The creature continues to advance on him.

Trey bends, grabs a coal shovel, brandishes it.

The creature knocks it aside like it's a matchstick—a gesture so fast it's blurry in my vision—and reaches for Trey's throat.

A *tat-tat-tat* rings like a snare drum in my ear, and searing heat zings past my cheek.

The creature arches its back. Bluish-green fluid stains its cloak, spreading like spilled ink. It collapses to the side, slips into the water, and disappears.

I whirl. It's Wyatt, holding the AR-15. Blood pours from a cut on his scalp.

Wyatt drops the gun, crumples to the deck.

I run toward him, heedless of my injured ankle. Footsteps pound behind me as Trey catches up. We reach him together and crouch beside him. His legs are sprawled, his back against the edge of the trough, his head lolled to the side. His breaths are short and shallow, like he's hyperventilating, and a sickly whistle stabs into my ear with each breath.

"Oh, god, Wyatt." Did he break a rib? Puncture a lung? That wheezing sound . . . I don't know what to do.

"Tell me where it hurts," Trey orders. "Or point if you can't talk."

Wyatt gasps out, "Inhaler."

His inhaler hurts?

But Trey understands right away. "Where?"

Wyatt pats the pocket of his coat, the ends of which stick out from under his life vest. "Pocket. But not there. Lost."

"Shit," Trey says. "Okay, buddy, I want you to breathe with me. We're going to breathe together, long and slow and calm, while Paige looks for your inhaler. Got it?"

Wyatt nods. It seems to me the skin of his face is a little blue.

I jump up and start looking, knowing it's likely futile. The inhaler is probably at the bottom of Lake Erie, but I have to try.

The shovel is in the trough where he dropped it, beside several half-buried propane tanks. Where, exactly, was Wyatt standing when I last saw him? *There,* I think, *in that hollowed-out spot.*

The barge is so huge, the coal so vast. It could be anywhere. I jump in, sweep my fingers through the coal, hoping to get lucky. If Wyatt lost the inhaler when he was outside of the trough, there's no chance of recovery; the waves have surely swept it away.

"Paige, hurry," Trey calls.

Shit. I search harder, but it would take an hour to thoroughly look through just this section of barge. I could be here all day.

Out of desperation, I reach for Wyatt's shovel. I'm just as likely to damage the inhaler with the shovel's blade as find it, but I'm running out of—

I let out a little yelp. There it us, right under the shovel, a plastic teal thing covering a metal canister, blackened with wet sediment.

I fish the inhaler out of its bed of coal and leap from the trough. My ankle is killing me, and the deck is slippery with waves, so I keep hold of the rail as I make my way back to Trey and Wyatt.

"Oh, thank god," Trey says, reaching for the inhaler, and I hand it to him. Trey wipes it down and gives the inhaler a good shake. "Here you go," he says, lifting it to Wyatt's mouth and depressing the canister.

Wyatt sucks on it like it's life itself. His chest expands, and he holds it there, refusing to exhale. Tears leak from his eyes.

This is why Wyatt never played football. This is why he

felt so bruised when Tanq called him "the weak link." He has serious asthma, and he's ashamed of it.

What an idiot. Wyatt could have so easily trusted us with this. We would have broken into a pharmacy for him. We would all be carrying extra, emergency inhalers by now—if he had just told us.

He exhales finally.

"Better?" Trey says, and Wyatt nods. "Okay, let's do another puff; then we'll get you off this boat."

They repeat the process. Wyatt's skin is already pinker, his wheeze less pronounced. The cut on his forehead bleeds badly, dripping into his ear and pooling there before oozing down his jaw. I don't have anything to mop it with, so I shake my sleeve off and press it to his scalp. Wyatt winces, but Trey says, "Thanks, Paige."

"He might have a concussion," I say. "But his skull feels intact. And this sleeve is not exactly sanitary."

"One thing at a time," Trey says.

The three of us stay like this, huddled together on the side of the barge. Manny watches from the upper deck of the towboat, his gaze skimming the water. Wyatt continues to breathe, guided by Trey. His wheezing gradually disappears as I keep pressure on his scalp wound. The wind is so angry now, whipping my hair into my mouth. Cold, fat drops of water splat onto my cheeks.

"We have to get under cover soon," I say. "That thing—or maybe its friends—could come back any moment."

"Can you walk, Wyatt?" Trey asks.

"Yeah."

"Paige, very slowly and gently pull your sleeve away. Let's see if the bleeding has slowed."

I do as Trey asks. Sure enough, a little blood wells up, but not nearly as much as before.

"Okay, let's move," Trey orders, and together he and I help Wyatt to his feet.

"How's that?" Trey asks him. "Any dizziness?"

"I think I'm okay," Wyatt says.

We make our way slowly up the barge toward Manny and the towboat. Eyes to the sky, Tanq and Trey have been saying, and I can't help scanning for dragonflies. But it turns out that danger comes from the deep, too. There is no safe place for us.

We're holed up in a beach house in Port Clinton. The *Tardis* is parked at the end of a long dock, hardly visible through the living-room window with the rain sheeting down. There might have been time to drive the barge back to Sandusky before the dragonflies started patrolling again, but this storm makes it too dangerous. And none of us were keen to be on the water anyway, after learning the walkers are also champion swimmers. Besides, we need to keep an eye on Wyatt for a while, make sure his breathing normalizes and that he doesn't have a concussion.

I wish there was a way to get in touch with Tanq, let her know we're taking an extra night to get the job done. She knew it was a possibility, but I can't imagine being all alone in that bunker, not knowing if my friends were okay. At least she has Emmaline.

"Okay, one more time," Manny says to me. "Go through it again. Don't leave out a single detail."

We're gathered in the living room on sandy-colored sofas that have seen better days. The room is paneled in dark wood, and taxidermied animal heads watch over us from the fireplace mantel: a black bear in full snarl, surrounded by a wolverine, a red fox, a six-point buck, and something whitish and scraggly that might once have been a rabbit.

I take a deep breath and give Manny the account all over again—the walker launching out of the lake like a porpoise, the way it glided toward me after it thought it had taken care of Wyatt, how it ignored me, like it hardly realized I was there. I describe its cloak touching my cheek—like fluffy cotton but wet and cold, cold, cold. I recount how I couldn't distract it from Trey until I threw coal at its back.

Manny is silent a long time.

"What does it mean, Manny?" Wyatt asks.

"You shouldn'ta done that, Paige," Trey slurs. We were so focused on taking care of Wyatt that we were slow to remove the projectile nail from Trey's shoulder. It's made his head a little fuzzy. Trey doesn't think it's serious. I slept through my own recovery from a Farmer projectile and felt fine afterward, so I hope he's right. "Was tryin' to get it away from you," he says.

"Thank you," I say. "That was very sweet."

He gives me a sloppy grin.

Manny leans forward and says, "Those who met with the Allies observed that they finished one another's thoughts, or that they would look at one another and come to a conclusion without speaking aloud at all. The Allies also told us at one point how careful they had to be, that hiding their intentions from the others was nearly impossible and extremely dangerous. We concluded from all this that they shared some kind of hive mind."

Wyatt says, "What does that have to do with—"

"They couldn't sense Paige," Manny says. "She was nearly invisible to them."

"I don't understand," I say.

"Have you ever seen them destroy an animal?" Manny says. "You watched them destroy your stepdad's car, right? But have you seen them go after a car that wasn't occupied? Or a boat?"

I think of all those ghost boats, drifting undisturbed across Lake Erie. "No," I say.

"You're saying they can sense people," Trey says.

"Except Paige."

"Why?" I say. "Why not me?"

"What's different about you, Paige? Think about it."

"Oh," I breathe. "I got sick. I didn't get the vaccine."

Rain gusts against the front window, sounding almost like hailstones. I grab a bottled water—which we retrieved earlier from the pantry—and take a sip. Not because I'm thirsty but because I need to sit with this information a moment, let it wash through me.

"The vaccine," Wyatt says. "You're saying *that's* what they're sensing?"

"It's a theory," Manny says.

Another theory, like the one that says dragonflies don't patrol the skies when the tower is down. What does it matter, if walkers can patrol the waters?

"Manny, you told us the cure is exta. . . extatewestial," Trey says.

"Extraterrestrial. That's right."

"So what if it came from *them*, from the Allies themselves? Something like, I dunno, the equivalent of blood plasma. That would explain its waw . . . rarity. And how difficult and dangerous it was to smuggle here."

I stare at him. Even slightly stoned, Trey's the smartest person in the room.

"Exactly," Manny says. "Maybe they can sense us all— except Paige—the way they sense each other."

Wyatt's eyes fly wide. "Wait. Are you saying they can read my thoughts?"

"I doubt it," Manny says. "That would require a lot more biological compatibility. I suspect this is more mechanical in nature. The virus is made of tiny machines, incomprehensible to us, but machines nevertheless. The cure is probably similar, a mechanized substance with some biological materials, which can act upon biological processes."

That sounds weird and complicated to me, but Trey is nodding along as though it makes perfect sense.

Manny's gaze turns distant. "I wonder . . ."

"About?" I press.

"If the virus or maybe even the cure would give us access to alien technology. If they're sensing us the way they sense each other . . . They're controlling those drones somehow, right?"

"Or they're automated," Trey says.

"What I want to know," I say, "is what we're going to do about that barge. Do we still try to get it to the tower?"

Silence greets my question.

Wyatt scratches at the scab forming on his scalp. "I don't see how," he says in a near whisper. "They're in the water. They could be on us before we even saw—"

"Your gun took care of one just fine," Trey says.

"Yeah. But that was lucky. I mean, I'm a pretty good shot, but AR-15's are notoriously inaccurate at distance, and it's really lucky I didn't shoot Paige instead. I wouldn't have risked it if I'd had any other choice."

He almost did hit me. I remember the bullet zinging past the skin of my cheek like a bright-hot wind.

"We can still protect the barge with that gun," Trey says. "We hang out in the driving cab; their fingernail projectiles couldn't penetrate my life jacket, so I bet they can't penetrate glass either. If one comes near, we shoot. We might not see any more at all. They're rare, right? An advance force, thinned out across the world."

I wouldn't be surprised if they started patrolling this area in greater numbers, given everything that's happened. But I'm the only one they may not be able to sense.

"The El Camino should be safe on the trip back, if we go during tower-down time," Manny says. "But we have two boats and only one gun."

"I really wish I'd brought that pistol," Trey says.

"We'll have to leave the *Tardis* behind," Wyatt says.

"No! We might need her. She's how we get to the barge and back, and she's . . ." Manny gazes longingly through the window toward his yacht, even though he can't possibly see a thing through that storm.

"Trey will drive the El Camino back to the bunker," I say. "Manny and Wyatt, you take the rifle and go back on the *Tardis*. I'll drive the towboat."

They all gape at me.

"They can't sense me, right? I'm the only one who can do it."

"Paige, it's a *theory*," Trey says. "No, worse. It's a preliminary hypothesis which needs further observation and study before we know it's true."

"Then I guess we better start experimenting," I tell him.

We all argue for a bit, but they come around. None of us wants to give up. We're still going to take down that tower somehow, which means we still need that barge.

If any of the others have figured out that I'm also the only one who can drive the barge into the tower undetected, they haven't mentioned it yet.

I swear this is the coldest, cloudiest April ever

TREY DOESN'T KISS ME GOOD-BYE BEFORE I HOP INTO THE *TARDIS* for my quick trip to the barge. But his fingers brush my hair from my face and linger on my cheek for a bit. He says, "I have something to be scared of all over again. Something to lose."

I nod, understanding exactly. I don't know what I'll do if something happens to him on the way back to the bunker. "Caring is scaring," I quip, but I can't even crack a smile.

Neither does he. Instead, Trey yanks me toward him and wraps his arms tight around me, his cheek resting on the top of my head. "Please be careful," he says.

He lets me go so abruptly that I stumble. He turns and strides away toward the El Camino without looking back once.

Within moments, Wyatt, Manny, and I are speeding toward the barge in the *Tardis*. My ears hurt from the chill, and my face feels chapped. But I'm warmer today because I traded the hoodie sweatshirt soaked in Wyatt's blood for a long wool overcoat I found in a closet at the beach house. It's something I never would have worn before the apocalypse. I feel like a giant, brown box.

The barge looks odd as we approach, crooked.

"Those troughs are lying too low in the water," Manny shouts over the sounds of engine and spray. "Storm nearly swamped them."

He's right. One in particular is barely above the water line.

We jump aboard the towboat. Manny orders me to turn the ignition to power everything up and then lock myself into the bridge cabin while he and Wyatt disappear into the deep belly of the ship. "We've got to find the barge pump," he says. "This will take a few minutes, so hang tight."

I do as he asks and wait. Gulls are flying again—a good sign that the storm has blown itself out for real—but the sky remains a dangerous gray. We finished loading the barge with propane tanks as dawn was cracking the sky. Trey and I did all the loading; Manny and Wyatt watched the water from the highest deck like bald eagles watching for the silver glint of fish, Wyatt holding his gun at the ready. Lighter-fluid canisters are stacked on the first deck near the barges; we chose not to soak the coal in lighter fluid just yet, thinking another storm would just dilute it or wash it away.

Minutes pass. Are the barges rising out of the water a bit? I mark a clump of zebra mussels attached to the side of the lowest barge, and sure enough, they rise higher and higher.

Whatever Manny and Wyatt are doing is working.

They return soon after.

"You're ready to go," Manny says. "Remember, no fancy driving. Just aim her true and trust her to get you there. We'll pick you up outside of Sandusky."

Wyatt grasps my hand. "Thanks for helping me. Yesterday."

I blink at him. "Of course. When we get a chance, we'll raid a pharmacy and get some backup inhalers for you. I'd be more comfortable if we all carried one."

Wyatt seems a little stunned at this. He says, "Yeah, okay," like it's no big deal. "Good luck, Paige. See you in Sandusky."

Moments later, they're gone, and I carefully, tremblingly hit the throttle.

Driving the barge is awkward and strange and terrifying and maybe one of the hardest things I've ever done. The water has calmed with the sunrise, though, or steering this thing would be even harder. But I'm all alone—unless you count the sailcloth-covered corpse of Captain Mercedes Wade. I don't even have Emmaline.

Some people loved life on the lake. I've heard of folks who worked year-round on boats like this, only stopping when the lake iced over too thick and hard to break through. Maybe Captain Wade was one of those.

It takes an hour to round Catawba Island, at which point I realize I have to pee. There's certainly some kind of facility on one of the lower decks, but I think of the alien creature jetting out of the water to attack Wyatt, and I decide to hold it.

Another thirty minutes or so puts me past the peninsula

that marks Sandusky Bay, and suddenly the giant roller coasters of Cedar Point are looming ahead, providing the perfect landmark. Ten more minutes take me within sight of the Yacht Club marina.

I turn off the ignition and drop anchor. Per Manny's instructions, I'm not supposed to get too close to shore, lest we risk running the barge aground all over again.

I wrap my arms around myself, preparing for a long wait. What if Wyatt and Manny don't come? It would mean something happened to them along the way.

But no, there they are, already sweeping toward me, the wake behind them making a perfect white *V*.

They're all smiles as they help me aboard the *Tardis*. We did it. We got the barge loaded with propane and back to Sandusky. It seemed like such an impossible task when we first conceived it.

As we speed toward the marina, I allow myself to fill with hope. With warmth. Trey will be waiting for us at the bunker, along with Tanq and Emmaline. Weird how the bunker is already feeling a little like home.

Sure enough, they're all outside the entrance to the tunnel. When the little dog sees me, she lets out a yip and plunges forward, practically wraps herself around my ankles.

"Up-up," I command, and she leaps into my arms and laps my face, quivering with excitement.

"You made it," Tanq breathes softly. "Every single one of you."

"Missed me, did you?" Wyatt says.

She turns away. "Whatever."

"Let's get inside," Manny says. "Not long until that tower comes back up."

Minutes later we're sitting on the bunks near the doorway to the kitchen, Trey and me on one, Tanq and Wyatt on the other. Manny stands between us, leaning against a bedpost. Emmaline sits at his feet, licking one of her paws. We've given Tanq the basic rundown of everything that happened during our barge-fetching mission. Talking about it makes me tired. I could fall over and take a nap this second.

"You're really going to do this," Tanq says, staring at the ground. "You're going to drive right up to that tower and crash into it on purpose."

"After pouring lighter fluid all over the coal and setting it on fire," I remind her.

"*If* the weather holds, we'll do it tomorrow," Manny says. "Rain means the plan is off."

"And you think you can drive up undetected," she says.

"Not all of us," I say.

"Just Paige," says Trey. "She didn't get the vaccine." He stares at me. "She has to do this alone."

"Yeah, I saw some notes about the hive mind thing in *The Book of Manny*," Tanq says, with a chin nod toward the giant binder on top of Manny's desk.

"You read that?" Manny asks. He seems both bothered and pleased.

"Some of it. That scrapbook of yours is . . . a *lot*. But I had plenty of time on my hands yesterday."

"I've been thinking about this," Wyatt says. "Paige can't go entirely alone. For one . . ." He ticks off a finger. "She needs a way off that barge after she's ignited the lighter fluid. For two, as soon the Farmers realize they're in danger, they'll attack the barge, whether they sense her or not, so she needs a distraction."

Trey is nodding along. "She needs cover and an exit strategy."

"Well, don't look at me," Tanq says. "I'm not going any—"

"You can help from right here, Tanq," Manny says. "You can set off the fireworks at Cedar Point when you see the barge come into view of the tower camera."

She cocks her head, considering. While we were gone, she showered again and applied thick black eyeliner with swooping wings. I have no idea where she got the eyeliner, but she looks amazing.

"I can do that," she says at last.

Emmaline hops up onto the bunk beside me, letting out a whine. It's an odd little vocalization I haven't heard much from her, and something about it gives me a chill. I scritch her head.

"So that's one distraction," Trey says. "Maybe the rest of us take the *Tardis* along, get close enough to be tempting, then run off and try to draw them away."

"That sounds really dangerous," I say.

"We have the guns," Wyatt reminds us. "The AR-15 and Paige's pistol. We can hold them off for a while."

"What if dragonflies destroy the *Tardis*?" I ask.

"We'll bail before that happens," Trey says. "We have—"

I follow his sudden shift in gaze to the monitor. The white tower has begun its daily journey out of the lake's surface and into the sky, pouring water.

"Uh, we have life jackets," Trey finishes.

"There was a small rowboat on the barge," Wyatt says.

I gape at them. We know the walkers can *swim*. Life vests won't protect us. And if a dragonfly can blow up a yacht, it can certainly blow up a rowboat. I'm about to tell them so, but I catch a look passing between them, and I realize it doesn't matter. They're committed to this plan, willing to risk their lives. They understand the dangers as well as I do.

"I'm going to grab some Red Vines," Tanq says, standing. "Anyone else want some?"

Emmaline whines again as Tanq steps toward the kitchen door.

"Sure," Wyatt says, but he's hardly paying attention because he's thinking so hard.

I say, "Hey, I'll take some too."

Tanq reaches for the door. Emmaline growls.

A scent wafts toward me—lake water, and hot metal, and something like talcum powder.

"Tanq, wait—"

She opens it. A walker stands in the doorway, dripping water and algae, bluish-green stains darkening its ephemeral cloak. In one "hand," it holds a round, metallic object that shifts in my vision like quicksilver.

It raises its other hand, points its shimmery black nails at Tanq's face.

I launch from the cot, but Manny gets there first, shoving Tanq aside. Her head knocks one of the bed frames and she crumples to the ground.

Manny's neck occupies the space where Tanq's face used to be. Before I can reach him, the creature darts its hand forward, plunges its nails into Manny's neck, rips out his throat.

Someone screams; it might be me. I'm trying to reach Manny but something makes the floor slippery and I can't get traction.

The creature steps toward me. "Who you?" it whispers. "Invissssible . . ."

"Paige, duck!" Trey yells.

I drop to my knees as a gun explodes in my ear. My head rings and my vision strobes, sending daggers of light into my brain. I have to get to my feet. I have to reach Manny. . . . I feel around for purchase, and my fingers encounter warm, sticky liquid. So much of it.

Large hands wrap my shoulders, yank me up. "It's okay, Paige," Trey whispers in my ear. "I got it. Are you hurt?"

I blink to clear strobing vision and wish I hadn't. There lies Manny, eyes wide open, his head cricked at an unnatural angle, blood spreading farther and farther across the floor. Beyond him is the creature, slumped against the doorway, a single bullet hole in its forehead. It twitches a little, as though not quite dead. And maybe it isn't. It's the same one from the barge; I'm sure of it. Bullet holes from Wyatt's gun mar its cloak. Somehow it survived. Followed us here, or even stowed away on the barge. Maybe its essential internal organs are in different places than human ones. Maybe they don't have any at all.

But Trey's shot seems to have done the trick. It struggles to breathe, its chin jerking sideways every few seconds. It can't last long.

On the floor by the cot, Tanq is curled into a ball, sobbing. Wyatt crouches down and whispers something in her ear.

"Trey," I whisper. "I can't . . ."

A hole is opening up in my heart to think of Manny, dead so fast. I knew him for only a few days, but I was already counting him a friend. We came here because of him. He answered our questions. Took care of us. Gave us a home.

This kind of death—fast like lightning, unspeakably painful and cruel—could be waiting for all of us.

"I know," Trey says, giving my shoulders a squeeze. "Just don't look."

"But we have to take care of . . ."

"We'll wait. Make *sure* that thing dies. Then we'll deal with . . . the mess. We'll find a way to say good-bye to Manny."

For once, Trey doesn't seem squeamish. His breathing is calm. The gun he just shot has been tossed onto the cot—my pistol, the one I pried out of Barry Stockton's hands.

"You should put another bullet into that thing," Tanq says, her voice muffled by sobbing, by Wyatt's arms. "And then another. Just unload it."

Trey says, "I don't know if that's a good id—"

Tanq launches up, dashes for the gun on the bed. "Then

I'll do it myself!" she yells. "For what it did to Manny, I'll . . ."

But Tanq freezes when the creature on the floor shifts, raises the hand still holding the strange metallic object. Its arm trembles with effort.

It lifts a blood-smeared finger and presses it against the top of the quicksilver cylinder. Something clicks.

The alien collapses, deathly still at last.

"Is that a bomb?" Wyatt says.

We're frozen, staring at the thing.

Nothing happens.

"Maybe it's a beacon," Trey says. "Transmitting our location."

"Bomb or a beacon, we have to get out of here," I say, snatching the floral purse from its spot at the foot of my bed.

"If it's a beacon, I can run with it," Trey says. "Draw them away."

He takes a step toward it, but I grab his arm. "No teammates left behind, remember? Let's go. The other tunnel, up the ladder. Emmaline, come!"

She trots over, and I scoop her up.

No one else is moving fast enough. "Let's go, let's go!" I yell. "Run, you idiots!"

That shocks everyone to action. Tanq grabs her pack and Manny's book, Wyatt his rifle, Trey the pistol. I'm not sure we have time to waste grabbing anything, but I'm so glad to see them all moving that I don't care.

Together, the four of us dash into the tunnel to the base of the ladder.

"Wyatt, you take that rifle and go first. Shoot anything you see."

He obliges, scrambling up like a spider. Tanq shoves the book into her pack and follows while I gently maneuver Emmaline into Hazel Jenkins's giant handbag. My dog barely fits, but she does. I sling the bag over my shoulder.

"I'll take up the rear," Trey says, and I know there's no use arguing so I hit the ladder and climb as fast as I can, the strap of the floral purse digging into my shoulder.

I crest the edge of the manhole and blink against sudden daylight. Only Wyatt is there; Tanq is already halfway across the parking lot, heading toward Barb's Barbecue. "Go on, Paige, follow Tanq," Wyatt orders.

I crouch down and let Emmaline out of the bag; she has a better chance of surviving if she can run on her own. Then I turn to make sure Trey made it out of the hole—

—and see three dragonflies bearing down on us, flying in formation, flashing silver against an angry gray sky.

"We have to *run*!" I scream, and I sprint with all my might toward Barb's.

Wyatt's and Trey's footsteps pound beside me. We pass cars, trample through bird droppings, duck under the awning, and launch ourselves through the broken window.

Tanq is already hiding behind a sales counter, and she peeks over the top, gesturing us over. "Hurry!" she says.

We dive behind the counter. There's barely room for all four of us and Emmaline.

A series of booms rock the world, concussive blasts so

intense they crash my teeth together and rattle my very bones.

The ensuing silence is eerie and sudden, like the world has died. I dare to peek over the countertop.

The manhole we just exited is gone. In its place is a massive sinkhole. The buildings forming the alley where we hid the day Wyatt found us are also gone, the places they occupied now part of the sinkhole. I watch, my stomach churning, as a chunk of asphalt the size of a car breaks free from the crater's edge and crashes down into the abyss. I don't hear it land.

Of the dragonflies, there is no sign. If Manny's theory is right, they can sense us, maybe even under cover. I feel as lost as ever when it comes to how to avoid them, how we can keep ourselves safe. I should make myself ponder it, reason it through.

But I can't think past this stabbing agony in my chest because our bunker—our one safe place—is gone. And our friend Manny with it.

April showers bring May flowers, or so I've always been told

WE'RE IN A FURNITURE STORE, SITTING ON A HUGE LEATHER sectional with multiple reclining seats and drink holders. Furniture spreads out all around us in this huge warehouse, grouped in cozy displays.

None of us wanted to be near the demolished bunker while we figure out what to do next. We chose this place because the giant store windows all have closing blinds, and because the entire rear section of the store is devoted to brand-new mattresses. At least we'll have comfy places to sleep tonight.

Tanq sits in a tight ball in one corner, knees held to her chest, her eyes wide and staring but seeing nothing. Emmaline is curled up beside her.

Wyatt is stretched out on a section all to himself, head against the armrest, eyes closed. The scab on his scalp has cracked and is now oozing blood mixed with clear fluid. He blots it occasionally with a paper towel he found in the men's room.

Wyatt had to take an extra puff on his inhaler after our flight from the bunker.

Trey and I sit side by side, his arm around me, both of us with our feet up on the coffee table. It's amazing, this feeling of caring for another person so much, knowing you're cared for in return. I don't know how I'd be doing right now if not for that.

"Wyatt, how many puffs do you have left on that thing?" I ask.

He pulls it from his pocket, checks the counter, and says, "Thirty-nine. I take it four times per day, unless I have an event, then I have to take more."

"So a week's worth, tops," I say. "We need to get you another inhaler."

"It should be our first priority," Trey says.

"Really?" Wyatt says.

"Why so surprised?" I say.

Wyatt stares at the ceiling. "I thought that maybe, you two being athletes, that you'd, I dunno, want to leave me behind or something. You know, once you found out about my . . . and then I was all weird to Trey. Manny explained why that was racist on the drive to the barge, and I really didn't mean it like that, but I wouldn't blame you all if—"

"Wyatt," Trey says. "I do need you to be not-racist. But I don't need you to be not-asthmatic. Okay?"

Wyatt swallows hard, and his jaw works overtime. Then he says, "Okay. There's a pharmacy two blocks over."

"So maybe we head there tonight," I suggest. "During tower-down time."

"Wouldn't hurt to grab some other supplies too," Trey says. "Some antibiotics, a painkiller, stuff for emergencies."

Tanq says nothing. She doesn't make eye contact, hardly even moves. I have no idea if she's paying attention to anything we're saying.

"I appreciate you all looking out for me," Wyatt says. "I do. But I guess what I really want to know is . . . what are we going to do next? Maybe Plan A wasn't so bad after all. We find a place to hole up, somewhere protected. Wait everything out as long as we can."

"Maybe you're right," Trey says, sounding defeated.

"Manny is dead because of what we did," Wyatt says. "We try to pull something like that again, another one of us could die. Or all of us."

"I don't want to go near that lake again, much less the tower," Trey says.

"Guys!" I practically shout. "We can't give up. Not now."

"Paige, we have to," Trey says, and I'm suddenly sick with disappointment that he's not backing me up. "We're back to square one with 'what we don't know might get us killed.' We thought we could avoid the Farmers by being still and quiet, staying under cover, but it turns out they can sense us—"

"Exactly," I interrupt. "If they can sense us, Plan A will

never work. We have to try to take them down, or we'll *never* be safe."

"Manny said taking down the tower would take care of the dragonflies," Wyatt says. "Not the walkers. He didn't say it would have any effect on them at all. And now that we know they can swim . . . that thing was probably underwater for hours, waiting . . ."

"We know how to kill walkers," I say. "Trey just showed us how. But those dragonflies . . . each one can take out a car. Just three of them together demolished a whole city block. They are by far our worst danger, and it's still worth it to take them out."

"True," Trey says, and I give him a look of gratitude. "I'm trying to figure out how it all works. Manny was certain the Farmers were attracted to motion and energy, but it sure seemed like Paige was invisible, even when she was yelling and waving her arms."

"Maybe it's a little of both?" Wyatt says. "They sense us, but they need motion to zero in on us. . . . Sorry, I don't know what I'm talking about."

"No, I think you're onto something," Trey says. "They're not of this world. It makes sense that their perceptions are not of this world either. Totally beyond our comprehension. We could be years and years figuring it out."

"Which is why we need to take down that tower," I insist. "So we buy ourselves time. It's the only way humanity will have a chance."

"Not if we die doing it," Wyatt says. "I know a lot of survival craft. We can head into the wilderness. Live a long time out there, unbothered. And yeah, maybe we don't save humanity, but we could last a while. Maybe they won't be able to sense us if we get far enough away."

"That's also a good point," Trey says.

I look back and forth between him and Wyatt. The wear of the last few days shows in their heavy eyelids, and their shoulders droop with exhaustion that I'm not sure is entirely physical. I don't blame them for being terrified and overwhelmed. I am, too.

But I don't do despair.

"I want to live," I say. "Except more than that. One of the reasons I wanted to go to the WNBA was because I wanted people to remember my name for years and years. I wanted to make a mark, do something important. I still do. And I still can."

I grab Hazel Jenkins's ridiculous floral purse and reach inside.

"And I want others to be remembered too. My stepdad, Paul, my brother, Ryan, my mom who probably spent her last breaths hooking me up to an IV so I could survive my coma. I don't have anything left of them. My house blew up. A dragonfly made Paul's car disappear, but look here."

I pull out the photo identification of Mrs. Carby and slap it down onto the coffee table.

"This is Suyin Carby," I say. "She made incredible chocolate chip oatmeal cookies, and she was devoted to training her dog. If not for her, we wouldn't have Emmaline. Finding

Emmaline may have saved my life, and Mrs. Carby deserves to be remembered."

I reach in for another ID and slap it down on the coffee table. A runny pink smile dares us to live.

"This is Hazel Jenkins. I took shelter in her house after mine blew up. I ate her food, slept on her bed. This ugly purse belonged to her. It's carried water, food, supplies, a gun, even my dog. Hazel Jenkins really loved pink, and she deserves to be remembered."

Wyatt sits up on the sofa. He stares at the IDs.

I grab another.

"Barry Stockton," I say, flipping out his driver's license like it's a playing card. "Grocery store manager. He sent his employees home and locked his store down tight when the virus hit. That meant Trey and I had all the supplies we could possibly need. That handgun was his, the one Trey used to kill a walker. We might all be dead if not for Barry Stockton. He deserves to be remembered.

"And this one," I say, "is Kenneth Anderson."

Tanq shoots up. She still holds herself apart, but she's looking. She's listening.

"Tanq's bio-dad," I explain. "He was an asshole who liked his fancy cars more than his own family. But we stayed in his house and ate his food and siphoned his fuel, and he might not deserve to be forgiven, but he deserves to be remembered.

"Here's Kent Williams. He gave us the El Camino. Tanq ate every single one of his corn chips."

I reach in one more time and grab the badge.

"Meet Captain Mercedes Wade," I say. The metal clasp attaching the badge to its lanyard clatters when I set it down. "Thanks to her, we have a coal barge with plenty of fuel. She must have run a tight ship, because it withstood a massive Lake Erie storm without breaking a sweat. Also, I think she ran the barge aground on purpose, so it wouldn't do any damage when she died. Captain Wade deserves to be remembered."

I stare at all the photos of the dead. The others stare too.

"Six people who helped us get this far. If we quit now, no one will know their names. Don't you see? It's not just humanity's future that's at stake here. It's our past. Everything we've ever been, everyone we've ever known."

"One more," comes a whisper. It's Tanq. She reaches down beside the sofa and hefts something—it's a giant binder filled with pages and clippings, all in plastic covers.

She thumps it onto the table beside Captain Wade's badge. "Armando Gomez," she says. "He got us to Sandusky. Before that, he spent years planning for our survival. He wrote pages and pages of notes. Everything he could think of, he wrote it down—for *us*. Did you know there's a section in here about edible wild plants? He literally devoted his life to helping us live. Right up until he saved me."

Tears pour from her eyes now, tinged black with eyeliner. "He *died* to save me. He deserves to be remembered."

We're silent a long time, collectively staring at the evidence that up until a few weeks ago, this planet had been covered with humans. Precious lives.

Trey says, "I want someone to remember Teena. And my mom."

Wyatt says, "My sister Willa was awesome. Maybe I can put a page about her in Manny's book."

"You see it now, right?" Tanq says. "We have to live. We *have* to. I wasn't sure before, but now . . ." She swallows hard, and suddenly the old Tanq is back. "I mean, people are probably still shit. But some of you assholes are worth saving."

"I want that on a T-shirt," Trey says. "'Asshole Worth Saving.'"

"AWS," I say. "We've just found our band name."

"Am . . . I . . . in your band?" Wyatt asks, his voice tentative.

Tanq reaches over the coffee table and punches him in the shoulder. "How are you such a moron?" she asks.

He grins.

Trey is fiddling with the piping on the couch cushion. Without looking up, he says, "It's just one tower. It saves humanity temporarily."

"There's always another Death Star," Wyatt says.

"But that's *life*," Tanq says. "At least, that's always been my life. You fight one battle so you can fight another."

Trey gets that faraway look I'm starting to recognize as his deep thought face. "I guess life is just a series of battles fought," he says.

"I'm going to keep fighting," I say. "Even if I have to do it alone. I'm driving that barge to the tower, and I'm going to blow it up. And I'm going to try really, really hard to live through it to fight again."

Trey shakes his head, and at first I think he's going to try to stop me but what he says is, "You're not going alone."

"We're with you, Paige," says Wyatt.

We all turn to Tanq.

She says, "Ethel Betts would never agree to this. But Tanq would." Then she grins. "Besides, I have to see this through because I have not yet consumed all the world's Red Vines."

Not even an alien shroud of greenish clouds can keep daffodils from blooming in Ohio. They're everywhere now.

WE GIVE OURSELVES TWO DAYS BECAUSE MY ANKLE STILL SMARTS from when it got stuck in the coal trough, and Wyatt's scab continues to ooze. We need rest and prep time.

Trey takes charge, making sure we use the time wisely. The first night during tower-down time, we break into the pharmacy and take three inhalers for Wyatt, along with some antibiotics, painkillers, and a few other things. I pretend not to notice when Trey grabs a handful of condoms. I'd rather use the pill, but there are so many different kinds on the shelf and I'm not sure what to take. After a moment of staring, I randomly grab a few packs.

Trey and I will have to have the contraception talk soon. If we make it through this.

As the sun comes up, we sneak over to the marina and

refuel the *Tardis* at the pumping station there. We also break into the boat house where rental keys are kept and liberate a Jet Ski. Tanq chooses the nicest one—metallic black with neon green racing stripes. Kenneth Anderson taught Tanq how to jet ski, before he decided she wasn't really his daughter, and Tanq insists that she'll be able to drive it just fine.

The next night, we hit pay dirt at a local ski shop, and everyone gets fitted with a wetsuit and deck shoes. We also find a doggy life vest for Emmaline; now that the bunker is destroyed, there's no leaving her behind.

Then we head to a sporting goods store, where Wyatt loads up on ammunition for the guns. "You're going to teach us to use those things safely, right?" Trey asks.

"Sure. But we won't have time for that before we hit the tower. The basics are: point and shoot. Never point at friendlies, even as a joke. Keep the safety on unless you're absolutely sure you're about to use it. Never store it loaded."

After that, Trey orders us all to try to get some sleep, but I can't. I lie awake on my bare store mattress, going over the plan. It's easy, though not exactly foolproof. I'll drive the barge right into the tower, do as much damage as I can. Then I'll ignite the coal, and as the fire races down the barge toward the bow piled with propane tanks, I'll bail out the side and get picked up by whoever reaches me first.

During my initial run at the tower, Tanq and Trey and Wyatt will circle around making nuisances of themselves, hopefully causing a distraction that will leave my path clear.

So many things can go wrong.

Eventually, I give up sleeping alone, and I crawl over to where Trey lies on his side, mouth open on his pillow. I stretch out behind him, put an arm around his waist.

He wakes momentarily, bracing with surprise, but then he grabs my hand with his and pulls it up to his chest.

I feel the gentle weight of Emmaline, curling up behind my knees.

Finally, I drift off.

The day is cloudy again, but it doesn't feel like rain coming, so the boys drive me to the barge in the *Tardis* and help me soak the coal in lighter fluid. We use up every single can, focusing on a line down the middle of each coal barge that will act as a fuse toward the propane tanks.

Emmaline has taken to boating like a champ, and after a brief hesitation over the *Tardis*'s rumbling engine, she was easily coaxed aboard. Now's she's locked in the bridge cabin of the barge, because I'm terrified she'll jump after us and misgauge the ever-shifting distance between the towboat and the flatboats.

Tanq maneuvers the Jet Ski like a pro, circling as we work, keeping an eye on the water. She seems fearless, even cheerful, and she still wears that backpack full of paints. The water is sure to ruin everything, but she refused to leave it behind.

I keep remembering the way the walker launched out of the lake and attacked Wyatt, and I find I can't bear to watch her zip around.

Too soon, we're done soaking the coal, and it's time to get underway.

Trey puts a hand on my shoulder and looks deep into my eyes, like he's about to say good-bye. "I just want you to know," he says, all solemnity, "that you are seriously hot in that wetsuit."

"Don't forget the deck shoes and the life vest," I say. "I hear this outfit is all the rage in the apocalypse."

He smiles slightly. "Luck, Paige. We've got your back. But remember, sometimes a point guard just has to drive to the basket, take the layup."

"Yeah, sure," I tell him, but I'm not sure what he's saying. That they're all going to die? That I might have to do this alone? I'm afraid to ask. "Good luck to you, too," I choke out.

Then he and Wyatt are heading off in the *Tardis*, and I am indeed all alone once again on what feels like a massive ship.

Emmaline spins circles around me when I return to the bridge, reminding me that I'm not so alone after all. Her nose is wet, and I realize she's been snarfling Captain Wade.

"Who's the grossest girl? You are!" I say as I turn the ignition and hit the throttle.

We spread out into a wide formation as we plunge across Lake Erie—Tanq in her Jet Ski a hundred yards to the north, probably near the invisible Canadian border. Trey and Wyatt ride on the south side to my right, each carrying a gun.

I hate that Tanq can't drive a Jet Ski and carry a weapon at the same time, but she's right; she's really good at this, and she whips along, zigzagging to compensate for the barge's slower speed.

I see the wave before I see the tower. We timed our operation so that we'd be on the lake before the dragonflies started patrolling, but I had forgotten the giant wave of displaced water created by the tower when it rose.

It's huge, at least thirty feet tall, and it will surely swamp the barge and wash away all that precious lighter fluid.

I hear Manny's voice in my head: *Don't avoid it. Steer into it.*

So I aim the barge to hit that monstrosity of water at a perfect, perpendicular angle.

That's it. Now give it a little gas as we crest the wave.

I hit the throttle a little early, because this ship is slow to accelerate. The wave approaches. The cargo barges ahead of me begin to lift. I clutch the steering wheel for dear life, holding it true.

The barges pierce the top of the wave; they buckle where they connect to the towboat and for a split second we are a *V* shape straddling the wave.

And suddenly, we're over, plunging down the other side. The tips of the barges are submerged for a horrible, breathless moment, but then they bop right back to the surface.

I hope it hasn't taken on too much water, and that not all the lighter fluid washed away. Those troughs are deep, the coal thick, as I discovered when I fell into one. Surely some of it remained dry. At least the propane tanks seem intact.

I cease to worry about all that, though, as the white alien tower looms ahead.

A quick check shows that Tanq and the boys all crested the

wave safely. As planned, they speed ahead of me to begin their distraction maneuvers.

But I don't know what difference that will make or how we ever thought we could do any damage to that thing because it is *huge*. Watching it on Manny's camera from the safety of our bunker didn't begin to do it justice. The tower is taller than any skyscraper I've ever seen, and made from a white material that looks like plastic at a quick glance but is most certainly not plastic because it shimmers and shifts in a way I can't understand. It's as though the tower is different, subtly changed every time I blink, but I can't say how.

The top opens, spreading iridescent white petals wide to the sky, and a beam of light thrusts upward, burning a hole in the clouds. It's unbearable, searing my eye sockets, and I'm forced to look away . . .

. . . only to find three dragonflies winging toward us. No, not us. The *Tardis*.

I give the throttle more gas. We have to get this over with as soon as possible or we're all going to die. But the barge is so huge and the towboat can only respond so fast, and my speed increases with agonizing slowness.

Tanq spots the dragonflies, too, and she rips through the waves toward the *Tardis*. I know she'll try to distract them, split their target, and I'm agape that the same girl who was nearly catatonic after the RAV4 was destroyed is capable of such courage now.

The *Tardis* is jetting away, drawing the dragonflies. Our distraction tactic is going to work; my path is clear. But maybe at the cost of my friends' lives, because those drones are closing the gap fast.

A *rat-tat-tat* sound wafts toward me on the breeze. Wyatt is pointing his rifle to the sky, trying to hit the dragonflies.

"More throttle," I murmur, but it's already as far forward as it will go. This barge won't go any faster.

One of the dragonflies jerks, spins on an invisible axis, spews green smoke as it plunges into the lake. A yell of triumph bursts from me, startling Emmaline.

That's one down.

But the other two are turning around for another pass at the *Tardis*. I watch in horror as they skim low. Wyatt shoots at them, and I'm too far away to see if any of the bullets are hitting. All I know is that it's really hard to hit a moving target, Wyatt must be a hell of a marksman to have taken one down, and it's unlikely he'll be able to do it again.

One dragonfly swoops so close it obscures my view of the boat. It releases something, not a laser or projectile, but more like a wave of energy that distorts the air around it, making it shimmer like a desert mirage.

Trey and Wyatt leap from the boat and disappear into the water.

The *Tardis* implodes on itself, becomes raw matter that spins around like a tiny hurricane, coalescing into a single point of space-time that suddenly winks out of existence. An impact crater lasts only a second before it's swamped, and the surface of the water appears as though the *Tardis* was never there at all.

"Trey," I whisper. I scan the surface of the lake for the

telltale orange of life vests. Trey and Wyatt could have so easily been caught in that energy beam. . . .

It's like all the breath leaves my body when I spot one, then two, orange motes bobbing in the water. From here, I can't tell if they're alive, but at least they're not . . . gone.

A dragonfly darts back and forth across the water, perhaps looking for them. Only one dragonfly. The boys must have shot down another one, and I was so preoccupied with the *Tardis* that I missed it.

The orange motes start to slowly drift my way. They're swimming for the barge. Which means they're alive!

Tanq is still speeding toward them. Maybe she intends to pick them up somehow, but no, she whips right past, waving one arm wildly. She's trying to get the drone's attention, lead it away from the boys.

But there could be walkers in the water, swimming in the dark depths like sharks, waiting to strike from below.

I dash out of the bridge cabin and down the ladder. I saw life preservers on the first deck; I'm sure of it. I can throw them out and pull the boys in. If that doesn't work, I'll take the rowboat and fetch them. I've never rowed before, but I'll do what I have to do.

Tanq has created some distance between her and the drone, and now she's circling back toward the boys flailing in the water. They're close enough now that I glimpse their faces between swells. They seem to be struggling, even with life vests and wetsuits. They're swamped with every wave, struggling to breathe. Wyatt's lungs must be on fire.

I make it down to the first deck. Where did I see those life preservers? Hanging against the wall maybe. The clatter of claws reaches me—Emmaline! I forgot to close the door behind me. No help for it now.

The Jet Ski slows as it approaches Trey. He reaches for the seat behind Tanq, starts to lug himself out of the water. The dragonfly screams toward them, flying low enough to create a wind wake on the water's surface.

"Hurry, Trey," I whisper.

He gets one leg up, then another, wraps his arms around Tanq's waist, curls himself over the bulk of her backpack.

Tanq looks toward Wyatt, back at the drone. She makes a decision and speeds away. Trey lifts his arm and points at the drone—he still has the hand gun! But can it actually fire after it's been soaked? Apparently so because a bang reaches me a second later. The dragonfly races after them, leaving Wyatt flailing alone in the lake.

There! A red-and-white life preserver, clipped to the wall. It's attached to a long rope.

My fingers are cold and clumsy as I unclip it. I run to the edge of the deck.

"Wyatt!" I scream. He's almost within range, but he's struggling. "Just a little closer."

I keep an eye on the dragonfly chasing Tanq and Trey; it seems distracted for now, but it could change its mind at any moment.

Wyatt does his best to stroke toward me. Then, incredibly, we get a bit of luck as a wave or current or something picks him up and carries him several yards.

This is my chance. I consider the life preserver for the briefest moment. I can't toss it like a basketball, so I treat it like a Frisbee. Making sure there's plenty of slack in the rope, I curl it behind my shoulder to wind it up, then fling it outward with all my might.

The rope creates drag, and the preserver wobbles as it sails through the air and plunks into the lake—far short of Wyatt's position.

But he aims for it anyway, doing his best against wind and wave. "C'mon, Wyatt, almost there."

I grab the rope, preparing to pull him in. In the distance, Tanq disappears around the far side of the tower. Emmaline runs back and forth along the side of the boat, occasionally leaping up on her hind legs. Her eyes are fixed on Wyatt, as if she's cheering him along.

Wyatt grabs the preserver and waves at me to indicate he has a good grip. So I pull the rope in with all the strength in me. Behind him, something in the water flashes silver. Or do I imagine it? I yank harder.

At last Wyatt is able to clutch the edge of the towboat. I hook his armpits and pull as hard as I can. Waves soak us both. Emmaline dances around me, as though this is all the greatest game.

One more heave, and together we collapse onto the deck. Wyatt chokes, spitting out water, then he gasps for air, and that horrible, sickly wheeze whistles from somewhere deep in his lungs.

"Inhaler?" I ask. He nods, so I dig into my pocket for one of the spares we got at the pharmacy. I shake it and hand it to him. He chest inflates as he takes a puff.

Wyatt squeezes his eyes shut as he holds the breath in place, and tears leak out of his eyes. His diaphragm contracts, jerking his whole body. I realize he's trying desperately not to cough.

At last he lets the breath out, and mine goes with it. Wyatt's head clunks backward against the siding, like he can hardly hold his own head on his neck. A chunk of wetsuit is torn away at his knee, revealing a jagged wound bleeding freely. He's weak, injured, and exhausted, but I dare to hope he'll be okay.

For now. Wyatt had the vaccine. With him aboard, the Farmers will come after us for sure. We've lost any advantage we may have had by having me drive this barge alone.

Emmaline whines, and my heart leaps into my throat. It was that soft, eerie sound she makes when a Farmer is near.

I launch to my feet, even as my eyes rove Wyatt for his rifle, but I don't see it anywhere.

"Gun?" I ask.

He shakes his head weakly. "Lost," he murmurs, then he takes another puff on his inhaler.

Emmaline's whine becomes a growl, and I search the boat, the sky, the water, for any sign, but there is nothing.

"Can you walk?" I ask Wyatt.

He shakes his head. "Maybe in a minute," he says. "My knee . . . "

His knee does look really bad. Whatever I do next, I'll have to do it alone.

The barge has started to drift to the side, pushed by current. "I'll be back!" I holler to Wyatt as I dash back up the steps to deck two, then again to the bridge. Emmaline trots inside after me as I grab the steering wheel—

—as three walkers missile out of the lake. They streak high into the sky, trailing streams of glistening water, and land with gentle precision on the bow near the propane tanks.

Three of them, and the one in the middle is a giant, half again as tall as the others, with a cloak that seems more corporeal than iridescent, in glittering, galaxy blue.

If the Farmers are a hive, this is definitely their queen.

I have no idea what to do. The barge is still at least two hundred yards away from the tower. I have no gun, nowhere to run. Wyatt is lying helplessly on the deck below.

I glance at the road flare lying on the console, the one I'm supposed to use to ignite the lighter fluid.

It's too soon. I'm not close enough.

But if I don't, those walkers will kill us for sure.

"Emmaline, stay." I grab the flare, skip down the steps, leap over the railing of the second deck, and land hard on the first.

As I sprint toward the coal troughs, I pop off the top of the flare. It streams fire.

The walkers begin to glide forward.

Tanq and Trey appear on the other side of the tower and jet toward us, but I wave the flare high to signal what I'm about to do. Tanq wisely veers wide, but she continues her approach at a more diagonal vector.

I reach the edge of the barge and hesitate. The walkers

hesitate too. If Manny's theory holds true, they can't quite pin-point my location. Maybe I have time to reach the tower.

But they start moving forward again. The dragonfly that was chasing Tanq and Trey veers away, heading toward me instead. The queen raises her arms. Her black nails are longer than eagle talons, but they're not as terrifying as the silvery, cylindrical object she holds—just like the one in the bunker.

Sure enough, the dragonfly bears toward me as though summoned, and I have no choice; I toss the flare into the near-est flatboat, right on top of the mountain of coal.

Fire bursts from the blackness, so much higher and hot-ter than I imagined, blowing my hair back and singeing my cheeks. It races down the barge like a hurricane wind, wild and free, making popping sounds that are louder than gunshots.

The wildfire reaches the propane tanks. Nothing happens.

The walkers press forward again, skirting the fire by staying to the edge of the barge, as far from the burning troughs as they can get. My heart sinks. I just blew our one chance to take down the tower in order to kill these things, and it didn't even work.

The dragonfly is nearly upon me, its nose skimming over the heads of the walkers.

The propane tanks explode, jerking the barge violently. My eardrums feel like they're bursting as a massive fireball boul-ders into the air. The walkers' mouths open in silent screams as the fire takes them, disintegrates them to nothing.

A chunk of shrapnel wings my way, and I barely duck in time to avoid it—as the fireball engulfs the dragonfly. The drone teeters in the air, its silvery hull turning red orange like the sun. Its sides begin to slip away, molten and dripping, until it loses control completely and drops like a stone, disappearing into the waters of Lake Erie.

I have no time for relief, because the end of the barge is drowning, sinking lower and lower, and it's going to drag the tugboat with it into the depths. I have to get Wyatt and Emmaline off this thing fast.

I sprint for the rowboat, which hangs alongside the first deck by chains on a pulley. But my feet feel heavier than lead and my heart is a stone. I've failed so utterly. I may have saved us temporarily, but that tower will keep rising every day, keep pouring methane into our atmosphere, and a few years from now, the full invading force will arrive and the earth as we know it will cease to exist.

I reach the rowboat as Tanq and Trey round the stern of the tow. I grab for the pulley, and I'm about to shout for Emmaline to come, but suddenly Trey is gesturing wildly from his spot behind Tanq on the Jet Ski.

"Keep going!" he shouts, pointing to the tower. "It could still work!"

I gape at him. The coal barge is sinking. It will be underwater soon, if the fire from the coal troughs doesn't get it first.

"Keep going!" he repeats.

I have no idea what he's thinking, but Trey is the smartest of all of us, and I've no doubt he understands something I don't. I sprint back to the bridge cabin. Emmaline is crouched behind the captain's seat, trembling, tail tucked as far between her legs as it will go. "Oh, Emmy, I'm so sorry, but I don't have time to comfort you now."

I aim the steering wheel and hit the throttle.

The barge responds even more slowly than usual. The drooping, burning coal troughs scoop water with every yard of progress, sinking lower and lower. The flames will all be engulfed soon.

And what a fire it is. The coal burns bright and hot, accelerated by the lighter fluid. Even way up here, in the protective shelter of the cabin, I feel like I'm inside a convection oven.

The barge gets closer and closer. The tower shimmers, reflecting light from the fire in prismatic shards. Waves lap against its sheer walls. Zebra mussels have already claimed territory, clumping against the whiteness right at the waterline.

I hit the throttle again, even though this boat is already going as fast as it ever will. It's not enough.

The impact surprises me, shivers up my legs and spine, knocking my hip against the piloting console. I peer out the window to see if we did any damage, but I just can't tell—the waves are too frothy, the fire so hot it makes a wavering mirage of the air around it.

Tanq scoops her Jet Ski around toward the tower, driving parallel. Trey reaches out with his gun and shoots at it. I have no idea if any of his shots penetrate.

But then they're flying back toward me and I hear Trey's voice over the waves. "Bail! Get off now!"

I don't second-guess. I grab Emmaline and rush out of the cabin, down to the first deck, toward Wyatt. "Time to go,

Wyatt," I holler, glad to see he's already on his feet.

I cast one longing glance toward the rowboat. But based on the urgency of Trey's voice, I don't have time for that. "We have to bail," I say. "Stay close. If you have trouble breathing, I'll do all the swimming for us, okay?"

He nods.

I have Emmaline in her doggy life vest in one arm. With my other hand, I grab Wyatt's hand. "On three," I say. "One, two—"

The world erupts.

A blast of something hits my back, and the three of us are flung into the lake. I lose my grip on Wyatt's hand, and my arm is suddenly empty of Emmaline as water closes over my head.

I flail for the surface, but blasts continue to hit over and over, swirling me around until I can't tell up from down. My lungs are on fire; I need air more than anything, for I had no time to take a breath. Then I remember to trust the life vest, and I stop struggling.

The vest lifts me, bobs me up to break the surface, and I gasp for air.

"Emmaline!" I scream. "Wyatt?"

Debris rains down around my head; something lands on my ear, searing my skin, and I duck my head under the water instinctively.

I resurface and scan the water for my dog, my friends. Bits of fiery shrapnel float around me, and finally I look back—just in time to watch the antenna that once stood proudly above the bridge cabin sink beneath the waves. The entire coal barge is gone.

Beyond it, the tower is in jagged ruins, rising less than a third of its original height, its top completely sheared off. I watch as another explosion blows a huge chunk out of its side. The remnant of the tower lists sideways and begins to sink.

"Paige!"

It's Tanq's voice, and I begin stroking toward it even before I pinpoint her location with my eyes. She rumbles toward me, taking it slow, avoiding flotsam when she can. Emmaline is curled up in her lap, bedraggled and frightened, but she seems okay. Wyatt clutches the Jet Ski near Tanq's feet, riding sidecar style. Trey looms over Tanq's back, pushing her forward as if he can make her go faster with the force of his body.

Tanq pulls up beside me.

"Hold on to the side," she says. "I'm going to get us out of here, but if the engine sucks up any of this debris, it'll choke, so be ready."

I nod, and Tanq shoots forward, nearly yanking my arm from my socket. I'm freezing cold now—my wetsuit must have torn somewhere—and I suspect I have small burns all over my body. But it feels like I can breathe again for the first time in days.

The tower is down. And we are alive.

The hull of Tanq's Jet Ski skids onto a pebbly shore, and I collapse, heedless of sharp edges poking through my wetsuit. I just lie here, breathing, grateful to feel solid ground again.

Emmaline hops off of Tanq's lap and shakes herself violently, spraying us all with water. Then she trots up the beach and squats.

The whole time we were trying to save humanity, Emmaline was holding it. I can't help myself; I start to laugh, and even though I'm not sure why, I can't seem to stop and I'm laughing and laughing until my sides pinch.

"Up you go," says Trey, and he lifts me by the armpit, helps me gain my feet.

On the other side of the Jet Ski, Wyatt stumbles up the beach. His knee is pretty banged up, but I'm glad to see him able to stand.

"Did we do it?" Tanq asks, swinging a leg over the seat to dismount. "We did it, right?"

"We did it," Trey confirms.

He puts his arm around me, and together we drip water onto the ground as we gaze back at our handiwork. I gasp.

Flotsam litters the lake, bits of metal and plastic-y stuff I couldn't begin to identify. High above the spot where the tower used to be, a giant tear rends the gray clouds. Their edges seem blackened with char, and they crackle with tiny fingers of lightning.

But beyond the tear in the clouds is blue, blue sky. Sunshine pours down in streamers, like waterfalls of light.

"I wish Manny could see this," Tanq says.

"Tanq," Wyatt says. "You were awesome out there."

"I know."

"How did you know that would work?" I ask Trey.

"Methane is highly combustible," he says. "If we compromised the integrity of the tower's hull and introduced oxygen and a heat source, then . . . what? What are you staring at?"

I gaze up at him, my heart surely in my eyes. "I'm fetishizing your brain," I say.

He grins.

Then he takes my face in his hands, leans down, and touches his lips to mine.

Somehow my arms end up around his neck and I'm kissing him back, and his hands are dropping low, pulling me against him, and nothing separates us but these damned wetsuits and I totally forget about anything but him and us and—

"It's about time," Tanq growls.

I ignore her and keep kissing Trey.

"Don't even think about it, Wyatt," Tanq adds. "I'm not kissing you or anyone."

It's a while before Trey and I come up for air, and when we do, my face is flushed and my lips feel swollen, or maybe a little bruised but mostly wonderful.

Trey takes my hand, pulls it to his lips. "You're the bravest person I know," he says.

"I'm one of the bravest people in the whole world," I tell him.

I'm suddenly aware that Tanq and Wyatt have disappeared with Emmaline. I glance around—there. Up the beach a way, toward a grassy area.

Trey and I link hands and go after them.

"Finally done sucking face?" Tanq says as we approach.

"For now," Trey says.

"Check this out," Wyatt say, pointing toward a marquee.

It's a big brown sign with gold lettering that says Ohio Historical Marker. Below that is a year: 1813, along with the words THE BATTLE OF . . .

But I don't get to see the rest because Tanq pulls a can of paint from her soaking wet pack. Quickly, she scrawls a near perfect oval with a line through it, the null sign in bright fuchsia, obscuring the date and the details.

"Hey, you're destroying a piece of history," I say. "I want to remember this stuff."

"I don't think that's what she's doing," Trey says. "Paige, do you know what day it is?"

I frown, considering. "April-ish?"

"Exactly. I don't know either."

"It's day one," Tanq says. "Of Year Zero. The year humanity starts over."

"Wouldn't it be Year One?" Wyatt says.

"Of course not," Tanq says. "Is a child one year old the day it's born? No, it is *not*. Besides, Year Zero sounds cooler."

Wyatt shrugs. "Okay, I buy that. Also, it's another possible band name."

"If I had a working camera," I say, "I'd take a selfie of all of us right now in front of this marker."

"We'll just have to remember," Trey says. "We have to remember everything." He turns back to gaze across the endless water of Lake Erie. Softly, he says, "We won a big battle today."

"I say we get started on Plan B," Wyatt says. "See if we can help each other out."

"Can we rest first?" Tanq says. "Also, I'm starving."

Trey puts an arm back around my shoulders. Gulls play in the gravel where waves lap the shore. Emmaline plunges into them, scattering them in all directions. For the first time in a long time, I don't see any crows.

"Hey, look at that," Trey says, pointing toward the tear in the clouds. It's widening, dissipating, revealing a normal, healthy blue. "I feel like we're watching the sun rise on a new era."

I laugh.

"What's so funny?"

"Melodrama makes me laugh."

"Well, how's this for melodrama? We did it. We made our mark. Made a difference. We saved the world, at least for now. I have to tell you, that might be even better than going to the NFL."

I gaze up at him, wondering if he's right. Would I have willingly given up all my hopes and dreams and loved ones to save the whole world? It's too big a question. Maybe I'll decide later.

But I squeeze his hand, because right or wrong, I appreciate the thought. I say, "Let's go find the rest of humanity."